NORA ROBERTS

"Nora Roberts is among the best."
—*The Washington Post*

"Roberts is indeed a word artist, painting her story and her characters with vitality and verve."
—*Los Angeles Daily News*

"You can't bottle wish fulfillment, but Nora Roberts certainly knows how to put it on the page."
—*New York Times*

"Her stories have fueled the dreams of twenty-five million readers."
—*Entertainment Weekly*

"With clear-eyed, concise vision and a sure pen, Roberts nails her characters and settings with awesome precision, drawing readers into a vividly rendered world of family-centered warmth and unquestionable magic."
—*Library Journal*

"Romance will never die as long as the megaselling Roberts keeps writing it."
—*Kirkus Reviews*

Together
For
Forever

Also available from Silhouette Books and Harlequin by

NORA ROBERTS

CATCH MY BREATH
Romance and trust and unravelling secrets

THE CALHOUN WAY
There's love in the *heir* for the Calhoun sisters

ACCIDENTALLY IN LOVE
The Stanislaskis are taking risks and trusting their hearts

SWEET STUBBORN LOVE
When worlds collide, romance blossoms

LOST LOVE FOUND
An irresistible contractor and talented Broadway musician make a pitch-perfect fit

ENCHANT MY HEART
Secret identities, magical secrets, and lots of love

For a full list of titles by Nora Roberts, please visit www.noraroberts.com.

NORA ROBERTS

Together For Forever

Includes *Megan's Mate* & *Irish Rebel*

Silhouette Books

If you purchased this book without a cover you should be aware that this book is stolen property. It was reported as "unsold and destroyed" to the publisher, and neither the author nor the publisher has received any payment for this "stripped book."

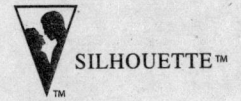

SILHOUETTE™

Recycling programs for this product may not exist in your area.

Together for Forever

ISBN-13: 978-1-335-44905-4

Copyright © 2025 by Harlequin Enterprises ULC

Megan's Mate
First published in 1996. This edition published in 2025.
Copyright © 1996 by Nora Roberts

Irish Rebel
First published in 2000. This edition published in 2025.
Copyright © 2000 by Nora Roberts

All rights reserved. No part of this book may be used or reproduced in any manner whatsoever without written permission.

Without limiting the exclusive rights of any author, contributor or the publisher of this publication, any unauthorized use of this publication to train generative artificial intelligence (AI) technologies is expressly prohibited. Harlequin also exercises their rights under Article 4(3) of the Digital Single Market Directive 2019/790 and expressly reserve this publication from the text and data mining exception.

This is a work of fiction. Names, characters, places, and incidents are either the product of the author's imagination or are used fictitiously. Any resemblance to actual persons, living or dead, businesses, companies, events or locales is entirely coincidental.

For questions and comments about the quality of this book, please contact us at CustomerService@Harlequin.com.

TM is a trademark of Harlequin Enterprises ULC.

Silhouette 22 Adelaide St. West, 41st Floor Toronto, Ontario M5H 4E3, Canada www.Harlequin.com	HarperCollins Publishers Macken House, 39/40 Mayor Street Upper, Dublin 1, D01 C9W8, Ireland www.HarperCollins.com

Printed in U.S.A.

CONTENTS

MEGAN'S MATE	1
IRISH REBEL	249

MEGAN'S MATE

For the Washington Romance Writers,
my extended family

Chapter 1

She wasn't a risk-taker. She was always absolutely sure a step was completed before she took the next. It was part of her personality—at least it had been for nearly ten years. She'd trained herself to be practical, to be cautious. Megan O'Riley was a woman who double-checked the locks at night.

To prepare for the flight from Oklahoma to Maine, she had meticulously packed carry-on bags for herself and her son, and had arranged for the rest of their belongings to be shipped. It was foolish, she thought, to waste time at baggage claim.

The move east wasn't an impulse. She had told herself that dozens of times during the past six months. It was both a practical and an advantageous step, not only for herself, but for Kevin, too. The adjustment shouldn't be too difficult, she thought as she glanced over to the window seat where her son was dozing. They had family in Bar Harbor, and Kevin had been beside himself with excitement ever since she'd told him she was considering moving near his uncle and his half brother and sister. And cousins, she thought.

Four new babies had been born since she and Kevin had first flown to Maine, to attend her brother's wedding to Amanda Calhoun.

She watched him sleep, her little boy. Not so little anymore, she realized. He was nearly nine. It would be good for him to be a part of a big family. The Calhouns were generous, God knew, with their affection.

She would never forget how Suzanna Calhoun Dumont, now Bradford, had welcomed her the year before. Even knowing that Megan had been Suzanna's husband's lover just prior to Suzanna's marriage, had borne Baxter Dumont a child, Suzanna had been warm and open.

Of course, Megan was a poor example of the classic other woman. She hadn't known Suzanna even existed when she fell for Baxter. She'd been only seventeen, naive, and ready to believe all the promises and the vows of undying love. No, she hadn't known Bax was engaged to Suzanna Calhoun.

When she'd given birth to Baxter's child, he'd been on his honeymoon. He had never seen or acknowledged the son Megan O'Riley had borne him.

Years later, when fate tossed Megan's brother, Sloan, and Suzanna's sister Amanda together, the story had come out.

Now, through the twists and turns of fate, Megan and her son would live in the house where Suzanna and her sisters had grown up. Kevin would have family—a half brother and sister, cousins, and a houseful of aunts and uncles. And what a house.

The Towers, Megan mused. The glorious old stone structure Kevin still called a castle. She wondered what it would be like to live there, to work there. Now that the renovations on The Towers Retreat were completed, a large portion of the house served as a hotel. A St. James hotel, she added thoughtfully, the brainstorm of Trenton St. James III, who had married the youngest Calhoun, Catherine.

St. James hotels were known worldwide for their quality and class. The offer to join the company as head accountant had, after much weighing and measuring, simply been too good to resist.

And she was dying to see her brother, Sloan, the rest of the family, The Towers itself.

If she was nervous, she told herself it was foolish to be. The move was a very practical, very logical step. Her new title, accounts manager, soothed frustrated ambitions, and though money had never been a problem, her new salary didn't hurt the ego, either.

And most important of all, she would have more time to spend with Kevin.

As the approach for landing was announced, Megan reached over, brushed a hand through Kevin's hair. His eyes, dark and sleepy, blinked open.

"Are we there yet?"

"Just about. Put your seat back up. Look, you can see the bay."

"We're going to go boating, right?" If he'd been fully awake, he might have remembered he was too old to bounce on his seat. But he bounced now, his face pressed to the window in his excitement. "And see whales. We'll go on Alex's new dad's boat."

The idea of boating made her stomach turn, but she smiled gamely. "You bet we will."

"And we're really going to live in that castle?" He turned back to her, her beautiful boy with his golden skin and tousled black hair.

"You'll have Alex's old room."

"And there's ghosts." He grinned, showing gaps where baby teeth had been.

"So they say. Friendly ones."

"Maybe not all of them." At least Kevin hoped not. "Alex says there's lots of them, and sometimes they moan and scream. And last year a man fell right out of the tower window and broke all his bones on the rocks."

She shuddered, knowing that part was sterling truth. The Calhoun emeralds, discovered a year before, had drawn out more than a legend and romance. They'd drawn out a thief and a murderer.

"That's over with now, Kevin. The Towers is safe."

"Yeah." But he was a boy, after all, and hoped for at least a little danger.

There was another boy who was already plotting adventures. It felt as though he'd been waiting forever at the airport gate for his brother to arrive. Alex had one hand in his mother's, the other in Jenny's—because, as his mother had told him, he was the oldest and had to keep his sister close.

His mother was holding the baby, his brand-new brother. Alex could hardly wait to show him off.

"Why aren't they here yet?"

"Because it takes time for people to get off the plane and out the gate."

"How come it's called a gate?" Jenny wanted to know. "It doesn't look like a gate."

"I think they used to have gates, so they still call them that." It was the best Suzanna could come up with after a frazzling half hour at the airport with three children in tow.

Then the baby cooed and made her smile.

"Look, Mom! There they are!"

Before Suzanna could respond, Alex had broken away and made a beeline toward Kevin, Jenny hot on his heels. She winced as they barely missed plowing into other passengers, then raised a resigned hand to wave at Megan.

"Hi!" Alex, having been schooled in airport procedure by his mother, manfully took Kevin's carry-on. "I'm supposed to take this 'cause we're picking you up." It bothered him a little that, even though his mother claimed he was growing like a weed, Kevin was still taller.

"Have you still got the fort?"

"We got the one at the big house," Alex told him. "*And* we got a new one at the cottage. We live at the cottage."

"With our dad," Jenny piped up. "We got new names and everything. He can fix anything, and he built me a new bedroom."

"It has pink curtains," Alex said with a sneer.

Knowing a brawl was dangerously close, Suzanna neatly stepped between her two children. "How was your flight?" She bent down, kissed Kevin, then straightened to kiss Megan.

"It was fine, thanks." Megan still didn't know quite how to respond to Suzanna's easy affection. There were still times she wanted to shout, *I slept with your husband. Don't you understand? Maybe he wasn't your husband yet, and I didn't know he would be, but facts are facts.* "A little delayed," she said instead. "I hope you haven't been waiting long."

"Hours," Alex claimed.

"Thirty minutes," Suzanna corrected with a laugh. "How about the rest of your stuff?"

"I had it shipped. This is it for now." Megan tapped her garment bag. Unable to resist, she peeked down at the bright-eyed baby in Suzanna's arms. He was all pink and smooth, with the dark blue eyes of a newborn and a shock of glossy black hair. She felt the foolish smile that comes over adults around babies spread over her face as he waved an impossibly small fist under her nose.

"Oh, he's beautiful. So tiny."

"He's three weeks old," Alex said importantly. "His name is Christian."

"'Cause that was our great-grandfather's name," Jenny supplied. "We have new cousins, too. Bianca and Cordelia—but we call her Delia—and Ethan."

Alex rolled his eyes. "Everybody had babies."

"He's nice," Kevin decided after a long look. "Is he my brother, too?"

"Absolutely," Suzanna said, before Megan could respond. "I'm afraid you've got an awfully big family now."

Kevin gave her a shy look and touched a testing finger to Christian's waving fist. "I don't mind."

Suzanna smiled over at Megan. "Want to trade?"

Megan hesitated a moment, then gave in. "I'd love to." She cradled the baby while Suzanna took the garment bag. "Oh, Lord." Unable to resist, she nuzzled. "It's easy to forget how tiny they are. How wonderful they smell. And you . . ." As they walked through the terminal, she took a good look at Suzanna. "How can you look so terrific, when you had a baby only three weeks ago?"

"Oh, bless you. I've been feeling like such a frump. Alex, no running."

"Same goes, Kevin. How's Sloan taking to fatherhood?" Megan wanted to know. "I hated not coming out when Mandy had the baby, but with selling the house and getting things in order to make the move, I just couldn't manage it."

"Everyone understood. And Sloan's a terrific daddy. He'd have Delia strapped on his back twenty-four hours a day if Amanda let him. He designed this incredible nursery for the babies. Window seats, cubbyholes, wonderful built-in cupboards for toys. Delia and Bianca share it, and when C.C. and Trent are in town—which, since The Retreat opened, is more often than not—Ethan's in there, too."

"It's wonderful that they'll all grow up together." She looked at Kevin, Alex and Jenny, thinking as much about them as about the babies.

Suzanna understood perfectly. "Yes, it is. I'm so glad you're here, Megan. It's like getting another sister." She watched Megan's lashes lower. Not quite ready for that, Suzanna surmised, and switched subjects. "And it's going to be a huge relief to hand over the books to you. Not only for The Retreat, but for the boat business, too."

"I'm looking forward to it."

Suzanna stopped by a new minivan, unlocked the doors. "Pile in," she told the kids, then slipped the baby out of Megan's arms. "I hope you say that after you get a look at the ledgers." Competently she strapped the baby into his car seat. "I'm afraid Holt's a pathetic record keeper. And Nathaniel . . ."

"Oh, that's right. Holt has a partner now. What did Sloan tell me? An old friend?"

"Holt and Nathaniel grew up together on the island. Nathaniel moved back a few months ago. He used to be in the merchant marine. There you go, sweetie." She kissed the baby, then shot an eagle eye over the rest of the children to make sure seat belts were securely buckled. She clicked the sliding door into place, then rounded the hood as Megan took the passenger seat. "He's quite a character," Suzanna said mildly. "You'll get a kick out of him."

The character was just finishing up an enormous lunch of fried chicken, potato salad and lemon meringue pie. With a sigh of satisfaction, he pushed back from the table and eyed his hostess lustfully.

"What do I have to do to get you to marry me, darling?"

She giggled, blushed and waved a hand at him. "You're such a tease, Nate."

"Who's teasing?" He rose, grabbed her fluttering hand and kissed it lavishly. She always smelled like a woman—soft, lush, glorious. He winked and skimmed his lips up to nibble on her wrist. "You know I'm crazy about you, Coco."

Cordelia Calhoun McPike gave another delighted giggle, then patted his cheek. "About my cooking."

"That, too." He grinned when she slipped away to pour him coffee. She was a hell of a woman, he thought. Tall, stately, striking. It amazed him that some smart man hadn't scooped up the widow McPike long ago. "Who do I have to fight off this week?"

"Now that The Retreat's open, I don't have time for romance." She might have sighed over it if she wasn't so pleased with her life. All her darling girls were married and happy, with babies of their own. She had grandnieces and grandnephews to spoil, nephews-in-law to coddle, and, most surprising of all, a full-fledged career as head chef for the St. James Towers Retreat. She offered Nathaniel the coffee and, because she caught him eyeing the pie, cut him another slice.

"You read my mind."

Now she did sigh a little. There was nothing quite so comforting to Coco as watching a man enjoy her food. And he was some man. When Nathaniel Fury rolled back into town, people had noticed. Who could overlook tall, dark and handsome? Certainly not Coco McPike. Particularly not when the combination came with smoky gray eyes, a cleft chin and wonderfully golden skin over sharp cheekbones—not to mention considerable charm.

The black T-shirt and jeans he wore accented an athletic, rangy body—broad shoulders, muscular arms, narrow hips.

Then there was that aura of mystery, a touch of the exotic. It went deeper than his looks, though the dark eyes and the waving mane of deep mahogany hair was exotic enough. It was a matter of presence, she supposed, the culmination of what he'd done and what had touched him in all those years he traveled to foreign ports.

If she'd been twenty years younger . . . Well, she thought, patting her rich chestnut hair, maybe ten.

But she wasn't, so she had given Nathaniel the place in her heart of the son she'd never had. She was determined to find the right woman for him and see him settled happily. Like her beautiful girls.

Since she felt she had personally arranged the romances and resulting unions of all four of her nieces, she was confident she could do the same for Nathaniel.

"I did your chart last night," she said casually, and checked the fish stew she had simmering for tonight's menu.

"Oh, yeah?" He scooped up more pie. God, the woman could cook.

"You're entering a new phase of your life, Nate."

He'd seen too much of the world to totally dismiss astrology—or anything else. So he smiled at her. "I'd say you're on target there, Coco. Got myself a business, a house on land, retired my seabag."

"No, this phase is more personal." She wiggled her slim brows. "It has to do with Venus."

He grinned at that. "So, are you going to marry me?"

She wagged a finger at him. "You're going to say that to someone, quite seriously, before the summer's over. Actually, I saw you falling in love twice. I'm not quite sure what that means." Her forehead wrinkled as she considered. "It didn't really seem as if you'd have to choose, though there was quite a bit of interference. Perhaps even danger."

"If a guy falls for two women, he's asking for trouble." And Nathaniel was content, at least for the moment, to have no females in his life. Women simply didn't come without expectations, and he planned to fulfill none but his own. "And since my heart already belongs to you . . ." He got up to go to the stove and kiss her cheek.

The tornado blew in without warning. The kitchen door slammed open, and three shrieking whirlwinds spun through.

"Aunt Coco! They're here!"

"Oh, my." Coco pressed a hand to her speeding heart. "Alex, you took a year off my life." But she smiled, studying the dark-eyed boy beside him. "Can this be Kevin? You've grown a foot! Don't you have a kiss for Aunt Coco?"

"Yes, ma'am." He went forward dutifully, still unsure of his ground. He was enveloped against soft breasts, in soft scents. It eased his somewhat nervous stomach.

"We're so glad you're here." Coco's eyes teared up sentimentally. "Now the whole family's in one place. Kevin, this is Mr. Fury. Nate, my grandnephew."

Nathaniel knew the story, how the scum Baxter Dumont had managed to get some naive kid pregnant shortly before he married Suzanna. The boy was eyeing him now, nervous but contained. Nathaniel realized Kevin knew the story, as well—or part of it.

"Welcome to Bar Harbor." He offered his hand, which Kevin took politely.

"Nate runs the boat shop and stuff with my dad." The novelty of saying "my dad" had yet to wear thin with Alex. "Kevin wants to see whales," he told Nathaniel. "He comes from Oklahoma, and they don't have any. They hardly have any water at all."

"We've got some." Kevin automatically defended his homeland. "And we've got cowboys," he added, one-upping Alex. "You don't have any of those."

"Uh-huh." This from Jenny. "I got a whole cowboy suit."

"Girl," Alex corrected. "It's a cowgirl, 'cause you're a girl."

"It is not."

"Is too."

Her eyes narrowed dangerously. "Is not."

"Well, I see everything's normal in here." Suzanna entered, aiming a warning look at both of her children. "Hello, Nate. I didn't expect to see you here."

"I got lucky." He slipped an arm around Coco's shoulders. "Spent an hour with my woman."

"Flirting with Aunt Coco again?" But Suzanna noted that his gaze had already shifted. She remembered that look from the first time they'd met. The way the gray eyes measured, assessed. Automatically she put a hand on Megan's arm. "Megan O'Riley, Nathaniel Fury, Holt's partner—and Aunt Coco's latest conquest."

"Nice to meet you." She was tired, Megan realized. Had to be, if that clear, steady gaze put her back up. She dismissed him, a little too abruptly for politeness, and smiled at Coco. "You look wonderful."

"Oh, and here I am in my apron. I didn't even freshen up." Coco gave her a hard, welcoming hug. "Let me fix you something. You must be worn-out after the flight."

"Just a little."

"We took the bags up, and I put Christian in the nursery." While Suzanna herded the children to the table and chatted, Nathaniel took a good long survey of Megan O'Riley.

Cool as an Atlantic breeze, he decided. A little frazzled and unnerved at the moment, he thought, but not willing to show it. The peach-toned skin and long, waving strawberry blond hair made an eye-catching combination.

Nathaniel usually preferred women who were dark and sultry, but there was something to be said for all that rose and gold. She had blue eyes, the color of a calm sea at dawn. Stubborn mouth, he mused, though it softened nicely when she smiled at her son.

A bit on the skinny side, he thought as he finished off his coffee. Needed some of Coco's cooking to help her fill out. Or maybe she just looked skinny—and prim—because she wore such a severely tailored jacket and slacks.

Well aware of his scrutiny, Megan forced herself to keep up her end of the conversation with Coco and the rest. She'd grown used to stares years before, when she was young, unmarried, and pregnant by another woman's husband.

She knew how some men reacted to her status as a single mother, how they assumed she was an easy mark. And she knew how to disabuse them of the notion.

She met Nathaniel's stare levelly, frostily. He didn't look away, as most would, but continued to watch her, unblinkingly, until her teeth clenched.

Good going, he thought. She might be skinny, but she had grit. He grinned, lifted his coffee mug in a silent toast, then turned to Coco. "I've got to go, got a tour to do. Thanks for lunch, Coco."

"Don't forget dinner. The whole family will be here. Eight o'clock."

He glanced back at Megan. "Wouldn't miss it."

"See that you don't." Coco looked at her watch, closed her eyes. "Where is that man? He's late again."

"The Dutchman?"

"Who else? I sent him to the butcher's two hours ago."

Nathaniel shrugged. His former shipmate, and The Towers' new assistant chef, ran on his own timetable. "If I see him down at the docks, I'll send him along."

"Kiss me goodbye," Jenny demanded, delighted when Nathaniel hauled her up.

"You're the prettiest cowboy on the island," he whispered in her ear. Jenny shot a smug look at her brother when her feet touched the floor again. "You let me know when you're ready for a sail," he said to Kevin. "Nice meeting you, Ms. O'Riley."

"Nate's a sailor," Jenny said importantly when Nathaniel strolled out. "He's been everywhere and done everything."

Megan didn't doubt it for a minute.

So much had changed at The Towers, though the family rooms on the first two floors and the east wing were much the same. Trent St. James, with Megan's brother, Sloan, as architect, had concentrated most of the time and effort on the ten suites in the west wing, the new guest dining area and the west tower. All of that area comprised the hotel.

From the quick tour Megan was given, she could see that none of the time and effort that had gone into the construction and renovations had been wasted.

Sloan had designed with an appreciation for the original fortresslike structure, retaining the high-ceilinged rooms and circular stairs, ensuring that the many fireplaces were working, preserving the mullioned windows and French doors that led out onto terraces, balconies, parapets.

The lobby was sumptuous, filled with antiques and

designed with a multitude of cozy corners that invited guests to lounge on a rainy or wintry day. The spectacular views of bay or cliffs or sea or Suzanna's fabulous gardens were there to be enjoyed, or tempted guests to stroll out onto terraces and balconies.

When Amanda, as hotel manager, took over the tour, Megan was told that each suite was unique. The storage rooms of The Towers had been full of old furniture, mementos and art. What hadn't been sold prior to Trent's having invested the St. James money in the transformation now graced the guest rooms.

Some suites were two levels, with an art deco staircase connecting the rooms, some had wainscoting or silk wallpaper. There was an Aubusson rug here, an old tapestry there. And all the rooms were infused with the legend of the Calhoun emeralds and the woman who had owned them.

The emeralds themselves, discovered after a difficult and dangerous search—some said with the help of the spirits of Bianca Calhoun and Christian Bradford, the artist who had loved her—resided now in a glass case in the lobby. Above the case was a portrait of Bianca, painted by Christian more than eighty years before.

"They're gorgeous," Megan whispered. "Stunning." The tiers of grass green emeralds and white diamonds almost pulsed with life.

"Sometimes I'll just stop and look at them," Amanda admitted, "and remember all we went through to find them. How Bianca tried to use them to escape with her children to Christian. It should make me sad, I suppose, but having them here, under her portrait, seems right."

"Yes, it does." Megan could feel the pull of them, even through the glass. "But isn't it risky, having them out here this way?"

"Holt arranged for security. Having an ex-cop in the family means nothing's left to chance. The glass is bulletproof." Amanda tapped her finger against it. "And wired to some high-tech sensor." Amanda checked her watch and judged that she had fifteen minutes before she had to resume her managerial duties. "I hope your rooms are all right. We've barely scratched the surface on the family renovations."

"They're fine." And the truth was, it relaxed Megan a bit to see cracked plaster and gnawed woodwork. It made it all less intimidating. "Kevin's in paradise. He's outside with Alex and Jenny, playing with the new puppy."

"Our Fred and Holt's Sadie are quite the proud parents." With a laugh, Amanda tossed back her swing of sable hair. "Eight pups."

"As Alex said, everyone's having babies. And your Delia is beautiful."

"She is, isn't she?" Maternal pride glowed in Amanda's eyes. "I can't believe how much she's grown already. You should have been around here six months ago. All four of us out to here." She laughed again as she held out her arms. "Waddling everywhere. The men strutting. Do you know they took bets to see if Lilah or I would deliver first? She beat me by two days." And since she'd bet twenty on herself, it still irritated her a little. "It's the first time I've known her to be in a hurry about anything."

"Her Bianca's beautiful, too. She was awake and

howling for attention when I was in the nursery. Your nanny has her hands full."

"Mrs. Billows can handle anything."

"Actually, I wasn't thinking about the babies. It was Max." She grinned remembering how Bianca's daddy had come running in, abandoning his new novel on the typewriter to scoop his daughter out of her crib.

"He's such a softie."

"Who's a softie?" Sloan strode into the room to swing his sister off her feet.

"Not you, O'Riley," Amanda murmured, watching the way his face softened like butter as he pressed his cheek to Megan's.

"You're here." He twirled her again. "I'm so glad you're here, Meg."

"Me too." She felt her eyes tear and squeezed him tight. "Daddy."

With a laugh, he set her down, slipped his free arm around his wife. "Did you see her yet?"

Megan feigned ignorance. "Who?"

"My girl. My Delia."

"Oh, her." Megan shrugged, chuckled, then kissed Sloan on his sulking mouth. "Not only did I see her, I held her, I sniffed her, and have already decided to spoil her at every opportunity. She's gorgeous, Sloan. She looks just like Amanda."

"Yeah, she does." He kissed his wife. "Except she's got my chin."

"That's a Calhoun chin," Amanda claimed.

"Nope, it's O'Riley all the way. And speaking of O'Rileys," he continued, before Amanda could argue, "where's Kevin?"

"Outside. I should probably go get him. We haven't even unpacked yet."

"We'll go with you," Sloan said.

"You go. I'm covering." Even as Amanda spoke, the phone on the mahogany front desk rang. "Break's over. See you at dinner, Megan." She leaned up to kiss Sloan again. "See you sooner, O'Riley."

"Mmm . . ." Sloan gave a satisfied sigh as he watched his wife stride off. "I do love the way that woman eats up the floor."

"You look at her just the way you did a year ago, at your wedding." Megan tucked her hand in his as they walked out of the lobby and onto the stone terrace steps. "It's nice."

"She's . . ." He searched for a word, then settled on the simplest truth. "Everything. I'd like you to be as happy as I am, Megan."

"I am happy." A breeze flitted through her hair. On it carried the sound of children's laughter. "Hearing that makes me happy. So does being here." They descended another level and turned west. "I have to admit I'm a little nervous. It's such a big step." She saw her son scramble to the top of the fort in the yard below, arms raised high in victory. "This is good for him."

"And you?"

"And me." She leaned against her brother. "I'll miss Mom and Dad, but they've already said that with both of us out here, it gives them twice as much reason to visit twice as often." She pushed the blowing hair from her face while Kevin played sniper, fighting off Alex and Jenny's assault on the fort. "He needs to know the rest of his family. And I . . . needed a change. And as to that—" she looked back at Sloan "—I tried to get Amanda to show me the setup."

"And she told you that you couldn't sharpen your pencils for a week."

"Something like that."

"We decided at the last family meeting that you'd have a week to settle in before you started hammering the adding machine."

"I don't need a week. I only need—"

"I know, I know. You'd give Amanda a run for the efficiency crown. But orders are you take a week off."

She arched a brow. "And just who gives the orders around here?"

"Everybody." Sloan grinned. "That's what makes it interesting."

Thoughtful, she looked out to sea. The sky was as clear as blown glass, and the breeze warm with early summer. From her perch at the wall, she could see the small clumps of islands far out in the diamond-bright water.

A different world, she thought, from the plains and prairies of home. A different life, perhaps, for her and her son.

A week. To relax, to explore, to take excursions with Kevin. Tempting, yes. But far from responsible. "I want to pull my weight."

"You will, believe me." He glanced out at the clear sound of a boat horn. "That's one of Holt and Nate's," Sloan told her, pointing to the long terraced boat that was gliding across the water. "The *Mariner*. Takes tourists out for whale-watching."

The kids were all atop the fort now, shouting and waving at the boat. When the horn blasted again, they cheered.

"You'll meet Nate at dinner," Sloan began.

"I met him already."

"Flirting a meal out of Coco?"

"It appeared that way."

Sloan shook his head. "That man can eat, let me tell you. What did you think?"

"Not much," she muttered. "He seemed a little rough-edged to me."

"You get used to him. He's one of the family now."

Megan made a noncommittal sound. Maybe he was, but that didn't mean he was part of hers.

Chapter 2

As far as Coco was concerned, Niels Van Horne was a thoroughly unpleasant man. He did not take constructive criticism, or the subtlest of suggestions for improvement, well at all. She tried to be courteous, God knew, as he was a member of the staff of The Towers and an old, dear friend of Nathaniel's.

But the man was a thorn in her side, an abrasive grain of sand in the cozy slipper of her contentment.

In the first place, he was simply too big. The hotel kitchen was gloriously streamlined and organized. She and Sloan had worked in tandem on the design, so that the finished product would suit her specifications and needs. She adored her huge stove, her convection and conventional ovens, the glint of polished stainless steel and glossy white counters, and her whisper-silent dishwasher. She loved the smells of cooking, the hum of her exhaust fans, the sparkling cleanliness of her tile floor.

And there was Van Horne—or Dutch, as he was called—a bull in her china shop, with his redwood-size shoulders and cinder-block arms rippling with tattoos.

He refused to wear the neat white bib aprons she'd ordered, with their elegant blue lettering, preferring his rolled-up shirts and tatty jeans held up by a hank of rope.

His salt-and-pepper hair was tied back in a stubby ponytail, and his face, usually scowling, was as big as the rest of him, scored with lines around his light green eyes. His nose, broken several times in the brawls he seemed so proud of, was mashed and crooked. His skin was brown, and leathery as an old saddle.

And his language . . . Well, Coco didn't consider herself a prude, but she was, after all, a lady.

But the man could cook. It was his only redeeming quality.

As Dutch worked at the stove, she supervised the two line chefs. The specials tonight were her New England fish stew and stuffed trout *à la française*. Everything appeared to be in order.

"Mr. Van Horne," she began, in a tone that never failed to put his back up. "You will be in charge while I'm downstairs. I don't foresee any problems, but should any arise, I'll be in the family dining room."

He cast one of his sneering looks over his shoulder. Woman was all slicked up tonight, like she was going to some opera or something, he thought. All red silk and pearls. He wanted to snort, but knew her damned perfume would interfere with the pleasure he gained from the smell of his curried rice.

"I cooked for three hundred men," he said in his raspy, sandpaper-edged voice. "I can deal with a couple dozen pasty-faced tourists."

"Our guests," she said between her teeth, "may be slightly more discriminating than sailors trapped on some rusty boat."

One of the busboys swung through, carrying plates. Dutch's eyes zeroed in on one that still held half an entrée. On *his* ship, men had cleaned their plates. "Not too damn hungry, were they?"

"Mr. Van Horne." Coco drew air through her nose. "You will remain in the kitchen at all times. I will not have you going out into the dining room again and berating our guests over their eating habits. A bit more garnish on that salad, please," she said to one of the line chefs, and glided out the door.

"Can't stand fancy-faced broads," Dutch muttered. And if it wasn't for Nate, he thought sourly, Dutch Van Horne wouldn't be taking orders from a dame.

Nathaniel didn't share his former shipmate's disdain of women. He loved them, one and all. He enjoyed their looks, their smells, their voices, and was more than satisfied to settle in the family parlor with six of the best-looking women it had been his pleasure to meet.

The Calhoun women were a constant delight to him. Suzanna, with her soft eyes, Lilah's lazy sexuality, Amanda's brisk practicality, C.C.'s cocky grin, not to mention Coco's feminine elegance.

They made The Towers Nathaniel's little slice of heaven.

And the sixth woman... He sipped his whiskey and water as he watched Megan O'Riley. Now there was a package he thought might be full of surprises. In the looks department, she didn't take second place to the fabulous Calhouns. And her voice, with its slow Oklahoma drawl, added its own appeal. What she lacked, he mused, was the easy warmth that flowed from the other women.

He hadn't decided as yet whether it was the result of a cold nature or simple shyness. Whatever it was, it ran deep. It was hard to be cold or shy in a room filled with laughing people, cooing babies and wrestling children.

He was holding one of his favorite females at the moment. Jenny was bouncing on his lap and barraging him with questions.

"Are you going to marry Aunt Coco?"

"She won't have me."

"I will." Jenny beamed up at him, an apprentice heartbreaker with a missing front tooth. "We can get married in the garden, like Mom and Daddy did. Then you can come live with us."

"Now that's the best offer I've had in a long time." He stroked a callused finger down her cheek.

"But you have to wait until I get big."

"It's always wise to make a man wait." This from Lilah, who slouched on a sofa, her head in the crook of her husband's arm, a baby in her own. "Don't let him rush you into anything, Jenny. Slow is always best."

"She'd know," Amanda commented. "Lilah's spent her life studying slow."

"I'm not ready to give up my girl." Holt scooped Jenny up. "Especially to a broken-down sailor."

"I can outpilot you blindfolded, Bradford."

"Nuh-uh." Alex popped up to defend the family honor. "Daddy sails the best. He can sail better than anybody. Even if bad guys were shooting at him." Territorial, Alex wrapped an arm around Holt's leg. "He even got shot. He's got a bullet hole in him."

Holt grinned at his friend. "Get your own cheering gallery, Nate."

"Did you ever get shot?" Alex wanted to know.

"Can't say that I have." Nathaniel swirled his whiskey. "But there was this Greek in Corfu that wanted to slit my throat."

Alex's eyes widened until they were like saucers. From his spot on the rug, Kevin inched closer. "Really?" Alex looked for signs of knife wounds. He knew Nathaniel had a tattoo of a fire-breathing dragon on his shoulder, but this was even better. "Did you stab him back and kill him dead?"

"Nope." Nathaniel caught the look of doubt and disapproval in Megan's eyes. "He missed and caught me in the shoulder, and the Dutchman knocked him cold with a bottle of ouzo."

Desperately impressed, Kevin slid closer. "Have you got a scar?"

"Sure do."

Amanda slapped Nathaniel's hand before he could tug up his shirt. "Cut it out, or every man in the room will be stripping to show off war wounds. Sloan's really proud of the one he got from barbed wire."

"It's a beaut," Sloan agreed. "But Meg's is even better."

"Shut up, Sloan."

"Hey, a man's gotta brag on his only sister." Enjoying himself, Sloan draped an arm around her shoulders. "She was twelve—hardheaded little brat. We had a mustang stallion nearly as bad-tempered as she was. She snuck him out one day, determined that she could break him. Well, she got about a half a mile before he shook her off."

"He did not shake me off," Megan said primly. "The bridle snapped."

"That's her story." Sloan gave her a quick squeeze.

"Fact is, that horse tossed her right into a barbed-wire fence. She landed on her rump. I don't believe you sat down for six weeks."

"It was two," she said, but her lips twitched.

"Got herself a hell of a scar." Sloan gave her butt a brotherly pat.

"Wouldn't mind taking a look at it," Nathaniel said under his breath, and earned an arched-eyebrow look from Suzanna.

"I think I'll put Christian down before dinner."

"Good idea." C.C. took Ethan from Trent just as the baby began to fuss. "Somebody's hungry."

"I know I am." Lilah rose.

Megan watched mothers and babies head upstairs to nurse, and was surprised by a quick tug of envy. Funny, she mused, she hadn't even thought of having more babies until she came here and found herself surrounded by them.

"So sorry I'm late." Coco glided into the room, patting her hair. "We had a few problems in the kitchen."

Nathaniel recognized the look of frustration on her face and fought back a grin. "Dutch giving you trouble, darling?"

"Well . . ." She didn't like to complain. "We simply have different views on how things should be done. Oh, bless you, Trent," she said when he offered her a glass. "Oh, dear, where is my head? I forgot the canapés."

"I'll get them." Max unfolded himself from the sofa and headed toward the family kitchen.

"Thank you, dear. Now . . ." She took Megan's hand, squeezed. "We've hardly had a moment to talk. What do you think of The Retreat?"

"It's wonderful, everything Sloan said it would be. Amanda tells me all ten suites are booked."

"It's been a wonderful first season." She beamed at Trent. "Hardly more than a year ago, I was in despair, so afraid my girls would lose their home. Though the cards told me differently. Did I ever tell you that I foresaw Trent in the tarot? I really must do a spread for you, dear, and see what your future holds."

"Well . . ."

"Perhaps I can just look at your palm."

Megan let go with a sigh of relief when Max came back with a tray and distracted Coco.

"Not interested in the future?" Nathaniel murmured.

Megan glanced over, surprised that he had moved beside her without her being aware of it. "I'm more interested in the present, one step at a time."

"A cynic." He took her hand and, though it went rigid in his, turned it palm up. "I met an old woman on the west coast of Ireland. Molly Duggin was her name. She said I had the sight." His smoky eyes stayed level with hers for a long moment before they shifted to her open palm. Megan felt something skitter down her spine. "A stubborn hand. Self-sufficient, for all its elegance."

He traced a finger over it. Now there was more than a skitter. There was a jolt.

"I don't believe in palmistry."

"You don't have to. Shy," he said quietly. "I wondered about that. The passions are there, but repressed." His thumb glided gently over her palm's mound of Venus. "Or channeled. You'd prefer to say channeled. Goal-oriented, practical. You'd rather make decisions

with your head, no matter what your heart tells you."
His eyes lifted to hers again. "How close am I?"

Much too close, she thought, but drew her hand coolly from his. "An interesting parlor game, Mr. Fury."

His eyes laughed at her as he tucked his thumbs in his pockets. "Isn't it?"

By noon the next day, Megan had run out of busywork. She hadn't the heart to refuse Kevin's plea to be allowed to spend the day with the Bradfords, though his departure had left her very much to her own devices.

She simply wasn't used to free time.

One trip to the hotel lobby had aborted her idea of convincing Amanda to let her study the books and files. Amanda, she was told by a cheerful desk clerk, was in the west tower, handling a small problem.

Coco wasn't an option, either. Megan had halted just outside the door of the kitchen when she heard the crash of pots and raised voices inside.

Since Lilah had gone back to work as a naturalist in the park, and C.C. was at her automotive shop in town, Megan was left on her own.

In a house as enormous as The Towers, she felt like the last living soul on the island.

She could read, she mused, or sit in the sun on one of the terraces and contemplate the view. She could wander down to the first floor of the family area and check out the progress of the renovations. And harass Sloan and Trent, she thought with a sigh, as they tried to get some work done.

She didn't consider disturbing Max in his studio, knowing he was working on his book. As she'd already spent an hour in the nursery playing with the babies, she felt another visit was out.

She wandered her room, smoothed down the already smooth coverlet on the marvelous four-poster. The rest of her things had arrived that morning, and in her perhaps too-efficient way, she'd already unpacked. Her clothes were neatly hung in the rosewood armoire or folded in the Chippendale bureau. Framed photos of her family smiled from the gateleg table under the window.

Her shoes were aligned, her jewelry was tucked away and her books were stored on the shelf.

And if she didn't find something to do, she would go mad.

With this in mind, she picked up her briefcase, checked the contents one last time and headed outside, to the car Sloan had left at her disposal.

The sedan ran like a top, courtesy of C.C.'s mechanical skills. Megan drove down the winding road toward the village.

She enjoyed the bright blue water of the bay, and the colorful throngs of tourists strolling up and down the sloped streets. But the glistening wares in the shop windows didn't tempt her to stop and do any strolling of her own.

Shopping was something she did out of necessity, not for pleasure.

Once, long ago, she'd loved the idle pleasure of window-shopping, the careless satisfaction of buying for fun. She'd enjoyed empty, endless summer days once, with nothing more to do than watch clouds or listen to the wind.

But that was before innocence had been lost, and responsibilities found.

She saw the sign for Shipshape Tours by the docks. There were a couple of small boats in drydock, but the *Mariner* and its sister ship, the *Island Queen*, were nowhere to be seen.

Her brows knit in annoyance. She'd hoped to catch Holt before he took one of the tours out. Still, there was no reason she couldn't poke inside the little tin-roofed building that housed the offices. After all, Shipshape was now one of her clients.

Megan pulled the sedan behind a long, long T-Bird convertible. She had to admire the lines of the car, and the glossy black paint job that highlighted the white interior.

She paused a moment, shielding her eyes as she watched a two-masted schooner glide over the water, its rust-colored sails full, its decks dotted with people.

There was no denying the beauty of the spot, though the smell and look of the water was so foreign, compared to what she'd known most of her life. The midday breeze was fresh and carried the scent of the sea and the aromas of lunch from the restaurants nearby.

She could be happy here, she told herself. No, she *would* be happy here. Resolutely she turned toward the building and rapped on the door.

"Yeah. It's open."

There was Nathaniel, his feet propped on a messy and ancient metal desk, a phone at his ear. His jeans were torn at the knee and smeared with something like motor oil. His mane of dark mahogany hair was tousled by the wind, or his hands. He crooked his finger in a come-ahead gesture, his eyes measuring her as he spoke on the phone.

"Teak's your best bet. I've got enough in stock, and can have the deck finished in two days. No, the engine just needed an overhaul. It's got a lot of life left in it. No problem." He picked up a smoldering cigar. "I'll give you a call when we're finished."

He hung up the phone, clamped the cigar between his teeth. Funny, he thought, Megan O'Riley had floated into his brain that morning, looking very much as she did at this moment. All spit and polish, that pretty rose-gold hair all tucked up, her face calm and cool.

"Just in the neighborhood?" he asked.

"I was looking for Holt."

"He's out with the *Queen*." Idly Nathaniel checked the diver's watch on his wrist. "Won't be back for about an hour and a half." His cocky mouth quirked up. "Looks like you're stuck with me."

She fought back the urge to shift her briefcase from hand to hand, to back away. "I'd like to see the books."

Nathaniel took a lazy puff on his cigar. "Thought you were on vacation."

She fell back on her best defense. Disdain. "Is there a problem with the books?" she said frostily.

"Couldn't prove it by me." In a fluid move, he reached down and opened a drawer in the desk. He took out a black-bound ledger. "You're the expert." He held it out to her. "Pull up a chair, Meg."

"Thank you." She took a folding chair on the other side of the desk, then slipped dark-framed reading glasses from her briefcase. Once they were on, she opened the ledger. Her accountant's heart contracted in horror at the mess of figures, cramped margin notes and scribbled-on Post-its. "These are your books?"

"Yeah." She looked prim and efficient in her practical glasses and scooped-up hair. She made his mouth water. "Holt and I sort of take turns with them—that's since Suzanna tossed up her hands and called us idiots." He smiled charmingly. "We figured, you know, with her being pregnant at the time, she didn't need any more stress."

"Hmmm . . ." Megan was already turning pages. For her, the state of the bookkeeping didn't bring on anxiety so much as a sense of challenge. "Your files?"

"We got 'em." Nathaniel jerked a thumb at the dented metal cabinet shoved in the corner. There was a small, greasy boat motor on top of it.

"Is there anything in them?" she said pleasantly.

"Last I looked there was." He couldn't help it. The more prim and efficient her voice, the more he wanted to razz her.

"Invoices?"

"Sure."

"Expense receipts?"

"Absolutely." He reached in another drawer and took out a large cigar box. "We got plenty of receipts."

She took the box, opened the lid and sighed. "This is how you run your business?"

"No. We run the business by taking people out to sea, or repairing their boats. Even building them." He leaned forward on the desk, mostly so he could catch a better whiff of that soft, elusive scent that clung to her skin. "Me, I've never been much on paperwork, and Holt had his fill of it when he was on the force." His smile spread. He didn't figure she wore prim glasses, pulled-back hair and buttoned-up blouses so that a man would yearn to toss aside, muss up and unbutton. But the result was the same. "Maybe that's why the accountant we hired to do the taxes this year developed this little tic." He tapped a finger beside his left eye. "I heard he moved to Jamaica to sell straw baskets."

She had to laugh. "I'm made of sterner stuff, I promise you."

"Never doubted it." He leaned back again, his swivel chair squeaking. "You've got a nice smile, Megan. When you use it."

She knew that tone, lightly flirtatious, unmistakably male. Her defenses locked down like a vault. "You're not paying me for my smile."

"I'd rather it came free, anyhow. How'd you come to be an accountant?"

"I'm good with numbers." She spread the ledger on the desk before opening her briefcase and taking out a calculator.

"So's a bookie. I mean, why'd you pick it?"

"Because it's a solid, dependable career." She began to run numbers, hoping to ignore him.

"And because numbers only add up one way?"

She couldn't ignore that—the faint hint of amusement in his voice. She slanted him a look, adjusted her glasses. "Accounting may be logical, Mr. Fury, but logic doesn't eliminate surprises."

"If you say so. Listen, we may have both come through the side door into the Calhouns' extended family, but we're there. Don't you feel stupid calling me Mr. Fury?"

Her smile had all the warmth of an Atlantic gale. "No, I don't."

"Is it me, or all men, you're determined to beat off with icicles?"

Patience, which she'd convinced herself she held in great store, was rapidly being depleted. "I'm here to do the books. That's all I'm here for."

"Never had a client for a friend?" He took a last puff on the cigar and stubbed it out. "You know, there's a funny thing about me."

"I'm sure you're about to tell me what it is."

"Right. I can have a pleasant conversation with a woman without being tempted to toss her on the floor and tear her clothes off. Now, you're a real treat to look at, Meg, but I can control my more primitive urges—especially when all the signals say stop."

Now she felt ridiculous. She'd been rude, or nearly so, since the moment she'd met him. Because, she admitted to herself, her reaction to him made her uncomfortable. But, damn it, he was the one who kept looking at her as though he'd like to nibble away.

"I'm sorry." The apology was sincere, if a trifle stiff. "I'm making a lot of adjustments right now, so I haven't felt very congenial. And the way you look at me puts me on edge."

"Fair enough. But I have to tell you I figure it's a man's right to look. Anything more takes an invitation—of one kind or the other."

"Then we can clear the air and start over, since I can tell you I won't be putting out the welcome mat. Now, Nathaniel—" it was a concession she made with a smile "—do you suppose you could dig up your tax returns?"

"I can probably put my hands on them." He scooted back his chair. The squeak of the wheels ended on a high-pitched yelp that had Megan jolting and scattering papers. "Damn it—forgot you were back there." He picked up a wriggling, whimpering black puppy. "He sleeps a lot, so I end up stepping on him or running the damn chair over his tail," he said to Megan as the pup licked frantically at his face. "Whenever I try to leave him home, he cries until I give in and bring him with me."

"He's darling." Her fingers were already itching to stroke. "He looks a lot like the one Coco has."

"Same litter." Because he could read the sentiment in Megan's eyes perfectly, Nathaniel handed the pup across the desk.

"Oh, aren't you sweet? Aren't you pretty?"

When she cooed to the dog, all defenses dropped, Nathaniel noted. She forgot to be businesslike and cool, and instead was all feminine warmth—those pretty hands stroking the pup's fur, her smile soft, her eyes alight with pleasure.

He had to remind himself the invitation was for a dog, not for him.

"What's his name?"

"Dog."

She looked up from the puppy's adoring eyes. "Dog? That's it?"

"He likes it. Hey, Dog." At the sound of his master's voice, Dog immediately cocked his head at Nathaniel and barked. "See?"

"Yes." She laughed and nuzzled. "It seems a bit unimaginative."

"On the contrary. How many dogs do you know named Dog?"

"I stand corrected. Down you go, and don't get any ideas about these receipts."

Nathaniel tossed a ball, and Dog gave joyful chase. "That'll keep him busy," he said as he came around the desk to help her gather up the scattered papers.

"You don't seem the puppy type to me."

"Always wanted one." He crouched down beside her and began to toss papers back into the cigar box. "Fact is, I used to play around with one of Dog's ancestors over at the Bradfords', when I was a kid. But it's hard to keep a dog aboard a ship. Got a bird, though."

"A bird?"

"A parrot I picked up in the Caribbean about five years ago. That's another reason I bring Dog along with me. Bird might eat him."

"Bird?" She glanced up, but the laugh froze in her throat. Why was he always closer than she anticipated? And why did those long, searching looks of his slide along her nerve ends like stroking fingers?

His gaze dropped to her mouth. The hesitant smile was still there, he noted. There was something very appealing about that touch of shyness, all wrapped up in stiff-necked confidence. Her eyes weren't cool now, but wary. Not an invitation, he reminded himself, but close. And damn tempting.

Testing his ground, he reached out to tuck a stray curl behind her ear. She was on her feet like a woman shot out of a cannon.

"You sure spook easily, Megan." After closing the lid on the cigar box, he rose. "But I can't say it isn't rewarding to know I make you nervous."

"You don't." But she didn't look at him as she said it. She'd never been a good liar. "I'm going to take all this back with me, if you don't mind. Once I have things organized, I'll be in touch with you, or Holt."

"Fine." The phone rang. He ignored it. "You know where to find us."

"Once I have the books in order, we'll need to set up a proper filing system."

Grinning, he eased a hip onto the corner of the desk. Lord, she was something. "You're the boss, sugar."

She snapped her briefcase closed. "No, you're the boss. And don't call me 'sugar.'" She marched outside, slipped into her car and eased away from the building and back into traffic. Competently she drove through the village, toward The Towers. Once she'd reached the bottom of the long, curving road that led home, she pulled the car over and stopped.

She needed a moment, she thought, before she faced anyone. With her eyes closed, she rested her head against the back of the seat. Her insides were still jittering, dancing with butterflies that willpower alone couldn't seem to swat away.

The weakness infuriated her. Nathaniel Fury infuriated her. After all this time, she mused, all this effort, it had taken no more than a few measuring looks to remind her, all too strongly, that she was still a woman.

Worse, much worse, she was sure he knew exactly what he was doing and how it affected her.

She'd been susceptible to a handsome face and smooth words before. Unlike those who loved her, she refused to blame her youth and inexperience for her reckless actions. Once upon a time, she'd listened to her heart, had believed absolutely in happy-ever-after. But no longer. Now she knew there were no princes, no pumpkins, no castles in the air. There was only reality, one a woman had to make for herself—and sometimes had to make for her child, as well.

She didn't want her pulse to race or her muscles to tense. She didn't want to feel that hot little curl in her stomach that was a yearning hunger crying to be filled. Not now. Not ever again.

All she wanted was to be a good mother to Kevin, to provide him with a happy, loving home. To earn her own way through her own skills. She wanted so badly to be strong and smart and self-sufficient.

Letting out a long sigh, she smiled to herself. And invulnerable.

Well, she might not quite achieve that, but she would be sensible. Never again would she permit a man the power to alter her life—and certainly not because he'd made her glands stand at attention.

Calmer, more confident, she started the car. She had work to do.

Chapter 3

"Have a heart, Mandy." Megan had sought her sister-in-law out the moment she returned to The Towers. "I just want to get a feel for my office and the routine."

Cocking her head, Amanda leaned back from her own pile of paperwork. "Horrible when everyone's busy and you're not, isn't it?"

Megan let out a heartfelt sigh. A kindred spirit. "Awful."

"Sloan wants you to relax," Amanda began, then laughed when Megan rolled her eyes. "But what does he know? Come on." Ready to oblige, she pushed back from the desk, skirted it. "You're practically next door." She led the way down the corridor to another thick, ornately carved door. "I think you've got just about everything you'll need. But if we've missed something, let me know."

Some women felt that frisson of excitement and anticipation on entering a department store. For some, that sensory click might occur at the smell of fresh paint, or the glint of candlelight, or the fizz of champagne just opened.

For Megan, it was the sight of a well-ordered office that caused that quick shiver of pleasure.

And here was everything she could have wanted.

The desk was glorious, gleaming Queen Anne, with a spotless rose-toned blotter and ebony desk set already in place. A multilined phone and a streamlined computer sat waiting.

She nearly purred.

There were wooden filing cabinets still smelling of lemon oil, their brass handles shining in the sunlight that poured through the many-paned windows. The Oriental rug picked up the hues of rose and slate blue in the upholstered chairs and love seat. There were shelves for her accounting books and ledgers, and a hunt table that held a coffeemaker, fax and personal copier.

Old-world charm and modern technology blended into tasteful efficiency.

"Mandy, it's perfect."

"I'd hoped you'd like it." Fussing, Amanda straightened the blotter, shifted the stapler. "I can't say I'm sorry to be handing over the books. It's more than a full-time job. I've filed everything, invoices, expenses, credit-card receipts, accounts payable, et cetera, by department." She opened a file drawer to demonstrate.

Megan's organized heart swelled at the sight of neatly color-coded file folders. Alphabetized, categorized, cross-referenced.

Glorious.

"Wonderful. Not a cigar box in sight."

Amanda hesitated, and then threw back her head and laughed. "You've seen Holt and Nate's accounting system, I take it."

Amused, and comfortable with Amanda, Megan

patted her briefcase. "I *have* their accounting system." Unable to resist, she sat in the high-backed swivel chair. "Now this is more like it." She took up a sharpened pencil, set it down again. "I don't know how to thank you for letting me join the team."

"Don't be silly. You're family. Besides, you may not be so grateful after a couple of weeks in chaos. I can't tell you how many interruptions—" Amanda broke off when she heard her name bellowed. Her brow lifted. "See what I mean?" She swung to the door to answer her husband's shout. "In here, O'Riley." She shook her head as Sloan and Trent trooped up to the door. Both of them were covered with dust. "I thought you were breaking down a wall or something."

"We were. Had some more old furniture to haul out of the way. And look what we found."

She examined what he held in his hands. "A moldy old book. That's wonderful, honey. Now why don't you and Trent go play construction?"

"Not just a book," Trent announced. "Fergus's account book. For the year of 1913."

"Oh." Amanda's heart gave one hard thud as she grabbed for the book.

Curiosity piqued, Megan rose to join them in the doorway. "Is it important?"

"It's the year Bianca died." Sloan laid a comforting hand on Amanda's shoulder. "You know the story, Meg. How Bianca was trapped in a loveless, abusive marriage. She met Christian Bradford, fell in love. She decided to take the children and leave Fergus, but he found out. They argued up in the tower. She fell through the window."

"And he destroyed everything that belonged to her."

Amanda's voice tightened, shook. "Everything—her clothes, her small treasures, her pictures. Everything but the emeralds. Because she'd hidden those. Now we have them, and the portrait Christian had painted. That's all we have of her." She let out a long breath. "I suppose it's fitting that we should have this of his. A ledger of profit and loss."

"Looks like he wrote in the margins here and there." Trent reached over to flip a page open. "Sort of an abbreviated journal."

Amanda frowned and read a portion of the cramped handwriting aloud.

"Too much waste in kitchen. Fired cook. B. too soft on staff. Purchased new cuff links. Diamond. Good choice for opera tonight. Showier than J. P. Getty's."

She let out a huff of breath. "It shows just what kind of man he was, doesn't it?"

"Darling, I wouldn't have brought it out if I'd known it would bother you."

Amanda shook her head. "No, the family will want it." But she set it down, because her fingers felt coated with more than dust and mold. "I was just showing Megan her new domain."

"So I see." Sloan's eyes narrowed. "What happened to relaxing?"

"This is how I relax," Megan responded. "Now why don't you go away and let me enjoy myself?"

"An excellent idea." Amanda gave her husband a kiss and a shove. "Scram." Even as she was hurrying the men along, Amanda's phone rang. "Give me a call if you need anything," she told Megan, and rushed to answer.

Feeling smug, Megan shut the door of her office. She was rubbing her hands together in anticipation as she crossed to her briefcase. She'd show Nathaniel Fury the true meaning of the word *shipshape*.

Three hours later, she was interrupted by the thunder of little feet. Obviously, she thought even before her door crashed open, someone had given Kevin the directions to her office.

"Hi, Mom!" He rushed into her arms for a kiss, and all thoughts of balancing accounts vanished from her mind. "We had the best time. We played with Sadie and Fred and had a war in the new fort. We got to go to Suzanna's flower place and water millions of plants."

Megan glanced down at Kevin's soggy sneakers. "And yourselves, I see."

He grinned. "We had a water battle, and I won."

"My hero."

"We had pizza for lunch, and Carolanne—she works for Suzanna—said I was a bottomless pit. And tomorrow Suzanna has to landscape, so we can't go with her, but we can go out on the whale boat if you want. You want to, don't you? I told Alex and Jenny you would."

She looked down at his dark, excited eyes. He was as happy as she'd ever seen him. At that moment, if he'd asked if she wanted to take a quick trip to Nairobi and hunt lions, she'd have been tempted to agree.

"You bet I do." She laughed when his arms flew around her and squeezed. "What time do we sail?"

At ten o'clock sharp the next morning, Megan had her three charges on the docks. Though the day was warm and balmy for June, she'd taken Suzanna's advice and brought along warm jackets and caps for the trip out into the Atlantic. She had binoculars, a camera, extra film.

Though she'd already downed a dose of motion-sickness pills, her landlubber's stomach tilted queasily as she studied the boat.

It looked sturdy. She could comfort herself with that. The white paint gleamed in the sun, the rails shone. When they stepped on board, she saw that there was a large interior cabin ringed with windows on the first deck. For the less hearty, she assumed. It boasted a concession stand, soft-drink machines and plenty of chairs and benches.

She gave it a last longing look as the children pulled her along. They wouldn't settle for a nice cozy cabin.

"We get to go to the bridge." Alex strutted along importantly, waving to one of the mates. "We own the *Mariner*. Us and Nate."

"Daddy says the bank owns it." Jenny scrambled up the iron steps, a red ribbon trailing from her hair. "But that's a joke. Dutch says it's a crying shame for a real sailor to haul around weak-bellied tourists. But Nate just laughs at him."

Megan merely lifted a brow. She had yet to meet the infamous Dutchman, but Jenny, clever as any parrot, would often quote him word for word. And all too often, those words were vividly blue.

"We're here." Alex burst onto the bridge, breathless with excitement. "Kevin, too."

"Welcome aboard." Nathaniel glanced up from the chart he was studying. His eyes fastened unerringly on Megan's.

"I was expecting Holt."

"He's helming the *Queen*." He picked up his cigar, clamped it between his teeth, grinned. "Don't worry, Meg, I won't run you aground."

She wasn't concerned about that. Exactly. In his black sweater and jeans, a black Greek fisherman's cap on his head and that gleam in his eye, he looked supremely competent. As a pirate might, she mused, upon boarding a merchant ship. "I started on your books." There, she thought, the ground was steady under her feet.

"I figured you would."

"They're a disorganized mess."

"Yeah. Kevin, come on over and take a look. I'll show you where we're heading."

Kevin hesitated, clinging to his mother's hand another moment. But the lure of those colorful charts was too much for him. He dashed over, dozens of questions tripping off his tongue.

"How many whales will we see? What happens if they bump the boat? Will they shoot water up from that hole on their back? Do you steer the boat from way up here?"

Megan started to interrupt and gently tell her son not to badger Mr. Fury, but Nathaniel was already answering questions, hauling Jenny up on one hip and taking Alex's finger to slide over the lines of the chart.

Pirate or not, she thought with a frown, he had a way with children.

"Ready to cast off, Captain."

Nathaniel nodded to the mate. "Quarter speed astern." Still holding Jenny, he walked to the wheel. "Pilot us out of here, sailor," he said to her, and guided her eager hands.

Curiosity got the better of Megan. She inched closer to study the instruments. Depth sounders, sonar, ship-to-shore radio. Those, and all the other equipment, were as foreign to her as the cockpit of a spaceship. She was a woman of the plains.

As the boat chugged gently away from the docks, her stomach lurched, reminding her why.

She clamped down on the nausea, annoyed with herself. It was in her mind, she insisted. A silly, imaginary weakness that could be overcome through willpower.

Besides, she'd taken seasickness pills, so, logically, she couldn't be seasick.

The children cheered as the boat made its long, slow turn in the bay. Megan's stomach turned with it.

Alex was generous enough to allow Kevin to blow the horn. Megan stared straight out the bridge window, her eyes focused above the calm blue water of Frenchman Bay.

It was beautiful, wasn't it? she told herself. And it was hardly tilting at all.

"You'll see The Towers on the starboard side," Nathaniel was saying.

"That's the right," Jenny announced. "Starboard's right and port's left."

"Stern's the back and the bow's in front," said Alex, not to be outdone. "We know all about boats."

Megan shifted her eyes to the cliffs, struggling to ignore another twist in her stomach. "There it is, Kevin." She gripped the brass rail beneath the starboard window for balance. "It looks like it's growing right out of the rock."

And it did look like a castle, she mused as she watched it with her son beside her. The turrets spearing up into the blue summer sky, the somber gray rock glistening with tiny flecks of mica. Even the scaffolding and the antlike figures of men working didn't detract from the fairy-tale aura. A fairy tale, she thought, with a dark side.

And that, she realized, was what made it all the more alluring. It was hardly any wonder that Sloan, with his love of buildings, adored it.

"Like something you'd expect to see on some lonely Irish coast." Nathaniel spoke from behind her. "Or on some foggy Scottish cliff."

"Yes. It's even more impressive from the sea." Her eyes drifted up, to Bianca's tower. She shivered.

"You may want to put your jacket on," Nathaniel told her. "It's going to get chillier when we get out to sea."

"No, I'm not cold. I was just thinking. When you've heard all the stories about Bianca, it's hard not to imagine what it was like."

"She'd sit up there and watch the cliffs for him. For Christian. And she'd dream—guiltily, I imagine, being a proper lady. But propriety doesn't have a snowball's chance in hell against love."

She shivered again. The statement hit much too close to home. She'd been in love once, and had tossed propriety aside, along with her innocence.

"She paid for it," Megan said flatly, and turned away. To distract herself, she wandered over to the charts. Not that she could make head or tail of them.

"We're heading north by northeast." As he had

with Alex, Nathaniel took Megan's hand and guided it along the chart. "We've got a clear day, good visibility, but there's a strong wind. It'll be a little choppy."

Terrific, she thought, and swallowed hard. "If you don't come up with whales, you're going to have some very disappointed kids."

"Oh, I think I can provide a few." She bumped against him as bay gave way to sea. His hands came up to steady her shoulders, and remained. The boat might have swayed, but he stood solid as a rock. "You want to brace your feet apart. Distribute the weight. You'll get your sea legs, Meg."

She didn't think so. Already she could feel the light coating of chilly sweat springing to her skin. Nausea rolled in an answering wave in her stomach. She would not, she promised herself, spoil Kevin's day, or humiliate herself, by being sick.

"It takes about an hour to get out, doesn't it?" Her voice wasn't as strong, or as steady, as she'd hoped.

"That's right."

She started to move away, but ended by leaning dizzily against him.

"Come about," he murmured, and turned her to face him. One look at her face had his brows drawing together. She was pale as a sheet, with an interesting tinge of green just under the surface. Dead sick, he thought with a shake of his head. And they were barely under way.

"Did you take anything?"

There was no use pretending. And she didn't have the strength to be brave. "Yes, but I don't think it did any good. I get sick in a canoe."

"So you came on a three-hour trek into the Atlantic."

"Kevin had his heart set—" She broke off when Nathaniel put a steadying arm around her waist and led her to a bench.

"Sit," he ordered.

Megan obeyed and, when she saw that the children were occupied staring out the windows, gave in and dropped her head between her legs.

Three hours, she thought. They'd have to pour her into a body bag in three hours. Maybe bury her at sea. God, what had made her think a couple of pills would steady her? She felt a tug on her hand.

"What? Is the ambulance here already?"

"Steady as she goes, sugar." Crouched in front of her, Nathaniel slipped narrow terry-cloth bands over her wrists.

"What's this?"

"Acupressure." He twisted the bands until small metal studs pressed lightly on a point on her wrist.

She would have laughed if she hadn't been moaning. "Great. I need a stretcher and you offer voodoo."

"A perfectly valid science. And I wouldn't knock voodoo, either. I've seen some pretty impressive results. Now breathe slow and easy. Just sit here." He slid open a window behind her and let in a blast of air. "I've got to get back to the helm."

She leaned back against the wall and let the fresh air slap her cheeks. On the other side of the bridge, the children huddled, hoping that Moby Dick lurked under each snowy whitecap. She watched the cliffs, but as they swayed to and fro, she closed her eyes in self-defense.

She sighed once, then began to formulate a complicated trigonometry problem in her mind. Oddly enough, by the time she'd worked it through to the solution, her stomach felt steady.

Probably because I've got my eyes closed, she thought. But she could hardly keep them closed for three hours, not when she was in charge of a trio of active children.

Experimentally, she opened one. The boat continued to rock, but her system remained steady. She opened the other. There was a moment of panic when the children weren't at the window. She jolted upright, illness forgotten, then saw them circled around Nathaniel at the helm.

A fine job she was doing, she thought in disgust, sitting there in a dizzy heap while Nathaniel piloted the ship and entertained three kids. She braced herself for the next slap of nausea as she took a step.

It didn't come.

Frowning, she took another step, and another. She felt a little weak, true, but no longer limp and clammy. Daring the ultimate test, she looked out the window at the rolling sea.

There was a tug, but a mild one. In fact, she realized, it was almost a pleasant sensation, like riding on a smooth-gaited horse. In amazement, she studied the terry-cloth bands on her wrists.

Nathaniel glanced over his shoulder. Her color was back, he noted. That pale peach was much more flattering than green. "Better?"

"Yes." She smiled, trying to dispel the embarrassment as easily as his magic bands had the seasickness. "Thank you."

He waited while she bundled the children, then herself, into jackets. On the Atlantic, summer vanished. "First time I shipped out, we hit a little squall. I spent the worst two hours of my life hanging over the rail. Come on. Take the wheel."

"The wheel? I couldn't."

"Sure you could."

"Do it, Mom. It's fun. It's really fun."

Propelled forward by three children, Megan found herself at the helm, her back pressed lightly into Nathaniel's chest, her hands covered by his.

Every nerve in her body began to throb. Nathaniel's body was hard as iron, and his hands were sure and firm. She could smell the sea, through the open windows and on him. No matter how much she tried to concentrate on the water flowing endlessly around them, he was there, just there. His chin brushing the top of her head, his heartbeat throbbing light and steady against her back.

"Nothing like being in control to settle the system," he commented, and she made some sound of agreement.

But this was nothing like being in control.

She began to imagine what it might be like to have those hard, clever hands somewhere other than on the backs of hers. If she turned so that they were face-to-face, and she tilted her head up at just the right angle . . .

Baffled by the way her mind was working, she set it to calculating algebra.

"Quarter speed," Nathaniel ordered, steering a few degrees to port.

The change of rhythm had Megan off balance. She was trying to regain it when Nathaniel turned her around. And now she was facing him, her head tilted up. The easy grin on his face made her wonder if he knew just where her mind had wandered.

"See the blips on the screen there, Kevin?" But he

was watching her, all but hypnotizing her with those unblinking slate-colored eyes. Sorcerer's eyes, she thought dimly. "Do you know what they mean?" And his lips curved—closer to hers than they should be. "There be whales there."

"Where? Where are they, Nate?" Kevin rushed to the window, goggle-eyed.

"Keep watching. We'll stop. Look off the port bow," he told Megan. "I think you'll get your money's worth."

Still dazed, she staggered away. The boat rocked more enthusiastically when stopped—or was it her system that was so thoroughly rocked? As Nathaniel spoke into the P.A. system, taking over the mate's lecture on whales, she slipped the camera and binoculars out of her shoulder bag.

"Look!" Kevin squealed, jumping like a spring as he pointed. "Mom, look!"

Everything cleared from her mind but wonder. She saw the massive body emerge from the choppy water. Rising, up and up, sleek and grand and otherworldly. She could hear the shouts and cheers from the people on the deck below, and her own strangled gasp.

It was surely some sort of magic, she thought, that something so huge, so magnificent, could lurk under the whitecapped sea. Her fingers rose to her lips, pressed there in awe as the sound of the whale displacing water crashed like thunder.

Water flew, sparkling like drops of diamond. Her camera stayed lowered, useless. She could only stare, an ache in her throat, tears in her eyes.

"His mate's coming up."

Nathaniel's voice broke through her frozen wonder.

Hurriedly she lifted the camera, snapping quickly as sea parted for whale.

They geysered from their spouts, causing the children to applaud madly. Megan was laughing as she hauled Jenny up for a better view and the three of them took impatient turns with the binoculars.

She pressed herself to the window as eagerly as the children while the boat cruised, following the glossy humps as they speared through the sea. Then the whales sounded, diving deep with a flap of their enormous tails. Below, people laughed and shouted as they were drenched with water.

Twice more the *Mariner* sought out and found pods, giving her passengers the show of a lifetime. Long after they turned and headed for home, Megan stayed at the window, hoping for one more glimpse.

"Beautiful, aren't they?"

She looked back at Nathaniel, eyes glowing. "Incredible. I had no idea. Photographs and movies don't quite do it."

"Nothing quite like seeing and doing for yourself." He cocked a brow. "Still steady?"

With a laugh, she glanced down at her wrists. "Another minor miracle. I would never have put stock in anything like this."

"'There are more things in heaven and earth, Horatio.'"

A black-suited pirate quoting Hamlet. "So it seems," she murmured. "There's The Towers." She smiled. "Off the port side."

"You're learning, sugar." He gave orders briskly and eased the *Mariner* into the calm waters of the bay.

"How long have you been sailing?"

"All my life. But I ran off and joined the merchant marine when I was eighteen."

"Ran off?" She smiled again. "Looking for adventure."

"For freedom." He turned away then, to ease the boat into its slip as smoothly as a foot slides into an old, comfortable shoe.

She wondered why a boy of eighteen would have to search for freedom. And she thought of herself at that age, a child with a child. She'd cast her freedom away. Now, more than nine years later, she could hardly regret it. Not when the price of her freedom had been a son.

"Can we go down and get a drink?" Kevin tugged on his mother's hand. "We're all thirsty."

"Sure. I'll take you."

"We can go by ourselves," Alex said earnestly. He knew they were much too big to need an overseer. "I got money and everything. We just want to sit downstairs and watch everybody get off."

"All right, then, but stay inside." She watched them rush off. "They start spreading their wings so soon."

"Your boy's going to be flying back to you for a long time yet."

"I hope so." She cut herself off before she voiced the rest: *He's all I have.* "This has been a terrific day for him. For me, too. Thanks."

"My pleasure." They were alone on the bridge now, the lines secured, the plank down and the passengers disembarking. "You'll come again."

"I don't think I could keep Kevin away. I'd better go down with them."

"They're fine." He stepped closer, before she could evade. "You know, Meg, you forget to be nervous when the kids are around."

"I'm not nervous."

"Jumpy as a fish on a line. It was a pure pleasure watching your face when we sighted whale. It's a pure pleasure anytime, but when you're laughing and the wind's in your hair, it could stop a man's heart."

He took another step and backed her up against the wheel. Maybe it wasn't fair, but he'd think about that later. It was going to take him a good long time to forget the way she'd felt, her back pressed against him, her hands soft and hesitant under his.

"Of course, there's something to be said about the way you're looking right now. All eyes. You've got the prettiest blue eyes I've ever seen. Then there's all that peaches-and-cream." He lifted a finger to her cheek, skimmed it down. She felt as though she'd stepped on a live wire. "Makes a man crave a nice long taste."

"I'm not susceptible to flattery." She'd wanted to sound firm and dismissive, not breathless.

"Just stating a fact." He leaned down until his mouth was a whisper from hers. "If you don't want me to kiss you, you'd better tell me not to."

She would have. Absolutely. If she'd been able to speak. But then his mouth was on hers, warm and firm and every bit as clever as his hands. She would tell herself later that her lips had parted with shock, to protest. But it was a lie.

They opened greedily, with a surge of hunger that went deep, that echoed on a groan that a woman might make who had her first sampling of rich cream after years of thin water.

Her body refused to go rigid in denial, instead humming like a harp string freshly plucked. Her hands dived into his hair and urged him to take the kiss deeper.

He'd expected a cool response, or at least a hesitant one. Perhaps he'd seen a flash of passion in her eyes, deep down, like the heat and rumble in the core of a volcano that seems dormant from the surface.

But nothing had prepared him for this blast of fire.

His mind went blank, then filled with woman. The scent and feel and taste of her, the sound of the moan that caught in her throat when he nipped on her full lower lip. He dragged her closer, craving more, and had the dizzying delight of feeling every slim curve and line of Megan pressed against his body.

The scent of the ocean through the window had him imagining taking her on some deserted beach, while the surf pounded and the gulls screamed.

She felt herself sinking, and gripped him for balance. There was too much, much too much, rioting through her system. It would take a great deal more than the little bands around her wrist to level her now.

It would take control, willpower, and, most of all . . . remembering.

She drew back, would have stumbled if his arms hadn't stayed clamped around her. "No."

He couldn't get his breath. He told himself he would analyze later why one kiss had knocked him flat, like a two-fisted punch. "You'll have to be more specific. No to what?"

"To this. To any of this." Panic kicked in and had her struggling away. "I wasn't thinking."

"Me, neither. It's a good sign you're doing it right, if you stop thinking when you're kissing."

"I don't want you to kiss me."

He slipped his hands into his pockets. Safer there, he decided, since the lady was thinking again. "Sugar, you were doing more than your share."

There was little use in hotly denying the obvious truth. She fell back on cool logic. "You're an attractive man, and I responded in a natural manner."

He had to grin. "Darling, if kissing like that's in your nature, I'm going to die happy."

"I don't intend for it to happen again."

"You know what they say about the road to hell and intentions, don't you?" She was tensed up again. He could see it in the set of her shoulders. He imagined her experience with Dumont had left plenty of scars. "Relax, Meg," he said, more kindly. "I'm not going to jump you. You want to take it slow, we'll take it slow."

The fact that his tone was so reasonable raised her hackles. "We're not going to take it any way at all."

Better, he decided. He didn't mind riling her. In fact, he was looking forward to doing it. Often.

"I'm going to have to say you're wrong. A man and woman set off a fire like that, they're going to keep coming back to the heat."

She was very much afraid he was right. Even now, part of her yearned to fan that blaze again. "I'm not interested in fires or in heat. I'm certainly not interested in an affair with a man I barely know."

"So, we'll get to know each other better before we have one," Nate responded, in an irritatingly reasonable tone.

Megan clamped her teeth together. "I'm not interested in an affair, period. I know that must be a blow to your ego, but you'll just have to deal with it. Now, if you'll excuse me, I'm going to get the children."

He stepped politely out of her way, waited until she'd reached the glass door leading onto the upper deck. "Meg?" It was only partly ego that pushed him to speak. The rest was pure determination. "The first time I make love with you, you won't think about him. You won't even remember his name."

Her eyes sliced at him, twin ice-edged swords. She abandoned dignity and slammed the door.

Chapter 4

"The woman'll be the death of me." Dutch took a bottle of Jamaican rum from his hidey-hole in the back of the pantry. "Mark my words, boy."

Nathaniel kicked back in the kitchen chair, sated and relaxed after the meal he'd enjoyed in the Calhoun dining room. The hotel kitchen was spotless, now that the dinner rush was over. And Coco, Nathaniel knew, was occupied with family. Otherwise, Dutch wouldn't have risked the rum.

"You're not thinking of jumping ship, are you, mate?"

Dutch snorted at the idea. As if he had to take French leave because he couldn't handle a fussy, snooty-nosed female. "I'm sticking." After one wary glance toward the door, he poured them both a healthy portion of rum. "But I'm warning you, boy, sooner or later that woman's going to get her comeuppance. And she's going to get it from yours truly." He stabbed a thick thumb at his wide chest.

Nathaniel downed a swig of rum, hissing through his teeth as it hit. Smooth as silk it wasn't. "Where's that bottle of Cruzan I got you?"

"Used it in a cake. This is plenty good enough for drinking."

"If you don't want a stomach lining," Nathaniel said under his breath. "So, what's the problem with Coco now?"

"Well, if it's not one thing, it's two." Dutch scowled at the kitchen phone when it rang. Room service, he thought with a sneer. Never had any damn room service aboard one of his ships. "Yeah, what?"

Nathaniel grinned into his rum. Tact and diplomacy weren't Dutch's strong points. He imagined that if Coco heard the man growl at guests that way, she'd faint. Or pop Dutch over the head with a skillet.

"I guess you think we've got nothing better to do down here?" he snarled into the phone. "You'll get it when it's ready." He hung up and snagged a plate. "Ordering champagne and fancy cake this time of night. Newlyweds. Ha! Haven't seen hide nor hair of the two in number three all week."

"Where's your romance, Dutch?"

"I leave that to you, lover boy." His ham-size fists delicately cut into the chocolate *gâteau*. "Seen the way you was eyeing that redhead."

"Strawberry blonde," Nathaniel corrected. "More gold than red." Bravely he took another sip of rum. "She's a looker, isn't she?"

"Never seen you go for one that wasn't." With an artist's flair, Dutch ladled vanilla sauce on the side of the twin slices of cake and garnished them with raspberries. "Got a kid, doesn't she?"

"Yeah." Nathaniel studied the cake and decided he could probably force down a small piece. "Kevin. Dark hair, tall for his age." A smile curved his lips. Damned if the boy hadn't gotten to him. "Big, curious eyes."

"Seen him." Dutch had a weakness for kids that he tried to hide. "Okay-looking boy. Comes around with those other two noisy brats, looking for handouts."

Which, Nathaniel knew, Dutch dispensed with great pleasure behind the mask of a scowl.

"Got herself in trouble pretty young."

Nathaniel frowned at that. It was a phrase, too often used to his way of thinking, that indicated the woman was solely responsible for the pregnancy. "It takes two, Dutch. And the bastard was stringing her along."

"I know. I know. I heard about it. Not much gets past me." It wasn't hard to finesse information out of Coco—if he pushed the right buttons. Though he'd never admit it, that was something he looked forward to doing daily. He buzzed for a waiter, taking delight in holding his thumb down until the kitchen door swung open. "Make up a tray for number three," Dutch ordered. "Two gato's, bottle of house champagne, two flutes, and don't forget the damn napkins."

That done, he tossed back his own rum. "Guess you'll be wanting a piece of this now."

"Wouldn't turn it down."

"Never known you to turn down food—or a female." Dutch cut a slice—a great deal larger than those he'd cut for the newlyweds—and shoved the plate in front of Nathaniel.

"I don't get any raspberries?"

"Eat what's in front of you. How come you ain't out there flirting with that skinny girl?"

"I'm working on it," Nathaniel said with a mouthful

of cake. "They're in the dining room, all of them. Family meeting." He rose, poured himself coffee, dumped the rest of his rum in it. "They found some old book. And she's not skinny." He had firsthand knowledge, now that he'd had Megan in his arms. "She's delicate."

"Yeah, right." He thought of Coco, those long, sturdy lines as fine as any well-crafted sloops. And snorted again. "All females are delicate—until they get a ring through your nose."

No one would have called the women in the dining room delicate—not with a typical Calhoun argument in full swing.

"I say we burn it." C.C. folded her arms across her chest and glared. "After everything we learned about Fergus from Bianca's journal, I don't know why we'd consider keeping his lousy account book around."

"We can't burn it," Amanda fired back. "It's part of our history."

"Bad vibes." Lilah narrowed her eyes at the book, now sitting in the center of the table. "Really bad vibes."

"That may be." Max shook his head. "But I can't go along with burning a book. Any kind of book."

"It's not exactly literature," C.C. mumbled.

Trent patted his wife's stiff shoulder. "We can always put it back where it came from—or give Sloan's suggestion some consideration."

"I think a room designed for artifacts, mementos—" Sloan glanced at Amanda "—the pieces of history that go with The Towers, would add something. Not only to the hotel, but for the family."

"I don't know." Suzanna pressed her lips together and tried to be objective. "I feel odd about displaying Fergus's things with Bianca's, or Aunt Colleen's, Uncle Sean's and Ethan's."

"He might have been a creep, but he's still a piece of the whole." Holt toyed with the last of his coffee. "I'm going with Sloan on this one."

That, of course, enticed a small riot of agreements, disagreements, alternate suggestions. Megan could only sit back and watch in amazement.

She hadn't wanted to be there at all. Not at a family meeting. But she'd been summarily outvoted. The Calhouns could unite when they chose.

As the argument swirled around her, she glanced at the object in question. When Amanda left it in her office, she'd eventually given in to temptation. After cleaning off the leather, she'd flipped through pages, idly totaling up columns, clucking her tongue at the occasional mistake in arithmetic. Of course, she'd scanned a few of the marginal notations, as well, and had found Fergus Calhoun a cold, ambitious and self-absorbed man.

But then, a simple account ledger hardly seemed worth this much trouble. Particularly when the last few pages of the books were merely numbers without any rhyme or reason.

She was reminding herself it wasn't her place to comment when she was put directly on the spot.

"What do you think, Megan, dear?" Coco's unexpected question had Megan blinking.

"Excuse me?"

"What do you think? You haven't told us. And you'd be the most qualified, after all."

"Qualified?"

"It's an account book," Coco pointed out. "You're an accountant."

Somehow, the logic in that defeated Megan. "It's really none of my business," she began, and was drowned out by a chorus of reasons why it certainly was. "Well, I . . ." She looked around the table, where all eyes were focused on her. "I imagine it would be an interesting memento—and it's kind of fascinating to review bookkeeping from so long ago. You know, expenses, and wages for the staff. It might be interesting to see how it adds up, what the income and outgo was for your family in 1913."

"Of course!" Coco clapped her hands. "Why, of course it would. I was thinking about you last night, Meg, while I was casting my runes. It kept coming back to me that you were to take on a project—one with numbers."

"Aunt Coco," C.C. said patiently, "Megan is our accountant."

"Well, I know that, darling." With a bright smile, Coco patted her hair. "So at first I didn't think much of it. But then I kept having this feeling that it was more than that. And I'm sure, somehow, that the project is going to lead to something wonderful. Something that will make all of us very happy. I'm so pleased you're going to do it."

"Do it?" Megan looked helplessly at her brother. She got a flash of a grin in return.

"Study Fergus's book. You could even put it all on computer, couldn't you? Sloan's told us how clever you are."

"I could, of course, but—"

She was interrupted by the cry of a baby through the monitor on the sideboard.

"Bianca?" Max said.

"Ethan," C.C. and Lilah said in unison.
And the meeting was adjourned.

What exactly, Megan wondered later, had she agreed to do? Somehow, though she'd barely said a word, she'd been placed in charge of Fergus's book. Surely that was a family matter.

She sighed as she pushed open the doors to her terrace and stepped outside. If she stated that obvious fact, in the most practical, logical of terms, she would be patted on the head, pinched on the cheek and told that she was family and that was all there was to it.

How could she argue?

She took a deep breath of the scented night air, and all but tasted Suzanna's freesias and roses. She could hear the sea in the distance, and the air she moved through was moist and lightly salty from it. Stars wheeled overheard, highlighted by a three-quarter moon, bright as a beacon.

Her son was dreaming in his bed, content and safe and surrounded by people who loved him.

Dissecting Fergus's book was a small favor that couldn't begin to repay what she'd been given.

Peace of mind. Yes, she thought, the Calhouns had opened the gates to that particular garden.

Too charmed by the night to close it out and sleep, she wandered down the curving stone steps to drift through the moon-kissed roses and star-sprinkled peonies, under an arbor where wisteria twisted triumphantly, raining tiny petals onto the path.

"'She was a phantom of delight when first she gleamed upon my sight.'"

Megan jolted, pressing a hand on her heart when a shadow separated itself from the other shadows.

"Did I startle you?" Nathaniel stepped closer, the red tip of his cigar glowing. "Wordsworth usually has a different effect."

"I didn't know you were there." And wouldn't have come out had she known. "I thought you'd gone home."

"I was passing a little time with Dutch and a bottle of rum." He stepped fully into the moonlight. "He likes to complain about Coco, and prefers an audience." He drew slowly on his cigar. For a moment, his face was misted by smoke, making it mysterious and beautiful. An angel cast from grace. "Nice night."

"Yes, it is. Well . . ."

"No need to run off. You wanted to walk in the garden." He smiled, reaching down to snap a pale pink peony from its bush. "Since it's nearly midnight, there's no better time for it."

She accepted the blossom, told herself she wouldn't be charmed. "I was admiring the flowers. I've never had much luck growing them."

"You have to put your heart in it—along with the water and fertilizer."

Her hair was down, waving softly over her shoulders. She still wore the neatly tailored blue jacket and slacks she'd had on at dinner. A pity, he thought. It would have suited the night, and his mood, if she'd drifted outside in a flowing robe. But then, Megan O'Riley wasn't the type of woman to wander midnight gardens in swirling silks.

Wouldn't let herself be.

The only way to combat those intrusive gray eyes, other than to run like a fool, was conversation. "So, do you garden, as well as sail and quote the classics?" she asked him.

"I've an affection for flowers, among other things." Nathaniel put a hand over the peony she held, and lifted it toward him so that he could enjoy its fragrance, and hers. He smiled at her over the feathered petals.

She found herself caught, as if in some slow-motion dream, between the man and the moonlight. The perfume of the garden seemed to rise up and swirl like the breeze, gently invading her senses. Shadows shifted over his face, highlighting all those fascinating clefts and ridges, luring her gaze to his mouth, curved now and inviting.

They seemed so completely alone, so totally cut off from the reality and responsibilities of day-to-day.

Just a man and a woman among star-dappled flowers and moonlit shadows, and the music of the distant sea.

Deliberately she lowered her lashes, as if to break the spell.

"I'm surprised you'd have time for poetry and flowers, with all the traveling."

"You can always make time for what counts."

The fact that the night held magic hadn't escaped him. But then, he was open to such things. There'd been times he'd seen water rise out of itself like a clenched fist, times he'd heard the siren song of mermaids through shifting fog—he believed in magic. Why else had he waited in the garden, knowing, somehow knowing, she would come?

He released the flower, but took her free hand, linking their fingers before she could think of a reason he shouldn't. "Walk with me, Meg. A night like this shouldn't be wasted."

"I'm going back in." She looked back up just as a breeze stirred in the air. Wisteria petals rained down.

"Soon."

So she was walking with him in the fairy-lit garden, with a flower in her hand and fragrant petals in her hair.

"I . . . really should check on Kevin."

"The boy have trouble sleeping?"

"No, but—"

"Bad dreams?"

"No."

"Well, then." Taking that as an answer, he continued his stroll down the narrow path. "Does having a man flirt with you always make you turn tail and run?"

"I certainly wasn't running. And I'm not interested in flirtations."

"Funny. When you were standing out on the terrace a bit ago, you looked like a woman ready for a little flirting."

She stopped dead. "You were watching me."

"Mmm." Nathaniel crushed his cigar out into the sand of a nearby urn. "I was thinking it was a shame I didn't have a lute."

Annoyance warred with curiosity. "A lute?"

"A pretty woman standing on a balcony in the moonlight—she should be serenaded."

She had to laugh at that. "I suppose you play the lute."

"Nope. Wished I did, though, when I saw you." He began to walk again. The cliff curved downward, toward the seawall. "I used to sail by here when I was a kid and look up at The Towers. I liked to think there was a dragon guarding it, and that I'd scale the cliffs and slay him."

"Kevin still calls it a castle," she murmured, looking back.

"When I got older and took note of the Calhoun sisters, I figured when I killed the dragon, they'd reward me. In the way a sixteen-year-old walking hormone fantasizes."

She laughed again. "Which one of them?"

"Oh, all of them." Grinning, he sat on the low wall, drew her down beside him. "They've always been . . . remarkable. Holt had this thing for Suzanna, though he wouldn't admit it. Being as he was my friend, I selflessly crossed her off my list. That left three for me after I conquered that dragon."

"But you never did face the dragon?"

A shadow passed over his face. "I had another to deal with. I guess you could say we left it at a draw, and I went to sea." He shook off the mood, and the uncomfortable past. "But I did have a brief and memorable interlude with the lovely Lilah."

Megan's eyes widened. "You and Lilah?"

"Right before I left the island. She set out to drive me crazy. I think she was practicing." He sighed at the memory. "She was damn good at it."

But they were so easy with each other, Megan thought. So relaxed and friendly.

"You're so easy to read, Meg." He chuckled and slipped his arm around her shoulders. "We weren't exactly Romeo and Juliet. I kissed her a few times, did my damnedest to convince her to do more. She didn't. And she didn't break my heart. Well, dented it a little, maybe," he mused.

"And Max isn't bothered?"

"Why would he be? He's got her. If we'd had a flaming affair—which we didn't—it would be a smoldering matchstick compared to what they've got."

He was right there. Each of the Calhoun women had found her match. "Still, it's interesting," she said quietly. "All these connections within connections."

"Are you thinking of me, or yourself?"

She stiffened, abruptly aware that she was sitting hip-to-hip with him, his arm around her. "That's not something I care to discuss."

"Still raw?" He tightened his arm, comforting. "From what I've heard of Dumont, I wouldn't think he'd be worth it. Settle down," he said when she jerked away. "We'll let it go. Too nice a night to uncover old wounds. Why don't you tell me how they talked you into taking on that old account book?"

"How do you know about that?"

"Holt and Suzanna filled me in." She was still rigid, he noted. But she wasn't running. "I saw them before they left."

She relaxed a little. It was comforting to discuss it with someone else who was just that small step outside the family. "I don't know how they talked me into it. I barely opened my mouth."

"Your first mistake."

She huffed out a breath. "I'd have had to shout to be heard. I don't know why they call it a meeting, when all they do is argue." Her brows knit. "Then they stop arguing and you realize you've been sucked in. If you try to pull yourself out, you find they've united in this solid wall that's impossible to beat."

"I know just what you mean. I still don't know if it was my idea to go into business with Holt. The notion came up, was debated, voted on and approved. The next thing I knew, I was signing papers."

Interesting, she mused, and studied his strong profile. "You don't strike me as someone who could be talked into anything."

"I could say the same."

She considered a moment, then gave up. "You're right. The book's fascinating. I can hardly wait to get at it."

"I hope you're not planning on letting it take up all your free time." He toyed with the ends of her blowing hair. No, not red, he mused. It was gold, enriched by quiet fire. "I want some of it."

Cautiously she inched away. "I explained to you, I'm not interested."

"What you are is worried because you are interested." He cupped a hand under her chin and turned her to face him. "I figure you had a rough time, and maybe it's helped you cope to lump all men in with the bastard who hurt you. That's why I said I'd be patient."

Fury flared in her eyes. "Don't tell me what I am or how I've coped. I'm not asking for your understanding or your patience."

"Okay."

He crushed his mouth to hers, without any patience at all. His lips were demanding, urgent, irresistible, conquering hers before she could draw the breath to deny it.

The embers that had smoldered inside her since the first time he'd kissed her burst into reckless flame. She wanted—craved—this flash point of feeling, this fireball of sensation. Hating herself for the weakness, she let herself burn.

He'd proved his point, Nathaniel thought as he tore his mouth from hers to press it against the thundering pulse in her throat. Proved his point, and wrapped himself up in nasty knots of need.

Needs that would have to wait, because she was far from ready. And because it mattered—she mattered—more than he'd expected.

"Now tell me you're not interested," he muttered against her lips, furious that he was unable to take what was so obviously his. "Tell me you didn't want me to touch you."

"I can't." Her voice broke in despair. She wanted him to touch her, to take her, to throw her on the ground and make wild love to her. And to take the decision, and the responsibility, out of her hands. That made her ashamed. That made her a coward. "But wanting's not enough." Shaken, she pushed away, lurched to her feet. "It's never going to be enough for me. I've wanted before." She stood trembling in the moonlight, her hair blowing free, her eyes fierce and afraid.

Nathaniel cursed himself, then her for good measure. "I'm not Dumont. And you're not a seventeen-year-old girl."

"I know who I am. I don't know who you are."

"You're hedging, Megan. We recognized each other from the first instant."

She stepped back, because she knew he was right. Because it terrified her. "You're talking about chemistry."

"Maybe I'm talking about fate." He said it softly, as he rose. He'd frightened her, and he despised himself for it. Unnerving a woman was one thing, bullying another. "You need time to think about that. So do I. I'll walk you back."

She put out a hand to stop him. "I can find my own way." She whirled and raced up the moonlit path.

Nathaniel swore under his breath. He sat again and took out a fresh cigar, lit it. There wasn't any use heading home yet. He already knew he wouldn't sleep.

Late the following afternoon, Megan roused herself from her ledgers when a knock sounded on her office door.

"Come in."

"Sorry to interrupt." Coco poked her head in the door—a head, Megan noted with surprise, that was now topped with sleek ebony hair—she apparently was a woman who changed her hair color as often as she changed moods. "You didn't break for lunch," Coco said as she stepped through the door with a large and laden silver tray.

"You didn't have to bother." Megan glanced at her watch and was stunned to see it was after three. "You've got enough to do without waiting on me."

"Just part of the service." After setting the tray on a table, Coco began to arrange a place setting. "We can't have you skipping meals." She glanced over at the computer screen, the open ledgers, the calculator and the neatly stacked files. "My goodness, such a lot of numbers. Numbers have always unsettled me. They're so . . . unyielding."

"You don't have to let them push you around," Megan said with a laugh. "Once you know that one and one always equals two, you can do anything."

Coco studied the screen doubtfully. "If you say so, dear."

"I've just finished up the first quarter on Shipshape. It was . . . a challenge."

"It's wonderful that you think so." Coco turned her back on the numbers before they could give her a headache. "But none of us wants you overdoing things. Now, here's some iced tea and a nice club sandwich."

It did look tempting, particularly since she'd had no appetite for breakfast. A residual effect, she knew, of her encounter with Nathaniel.

"Thank you, Coco. I'm sorry I took you away from your work."

"Oh." Coco waved a dismissive hand as Megan rose to pick up her plate. "Don't give it a thought. To be frank, dear, I simply had to get out—away from that man."

"The Dutchman?" Megan smiled over her first bite of sandwich. "I met him this morning, when I was coming down. I made a wrong turn and ended up in the hotel wing."

Restless, Coco began to fiddle with the thick gold links around her throat. "I hope he didn't say anything to offend you. He's a bit . . . rough."

"No." Megan poured two glasses of tea, offered one to Coco. "He sort of glowered and told me I needed some meat on my bones. I thought he was going to start stuffing me with the Greek omelet he was fixing, but one of the busboys dropped a plate. I escaped while he was swearing at the poor kid."

"His language." Coco seated herself, smoothed down her silk trouser leg. "Deplorable. And he's always contradicting me on recipes." She shut her eyes, shuddered. "I've always considered myself a patient woman—and, if I can be immodest for a moment, a clever one. I had to be both to raise four lively girls." Sighing, she tossed up her hands in a gesture of surrender. "But as far as that man's concerned, I'm at my wits' end."

"I suppose you could let him go," Megan said tentatively.

"Impossible. The man's like a father to Nathaniel, and the children, for reasons that escape me, are terribly fond of him." She opened her eyes again and smiled bravely. "I can cope, dear, and I must admit the man has a way with certain rudimentary dishes." She patted her new hairdo. "And I find little ways to distract myself."

But Megan's attention was stuck back at Coco's first statement. "I suppose Mr. Van Horne has known Nathaniel for some time."

"Oh, more than fifteen years, I believe. They served together, sailed together, whatever you call it. I believe Mr. Van Horn took Nate under his wing. Which is something in his favor, I suppose. God knows the boy needed someone, after the miserable childhood he had."

"Oh?" It wasn't in Megan's nature to probe, but Coco needed little prompting.

"His mother died when he was very young, poor boy. And his father." Her lovely mouth went grim. "Well, the man was little more than a beast really. I barely knew John Fury, but there was always talk in the village. And now and then Nathaniel would come along with Holt when Holt brought us fish. I'd see the bruises for myself."

"Bruises," Megan repeated, horrified. "His father beat him?"

Coco's soft heart had tears swimming in her eyes. "I'm very much afraid so."

"But—didn't anyone do anything about it?"

"Whenever there were questions, the man would claim the boy had fallen, or gotten into a fight with another child. Nathaniel never contradicted him. Sad to say, abuse was something people often overlooked back then. Still is, I'm afraid." Tears threatened her mascara. She dabbed at them with Megan's napkin. "Nathaniel ran off to sea the moment he was of age. His father died a few years back. Nate sent money for the funeral, but didn't come. It was hard to blame him."

Coco sighed, shook herself. "I didn't mean to come in with such a sad story. But it has a good ending. Nate turned out to be a fine man." Coco's damp eyes were deceptively guileless. "All he needs is the right woman. He's terribly handsome, don't you think?"

"Yes," Megan said cautiously. She was still trying to equate the abused child with the confident man.

"And dependable. Romantic, too, with all those tales of the sea, and that air of mystery around him. A woman would be very lucky to catch his eye."

Megan blinked her own eyes as the not-so-subtle hint got through. "I couldn't say. I don't know him very well, and I don't really think about men that way."

"Nonsense." Confident in her own matchmaking skills, Coco patted Megan's knee. "You're young, beautiful, intelligent. Having a man in your life doesn't diminish those things, dear—or a woman's independence. The right man enhances them. And I have a feeling that you'll be finding that out, very soon. Now—" she leaned over and kissed Megan's cheek "—I have to get back to the kitchen, before that man does something horrid to my salmon patties."

She started out the door, then paused—timing it, Coco thought, rather beautifully. "Oh, dear, I'm such a scatterbrain. I was supposed to tell you about Kevin."

"Kevin?" Automatically Megan's gaze shifted to the window. "Isn't he outside with Alex and Jenny?"

"Well, yes, but not here." Coco smiled distractedly—it was a pose she'd practiced for years. "It's Nathaniel's day off, and he was by for lunch. Such a wonderful appetite he has, and never seems to gain an ounce. Of course, he does keep active. That's why he has all those marvelous muscles. They are marvelous, aren't they?"

"Coco, where is Kevin?"

"Oh, there I go, running off again. Kevin's with Nate. All of them are. He took the children with him."

Megan was already on her feet. "With him? Where? On a boat?" Visions of squalls and towering waves of water swam through her head, despite the calm, cloudless blue of the sky.

"No, no, to his house. He's building a deck or something, and the children were dying to go along and help. It would be such a favor to me if you could go by and pick them up." And, of course, Coco thought cannily, Megan would then see Nate's lovely little home, and his charming way with children. "Suzanna expects the children to be here, you see, but I didn't have the heart to deny them. She won't be back until five, so there's no hurry."

"But, I—"

"You know where Suzanna and Holt's cottage is, don't you, darling? Nathaniel's is only a half a mile past it. Charming place. You can't miss it."

Before Megan could form another word, the door closed gently in her face.

A job, Coco thought as she strode down the corridor, very well done.

Chapter 5

Kevin didn't know which was the coolest. It was a very close call between the small fire-breathing dragon on the back of Nathaniel's shoulder and the puckered white scar on the front. The scar was the result of the knife wound, which ought to have put it far ahead in the running. But a tattoo, a tattoo of a *dragon*, was pretty hard to beat.

There was another scar, just above Nathaniel's waistline, near the hip. At Alex's eager questioning, Nathaniel had said it was from a moray eel he'd tangled with in the South Pacific.

Kevin could easily imagine Nathaniel, armed with only a knife clenched between his teeth, fighting to the death with a sea creature on the scale of the Loch Ness monster.

And Nathaniel had a parrot, a big, colorful bird who sat right inside the house on a wooden perch and talked. Kevin's current favorite was "Off with her head."

Kevin figured Nathaniel Fury was about the coolest man he'd ever met—a man who had traveled the seven seas like Sinbad, and had the scars and stories to prove it. A man who liked puppies and talking birds.

He didn't seem to mind when Kevin hung back while Alex and Jenny raced around the yard with the puppy and killed each other with imaginary laser pistols. It was more fun to crouch close while Nathaniel hammered nails into boards.

It took Kevin about six boards to start asking questions.

"How come you want a deck out here?"

"So I can sit on it." Nathaniel set another board in place.

"But you've already got one in the back."

"I'll still have it." Three strikes of the hammer and the nail was through board and joist. Nathaniel sat back on his haunches. He wore nothing but a bandanna twisted around his head and a pair of ragged cutoff jeans. His skin was bronzed by the sun and coated lightly with sweat. "See how the frame goes?"

Kevin followed the direction of the deck frame as it skirted around the side of the house. "Uh-huh."

"Well, we'll keep going till we meet the other deck."

Kevin's eyes brightened. "So it'll go all around, like a circle."

"You got it." Nathaniel hammered the next nail, and the next, then shifted positions. "How do you like the island?"

He asked the question in such a natural, adult fashion that Kevin first glanced around to see if Nathaniel was speaking to him. "I like it. I like it a lot. We get to live in the castle, and I can play with Alex and Jenny anytime."

"You had friends back in Oklahoma, too, right?"

"Sure. My best friend is John Curtis Silverhorn. He's part Comanche. My mom said he could come visit anytime, and that we can write letters all we want. I already wrote him about the whale." Kevin smiled shyly. "I liked that the best."

"We'll have to go out again."

"Really? When?"

Nathaniel stopped hammering and looked at the boy. He realized he should have remembered from his exposure to Alex and Jenny that when children were raised with love and trust, they believed just about everything you told them.

"You can come out with me whenever you want. 'Long as your mother gives the go-ahead."

His reward for the careless offer was a brilliant smile. "Maybe I can steer the boat again?"

"Yeah." Nathaniel grinned and turned Kevin's baseball cap backward. "You could do that. Want to nail some boards?"

Kevin's eyes widened and glowed. "Okay!"

"Here." Nathaniel scooted back so that Kevin could kneel in front of him. "Hold the nail like this." He wrapped his hands over Kevin's, showing him how to hold both the hammer and the nail to guide the stroke.

"Hey!" Alex rose from the dead on Planet Zero and raced over. "Can I do it?"

"Me too." Jenny leaped on Nathaniel's back, knowing she was always welcome.

"I guess I got me a crew." Nathaniel figured that with all the extra help it would only take about twice as long to finish.

An hour later, Megan pulled up beside the long, classic lines of the T-Bird and stared. The house itself surprised her. The charming two-story cottage, with its neatly painted blue shutters and its window boxes bright with pansies, wasn't exactly the image she had of Nathaniel Fury. Nor was the tidy green lawn, the trimmed hedge, the fat barking puppy.

But it was Nathaniel who surprised her most. She was a bit taken aback by all that exposed golden skin, the lithe, muscled body. She was human, after all. But it was what he was doing that really captured her attention.

He was crouched over her son on the partially finished deck, their heads close, his big hand over Kevin's small one. Jenny was sitting adoringly beside him, and Alex was playing highwire on a joist.

"Hi, Megan! Look, I'm the death-defying Alex." In his excitement, Alex nearly lost his balance and almost plunged a harrowing eight inches to the ground. He pinwheeled his arms and avoided disaster.

"Close call," she said, and grinned at him.

"I'm in the center ring, without a net."

"Mom, we're building a deck." Kevin caught his bottom lip between his teeth and pounded a nail. "See?"

"Yes, I do." Briefcase in tow, Megan stopped to pet the eager puppy, who fell over backward in enthusiasm.

"And it's my turn next." Jenny batted her eyes at Nathaniel. "Isn't it?"

"That's right, sugar. Okay, Captain. Let's drive that baby home."

With a grunt of effort, Kevin sent the nail into the board. "I did it. I did the whole board." Proudly Kevin looked back at his mother. "We each get to do a board. This is my third one."

"It looks like you're doing a good job." To give the

devil his due, she smiled at Nathaniel. "Not everyone could handle it."

"Just takes a steady eye and a sure hand. Hey, mates, where's my timber?"

"We'll get it." Alex and Kevin scrambled together to heave the next plank.

Standing back, Megan watched the routine they'd worked out. Nathaniel took the board, sighted down it, set it in place. He tapped, shifted, using a small block of wood to measure the distance between the last board and the new one. Once he was satisfied, Jenny wriggled in front of him.

She wrapped both little hands around the hammer, and Nathaniel, a braver soul than Megan had imagined, held the nail.

"Keep your eye on the target," Nathaniel warned, then sat patiently while her little strokes gradually anchored the nail. Then, wrapping his hand over hers, he rammed it home. "Thirsty work," he said casually. "Isn't it, mates?"

"Aye, aye." Alex put his hands to his throat and gagged.

Nathaniel held the next nail. "There's some lemonade in the kitchen. If someone was to go fetch the pitcher and a few glasses . . ."

Four pairs of eyes turned on her, putting Megan firmly in her place. If she wasn't going to be a carpenter, she'd have to be a gofer.

"All right." She set the briefcase down and crossed the finished portion of the deck to the front door.

Nathaniel said nothing, waited.

Seconds later, a shrill wolf whistle sounded from inside, followed by a muffled scream. He was grinning by the time Bird squawked out his invitation: "Hey, sugar, buy you a drink? Here's looking at you, kid." When Bird began to sing a chorus of "There Is Nothing Like a Dame," the children collapsed into fits of laughter.

A few minutes later, Megan carried out a tray of drinks. Bird's voice followed her. "'Give me a kiss, and to that kiss a score!'"

She arched a brow as she set the tray on the deck. "Bogart, show tunes and poetry. That's quite a bird."

"He has an eye for pretty women." Nathaniel picked up a glass and downed half the contents. He scanned Megan, taking in the tidy French twist, the crisp blouse and slacks. "Can't say I blame him."

"Aunt Coco says Nate needs a woman." Alex smacked his lips over the tart lemonade. "I don't know why."

"To sleep with him," Jenny said, and caused both Nathaniel and Megan to gape. "Grown-ups get lonely at night, and they like to have someone to sleep with. Like Mom and Daddy do. I have my bear," she continued, referring to her favorite stuffed animal. "So I don't get lonely."

"Break time." Nathaniel gamely swallowed his choke of laughter. "Why don't you guys take Dog for a walk down by the water?"

The idea met with unanimous approval. With war whoops and slapping feet, they raced off.

"Kid's got a point." Nathaniel rubbed the cold glass over his sweaty brow. "Nights can get lonely."

"I'm sure Jenny will lend you her bear." Megan stepped away from him, as if studying the house. "It's a very nice place, Nathaniel." She flicked a finger over the sassy petals of a pansy. "Homey."

"You were expecting a crow's nest, some oilcloth?"

She had to smile. "Something like that. I want to thank you for letting Kevin spend the day."

"I'd say the three of them are working as a team these days."

Her smile softened. She could hear their laughter from behind the house. "Yes, you're right."

"I like having them around. They're good company." He shifted on the deck, folding his legs under him. "The boy's got your eyes."

Her smile faded. "No, Kevin's are brown." Like his father's.

"No, not the color. The look in them. Goes a lot deeper than brown or blue. How much have you told him?"

"I—" She brought herself back, angled her chin. "I didn't come here to discuss my personal life with you."

"What did you come here to discuss?"

"I came to get the children, and to go over your books."

Nathaniel nodded at her briefcase. "Got them in there?"

"Yes." She retrieved it, then, because she saw little choice, sat on the deck facing him. "I've finished the first quarter—that's January, February, March. Your outlay exceeded your income during that period, though you did have some cash flow through boat repairs. There is an outstanding account payable from February." She took out files, flipped through the neat computer-generated sheets. "A Mr. Jacques LaRue, in the amount of twelve hundred and thirty-two dollars and thirty-six cents."

"LaRue's had a tough year." Nathaniel poured more

lemonade. "Holt and I agreed to give him some more time."

"That's your business, of course. Traditionally there would be late charges on any outstanding account after thirty days."

"Traditionally, on the island, we're a little friendlier."

"Your choice." She adjusted her glasses. "Now, as you can see, I've arranged the books into logical columns. Expenses—rent, utilities, office supplies, advertising and so forth. Then we have wages and withholding."

"New perfume."

She glanced over. "What?"

"You're wearing a new perfume. There's a hint of jasmine in it."

Distracted, she stared at him. "Coco gave it to me."

"I like it." He leaned closer. "A lot."

"Well." She cleared her throat, flipped a page. "And here we have income. I've added the weekly ticket sales from the tours to give you a month-by-month total, and a year-to-date. I see that you run a package deal with The Retreat, discounting your tour for hotel guests."

"Seemed friendly—and like good business."

"Yes, it's very smart business. On the average, eighty percent of the hotel guests take advantage of the package. I . . . Do you have to sit so close?"

"Yeah. Have dinner with me tonight, Meg."

"No."

"Afraid to be alone with me?"

"Yes. Now, as you can see, in March your income began an upswing—"

"Bring the boy."

"What?"

"Am I mumbling?" He smiled at her and slipped her glasses off her nose. "I said bring Kevin along. We'll take a drive out to this place I know. Great lobster rolls." He gave the word *lobster* a broad New England twist that made her smile. "I can't claim they're up to Coco's standards, but there's plenty of local color."

"We'll see."

"Uh-uh. Parental cop-out."

She sighed, shrugged. "All right. Kevin would enjoy it."

"Good." He handed her glasses back before he rose to heft another board. "Tonight, then."

"Tonight?"

"Why wait? You can call Suzanna, tell her we'll drop the kids off at her house on the way."

"I suppose I could." Now that his back was to her, she had no choice but to watch the ripple of muscles play as he set the board. She ignored the quick tug at her midsection, and reminded herself that her son would be along as chaperon. "I've never had a lobster roll."

"Then you're in for a treat."

He was absolutely right. The long, winding drive in the spectacular T-Bird was joy enough. The little villages they passed through were as scenic as any postcard. The sun dipped down toward the horizon in the west, and the breeze in the open car smelled of fish, then flowers, then sea.

The restaurant was hardly more than a diner, a square of faded gray wood set on stilts in the water, across a rickety gangplank. The interior decoration ran to torn fishnets and battered lobster buoys.

Scarred tables dotted the equally scarred floor. The booths were designed to rip the hell out of panty hose. A dubious effort at romantic atmosphere was added by the painted tuna can and hurricane globe set in the center of each table. The candles globbed in the base of the cans were unlit. Today's menu was scrawled on a chalkboard hanging beside the open kitchen.

"We got lobster rolls, lobster salad and lobster lobster," a waitress explained to an obviously frazzled family of four. "We got beer, we got milk, iced tea and soft drinks. There's French fries and coleslaw, and no ice cream 'cause the machine's not working. What'll you have?"

When she spotted Nathaniel, she abandoned her customers and gave him a hard punch in the chest. "Where you been, Captain?"

"Oh, out and about, Jule. Got me a taste for lobster roll."

"You came to the right place." The waitress, scarecrow-thin with a puff of steel-gray hair, eyed Megan craftily. "So, who's this?"

"Megan O'Riley, her son Kevin. This is Julie Peterson. The best lobster cook on Mount Desert Island."

"The new accountant from The Towers." Julie gave a brisk nod. "Well, sit down, sit down. I'll fix you up when I get a minute." She swiveled back to her other customers. "You make up your mind yet, or are you just going to sit and take the air?"

"The food's better than the service." Nathaniel winked at Kevin as he led them to a booth. "You've just met one of the monuments of the island, Kevin. Mrs. Peterson's family has been trapping lobster and cooking them up for over a hundred years."

"Wow." He eyed the waitress, who, to almost-nine-year-old eyes, seemed old enough to have been handling that job personally for at least a century.

"I worked here some when I was a kid. Swabbing the decks." And she'd been kind to him, Nathaniel remembered. Giving him ice or salve for his bruises, saying nothing.

"I thought you worked with Holt's family—" Megan began, then cursed herself when he lifted a brow at her. "Coco mentioned it."

"I put in some time with the Bradfords."

"Did you know Holt's grandfather?" Kevin wanted to know. "He's one of the ghosts."

"Sure. He used to sit on the porch of the house where Alex and Jenny live now. Sometimes he'd walk up to the cliffs over by The Towers. Looking for Bianca."

"Lilah says they walk there together now. I haven't seen them." And it was a crushing disappointment. "Have you ever seen a ghost?"

"More than once." Nathaniel ignored the stiff kick Megan gave him under the table. "In Cornwall, where the cliffs are deadly and the fogs roll in like something alive, I saw a woman standing, looking out to sea. She wore a cape with a hood, and there were tears in her eyes."

Kevin was leaning forward now, rapt and eager.

"I started toward her, through the mist, and she turned. She was beautiful, and sad. 'Lost,' was what she said to me. 'He's lost. And so am I.' Then she vanished. Like smoke."

"Honest?" Kevin said in an awed whisper.

Honest wasn't the point, Nathaniel knew. The pull of the story was. "They called her the Captain's Lady, and legend is that her husband and his ship went down in a storm in the Irish Sea. Night after night while she lived, and long after, she walked the cliffs weeping for him."

"Maybe you should be writing books, like Max," Megan murmured, surprised and annoyed at the shiver that raced down her spine.

"Oh, he can spin a tale, Nate can." Julie plopped two beers and a soft drink on the table. "Used to badger me about all the places he was going to see. Well, guess you saw them, didn't you, Captain?"

"Guess I did." Nathaniel lifted the bottle to his lips. "But I never forgot you, darling."

Julie gave another cackling laugh, punched his shoulder. "Sweet-talker," she said, and shuffled off.

Megan studied her beer. "She didn't take our order."

"She won't. She'll bring us what she wants us to have." He took another pull of the beer. "Because she likes me. If you're not up for beer, I can charm her into switching it."

"No, it's fine. I suppose you know a lot of people on the island, since you grew up here."

"A few. I was gone a long time."

"Nate sailed around the whole world. Twice." Kevin slurped soda through his straw. "Through hurricanes and typhoons and everything."

"It must have been exciting."

"It had its moments."

"Do you miss it?"

"I sailed on another man's ship for more than fifteen years. Now I sail my own. Things change." Nathaniel draped his arm over the back of the booth. "Like you coming here."

"We like it." Kevin began to stab his straw in the ice. "Mom's boss in Oklahoma was a skinflint."

"Kevin."

"Granddad said so. And he didn't appreciate you. You were hiding your light under a bushel." Kevin didn't know what that meant, but his grandmother had said so.

"Granddad's biased." She smiled and ruffled her son's hair. "But we do like it here."

"Eat hearty," Julie ordered, and dropped three enormous platters on the table.

The long rolls of crusty bread were filled with chunks of lobster and flanked by a mound of coleslaw and a small mountain of French fries.

"Girl needs weight," Julie proclaimed. "Boy, too. Didn't know you liked 'em skinny, Captain."

"I like them any way I can get them," Nathaniel corrected, which sent Julie off into another gale of laughter.

"We'll never eat all of this." Megan stared, daunted, at her plate.

Nathaniel had already dug in. "Sure we will. So, have you looked over Fergus's book yet?"

"Not really." Megan sampled the first bite. Whatever the atmosphere, the food was four-star. "I want to get the backlog caught up first. Since Shipshape's books were the worst, I dealt with them first. I still have to work on your second quarter, and The Retreat's."

"Your mother's a practical woman, Kev."

"Yeah." Kevin managed to swallow a giant bite of lobster roll. "Granddad says she needs to get out more."

"Kevin."

But the warning came too late. Nathaniel was already grinning.

"Does he? What else does Granddad say?"

"She should live a little." Kevin attacked his French fries with the single-minded determination of a child. "'Cause she's too young to hole up like a hermit."

"Your granddad's a smart man."

"Oh, yeah. He knows everything. He's got oil for blood and horses on the brain."

"A quote from my mother," Megan said dryly. "She knows everything, too. But you were asking about Fergus's book."

"Just wondered if it had scratched your curiosity."

"Some. I thought I might take an hour or so at night to work on it."

"I don't think that's what your daddy meant by living a little, Meg."

"Regardless." She turned back to the safer topic of the account book. "Some of the pages are faded badly, but other than a few minor mistakes, the accounts are very accurate. Except for the last couple of pages, where there are just numbers without any logic."

"Really. They don't add up?"

"They don't seem to, but I need to take a closer look."

"Sometimes you miss more by looking too close." Nathaniel winked at Julie as she set another round of drinks on the table. It was coffee for him this time. She knew that when he was driving he kept it to one beer. "I wouldn't mind taking a look at it."

Megan frowned at her. "Why?"

"I like puzzles."

"I don't think it's much of a puzzle, but if it's all right with the family, I don't have any objection." She leaned back, sighed. "Sorry, I just can't eat any more."

"It's okay." Nathaniel switched his empty plate with hers. "I can."

To Megan's amazement, he could. It wasn't much of a surprise that Kevin had managed to clean his plate. The way he was growing he often seemed in danger of eating china and all when he sat down for a meal. But Nathaniel ate his meal, then half of hers, without a blink.

"Have you always eaten like that?" Megan asked when they were driving away from the restaurant.

"Nope. Always wanted to, though. Never could seem to fill up as a kid." Of course, that might have been because there was little to fill up on. "At sea, you learn to eat anything, and plenty of it, while it's there."

"You should weigh three hundred pounds."

"Some people burn it off." He shifted his eyes to hers. "Like you. All that nervous energy you've got just eats up those calories."

"I'm not skinny," she muttered.

"Nope. Thought you were myself, till I got ahold of you. It's more like willowy—and you've got a real soft feel to you when you're pressed up against a man."

She hissed, started to look over her shoulder.

"He conked out the minute I turned on the engine," Nathaniel told her. And, indeed, she could see Kevin stretched out in the back, his head pillowed on his arms, sleeping soundly. "Though I don't see what harm there is for the boy to know a man's interested in his mother."

"He's a child." She turned back, the gentle look in her eyes gone. "I won't have him think that I'm—"

"Human?"

"It's not your affair. He's my son."

"That he is," Nathaniel agreed easily. "And you've done a hell of a job with him."

She slanted him a cautious look. "Thank you."

"No need to. Just a fact. It's tough raising a kid on your own. You found the way to do it right."

It was impossible to stay irritated with him, especially when she remembered what Coco had told her. "You lost your mother when you were young. Ah . . . Coco mentioned it."

"Coco's been mentioning a lot of things."

"She didn't mean any harm. You know how she is, better than I. She cares so much about people, and wants to see them . . ."

"Lined up two by two? Yeah, I know her. She picked you out for me."

"She—" Words failed her. "That's ridiculous."

"Not to Coco." He steered easily around a curve. "Of course, she doesn't know that I know she's already got me scheduled to go down on one knee."

"It's fortunate, isn't it, that you're forewarned?"

Her indignant tone had a smile twitching at his lips. "Sure is. She's been singing your praises for months. And you almost live up to the advance publicity."

She hissed like a snake and turned to him. His grin, and the absurdity of the situation, changed indignation to amusement. "Thank you." She stretched out her legs, leaned back and decided to enjoy the ride. "I'd hate to have disappointed you."

"Oh, you didn't, sugar."

"I've been told you're mysterious, romantic and charming."

"And?"

"You almost live up to the advance publicity."

"Sugar—" he took her hand and kissed it lavishly "—I can be a lot better."

"I'm sure you can." She drew her hand away, refusing to acknowledge the rippling thrill up her arm. "If I wasn't so fond of her, I'd be annoyed. But she's so kind."

"She has the truest heart of anyone I've ever met. I used to wish she was my mother."

"I'm sorry." Before she could resist the urge, Megan laid a hand on his. "It must have been so hard, losing your mother when you were only a child."

"It's all right. It was a long time ago." Much too long for him to grieve. "I still remember seeing Coco in the village, or when I'd tag along with Holt to take fish up to The Towers. There she'd be, this gorgeous woman—looked like a queen. Never knew what color her hair would be from one week to the next."

"She's a brunette today," Megan said, and made him laugh.

"First woman I ever fell for. She came to the house a couple times, read my old man the riot act about his drinking. Guess she thought if he was sober he wouldn't knock me around so much." He took his eyes off the road again, met hers. "I imagine she mentioned that, too?"

"Yes." Uncomfortable, Megan looked away. "I'm sorry, Nathaniel. I hate when people discuss me, no matter how good their intentions. It's so intrusive."

"I'm not that sensitive, Meg. Everybody knew what my old man was like." He could remember, too well, the pitying looks, the glances that slid uneasily away. "It bothered me back then, but not anymore."

She struggled to find the right words. "Did Coco—did it do any good?"

He was silent a moment, staring out at the lowering sun and the bloodred light it poured into the water. "He was afraid of her, so he beat the hell out of me when she left."

"Oh, God."

"I'd just as soon she didn't know that."

"No." Megan had to swallow the hot tears lodged in her throat. "I won't tell her. That's why you ran away to sea, isn't it? To get away from him."

"That's one of the reasons." He reached over, ran a fingertip down her cheek. "You know, if I'd figured out the way to get to you was to tell you I'd taken a strap a few times, I'd have brought it up sooner."

"It's nothing to joke about." Megan's voice was low and furious. "There's no excuse for treating a child that way."

"Hey, I lived through it."

"Did you?" She shifted back to him, eyes steady. "Did you ever stop hating him?"

"No." He said it quietly. "No, I didn't. But I stopped letting it be important, and maybe that's healthier." He stopped the car in front of The Towers, turned to her. "Someone hurts you, in a permanent way, you don't forget it. But the best revenge is seeing that it doesn't matter."

"You're talking about Kevin's father, and it's not at all the same. I wasn't a helpless child."

"Depends on where you draw the line between helpless and innocent." Nathaniel opened the car door. "I'll carry Kevin in for you."

"You don't have to." She hurried out herself, but Nathaniel already had the boy in his arms.

They stood there for a moment, in the last glow of the day, the boy between them, his head resting securely on Nathaniel's shoulder, dark hair to dark hair, honed muscle to young limbs.

Something locked deep inside her swelled, tried to burst free. She sighed it away, stroked a hand over her son's back and felt the steady rhythm of his breathing.

"He's had a long day."

"So have you, Meg. There are shadows under your eyes. Since that means you didn't sleep any better than I did last night, I can't say I mind seeing them there."

It was hard, she thought, so very hard, to keep pulling away from the current that drew her to him. "I'm not ready for this, Nathaniel."

"Sometimes a wind comes up, blows you off course. You're not ready for it, but if you're lucky, you end up in a more interesting place than you'd planned."

"I don't like to depend on luck."

"That's okay. I do." He shifted the boy more comfortably, and carried him to the house.

Chapter 6

"Don't see what all the damn to-do's about," Dutch grumbled as he whipped a delicate egg froth for his angel food cake surprise.

"Trenton St. James II is a member of the family." Running on nerves, Coco checked the temperature on her prime rib. She had a dozen things to deal with since the cucumber facial she'd indulged in had thrown off her timetable. "And the president of the St. James hotels." Satisfied that the beef was coming along nicely, she basted her roast duck. "As this is his first visit to The Retreat, it's important that everything run smoothly."

"Some rich bastard coming around to freeload."

"Mr. Van Horne!" Coco's heart lurched. After six months, she knew she shouldn't be shocked by the man. But, *really*. "I've known Mr. St. James for . . . well, a great number of years. I can assure you he is a successful businessman, an entrepreneur. *Not* a freeloader."

Dutch sniffed, gave Coco the once-over. She'd done herself up good and proper, he noted. The fancyshmancy dress glittered and flowed down, stopping plenty short to show off her legs. Her cheeks were all pink, too. And he didn't think it was from kitchen heat. His lips curled back in a sneer.

"So what's he, your boyfriend?"

The pink deepened to rose. "Certainly not. A woman of my . . . experience doesn't have boyfriends." Surreptitiously she checked her face in the stainless-steel exhaust hood on the stove. "Beaux, perhaps."

Beaux. Ha! "I hear he's been married four times and pays enough alimony to balance the national debt. You looking to be number five?"

Speechless, Coco pressed a hand to her heart. "You are—" She stumbled, stuttered, over the words. "Impossibly rude. Impossibly crude."

"Hey, ain't none of my never-mind if you want to land yourself a rich fish."

She squeaked. Though the rolling temper that caused red dots to swim in front of her eyes appalled her—she was, after all, a civilized woman—she surged forward to ram a coral-tipped nail into his massive chest. "I will not tolerate any more of your insults."

"Yeah?" He poked her right back. "Whatcha gonna do about it?"

She leaned forward until they were nose-to-nose. "I will fire you."

"Now that'll break my heart. Go ahead, fancy face, give me the boot. See how you get by with tonight's dinner rush."

"I assure you, I will 'get by' delightfully." Her heart was beating too fast. Coco wondered it didn't soar right out of her breast.

"Like hell." He hated her perfume. Hated that it made his nostrils twitch and his mouth water. "When I came on board, you were barely treading water."

She couldn't get her breath, simply couldn't. "This kitchen doesn't need you, Mr. Van Horne. And neither do I."

"You need me plenty." How had his hands gotten onto her shoulders? Why were hers pressed to his chest? The hell with how or why, he thought. He'd show her what was what.

Her eyes popped hard when his hard, sneering mouth crushed down on hers in a very thorough kiss. But she didn't see a thing. Her world, so beautifully secure, tilted under her feet. That was why—naturally that was why—she clung to him.

She would slap his face. She certainly would.

In just a few minutes.

Damn women, Dutch thought. Damn them all. Especially tall, curvy, sweet-smelling females with lips like . . . cooking cherries. He'd always had a weakness for tartness.

He jerked her away, but kept his big hands firm on her shoulders. "Let's get something straight . . ." he began.

"Now look here . . ." she said at the same time.

They both leaped apart like guilty children when the kitchen door swung open.

Megan stood frozen in the doorway, her jaw dropping. Surely she hadn't seen what she thought she'd seen. Coco was checking the oven, and Dutch was measuring flour into a bowl. They couldn't have been . . . embracing. Yet both of them were a rather startling shade of pink.

"Excuse me," she managed. "I'm sorry to, ah . . ."

"Oh, Megan, dear." Flustered, Coco patted her hair.

She was tingling, she realized. From embarrassment—and annoyance, she assured herself. "What can I do for you?"

"I just wanted to check a couple of the kitchen expenses." She was still goggling, her eyes shifting from Coco to Dutch and back. The tension in the room was thicker than Coco's split-pea soup. "But if you're busy, we can do it later."

"Nonsense." Coco wiped her sweaty palms on her apron. "We're just a little frantic preparing for Trenton's arrival."

"Trenton? Oh, I'd forgotten. Trent's father's expected." She was cautiously backing out of the room. "We don't need to do this now."

"No, no." Oh, Lord, Coco thought, don't leave me. "Now's a perfect time. We're under control here. Let's do it in your office, shall we?" She took Megan firmly by the arm. "Mr. Van Horne can handle things for a few minutes." Without waiting for his assent, she hurried from the room. "Details, details," Coco said gaily, and clung to Megan as though she were a life raft in a churning sea. "It seems the more you handle, the more there are."

"Coco, are you all right?"

"Oh, of course." But she pressed a hand to her heart. "Just a little contretemps with Mr. Van Horne. But that's nothing I can't deal with." She hoped. "How are your accounts coming along, dear? I must say I'd hoped you'd find time to glance at Fergus's book."

"Actually, I have—"

"Not that we want you working too hard." With the buzz going on in Coco's head, she didn't hear a word Megan said. "We want you to feel right at home here, to enjoy yourself. To relax. After all the trouble and excitement last year, we all want to relax. I don't think any of us could stand any more crises."

"I do not have, nor do I require, a reservation."

The crackling, irate voice stopped Coco in her tracks. The becoming flush in her cheeks faded to a dead white.

"Dear God, no. It can't be."

"Coco?" Megan took a firmer grip on Coco's arm. She felt the tremor and wondered if she could hold the woman up if she fainted.

"Young man." The voice rose, echoing off the walls. "Do you know who I am?"

"Aunt Colleen," Coco said in a shaky whisper. She let go one last shuddering moan, drew in a bracing breath, then walked bravely into the lobby. "Aunt Colleen," she said in an entirely different tone. "What a lovely surprise."

"Shock, you mean." Colleen accepted her niece's kiss, then rapped her cane on the floor. She was tall, thin as a rail and formidable as iron in a raw-silk suit and pearls as white as her hair. "I see you've filled the place with strangers. Better to have it burned to the ground. Tell this insolent boy to have my bags taken up."

"Of course." Coco gestured for a bellman herself. "In the family wing, second floor, first room on the right," she instructed.

"And don't toss those bags around, boy." Colleen leaned on her gold-tipped cane and studied Megan. "Who's this?"

"You remember Megan, Aunt Colleen. Sloan's sister? You met at Amanda's wedding."

"Yes, yes." Colleen's eyes narrowed, measured.

"Got a son, don't you?" Colleen knew all there was to know about Kevin. Had made it her business to know.

"Yes, I do. It's nice to see you again, Miss Calhoun."

"Ha. You'd be the only one of this lot who thinks so." Ignoring them both, she walked to Bianca's portrait, studied it and the emeralds glistening in their case. She sighed, but so quietly no one could hear.

"I want brandy, Cordelia, before I take a look at what you've done to this place."

"Of course. We'll just go into the family wing. Megan, please, join us."

It was impossible to deny the plea in Coco's eyes.

A few moments later, they had settled into the family parlor. Here, the wallpaper was still faded, peeling in spots. There were scars on the floor in front of the fireplace where errant embers had seared and burned.

"Nothing's changed here, I see." Colleen sat like a queen in a wing chair.

"We've concentrated on the hotel wing." Nervous and babbling, Coco poured brandy. "Now that it's done, we're beginning renovations. Two of the bedrooms are finished. And the nursery's lovely."

"Humph." She'd come specifically to see the children—and only secondarily to drive Coco mad. "Where is everyone? I come to see my family and find nothing but strangers."

"They'll be along. We're having a dinner party tonight, Aunt Colleen." Coco kept the brilliant smile plastered on her face. "Trent's father's joining us for a few days."

"Aging playboy," Colleen mumbled into her brandy. "You." She pointed at Megan. "Accountant, aren't you?"

"Yes, ma'am."

"Megan's a whiz with figures," Coco said desperately. "We're so grateful she's here. And Kevin, too, of course. He's a darling boy."

"I'm talking to the girl, Cordelia. Go fuss in the kitchen."

"But—"

"Go on, go on."

With an apologetic look for Megan, Coco fled.

"The boy'll be nine soon?"

"Yes, in a couple of months." She was prepared, braced, for a scathing comment on his lineage.

Tapping her fingers on the arm of the chair, Colleen nodded. "Get along with Suzanna's brood, does he?"

"Very well. They've rarely been apart since we arrived." Megan did her best not to squirm. "It's been wonderful for him. And for me."

"Dumont bothering you?"

Megan blinked. "I beg your pardon?"

"Don't be a fool, girl, I asked if that excuse for a human being has been bothering you."

Megan's spine straightened like a steel rod. "No. I haven't seen or heard from Baxter since before Kevin was born."

"You will." Colleen scowled and leaned forward. She wanted to get a handle on this Megan O'Riley. "He's been making inquiries."

Megan's fingers clenched on the snifter of brandy. "I don't understand."

"Poking his nose in, asking questions." Colleen gave her cane an imperious thump.

"How do you know?"

"I keep my ear to the ground when it comes to family." Eyes bright, Colleen waited for a reaction, got none. "You moved here, didn't you? Your son's been accepted as Alex and Jenny—and Christian's—brother."

Ice was forming in Megan's stomach, thin, brittle strips of it. "That has nothing to do with him."

"Don't be a fool. A man like Dumont thinks the world revolves around him. His eye's on politics, girl, and the way that particular circus is running, a few well-chosen words from you to the right reporter . . ." The idea was pleasant enough to make Colleen smile. "Well, his road to Washington would be a steeper climb."

"I've no intention of going to the press, of exposing Kevin to public attention."

"Wise." Colleen sipped again. "A pity, but wise. You tell me if he tries anything. I'd like to tangle with him again."

"I can handle it myself."

Colleen lifted one snowy brow. "Perhaps you can."

"How come I have to wear a dumb tie?" Kevin squirmed while Megan fumbled with the knot. Her fingers had been stiff and cold ever since her talk with Colleen.

"Because it's a special dinner and you need to look your best."

"Ties are stupid. I bet Alex doesn't have to wear a stupid tie."

"I don't know what Alex is wearing," Megan said, with the last of her patience. "But you're doing as you're told."

The sharp tone, rarely heard, had his bottom lip poking out. "I'd rather have pizza."

"Well, you're not having pizza. Damn it, Kevin, hold still!"

"It's choking me."

"*I'm* going to choke you in a minute." She blew her hair out of her eyes and secured the knot. "There. You look very handsome."

"I look like a dork."

"Fine, you look like a dork. Now put your shoes on."

Kevin scowled at the shiny black loafers. "I hate those shoes. I want to wear my sneakers."

Exasperated, she leaned down until their faces were level. "Young man, you will put your shoes on, and you will watch your tone of voice. Or you'll find yourself in very hot water."

Megan marched out of his room and across the hall to her own. Snatching her brush from the dresser, she began to drag it through her hair. She didn't want to go to the damn dinner party, either. The aspirin she'd downed an hour before hadn't even touched the splitting headache slicing through her skull. But she had to put on her party face and go down, pretend she wasn't terrified and angry and sick with worry over Baxter Dumont.

Colleen might be wrong, she thought. After all, it had been nearly a decade. Why would Baxter bother with her and Kevin now?

Because he wanted to be a United States senator. Megan closed her eyes. She read the paper, didn't she? Baxter had already begun his campaign for the seat. And an illegitimate son, never acknowledged, hardly fit the straight-arrow platform he'd chosen.

"Mom."

She saw Kevin's reflection in the mirror. His shoes

were on—and his chin was on his chest. Guilt squeezed its sticky fingers around her heart. "Yes, Kevin."

"How come you're so mad at everything?"

"I'm not." Wearily she sat on the edge of the bed. "I've just got a little headache. I'm sorry I snapped at you." She held out her arms, sighing when he filled them. "You're such a handsome dork, Kev." When he laughed, she kissed the top of his head. "Let's go down. Maybe Alex and Jenny are here."

They were, and Alex was just as disgusted with his tie as Kevin was with his. But there was too much going on for the boys to sulk for long. There were canapés to gobble, babies to play with and adventures to plan.

Everyone, naturally, was talking at once.

The volume in the room cut through Megan's aching head like a rusty saw. She accepted the flute of champagne Trenton II offered her, and did her best to pretend an interest in his flirtation. He was trim and tall and tanned, glossily handsome and charming. And Megan was desperately relieved when he turned his attentions on Coco.

"Make a nice couple, don't they?" Nathaniel murmured in her ear.

"Striking." She took a cube of cheese and forced it down.

"You don't look in the party mood, Meg."

"I'm fine." To distract him, she changed the subject. "You might be interested in what I think I might have walked in on this afternoon."

"Oh?" Taking her arm, he steered her toward the open terrace doors.

"Coco and Dutch."

"Fighting again? Saucepans at twenty paces?"

"Not exactly." She took a deep breath of air, hoping it would clear her head. "They were . . . at least I think they were . . ."

Nathaniel's brows shot up. He could fill in the blanks himself. "You're joking."

"No. They were nose-to-nose, with their arms around each other." She managed to smile even as she rubbed at the throbbing in her temple. "At my unexpected and ill-timed entrance, they jumped apart as if they'd been planning murder. And they were blushing. Both of them."

"The Dutchman, blushing?" Nathaniel started to laugh, but it began to sink in. "Good God."

"I think it's sweet."

"Sweet." He looked back inside, where Coco, regally elegant, was laughing over something Trenton had whispered in her ear. "She's out of his league. She'll break his heart."

"What a ridiculous thing to say." Lord, why didn't her head just fall off her shoulders and give her some relief? "Sporting events have leagues, not romances."

"The Dutchman and Coco." It worried him, because they were two of the very few people in the world he could say he loved. "You're the accountant, sugar, and you're going to tell me that adds up?"

"I'm not telling you anything," she shot back. "Except I think they're attracted to each other. And stop calling me 'sugar.'"

"Okay, simmer down." He looked back down at her, focused on her. "What's the matter?"

Guiltily she dropped her hand. She'd been massaging her temple again. "Nothing."

With an impatient oath, he turned her fully to face him, looked into her eyes. "Headache, huh? Bad one?"

"No, it's—Yes," she admitted. "Vicious."

"You're all tensed up." He began to knead her shoulders. "Tight as a spring."

"Don't."

"This is purely therapeutic." He rubbed his thumbs in gentle circles over her collarbone. "Any pleasure either of us gets out of it is incidental. Have you always been prone to headaches?"

His fingers were strong and male and magical. It was impossible not to stretch under them. "I'm not prone to headaches."

"Too much stress." His hands skimmed lightly up to her temples. She closed her eyes with a sigh. "You bottle too much up, Meg. Your body makes you pay for it. Turn around, let me work on those shoulders."

"It's not—" But the protest died away when his hands began to knead at the knots.

"Relax. Pretty night, isn't it? Moon's full, stars are out. Ever walk up on the cliffs in the moonlight, Megan?"

"No."

"Wildflowers growing right out of the rock, the water thundering. You can imagine those ghosts Kevin's so fond of strolling hand in hand. Some people think it's a lonely place, but it's not."

His voice and his hands were so soothing. She could almost believe there was nothing to worry about. "There's a painting at Suzanna's of the cliffs in moonlight," Megan offered, trying to focus on the conversation.

"Christian Bradford's work—I've seen it. He had a feel for that spot. But there's nothing like the real thing. You could walk with me there after dinner. I'll show you."

"This isn't the time to fool around with the girl." Colleen's voice cut through the evening air, and she stamped her cane in the doorway.

Though Megan tensed again, Nathaniel kept his hands where they were and grinned. "Seems like a fine time to me, Miss Colleen."

"Ha! Scoundrel." Colleen's lips twitched. Nothing she liked better than a handsome scoundrel. "Always were. I remember you, running wild through the village. Looks like the sea made a man of you, all right. Stop fidgeting, girl. He's not going to let loose of you. If you're lucky."

Nathaniel kissed the top of Megan's head. "She's shy."

"Well, she'll have to get over it, won't she? Cordelia's finally going to feed us. I want you to sit with me, talk about boats."

"It would be a pleasure."

"Well, come on, bring her. Lived on cruise ships half my life or more," Colleen began. "I'll wager I've seen more of the sea than you, boy."

"I wouldn't doubt it, ma'am." Nathaniel kept one hand on Megan and offered Colleen his arm. "With a trail of broken hearts in your wake."

She gave a hoot of laughter. "Damn right."

The dining room was full of the scents of food and flowers and candle wax. The moment everyone was settled, Trenton II rose, glass in hand.

"I'd like to make a toast." His voice was as cultured

as his dinner suit. "To Cordelia, a woman of extraordinary talents and beauty."

Glasses were clinked. From his spy hole at the crack in the doorway, Dutch snorted, scowled, then stomped back to his own kitchen.

"Trent." C.C. leaned toward her husband, her voice low. "You know I love you."

He thought he knew what was coming. "Yes, I do."

"And I adore your father."

"Mmm-hmm . . ."

"And if he puts the moves on Aunt Coco, I'm going to have to kill him."

"Right." Trent smiled weakly and began on the first course.

At the other end of the table, sublimely ignorant of the threat, Trenton beamed at Colleen. "What do you think of The Retreat, Miss Calhoun?"

"I dislike hotels. Never use them."

"Aunt Colleen." Coco fluttered her hands. "The St. James hotels are world-famous for their luxury and taste."

"Can't stand them," Colleen said complacently as she spooned up soup. "What's this stuff?"

"It's lobster bisque, Aunt Colleen."

"Needs salt," she said, for the devil of it. "You, boy." She jabbed a finger down the table at Kevin. "Don't slouch. You want your bones to grow crooked?"

"No, ma'am."

"Got any ambitions?"

Kevin stared helplessly, and was relieved when his mother's hand closed over his. "I could be a sailor," he blurted out. "I steered the *Mariner*."

"Ha!" Pleased, she picked up her wine. "Good for you. I won't tolerate any idlers in my family. Too thin. Eat your soup, such as it is."

With a quiet moan, Coco rang for the second course.

"She never changes." Lazily content, Lilah rocked while Bianca suckled hungrily at her breast. The nursery was quiet, the lights were low. Megan had headed for it, figuring it would be the perfect escape hatch.

"She's . . ." Megan searched for a diplomatic phrase. "Quite a lady."

"She's a nosy old nuisance." Lilah laughed lightly. "But we love her."

In the next rocker, Amanda sighed. "As soon as she hears about Fergus's book, she's going to start nagging you."

"And badgering," C.C. put in, cradling Ethan.

"And hounding," Suzanna finished up as she changed Christian's diaper.

"That sounds promising."

"Don't worry." With a laugh, Suzanna slipped Christian into his sleeper. "We're right behind you."

"Notice," Lilah added with a smile, "the direction is *behind*."

"About the book." Megan flicked a finger over a dancing giraffe on a mobile. "I've made copies of several pages I thought you'd be interested in. He made a lot of notations, about business deals, personal business, purchases. At one point he inventories jewelry—Bianca's, I assume—for insurance purposes."

"The emeralds?" Amanda's brow rose at Megan's nod. "And to think of all the hours we spent going through papers, trying to find proof that they existed."

"There's a number of other pieces—hundreds of thousands of dollars' worth in 1913 dollars."

"He sold nearly everything," C.C. murmured. "We found the documents of sale. He got rid of anything that reminded him of Bianca."

"It still hurts," Lilah admitted. "Not the money, though God knows we could have used it. It's the loss of what was hers, what we won't be able to pass on."

"I'm sorry."

"Don't be." Amanda rose to lay a sleeping Delia in her crib. "We're too sentimental. I suppose we all feel such a close connection with Bianca."

"I know what you mean." It felt odd to admit it, but Megan was compelled. "I feel it, too. I suppose from seeing the references to her in the old book, and having her portrait right there in the lobby." A bit embarrassed, she laughed. "Sometimes, when you walk down the halls at night, it's almost as if you could sense her."

"Of course," Lilah said easily. "She's here."

"Excuse me, ladies." Nathaniel stepped inside, obviously comfortable in a nursery inhabited by babies and nursing mothers.

Lilah smiled slowly. "Well, hello, handsome. What brings you to the maternity wing?"

"Just coming to fetch my date."

When he took Megan's arm, she drew back. "We don't have a date."

"A walk, remember?"

"I never said—"

"It's a lovely night for it." Suzanna lifted Christian into her arms, cooed to him.

"I have to put Kevin to bed."

She was digging in her heels, but it didn't seem to be doing any good.

"I've already tucked him in." Nathaniel propelled her toward the doors.

"You put Kevin to bed?"

"Since he'd fallen asleep in my lap, it seemed the thing to do. Oh, Suzanna, Holt said the kids are ready whenever you are."

"I'm on my way." Suzanna waited until Megan and Nate were out of earshot before she turned to her sisters. "What do you think?"

Amanda smiled smugly. "I think it's working perfectly."

"I have to agree." C.C. settled Ethan comfortably in his crib. "I thought Lilah had lost her mind when she came up with the idea of getting those two together."

Lilah yawned, sighed. "I'm never wrong." Then her eyes lit. "I bet we can see them from the window."

"*Spy* on them?" Amanda arched her brows. "Good idea," she said, and darted to the window.

They were outlined in the moonlight that sprinkled the lawn.

"You're complicating things, Nathaniel."

"Simplifying," he corrected. "Nothing simpler than a walk in the moonlight."

"That's not where you expect all this to end."

"Nope. But we're still moving at your pace, Meg." He brought her hand to his lips, kissed it absently, when they began the climb. "I seem to have this need to be around you. It's the damnedest thing. Can't shake it. So I figure, why try? Why not just roll with it?"

"I'm not a simple woman." She wished she could

be, just for tonight, just for an hour in the starlight. "I have baggage and resentments and insecurities I didn't even realize were there until I met you. I'm not going to let myself be hurt again."

"No one's going to hurt you." In a subtle gesture of protection, he slipped an arm around her and looked up at the sky. "Look how big the moon is tonight. Just hanging there. You can see Venus, and the little star that dogs her. There's Orion." He lifted her hand, tracing the sky with it as he had once traced his charts. "And the Twins. See?"

"Yes." She watched their joined hands connect stars while the breeze lifted lovingly off the water and stirred the flowers that grew wild in the rock.

Romantic, mysterious, Coco had said. Yes, he was, and Megan realized she was much more susceptible to both than she would have believed.

For she was here, wasn't she, standing on a cliff with a seafaring man whose callused hand held hers, whose voice helped her see the pictures painted by the stars. His body was warm and solid against hers. And her blood was pumping fast and free in her veins.

Alive. The wind and the sea and the man made her feel so alive.

And perhaps there was something more—those ghosts of the Calhouns'. The cliffs seemed to invite spirits to walk, the air filled with contentment. And the glow of love that had outlasted time.

"I shouldn't be here like this." But she didn't move away, not even when his lips brushed over her hair.

"Listen," he murmured. "Close your eyes and listen, and you can hear the stars breathing."

She obeyed, and listened to the whisper and throb of

the air. And of her own heart. "Why do you make me feel this way?"

"I don't have an answer. Not everything adds up neat, Meg." Because he had a great need to see her face, he turned her gently. "Not everything has to." And kissed her. His lips skimmed hers, journeyed up to her temple, over her brow and down. "How's the headache?"

"It's gone. Nearly."

"No. Keep your eyes closed." His lips traced over them, soft as air, before trailing slowly over her face. "Kiss me back, will you?"

How could she not, when his mouth was so tempting on hers? With a small sound of surrender, she let her heart lead. Just for tonight, she promised herself. Just for a moment.

That slow, melting change almost undid him. She went pliant in his arms, those hesitant lips heating, parting, offering. It took all his willpower not to drag her against him and plunder.

She wouldn't resist. Perhaps he'd known that there would be enough magic on those cliffs to bewitch them both, to seduce her into surrender—and to remind him to take care.

"I want you, Megan." He took his lips down her throat, up over her jaw. "I want you so much it's got me tied in knots."

"I know. I wish . . ." She pressed her face to his shoulder. "I'm not playing games, Nathaniel."

"I know." He stroked a hand down her hair. "It would be easier if you were, because I know all the rules." Cupping her face, he lifted it. "And how to break them." He sighed, kissed her again, lightly. "They make it damn hard for me, those eyes of yours." He stepped back. "I'd better take you in."

"Nathaniel." She laid a hand on his chest. "You're the first man who's made me . . . who I've wanted to be with since Kevin was born."

Something flashed in his eyes, wild, dangerous, before he banked it. "Do you think it makes it easier on me, knowing that?" He would have laughed, if he hadn't felt so much like exploding. "Megan, you're killing me." But he swung an arm around her shoulders and led her down the cliff path.

"I don't know how to handle this," she said under her breath. "I haven't had to handle anything like this before."

"Keep it up," he warned, "and you're over my shoulder, shanghaied straight to bed. Mine."

The image gave her a quick thrill, and a guilty one. "I'm just trying to be honest."

"Try lying," he said with a grimace. "Make it easier on me."

"I'm a lousy liar." She slanted a look at him. Wasn't it interesting, she mused, that for once he was the one at a disadvantage? "It doesn't seem logical that it would bother you to know what I'm feeling."

"I'm having a lot of trouble dealing with what I'm feeling." He took a long, steadying breath. "And I'm not feeling logical." Nor, he thought ruefully, would he sleep tonight. "'Desire hath no rest.'"

"What?"

"Robert Burton. Nothing."

They walked toward the lights of The Towers. The shouting reached them before they crossed the lawn.

"Coco," Megan said.

"Dutch." Taking firm hold of Megan's hand, Nathaniel quickened his pace.

"You're insulting and obnoxious," Coco snapped at Dutch, her chin up, her hands planted on her hips.

His massive arms were folded across his barrel of a chest. "I saw what I saw, said what I said."

"I was not draped all over Trenton like a . . . a . . ."

"Barnacle," Dutch said with relish. "Like a barnacle on the hull of a fancy yacht."

"We happen to have been dancing."

"Ha! That's what you call it. We got another name for it. Where I come from, we call it—"

"Dutch!" Nathaniel cut off the undoubtedly crude description.

"There." Mortified, Coco smoothed down her dress. "You've made a scene."

"You were the one making a scene, with that smooth-skinned rich boy. Flaunting yourself."

"F-f-flaunting." Enraged, she drew herself up to her full, and considerable, height. "I have never flaunted in my life. You, sir, are despicable."

"I'll show you despicable, lady."

"Cut it out." Prepared for fists to fly, Nathaniel stepped between them. "Dutch, what the hell's wrong with you? Are you drunk?"

"A nip or two of rum never rattled my brain." He glared over Nathaniel's shoulder at Coco. "It's her that's acting snockered. Out of my way, boy, I've got a thing or two left to say."

"You've finished," Nathaniel corrected.

"Out of his way." All eyes turned to Coco. She was

flushed, bright-eyed, and regal as a duchess. "I prefer to handle this matter myself."

Megan tugged gently on her arm. "Coco, don't you think you should go inside?"

"I do not." She caught herself and added a friendly pat. "Now, dear, you and Nate run along. Mr. Van Horne and I prefer to handle this privately."

"But—"

"Nathaniel," Coco said, interrupting her, "take Megan inside now."

"Yes, ma'am."

"Are you sure we should leave them alone?"

Nathaniel continued to steer Megan to the terrace doors. "You want to get in the middle of that?"

Megan glanced back over her shoulder. "No." She chuckled, shook her head. "No, I don't think so."

"Well, Mr. Van Horne," Coco began, when she was certain they were alone again. "Do you have something more to say?"

"I got plenty." Prepared for battle, he stepped forward. "You tell that slick-talking rich boy to keep his hands to himself."

She tossed back her head and enjoyed the mad flutter of her heart when her eyes met his. "And if I don't?"

Dutch growled like a wolf—like a wolf, Coco thought, challenging his mate. "I'll break his puny arms like matchsticks."

Oh, my, she thought. Oh, my goodness. "Will you, really?"

"Just you try me." He gave her a jerk, and she let herself tumble into his arms.

This time she was ready for the kiss, and met it

head-on. By the time they broke apart, they were both breathless and stunned.

Sometimes, Coco realized, it was up to the woman. She moistened her lips, swallowed hard.

"My room's on the second floor."

"I know where it is." A ghost of a smile flitted around his mouth. "Mine's closer." He swept her into his arms—very much, Coco thought dreamily, like a pirate taking his hostage.

"You're a fine, sturdy woman, Coco."

She pressed a hand on her thundering heart. "Oh, Niels."

Chapter 7

It wasn't like Megan to daydream. Years of discipline had taught her that dreams were for sleeping, not for rainy mornings when the fog was drifting around the house and the windows ran wet, as if with tears. But her computer hummed, unattended, and her chin was on her fist as her mind wandered back, as it had several times over the past few days, toward moonlight and wildflowers and the distant thunder of surf.

Now and again she caught herself and fell back on logic. It wouldn't pay to forget that the only romance in her life had been an illusion, a lie that betrayed her innocence, her emotions and her future. She'd thought herself immune, been content to be immune. Until Nathaniel.

What should she do, now that her life had taken this fast, unexpected swing? After all, she was no longer a child who believed in or needed promises and coaxing words. Now that her needs had been stirred, could she satisfy them without being hurt?

Oh, how she wished her heart wasn't involved. How she wished she could be smart and savvy and sophisticated and indulge in a purely physical affair, without emotion weighing in so heavily.

Why couldn't attraction, leavened with affection and respect, be enough? It should be such a simple equation. Two consenting adults, plus desire, times understanding and passion, equals mutual pleasure.

She just wished she could be sure there wasn't some hidden fraction that would throw off the simple solution.

"Megan?"

"Hmm?" Dreamily she turned toward the sound of the voice. Her imaginings shattered when she saw Suzanna inside the office, smiling at her. "Oh, I didn't hear you come in."

"You were miles away."

Caught drifting, Megan fought back embarrassment and shuffled papers. "I suppose I was. Something about the rain."

"It's lovely—always sets my mind wandering." Suzanna thought she knew just where Megan's mind had wandered. "Though I doubt the tourists or the children think so."

"Kevin thought the fog was great—until I told him he couldn't climb on the cliffs in it."

"And Alex and Jenny's plans for an assault on Fort O'Riley have been postponed. The kids are in Kevin's room, defending the planet against aliens. It's wonderful watching them together."

"I know. They've blended together so well."

"Like a mud ball," Suzanna said with a laugh, and eased a jean-clad hip on the edge of Megan's desk. "How's the work coming?"

"It's moving along. Amanda kept everything in order, so it's just a matter of shifting it into my own system and computerizing."

"It's a tremendous relief for her, having you take it over. Some days she'd be doing the books with a phone at her ear and Delia at her breast."

The image made Megan grin. "I can see it. She's amazingly organized."

"An expert juggler. Nothing she hates more than to bobble a ball. You'd understand that."

"Yeah, I do." Megan picked up a pencil and ran it between her fingers. "I worried about coming here, Suzanna, bringing Kevin. I was afraid I'd not only bobble a ball, but drop all of them, because I'd be so anxious not to say anything, even think anything, that would make you uncomfortable."

"Aren't we past that, Megan?"

"You were." Sighing, Megan set the pencil down again. "Maybe it's a little harder, being the other woman."

"Were you?" Suzanna said gently. "Or was I?"

Megan could only shake her head. "I can't say I wish I could go back and change things, because if I did I wouldn't have Kevin." She took a long breath, met Suzanna's eyes levelly. "I know you consider Kevin a brother to your children, and that you love him."

"Yes, I do."

"I want you to know that I think of your children as my family and I love them."

Suzanna reached over to lay a hand over Megan's. "I know you do. One of the reasons I dropped in was to ask if you'd mind if Kevin came along with us. I'm going to do some greenhouse work today. Alex and Jenny always enjoy it—especially since it includes pizza for lunch."

"I can't think of anything he'd rather do. And it would make up for having to wear a tie the other night."

Suzanna's eyes lit with humor. "I nearly had to strangle Alex to get him into his. I hope Aunt Coco doesn't plan any more formal dinner parties for some time to come." She tilted her head. "Speaking of Aunt Coco, have you seen her today?"

"Only for a minute, right after breakfast. Why?"

"Was she singing?"

"As a matter of fact, she was." Megan touched her tongue to her top lip. "She's been singing in the morning for several days now."

"She was singing just now, too. And wearing her best perfume." Uneasy, Suzanna nibbled her lip. "I was wondering if Trent's father . . . Of course, he's gone back to Boston now, so I thought there was nothing to worry about. He's a lovely man, and we're all very fond of him, but, well, he's been married four times, and he doesn't seem able to keep his eye from roving."

"I noticed." After a quick debate on privacy versus disclosure, Megan cleared her throat. "Actually, I don't think Coco's looking in that direction."

"No?"

"Dutch," Megan said, and watched Suzanna's eyes go blank.

"Excuse me?"

"I think she and Dutch are . . . infatuated."

"Dutch? Our Dutch? But she's always complaining about him, and he's snarling at her every chance he gets. They're always fighting, and . . ." She trailed off, pressed her hands to her lips. "Oh . . ." she said, while her eyes danced over them. "Oh, oh, oh . . ."

They stared at each other, struggled dutifully for perhaps three seconds before bursting into laughter. Megan fell easily into the sisterly pleasure of discussing a family member. After she told Suzanna about walking in on Coco and Dutch in the kitchen, she followed it up with the scene on the terrace.

"There were sparks flying, Suzanna. At first I thought they were going to come to blows, then I realized it was more of a—well, a mating ritual."

"A mating ritual," Suzanna repeated in a shaky voice. "Do you really think they—?"

"Well." Megan wriggled her eyebrows. "She's been doing a lot of singing lately."

"She certainly has." Suzanna let the idea stew for a moment, found it simmered nicely. "I think I'll drop by the kitchen before I go. Check out the atmosphere."

"I hope I can count on a full report."

"Absolutely." Still chuckling, Suzanna rose to go to the door. "I guess that was some moon the other night."

"It was," Megan murmured. "Some moon."

Suzanna paused with her hand on the knob. "And Nathaniel's some man."

"I thought we were talking about Dutch."

"We were talking about romance," Suzanna corrected. "I'll see you later."

Megan frowned at the closed door. Good Lord, she thought, was she that obvious?

After spending the rest of the morning and the first part of the afternoon on The Retreat's accounts, Megan gave herself the small reward of an hour with Fergus's book. She enjoyed tallying up the costs of stabling horses, maintaining carriages. It was an eye-opener to see how much expense was involved in giving a ball at The Towers in 1913. And, by reading Fergus's margin notes, to come to understand his motives.

> Invitations all accepted. No one dare decline. B. ordered flowers—argued about ostentation. Told her big display equals success and wife must never question husband. She will wear emeralds, not pearl choker as she suggested, show society my taste and means, remind her of her place.

Her place, Megan thought with pity for Bianca, had been with Christian. How sad that it had taken death to unite them.

Wanting to dispel the gloom, she flipped to the back pages. The numbers simply didn't make sense. Not expenses, she mused. Not dates. Account numbers, perhaps. Stock-market prices, lot numbers?

Perhaps it would be worth a trip to the library to see if she could unearth any information from 1913 that correlated. And on the way she could stop by Shipshape to drop off the completed spreadsheet for April and pick up any more receipts.

If she happened to run into Nathaniel, it would be purely coincidental.

It was a pleasure to drive in the rain. The slow, steady stream of drops had most of the summer people seeking indoor entertainment. A few pedestrians wandered the sidewalks, window-shopping under umbrellas. The water in Frenchman Bay was gray and misted, with the masts and sails of ships spearing through the heavy air.

She could hear the ring of bell buoys, the drone of foghorns. It was as if the entire island were tucked under a blanket, snug and safe and solitary. She was tempted to keep driving, to take the twisting road to Acadia National Park, or the meandering one along the shore.

Maybe she would, she thought. After she completed the day's business, she would take that drive, explore her new home. And maybe she would ask Nathaniel to join her.

But she didn't see his car outside Shipshape. Ridiculous to say it didn't matter whether she saw him or not, she realized. Because it did matter. She wanted to see him, to watch the way his eyes deepened and locked on hers. The way his lips curved.

Maybe he'd parked around the corner, out of sight. Snagging her briefcase, she dashed from her car into the office. It was empty.

The first slap of disappointment was stunning. She hadn't realized just how much she'd counted on him being there until he wasn't. Then she heard, faintly, through the rear wall, the throb of bass from a radio. Someone was in the shop attached to the back of the building, she concluded. Probably working on repairs as the seas were too rough for tours.

She wasn't going to check out who was back there, she told herself firmly. She'd come on legitimate business and she took out the latest spreadsheet and set it on the overburdened desk. But on a purely practical level, she would need to go over, with at least one of them, the second quarter and the projections for the rest of the year. But she supposed it could wait.

A long look around showed her a disorder she couldn't comprehend. How could anyone work, or hope to concentrate, in such a mess?

She was tempted to organize, but turned her back on the chaos and walked to the filing cabinets. She'd take what she needed and leave the rest. Then she would, casually, wander around back, to the shop.

When she heard the door open, she turned, ready with a smile. It faded a little when she saw a stranger in the doorway. "May I help you?"

The man stepped fully inside and shut the door behind him. When he smiled, something jittered inside Megan's brain. "Hello, Megan."

For an instant, time froze, and then it rewound. Slow motion for five years, six, then back a decade, to a time when she'd been young and careless and ready to believe in love at first sight.

"Baxter," she whispered. How odd, she thought dully, that she hadn't recognized him. He'd hardly changed in ten years. He was as handsome, as smooth and polished, as he'd been when she first saw him. A trim, Savile Row–suited Prince Charming with lies on his lips.

Baxter smiled down at Megan. For days he'd been trying to catch her alone. Frustration had pushed him to approach her here and now. Because he was a man concerned with his image, he'd checked the office thoroughly before he stepped through the door. It was easy to see she was alone in the small space. There were things he intended to settle with her once and for all. Calmly, of course, he thought as she stared at him. Reasonably. Privately.

"Pretty as ever, aren't you?" It pleased him to see her eyes go blank with shock. The advantage was with him, as he preferred it. After all, he'd been planning this reunion for several weeks now. "The years have improved your looks, Megan. You've lost that charming baby fat, and you've become almost elegant. My compliments."

When he stepped closer, she didn't move, couldn't make her legs or her brain respond. Not even when he lifted a finger and trailed it down her cheek, under her chin, to tip it up in an old habit she'd made herself forget.

"You were always a beauty, Megan, with that wide-eyed innocence that makes a man want to corrupt."

She shuddered. He smiled.

"What are you doing here?" *Kevin* was all she could think. Thank God Kevin wasn't with her.

"Funny, I was going to ask you the same. Just what are you doing here, Megan?"

"I live here." She hated hearing the hesitancy in her voice, like the throb of an old scar. "I work here."

"Tired of Oklahoma, were you? Wanted a change of scene?" He leaned closer, until she backed into the filing cabinet. Bribery, he knew, wouldn't work with her. Not with the O'Riley money behind her. Intimidation was the next logical choice. "Don't take me for a fool, Megan. It would be a terrible, costly mistake."

When her back hit the filing cabinet, she realized she was cringing, and her shock melted away, her spine stiffening. She wasn't a child now, she reminded herself, but a woman. Aware, responsible. "It's none of your business why I moved here."

"Oh, but it is." His voice was silky, quiet, reasonable. "I prefer you in Oklahoma, Megan. Working at your nice, steady job, in the midst of your loving family. I really much prefer it."

His eyes were so cold, she thought with dull wonder. Odd, she'd never seen that, didn't remember that. "Your preferences mean nothing to me, Baxter."

"Did you think I wouldn't find out that you'd thrown your lot in with my ex-wife and her family?" he continued, in that same reasonable tone. "That I haven't kept tabs on you over the years?"

With an effort, she steadied her breathing, but when she tried to shift away, he blocked her. She wasn't afraid, yet, but the temper she'd worked so hard to erase from her character was beginning to bubble up toward the surface.

"I never gave a thought to what you'd find out. And no, I wasn't aware you were keeping tabs. Why should you? Neither Kevin nor I ever meant anything to you."

"You've waited a long time to make your move." Baxter paused, struggling to control the fury that had clawed its way into his throat. He'd worked too hard, done too much, to see some old, forgotten mistake rear up and slap him down. "Clever of you, Megan, more clever than I gave you credit for."

"I don't know what you're talking about."

"Do you seriously want me to believe you know nothing about my campaign? I'm not going to tolerate this pathetic stab at revenge."

Her voice was cooler now, despite the fact that she could feel her skin start to tremble with an intense mixture of emotions. "At the risk of repeating myself, I don't know what you're talking about. My life is of no concern to you, Baxter, and yours none of mine. You made that clear a long time ago, when you refused to acknowledge me or Kevin."

"Is that the tack you're going to take?" He'd wanted to be calm, but rage was working through him. Intimidation, he realized, simply wouldn't be enough. "The young, innocent girl, seduced, betrayed, abandoned? Left behind, pregnant and brokenhearted? Please, spare me."

"That's not a tack, it's truth."

"You were young, Megan, but innocent?" His teeth flashed. "Now, that's a different matter. You were willing enough, even eager."

"I believed you!" She shouted it—a mistake, as her own voice tore her composure to pieces. "I believed you loved me, that you wanted to marry me. And you played on that. You never had any intention of making a future with me. You were already engaged. I was just an easy mark."

"You certainly were easy." He pushed her back against the cabinet, kept his hands hard on her shoulders. "And very, very tempting. Sweet, Megan. Very sweet."

"Take your hands off me."

"Not quite yet. You're going to listen to me, carefully. I know why you've come here, linked yourself with the Calhouns. First there'll be whispers, rumors, then a sad story to a sympathetic reporter. The old lady put pressure on me about Suzanna." He thought of Colleen with loathing. "But I've made that work for me. In the interest of the children," he murmured. "Letting Bradford adopt them, selflessly giving up my rights, so the children could be secure in a traditional family."

"You never cared about them, either, did you?" Megan said in a husky voice. "Alex and Jenny never mattered to you, any more than Kevin."

"The point is," he continued, "the old woman has no reason to bother about you. So, Megan, you'd better mind your step and listen to me. Things aren't working out for you here, so you're going to move back to Oklahoma."

"I'm not going anywhere," she began, then gasped when his fingers dug in.

"You're going back to your quiet life, away from here. There will be no rumors, no tearful interviews with reporters. If you try to undermine me, to implicate me in any way, I'll ruin you. When I've finished—and believe me, with the Dumont money I can hire plenty of willing men who'll swear they've enjoyed you—when I've finished," he repeated, "you'll be nothing more than an opportunistic slut with a bastard son."

Her vision hazed. It wasn't the threat that frightened her, or even infuriated her so very much. It was the term *bastard* in connection with her little boy.

Before she fully realized her intent, her hand was swinging up and slapping hard across his face. "Don't you ever speak about my son that way."

When his hand cracked across her cheek, it wasn't pain she felt, or even shock, but rage.

"Don't push me, Megan," he said, breathing hard. "Don't push me, because you'll be the one to take the fall. You, and the boy."

As crazed as any mother protecting her cub, she lunged at him. The power of the attack rammed them both against the wall. She landed two solid blows before he threw her off.

"You still have that passionate nature, I see." He dragged her against him, infuriated, aroused. "I remember how to channel it."

She struck out again, a glancing blow, before he caught her arms and pinned them against her body. So she used her teeth. Even as Baxter cursed in pain, the door burst in.

Nathaniel plucked him off the floor as he might a flea off a dog. Through the haze of her own vision, Megan saw there was murder in his eye. Hot-blooded. Deadly.

"Nathaniel."

But he didn't look at her. Instead, he rapped Baxter hard against the wall. "Dumont, isn't it?" His voice was viciously quiet, terrifyingly pleasant. "I've heard how you like pushing women around."

Baxter struggled for dignity, though his feet were inches off the ground. "Who the hell are you?"

"Well, now, it seems only fair you should know the name of the man who's going to rip out your damn heart with his bare hands." He had the pleasure of seeing Baxter blanch. "It's Fury, Nathaniel Fury. You won't forget it—" he rammed a fist low, into the kidneys "—will you?"

When Baxter could breathe again, his words struggling out weakly, he wheezed, "You'll be in jail before the night's out."

"I don't think so." His head snapped around when Megan started forward. "Stay back," he said between his teeth. The hot leap of fire in his eyes had her coming to a stop.

"Nathaniel." She swallowed hard. "Don't kill him."

"Any particular reason you want him alive?"

She opened her mouth, shut it again. The answer seemed desperately important, so she offered the truth. "No."

Baxter drew in his breath to scream. Nathaniel cut it off neatly with a hand over the windpipe. "You're a lucky man, Dumont. The lady doesn't want me to kill you, and I don't like to disappoint her. We'll leave it to fate." He dragged Baxter outside, hauling him along as if the man were nothing more than a heavily packed seabag.

Megan raced to the door. "Holt." A shiver of relief worked down her spine when she spotted Suzanna's husband near the pier. "Do something."

Holt merely shrugged. "Fury beat me to it. You should go back in, you're getting wet."

"But—he's not really going to kill him, is he?"

Holt considered a moment, narrowing his eyes against the rain as Nathaniel carted Baxter down the pier. "Probably not."

"I hope to God you can't swim," Nathaniel muttered, then threw Baxter off the pier. He turned away and was striding to Megan before the sound of the splash. "Come on."

"But—"

He simply scooped her up in his arms. "I'm knocking off for the day."

"Fine." Holt stood, his thumbs in his pockets, a look of unholy glee in his eyes. "See you tomorrow."

"Nathaniel, you can't—"

"Shut up, Meg." He dumped her in the car. She craned her neck, and wasn't sure whether she was relieved or disappointed to see Baxter heaving himself back onto the pier.

He needed quiet to pull himself back from violence. He detested the temper that lurked inside him, that made him want to raise his fists and pummel. He could rationalize it, under the circumstances, but it always left him sick inside to know what he was capable of if pushed.

There was no doubt in his mind that he would have come very close to murder if Megan hadn't stopped him.

He'd trained himself to use words and wit to resolve a fight. It usually worked. When it didn't, well, it didn't. But he continued, years after the last blow he'd taken from his father, to remember, and regret.

She was shivering by the time he parked the car in his driveway. It didn't occur to him until that moment that he'd forgotten Dog. Holt would see to him, Nathaniel figured, and plucked Megan from her seat.

"I don't—"

"Just be quiet." He carried her in, past the bird, who squawked greetings, and up the stairs. Megan was ready to babble in shock by the time he dumped her in a chair in the bedroom. Without a word, he turned away to rummage through his dresser drawers. "Get out of those wet clothes," he ordered, tossing her a sweatshirt and sweatpants. "I'm going to go down and make you some tea."

"Nathaniel—"

"Just do it!" he shouted, gritting his teeth. "Just do it," he repeated quietly, and shut the door.

He didn't slam it; nor, when he was down in the kitchen, did he put his fist through a wall. He thought about it. But instead, he put on the kettle, got out the brandy. After a moment's consideration, he took a pull of the fiery liquid, straight from the bottle. It didn't calm him very much, but it took the edge off his sense of self-disgust.

When he heard Bird whistle and invite Megan to come to the Casbah, he set her spiked tea on the table.

She was pale, he noted, and her eyes were too big. So were the sweats. He nearly smiled at the picture she made, hesitating in the doorway, with the shirt drooping off her shoulders and the pants bagging at her ankles.

"Sit down and have something to drink. You'll feel better."

"I'm all right, really." But she sat, and lifted the mug in both hands, because they tended to shake. The first sip had her sucking in her breath. "I thought this was tea."

"It is. I just gave it a little help." He sat across from her, waited until she sipped again. "Did he hurt you?"

She stared down at the table. The wood was polished so brightly she could see her own face in it. "Yes."

She said it calmly. She thought she was calm, until Nathaniel put his hand over hers. Her breath hitched once, twice, and then she put her head on the table and wept.

So much washed out with the tears—the hopes she'd once had, the dreams, the betrayal and the disillusionment, the fears and the bitterness. He didn't try to stop her, only waited it out.

"I'm sorry." She let her cheek rest against the table a moment, comforted by the cool, smooth feel of the wood on her skin and Nathaniel's hand on her hair. "It all seemed to happen so fast, and I wasn't prepared." She straightened, started to wipe the tears away, when a new fear glazed her eyes. "Kevin. Oh, God, if Bax—"

"Holt will take care of Kevin. Dumont won't get near him."

"You're right." She gave a shuddering sigh. "Of course, you're right. Holt would see to Suzanna and all the children right away. And all Baxter wanted to do in any case was frighten me."

"Did he?"

Her eyes were still wet, but they were steady. "No. He hurt me, and he infuriated me, and he made me sick that I'd ever let him touch me. But he didn't frighten me. He can't."

"Attagirl."

She sniffled, smiled weakly. "But I frightened him. That's why he came here today, after all this time. Because he's frightened."

"Of what?"

"Of the past, the consequences." She drew another, deeper breath and smelled Nathaniel—tobacco and salt spray. How oddly comforting it was. "He thinks our coming here is some sort of plot against him. He's been keeping track of me all this time. I didn't know."

"He's never contacted you until today?"

"No, never. I suppose he felt safe when I was in Oklahoma and hadn't any connection with Suzanna. Now, not only is there a connection, but I'm living here. And Kevin and Alex and Jenny . . . Well, he doesn't seem to understand it has nothing to do with him."

She picked up her tea again. Nathaniel hadn't asked anything, he'd simply sat and held her hand. Perhaps that was why she felt compelled to tell him.

"I met him in New York. I was seventeen, and it was my first real trip away from home. It was during the winter break, and several of us went. One of my friends had relatives there. I guess you've been to New York."

"A time or two."

"I'd never experienced anything like it. The people, the buildings. The city was so exciting, and so unlike the West. Everything crowded in and colorful. I loved it—rushing along Fifth Avenue, having coffee in some hole-in-the-wall in Greenwich Village. Gawking. It sounds silly."

"No, it sounds normal."

"I guess it was," she said with a sigh. "Everything was normal, and simple, before . . . It was at this party, and he looked so handsome and romantic, I suppose. A young girl's dream, with those movie-star looks and that sheen of sophistication. And he was older—just enough older to be fascinating. He'd been to Europe." She stopped herself, squeezed her eyes shut. "Oh, God, how pathetic."

"You know you don't have to do this now, Meg."

"No, I think I do." Steadying herself, she opened her eyes again. "If you can stand listening to it."

"I'm not going anywhere." He gave her hand a comforting squeeze. "Go ahead, then, get rid of it."

"He said all the right things, made all the right moves. He sent a dozen roses the next day, and an invitation to dinner."

She paused to choose her words and pushed absently at a pin that had loosened in her hair. It wasn't so horrible, she realized, to look back. It seemed almost like a play, with her as both actor and audience. Vitally involved and breezily detached.

"So I went. There was candlelight, and we danced.

I felt so grown-up. I think you only really feel that way when you're seventeen. We went to museums and window-shopping and to shows. He told me he loved me, and he bought me a ring. It had two little diamond hearts, interconnected. It was very romantic. He slipped it on my finger, and I slipped into his bed."

She stopped, waited for Nathaniel to comment. When he didn't, she worked up the courage to continue.

"He said he would come to Oklahoma, and we'd make our plans for the future. But, of course, he didn't come. At first, when I called, he said he'd been delayed. Then he stopped answering my calls altogether. I found out I was pregnant, and I called, I wrote. Then I heard that he was engaged, that he'd been engaged all along. At first I didn't believe it, then I just went numb. It took me a while before I made myself believe it, made myself understand and deal with it. My family was wonderful. I never would have gotten through it without them. When Kevin was born, I realized I couldn't just feel grown-up. I had to *be* grown-up. Later on, I tried to contact Bax one last time. I thought he should know about Kevin, and that Kevin should have some sort of relationship with his father. But . . ." She trailed off. "When there was absolutely no interest, only anger and hostility, I began to understand that it was best that that didn't happen. Today, maybe for the first time, I was absolutely sure of it."

"He doesn't deserve either of you."

"No, he doesn't." She managed a small smile. Now that she'd said it all, for the first time in so very long, she felt hollowed out. Not limp, she realized. Just free. "I want to thank you for charging to the rescue."

"My pleasure. He won't touch you again, Meg." He took her hand, brought it to his lips. "You or Kevin. Trust me."

"I do." She turned her hand in his, gripped. "I do trust you." Her pulse was starting to skip, but she kept her eyes on his. "I thought, when you carried me in and upstairs . . . Well, I didn't think you were going to make me tea."

"Neither did I. But you were trembling, and I knew if I touched you before I cooled off, I'd be rough. That it wouldn't be right, for either of us."

Her heart stuttered, then picked up its pace. "Are you cooled off now?"

His eyes darkened. "Mostly." Slowly, he rose, drew her to her feet. "Is that an invitation, Megan?"

"I—" He was waiting, she realized, for her to agree or refuse. No seduction, no pretty promising words. No illusions. "Yes," she said, and met his lips with hers.

When he swept her up this time, she gave a quick, nervous laugh. It slid back down her throat when she met the look in his eyes.

"You won't think of him," Nathaniel said quietly. "You won't think of anything but us."

Chapter 8

She could hear her own heartbeat pounding, pounding, in counterpoint to the rain that pounded against the windows. She wondered whether Nathaniel could hear it, too, and if he did, whether he knew that she was afraid. His arms were so strong, his mouth was so sure each time it swooped down to claim hers again.

He carried her up the stairs as if she weighed no more than the mist that swirled outside the cottage.

She would make a mistake, she would do something foolish, she wouldn't be what either of them wanted. The doubts pinched at her like fingers as he swept her into his bedroom, where the light was dim and the air was sweet with wisteria.

She saw the spear of purple blooms in an old bottle on a scarred wooden chest, the undraped windows that were opened to welcome the moist breeze. And the bed, with its sturdy iron headboard and taut cotton spread.

He set her down beside it, so that she was all too aware of the weakness in her knees. But she kept her eyes on his and waited, terrified and aching, for him to make the first move.

"You're trembling again." His voice was quiet, the fingers he lifted to stroke her cheek were soothing. Did she think he couldn't see all those fears in her eyes? She couldn't know that they stirred his own.

"I don't know what to do." The moment the words were out, she closed her eyes. She'd done it already, she realized. The first mistake. Determined, she dragged his head down to hers for an aggressive kiss.

A fire kindled in his gut, flames leaping and licking at the ready fuel of his need. Muscles tensed in reaction, he fought back the urge to shove her back on the bed and take, take quickly, fiercely. He kept his hands easy, stroking her face, her shoulders, her back, until she quieted.

"Nathaniel."

"Do you know what I want, Meg?"

"Yes—No." She reached for him again, but he caught her hands, kissed them, fingertip by fingertip.

"I want to watch you relax. I want to watch you enjoy." His eyes on hers, he lowered her hands to her sides. "I want to watch you fill up with me." Slowly he began to take the pins from her hair, setting them on the table beside the bed. "I want to hear you say my name when I'm inside you."

He combed his fingers through her hair, contenting himself with the silky texture. "I want you to let me do all the things I've been dreaming of since I first laid eyes on you. Let me show you."

He kissed her first, his mouth soft, smooth, seductive. Endlessly patient, he parted hers with teasing nips and nibbles, with the persuasive caress of his tongue. Degree by torturous degree, he deepened the kiss, until her hands clutched weakly at his waist and her shudders gave way to pliancy.

The lingering taste of brandy, the faint and very male scrape of a day's beard against her cheek, the patter of rain and the drifting scent of flowers. All this whirled in her head like a drug, both potent and possessing.

His lips left hers to journey over her face, to trace the line of her jaw, to nuzzle at her ear, waiting, patiently waiting, until he felt her slip over to the next stage of surrender.

He stepped back, only an inch, and slipped the shirt up her torso, over her head, let it drop to the floor. His muscles coiled like a snake. She thought she saw the lightning flash of desire that darkened his eyes to soot. But he only skimmed a fingertip down her throat, to the aching tip of her breast.

Her breath caught; her head lolled back.

"You're so beautiful, Meg. So soft." He pressed a kiss to her shoulder while his hands gently molded, caressed, aroused. "So sweet."

He was afraid his hands were too big, too rough. As a result, his touch was stunningly tender, humming over her heating skin. They slicked down her sides, leaving tremors in their wake as he eased the loose pants from her hips.

Then those fingertips moved over her, gliding over curves until her shaking breathing turned to unsteady moans.

He undressed, watching her heavy eyes flutter open, seeing the misty blue focus on him, the pupils dilate.

Now, she thought, and her heart stuttered madly in her throat. He would take her now, and ease this glorious ache he'd stirred to life inside her. Sweet and eager, her mouth lifted to his. He gathered her close, laid her on the bed as gently as he might have laid her in a pool of rose petals. She arched to him, accepting, braced for the torrent. He used only his lips, soft as the rain, savoring her flesh as though it were a banquet of the most delicate flavors. Then his hands, big and hard-palmed, skimmed, lingered, discovered.

Nothing could have prepared her. If she'd had a hundred lovers, none could have given more, or taken more. She was lost in a gently rocking sea of sensation, undone by patience, weakened by tenderness.

Her breathing slowed, deepened, even as her heart rate soared. She felt the brush of his hair on her breast before his mouth claimed it, heard his quiet, satisfied groan of pleasure as he suckled. Heard his sigh as he circled and teased with his tongue.

She sank, fathoms deep, in warm, clear waters.

She didn't know when those waters began to churn. The storm gathered so slowly, so subtly. It seemed one moment she was drifting, and the next floundering. She couldn't get her breath, no matter how deeply she gasped for air. Her mind, suddenly reeling, struggled for the surface, even as her body coiled and tensed.

"Nathaniel." She grabbed at him, her fingers digging into his flesh. "I can't—"

But he covered her mouth with his, swallowing her gasps, savoring her moan, as the first dizzy climax racked her.

She reared against his hand, instinctively urging him on as hot red waves of pleasure swept her up. Her neat, rounded nails scored his shoulders before her hands, her body, even her mind, went limp.

"Megan. God." She was so hot, so wet. He pressed his lips to her throat as he fought to level his own breathing. Pleasuring a woman had always pleasured him. But not like this. Never like this. He felt like a king and a beggar all at once.

Her stunned response aroused him unbearably. All he could do was wallow in her, absorbing her shock waves, and his own, feeling each and every nerve in his body sizzle and spark.

He wanted to give her more. Had to give her more. Strapping down his own grinding needs, he slipped inside her, letting himself rock with the pleasure of her quick shudder, her broken sigh.

She was so small. He had to remind himself again and again that she was small, all delicate bones and fragile skin. That she was innocent, and nearly as untouched as a virgin. So while the blood pounded in his head, his heart, his loins, he took her gently, his hands fisted on the bedspread for fear he would touch her and bruise.

He felt her body contract, explode. And then she said his name.

He pressed his lips to hers again, and followed her over.

The rain was still drumming. As she slowly swam back to reality, she heard its steady beat on the roof. She lay still, her hand tangled in Nathaniel's hair, her body glowing. She realized she had a smile on her face.

She began to hum.

Nathaniel stirred himself, pushed back lazily to lean on his elbow. "What are you doing?"

"Singing. Sort of."

He grinned, studying her. "I like your looks, sugar."

"I'm getting used to yours." She traced the cleft in his chin with a fingertip. Her lashes lowered. "It was all right, wasn't it?"

"What?" He waited, wisely holding back a chuckle until she looked at him again. "Oh, that. Sure, it was okay for a start."

She opened her mouth, closed it again with a little humming sound that wasn't at all musical. "You could be a little more . . . flattering."

"You could be a little less stupid." He kissed her frowning mouth. "Making love isn't a quiz, Meg. You don't get graded."

"What I meant was . . . Never mind."

"What you meant was . . ." He hauled her over until she was splayed on top of him. "On a scale of one to ten . . ."

"Cut it out, Nathaniel." She laid her cheek on his chest. "I hate it when you make me feel ridiculous."

"I don't." Possessively he ran a hand down her back. "I love to make you feel ridiculous. I love to make you feel."

He nearly followed that up with a very simple "I love you." But she wouldn't have accepted it. He'd barely done so himself.

"You did." She kept her head over his heart. "You made me feel things I never have before. I was afraid."

Trouble clouded his eyes. "I don't want you to be afraid of me."

"I was afraid of me," she corrected. "Of us. Of letting this happen. I'm glad it did." It was easier than she'd imagined to shift, to smile, to press her mouth to his. For a moment, she thought he tensed, but she dismissed that as foolish and kissed him again.

His system snapped to full alert. How could he want her again, so desperately, so quickly? he wondered. How could he resist those sweet, tantalizing lips?

"Keep that up," he managed, "and it's going to happen again."

The shiver of excitement was glorious. "Okay." She shared her anticipation in the kiss, torturing his mouth, teasing his tongue. Amazed that there could be more, she gave a low sound of delight when he rolled, shoving her beneath him and crushing her mouth.

For a heady moment, he let those violent needs hold sway, trapping her beneath him, devouring her lips, her skin, dragging a hand through her tousled hair until her throat was exposed to his hungry teeth and tongue.

She moaned, writhed under him. Whimpered.

Rolling away, he lay on his back, cursing himself, while his heart pounded the blood through his veins.

Confused, shivering with needs freshly aroused but unmet, Megan laid a tentative hand on his arm. He jerked away.

"Don't." The order came out harsh. "I need a minute."

Her eyes went dead. "I'm sorry. I did something wrong."

"No, you didn't." He scrubbed his hands over his face and sat up. "I'm just not ready. Look, why don't I go down and rustle us up something to eat?"

He was only inches away. It might as well have been miles, and she felt the sharp sting of rejection. "No, that's all right." Her voice was cool and calm again. "I really should get going. I need to pick up Kevin."

"Kevin's fine."

"Regardless." She brushed at her hair, tried to smooth it. She wished desperately for something to wrap around her nakedness.

"Don't pull that door shut on me now." He battled back fury, and a much more dangerous passion.

"I haven't shut any door. I thought—that is, I assumed you wanted me to stay. Since you don't, I'll—"

"Of course I want you to stay. Damn it, Megan." He whirled on her, and wasn't surprised when she jerked back. "I need a bloody minute. I could eat you alive, I want you so much."

In defense, she crossed an arm over her breasts. "I don't understand you."

"Damn right you don't understand me. You'd run like hell if you did." He fought for control, gained a slippery hold. "We'll be fine, Meg, if you wait until I pull myself together."

"What are you talking about?"

Gripped by frustration, he grabbed her hand, pressed it against his, palm to palm. "I've got big hands, Megan. Got them from my father. I know the right way to use them—and the wrong way."

There was a glint in his eyes, like the honed edge of a sword. It should have frightened her, but it only excited. "You're afraid of me," she said quietly. "Afraid you'll hurt me."

"I won't hurt you." He dropped his hand, left it fisted on the bed.

"No, you won't." She lifted a hand to touch his cheek. His jaw was tight, urging her fingers to stroke and soothe. There was a power here, she realized, a power she'd been unaware of possessing. She wondered what they could make between them if she set it free.

"You want me." Feeling reckless, she edged closer, until her mouth slid over his. "You want to touch me." She lifted his fisted hand to her breast, her heart pounding like a drum as his fingers opened, cupped. "And for me to touch you." Her hands stroked down his chest, felt the quiver of his stomach muscles. So much strength, she thought, so ruthlessly chained. What would it be like if those links snapped free?

She wanted to know.

"Make love with me now, Nathaniel." Eyes half-closed, she linked her arms around his neck, pressed her eager body to his. "Show me how much you want me."

He held himself in check, concentrating on the flavor of her mouth. It would be enough, he told himself, to make her float again.

But she had learned quickly. When he sought to soothe, she enticed. Where he tried to gentle, she enraged.

With an oath, he dragged her up until they were kneeling, body-to-body. And his mouth was wild.

She answered avidly each urgent demand, each desperate moan. His hands were everywhere, hard and possessive, taking more only when she cried out for it. There was no calm water to sink in now, but a violent tempest that spun them both over the bed in a tangle of hot flesh and raging needs.

He couldn't stop, no longer gave a damn about control. She was his, and by God, he would have all of her. With something like a snarl, he clamped her hands above her head and ravished her flesh.

She arched like a bow, twisted, and still he plundered, invading that hot, wet core with probing tongue until she was sobbing his name.

And more, still more, wrestling over the bed with her hands as rough and ready as his, her mouth as bold and ravenous.

He drove himself into her, hard and deep, hissing with triumph, eyes glazed and dark. His hands locked on hers as she rose to meet him.

She would remember the speed, and the wild freedom, of their mindless mating. And she would remember the heady flavor of power as they plunged recklessly off the edge together.

She must have slept. When she woke, she was sprawled on her stomach across the bed. The rain had stopped and night had fallen. When her mind cleared, she became aware of dozens of small aches, and a drugged sense of satisfaction.

She thought of rolling over, but it seemed like too much trouble. Instead, she stretched out her arms, searching the tumbled bed, knowing already that she was alone.

She heard the bird squawk slyly. "You know how to whistle, don't you, Steve?"

She was still chuckling when Nathaniel stepped back into the room.

"What do you do, run old movies for him all day?"

"He's a Bogart fan. What can I tell you?" It amazed him that he felt awkward, holding a dinner tray while a naked woman lolled in his bed. "That's a pretty good scar you've got there, sugar."

She was much too content to be embarrassed when

she saw where his eyes had focused. "I earned it. That's a pretty good dragon you've got."

"I was eighteen, stupid, and more than a little buzzed on beer. But I guess I earned it, too."

"Suits you. What have you got there?"

"Thought you might be hungry."

"I'm starving." She braced herself on both elbows and smiled at him. "That smells terrific. I didn't know you cooked."

"I don't. Dutch does. I cadge handouts from the kitchen, then nuke them."

"Nuke them?"

"Zap them in the microwave." He set the tray down on the sea chest at the foot of the bed. "We've got some Cajun chicken, some wine."

"Mmm . . ." She roused herself enough to lean over and peer at it. "Looks wonderful. But I really need to get Kevin."

"I talked to Suzanna." He wondered if he could talk her into eating dinner just as she was, gloriously naked. "Unless she hears from you, Kevin's set to spend the night with them."

"Oh. Well."

"She says he's already knee-deep in video games with Alex and Jenny."

"And if I called, I'd spoil his party."

"Pretty much." He sat on the edge of the bed, ran a fingertip down her spine. "So, how about it? Sleep with me tonight?"

"I don't even have a toothbrush."

"I can dig up an extra." He broke off a piece of chicken, fed it to her.

"Oh." She swallowed, blew out a breath. "Spicy."

"Yeah." He leaned down to sample her lips, then lifted a glass of wine to them. "Better?"

"It's wonderful."

He tipped the glass so that a few drops of wine spilled on her shoulder. "Oops. Better clean that up." He did so with a lingering lick of his tongue. "What do I have to do to convince you to stay?"

She forgot the food and rolled into his arms. "You just did."

In the morning, the mists had cleared. Nathaniel watched Megan pin up her hair in a beam of sunlight. It seemed only right that he move behind her and press his lips to the base of her neck.

He thought it was a sweetly ordinary, sweetly intimate gesture that could become a habit.

"I love the way you polish yourself up, sugar."

"Polish myself up?" Her curious eyes met his in the glass. She had on the same tailored suit she'd worn the day before—now slightly wrinkled. Her makeup was sketchy at best, courtesy of the small emergency cosmetic kit she carried in her purse, and her hair was giving her trouble, as she'd lost half of her pins.

"Like you are now. Like some pretty little cupcake behind the bakery window."

"Cupcake." She nearly choked. "I'm certainly not a cupcake."

"I've got a real sweet tooth." To prove it, he nibbled his way to her ear.

"I've noticed." She turned, but put her hands against his chest to hold him off. "I have to go."

"Yeah, me too. I don't suppose I could talk you into coming with me."

"To sight whales?" She cocked her head. "No more than I could talk you into sitting with me in my office all day, running figures."

He winced. "Guess not. How about tonight?"

She yearned, wished, longed. "I have to think of Kevin. I can't spend my nights here with you while he spends them somewhere else."

"I had that figured. I was thinking if you were to leave your terrace doors open . . ."

"You could come sneaking in?" she asked archly.

"More or less."

"Good thinking." She laughed and drew away. "Now, are you going to drive me back to my car?"

"Looks that way." He took her hand, holding it as they walked downstairs. "Megan . . ." He hated to bring it up when the sun was shining and his mood was light. "If you hear from Dumont, if he tries to see you or Kevin, if he calls, sends a damn smoke signal, does anything, I want you to tell me."

She gave his hand a reassuring squeeze. "I doubt I will, after the dunking you gave him. But don't worry, Nathaniel, I can handle Baxter."

"Off with his head," Bird suggested, but Nathaniel didn't smile.

"It's not a matter of what you can handle." He pushed the door open, stepped outside. "Maybe you don't figure that last night gives me the right to look out for you and your boy, but I do. I will. So we'll put it this way." He opened the car door for her. "Either you promise me that you'll tell me, or I go after him now."

She started to protest, but the image, absolutely vivid, of the look on Nathaniel's face when he'd rammed Baxter against the wall stopped her. "You would."

"Bank on it."

She tried to separate annoyance from the simple pleasure of being protected. And couldn't. "I want to say I appreciate the concern, but I'm not sure I do. I've been taking care of myself, and of Kevin, for a long time."

"Things change."

"Yes," she said carefully, wondering what was behind those calm, unblinking gray eyes. "I'm more comfortable when they change slowly."

"I'm doing my best to keep at your pace, Meg." Whatever frustrations he had, he told himself, he could handle. "Just a simple yes or no on this'll do."

It wasn't just herself, Megan thought. There was Kevin. And Nathaniel was offering them both a strong, protecting arm. Pride meant nothing when compared to the welfare of her son.

Not at all sure why she was amused, she turned to him once he'd settled into the driver's seat. "You have an uncanny knack for getting your own way. And when you do, you just accept it as inevitable."

"It usually is." He backed out of the drive and headed for Shipshape.

There was a small greeting party waiting for them. Holt and, to Megan's surprise, her brother, Sloan.

"I dropped the kids off at The Towers," Holt told her, before she could ask. "They've got your dog, Nate."

"Thanks." She'd barely stepped from the car when Sloan grabbed her by the shoulders, stared hard into her eyes.

"Are you all right? Why the hell didn't you call me? Did he put his hands on you?"

"I'm fine. Sloan, I'm fine." Instinctively she cupped his face, kissed him. "I didn't call because I already had two white knights charging into battle. And he may have put his hands on me, but I put my fists on him. I think I split his lip."

Sloan said something particularly foul about Dumont and hugged Megan close. "I should have killed him when you first told me about him."

"Stop it." She pressed her cheek to his. "It's over. I want it put aside. Kevin's not to hear about it. Now come on, I'll drive you back to the house."

"I've got some things to do." He gave Nathaniel a steely stare over Megan's shoulder. "You go on up, Meg. I'll be along later."

"All right, then." She kissed him again. "Holt, thanks again for looking after Kevin."

"No problem." Holt tucked his tongue in his cheek when Nathaniel scooped Megan up for a long, lingering kiss. A glance at Sloan's narrowed eyes had him biting that tongue to keep from grinning.

"See you, sugar."

Megan flushed, cleared her throat. "Yes . . . well. Bye."

Nathaniel tucked his thumbs in his pockets, waited until she'd driven off before he turned to Sloan. "Guess you want to talk to me."

"Damn right I want to talk to you."

"You'll have to come up to the bridge. We've got a tour going out."

"Want a referee?" Holt offered, and earned two deadly glances. "Too bad. I hate to miss it."

Smoldering, Sloan followed Nathaniel up the gangplank, waited restlessly while he gave orders. Once they were on the bridge, Nathaniel glanced over the charts and dismissed the mate.

"If this is going to take longer than fifteen minutes, you're in for a ride."

"I've got plenty of time." Sloan stepped closer, braced his legs like a gunslinger at high noon. "What the hell were you doing with my sister?"

"I think you have that figured out," Nathaniel said coolly.

Sloan bared his teeth. "If you think I'm going to stand back while you move in on her, you're dead wrong. I wasn't around when she got tangled up with Dumont, but I'm here now."

"I'm not Dumont." Nathaniel's own temper threatened to snap, a dry twig of control. "You want to take out what he did to her on me, that's fine. I've been looking to kick someone's ass ever since I caught that bastard tossing her around. So you want to take me on?" he said invitingly. "Do it."

Though the invitation tempted some elemental male urge, Sloan pulled back. "What do you mean, he was tossing her around?"

"Just what I said. He had her up against the wall." The rage swept back, almost drowning him. "I thought about killing him, but I didn't think she could handle it."

Sloan breathed deep to steady himself. "So you threw him off the pier."

"Well, I punched him a few times first, then I figured there was a chance he couldn't swim."

Calmer, and grateful, Sloan nodded. "Holt had a few words with him when he dragged his sorry butt out. They've tangled before." He'd missed his chance that time, as well, he thought, thoroughly disgusted. "I don't think Dumont'll come back, chance running into any of us again." Sloan knew he should be glad of it, but he regretted, bitterly, not getting his own licks in.

"I appreciate you looking out for her," he said stiffly. "But that doesn't get us past the rest. She'd have been upset, vulnerable. I don't like a man who takes advantage of that."

"I gave her tea and dry clothes," Nathaniel said between his teeth. "It would have stopped right there, if that was what she wanted. Staying with me was her choice."

"I'm not going to see her hurt again. You might look at her and see an available woman, but she's my sister."

"I'm in love with your sister." Nathaniel snapped his head around when the bridge door opened.

"Ready to cast off, Captain."

"Cast off." He cursed under his breath as he stalked to the wheel.

Sloan stood back while he gave orders and piloted the boat into the bay.

"You want to run that by me again?"

"Have you got a problem with plain English?" Nathaniel tossed back. "I'm in love with her. Damn it."

"Well, now." More than a little taken aback, Sloan sat on the bench closest to the helm.

He wanted to think that one through. After all, Megan had barely met the man. Then again, he remembered, he'd fallen for Amanda in little more time than it took her to snap his head off. If he'd been able to choose a man for his sister, it might have been someone very much like Nathaniel Fury.

"Have you told her that?" Sloan asked, his tone considerably less belligerent.

"Go to hell."

"Haven't," he decided, and braced his booted foot on his knee. "Does she feel the same way about you?"

"She will." Nathaniel set his teeth. "She needs time to work it out, that's all."

"Is that what she said?"

"That's what I say." Nathaniel ran a frustrated hand through his hair. "Look, O'Riley, either mind your own damn business or take a punch at me. I've had enough."

Sloan's smile spread slow and easy. "Crazy about her, aren't you?"

Nathaniel merely grunted and started out to sea.

"What about Kevin?" Sloan studied Nathaniel's profile as he probed. "Some might have a problem taking on another man's son."

"Kevin's Megan's son." His eyes flashed to Sloan's, burned. "He'll be mine."

Sloan waited a moment until he was sure. "So, you're going to take on the whole package."

"That's right." Nathaniel pulled out a cigar, lit it. "You got a problem with that?"

"Can't say as I do." Sloan grinned and accepted the cigar Nathaniel belatedly offered him. "You might, though. My sister's a damn stubborn woman. But seeing as you're almost a member of the family, I'll be glad to offer any help."

A smile finally twitched at Nathaniel's mouth. "Thanks, but I'd like to handle it on my own."

"Suit yourself." Sloan settled back to enjoy the ride.

"Are you sure you're all right?"

Megan had no more than stepped in the door of The Towers when she found herself surrounded by concern.

"I'm fine, really." Her protests hadn't prevented the Calhouns from herding her into the family kitchen and plying her with tea and sympathy. "This has gotten blown out of proportion."

"When somebody messes with one of us," C.C. corrected, "he messes with all of us."

She glanced outside, where the children were playing happily in the yard. "I appreciate it. Really. But I don't think there's anything more to worry about."

"There won't be." Colleen stepped into the room, her gaze scanning each face in turn. "What are you all doing in here, smothering the girl? Get out."

"Aunt Colleen . . ." Coco began.

"Out, I said, all of you. You, go back to your kitchen and flirt with that big Dutchman you've got sneaking into your room at night."

"Why, I—"

"Go. And you." Now her cane gestured threateningly at Amanda. "You've got a hotel to run, don't you? Go weed some flowers," she ordered Suzanna. "And you go tinker with an engine." She flicked her gaze from C.C. to Lilah.

"Tougher with me, isn't it, Auntie?" Lilah said lazily.

"Take a nap," Colleen snapped.

"Got me," Lilah said with a sigh. "Come on, ladies, we've been dismissed."

Satisfied when the door swung shut behind them, Colleen sat heavily at the table. "Get me some of that tea," she ordered Megan. "See that it's hot."

Though she moved to obey, Megan wasn't cowed. "Do you always find rudeness works to your advantage, Miss Calhoun?"

"That, old age, and a hefty portfolio." She took the

tea Megan set in front of her, sipped, nodded grudgingly when she found it hot and strong. "Now then, sit down and listen to what I have to say. And don't prim your mouth at me, young lady."

"I'm very fond of Coco," Megan told her. "You embarrassed her."

"Embarrassed her? Ha! She and that tattooed hulk have been mooning around after each other for days. Gave her a prod is what I did." But she eyed Megan craftily. "Loyal when it's deserved, are you?"

"I am."

"And so am I. I made a few calls this morning, to some friends in Boston. Influential friends. Hush," she ordered when Megan started to speak. "Detest politics myself, but it's often necessary to dance with the devil. Dumont should be being made aware, at this moment, that any contact with you, or your son, will fatally jeopardize his ambitions. He will not trouble you again."

Megan pressed her lips together. She wanted her voice to be steady. No matter what she had said, how she had pretended, there had been an icy fear, like a cold ax balanced over her head, of what Baxter might do. In one stroke, Colleen had removed it.

"Why did you do it?"

"I loathe bullies. I particularly loathe bullies who interfere with the contentment of my family."

"I'm not your family," Megan said softly.

"Ha! Think again. You stuck your toe in Calhoun waters, girl. We're like quicksand. You're a Calhoun now, and you're stuck."

Tears rushed into her eyes, blinding her. "Miss Calhoun—" Megan's words were cut off by the impatient rap of Colleen's cane. After a sniffle, Megan began again. "Aunt Colleen," she corrected, understanding. "I'm very grateful."

"So you should be." Colleen coughed to clear her own husky voice. Then she raised it to a shout. "Come back in here, the lot of you! Stop listening at the door!"

It swung open, Coco leading the way. She walked to Colleen, bent, kissed the papery cheek.

"Stop all this nonsense." She waved her grandnieces away. "I want the girl to tell me how that strapping young man tossed that bully in the drink."

Megan laughed, wiped her eyes. "He choked him first."

"Ha!" Colleen rapped her cane in appreciation. "Don't spare the details."

Chapter 9

> B. behaving oddly. Since return to island for summer she is absentminded, daydreaming. Arrived late for tea, forgot luncheon appointment. Intolerable. Unrest in Mexico annoying. Dismissed valet. Excess starch in shirts.

Unbelievable, Megan thought, staring at the notes Fergus had written in his crabbed hand beside stock quotations. He could speak of his wife, a potential war and his valet in the same faintly irritated tone. What a miserable life Bianca must have had. How terrible to be trapped in a marriage, ruled by a despot and without any power to captain your own destiny.

How much worse, she thought, if Bianca had loved him.

As she often did in the quiet hours before sleep, Megan flipped through the pages to the series of numbers. She had time now to regret that she'd never made it to the library.

Or perhaps Amanda was a better bet. Amanda might

know whether Fergus had had foreign bank accounts, safe-deposit boxes.

Peering down, she wondered whether that was the answer. The man had had homes in Maine and in New York. These could be the numbers of various safe-deposit boxes. Even combinations to safes he'd kept in his homes.

That idea appealed to her, a straightforward answer to a small but nagging puzzle. A man as obsessed with his wealth and the making of money as Fergus Calhoun had been would very likely have kept a few secret stores.

Wouldn't it be fantastic, she thought, if there was some dusty deposit box in an old bank vault? Unopened all these years, she imagined. The key lost or discarded. The contents? Oh . . . priceless rubies or fat, negotiable bonds. A single faded photograph. A lock of hair wound with a gold ribbon.

She rolled her eyes and laughed at herself. "Imagination's in gear, Megan," she murmured. "Too bad it's so farfetched."

"What is?"

She jumped like a rabbit, her glasses sliding down to her chin. "Damn. Nathaniel."

He was grinning as he closed and locked the terrace doors at his back. "I thought you'd be happy to see me."

"I am. But you didn't have to sneak up on me that way."

"When a man comes through a woman's window at night, he's supposed to sneak."

She shoved her glasses back in place. "They're doors."

"And you're too literal." He leaned over the back of

the chair where she sat and kissed her like a starving man. "I'm glad you talk to yourself."

"I do not."

"You were, just now. That's why I decided to stop watching you and come in." He strolled to the hallway door, locked it. "You looked incredibly sexy sitting there at your neat little desk, your hair scooped up, your glasses sliding down your nose. In that cute, no-nonsense robe."

She wished heartily that the practical terry cloth could transform into silk and lace. But she had nothing seductive to adorn herself in, and had settled for the robe and Coco's perfume.

"I didn't think you were coming after all. It's getting late."

"I figured there'd be some hoopla over yesterday, and that you'd need to settle Kevin for the night. He didn't get wind of it, did he?"

"No." It touched her that he would ask, that it would matter to him. "None of the children know. Everyone else has been wonderful. It's like thinking you're alone in a battle and then finding yourself surrounded by a circle of shields." She smiled, tilted her head. "Are you holding something behind your back?"

His brows rose, as if in surprise. "Apparently I am." He drew out a peony, a twin to the one he'd given her before. "'A rose,'" he said, "'without a thorn.'"

He crossed to her as he spoke, and all she could think for one awed moment was that this man, this fascinating man, wanted her. He started to take its faded twin from the bud vase on her desk.

"Don't." She felt foolish, but stayed his hand. "Don't throw it out."

"Sentimental, Meg?" Moved that she had kept his

token, he slipped the new bud in with the old. "Did you sit here, working late, looking at the flower and thinking of me?"

"I might have." She couldn't fight the smile in his eyes. "Yes, I thought of you. Not always kindly."

"Thinking's enough." He lifted her hand, kissed her palm. "Nearly." To her surprise, he plucked her from the chair, sat himself down and nestled her in his lap. "But this is a whole lot better."

It seemed foolish to disagree, so she rested her head on his shoulder.

"Everyone's getting prepped for the big Fourth of July celebration," she told him idly. "Coco and Dutch are arguing about recipes for barbecue sauce and the kids are bitterly disappointed we won't let them have small, colorful bombs to set off."

"They'll end up making two kinds of sauce and asking everyone to take sides." It was nice sitting like this, he thought, alone and quiet at the end of the day. "And the kids won't be disappointed after they see the fireworks display Trent organized."

Kevin had talked of nothing else all evening, she remembered. "I've heard it's going to be quite a show."

"Count on it. This bunch won't do anything halfway. Like fireworks, do you, sugar?"

"Almost as much as the kids." She laughed and snuggled against him. "I can't believe it's July already. All I have to do is get about two dozen things out of the way so I can compete in the great barbecue showdown, keep the kids from setting themselves on fire and enjoy the show."

"Business first," he murmured. "Working on Fergus's book?"

"Mmm-hmm... I had no idea how much of a fortune he'd amassed, or how little he considered people. Look here." She tapped her finger to the page. "Whenever he made a note about Bianca, it's as if she were a servant or, worse, a possession. He checked over the household accounts every day, to the penny. There's a notation about how he docked the cook thirty-three cents for a kitchen discrepancy."

"A lot of people think more of money than souls." He flipped idly through the book. "I can be sure you're not sitting on my lap because of my bank balance—since you know it down to the last nickel."

"You're in the black."

"Barely."

"Cash flow is usually thin the first few years in any business—and when you add in the outlay in equipment you've purchased, the down payment for the cottage, insurance premiums and licensing fees—"

"God, I love it when you talk profit and loss." Letting the book close, he nipped playfully at her ear. "Talk to me about checks and balances, or quarterly returns. Quarterly returns make me crazy."

"Then you'll be happy to know you and Holt underestimated your federal payments."

"Mmm..." He stopped, narrowed his eyes. "What do you mean?"

"You owe the government another two hundred and thirty dollars, which can be added to your next quarter due, or, more wisely, I can file an amended return."

He swore halfheartedly. "How come we have to pay them in advance, anyway?"

She gave him a light kiss in sympathy. "Because, Nathaniel, if you don't, the IRS will make your life a living hell. I'm here to save you from them. I'm also, if your system can take the excitement, going to suggest you open a Keogh—a retirement account for the self-employed."

"Retirement? Hell, Meg, I'm thirty-three."

"And not getting a day younger. Do you know what the cost-of-living projections are for your golden years, Mr. Fury?"

"I changed my mind. I don't like it when you talk accountant to me."

"It's also good tax sense," she persisted. "The money you put in won't be taxable until you're of retirement age. When, usually, your bracket is lower. Besides, planning for the future might not be romantic, but it is rewarding."

He slid a hand under the terry cloth. "I'd rather have instant gratification."

Her pulse scrambled. "I have the necessary form."

"Damn right you do."

"For the Keogh. All you need to—Oh." The terry cloth parted like water under his clever hands. She gasped, shuddered, melted. "How did you do that?"

"Come to bed." He lifted her. "I'll show you."

Just past dawn, Nathaniel strolled down the curve of the terrace steps, his hands in his pockets and a whistle on his lips. Dutch, in a similar pose, descended the opposite curve. Both men stopped dead when they met in the center.

They stared, swore.

"What are you doing here at this hour?" Dutch demanded.

"I could ask you the same question."

"I live here, remember?"

Nathaniel inclined his head. "You live down there." He pointed toward the kitchen level.

"I'm taking the air," Dutch said, after a fumble for inspiration.

"Me too."

Dutch flicked a glance toward Megan's terrace. Nathaniel gave Coco's a studying look. Each decided to leave well enough alone.

"Well, then. Suppose you want some breakfast."

Nathaniel ran his tongue around his teeth. "I could do with some."

"Come on, can't dawdle out here all morning."

Relieved with the solution, they walked down together in perfect agreement.

She overslept. It was a breach in character that had her racing out of her room, still buttoning her blouse. She stopped to peek into Kevin's bedroom, spotted the haphazardly made bed and sighed.

Everyone was up and about, it seemed, but her.

She made a dash toward her office, crossing breakfast with her son off her list of small pleasures for the day.

"Oh, dear." Coco fluttered her hands when Megan nearly mowed her down in the lobby. "Is something wrong?"

"No, I'm sorry. I'm just late."

"Did you have an appointment?"

"No." Megan caught her breath. "I meant I was late for work."

"Oh, my, I thought there was a problem. I just this minute left a memo on your desk. Go ahead in, dear, I don't want to hold you up."

"But—" Megan found herself addressing Coco's retreating back, so she turned into her office to read the message.

Coco's idea of an interoffice memo was something less than professional.

> Megan, dear, I hope you slept well. There's fresh coffee in your machine, and I've left you a nice basket of muffins. You really shouldn't skip breakfast. Kevin ate like a young wolf. It's so rewarding to see a boy enjoy his food. He and Nate will be back in a few hours. Don't work too hard.
>
> Love, Coco
> P.S. The cards say you have two important questions to answer. One with your heart, one with your head. Isn't that interesting?

Megan blew out a breath, and was reading the memo again when Amanda popped in. "Got a minute?"

"Sure." She handed over the paper she held. "Do you think you could interpret this for me?"

"Ah, one of Aunt Coco's convoluted messages." Lips pursed, Amanda studied it. "Well, the coffee and muffins are easy."

"I got that part." In fact, Megan helped herself to both. "Want some?"

"No, thanks, she already delivered mine. Kevin ate a good breakfast. I can vouch for that. When I saw him, he was scarfing down French toast, with Nathaniel battling him for the last piece."

Megan bobbled her coffee. "Nathaniel was here for breakfast?"

"Eating and charming Aunt Coco, while telling Kevin some story about a giant squid. They'll be back in a few hours," she continued, tapping the note, "because Kevin talked Nate into taking him out on the tour again. It didn't take much talking," she added with a smile. "And we didn't think you'd mind."

"No, of course not."

"And the bit about the cards defies interpretation. That's pure Aunt Coco." Amanda set the memo down again. "It's spooky, though, just how often she hits the mark. Been asked any questions lately?"

"No, nothing in particular."

Amanda thought of what Sloan had related to her about Nathaniel's feelings. "Are you sure?"

"Hmmm? Yes. I was thinking about Fergus's book. I suppose it could loosely be considered a question. At least there's one I want to ask you."

Amanda made herself comfortable. "Shoot."

"The numbers in the back. I mentioned them before." She opened a file, handing a copy of the list to Amanda. "I was wondering if they might be passbook numbers, or safe-deposit boxes, safe combinations. Lot numbers, maybe, on some real estate deal?" She moved her shoulders. "I know it's silly to get so hung up on them."

"No." Amanda waved the notion away. "I know just what you mean. I hate it when things don't fit into place. We went through most of the papers from this year when we were looking for clues to find the necklace. I don't recall anything that these figures might connect to, but I can look through the material again."

"Let me do it," Megan said quickly. "I feel like it's my baby."

Megan's Mate 171

"Glad to. I've got more than enough on my plate, and with the big holiday tomorrow, barely time to clean up. Everything you'd want is in the storeroom under Bianca's tower room. We've got it all boxed according to year and content, but it's still a nasty, time-consuming job."

"I live for nasty, time-consuming jobs."

"Then you'll be in heaven. Megan, I hate to ask, but it's the nanny's day off, and Sloan's up to his ears in plywood or something. We've been playing pass-the-babies this morning, but I've got an appointment in the village this afternoon. I could reschedule."

"You want me to baby-sit."

"I know you're busy, but—"

"Mandy, I thought you'd never ask me." Megan's eyes lit up. "When can I get my hands on her?"

Kevin figured this was the best summer of his life. He missed his grandparents, and the horses, and his best friend, John Silverhorn, but there was too much to do for him to be really homesick.

He got to play with Alex and Jenny every day, had his own fort, and lived in a castle. There were boats to sail, and rocks to climb—and Coco or Mr. Dutch always had a snack waiting in the kitchen. Max told him really neat stories. Sloan and Trent sometimes let him help with the renovations, and Holt had let him drive the little powerboat.

All his new aunts played games with him, and sometimes, if he was really, really careful, they let him hold one of the babies.

It was, to Kevin's thinking, a really good deal.

Then there was Nathaniel. He snuck a look at the

man who sat beside him, driving the big convertible up the winding road to The Towers. Kevin had decided that Nathaniel knew something about everything. He had muscles and a tattoo and most always smelled like the sea.

When he stood at the helm of the big tour boat, his eyes narrowed against the sun and his broad hands on the wheel, he was every little boy's idea of a hero.

"Maybe . . ." Kevin trailed off until Nathaniel glanced down at him.

"Maybe what, mate?"

"Maybe I could go back out with you sometime," Kevin blurted out. "I won't ask so many questions next time, or get in the way."

Was there ever a man, Nathaniel wondered, who could defend himself against the sweetness of a child? He stopped the car at the family entrance. "I'll pipe you aboard my ship anytime." He flicked a finger down the brim of the captain's hat he'd carelessly dropped on Kevin's head. "And you can ask all the questions you want."

"Really?" Kevin pushed the brim back up, so that he could see.

"Really."

"Thanks!" Kevin threw his arms around Nathaniel in a spontaneous hug that had Nathaniel's heart sliding down the slippery chute toward love. "I gotta tell Mom. Are you going to come in?"

"Yeah." He let his hands linger on the boy a moment before they dropped away.

"Come on." Bursting with tidings, Kevin scrambled out of the car and up the steps. He hit the door running. "Mom! I'm back!"

"What a quiet, dignified child," Megan commented as she stepped into the hallway from the parlor. "It must be my Kevin."

With a giggle, Kevin darted to her, rising on his toes to see which baby she was holding. "Is that Bianca?"

"Delia."

Kevin squinted and studied. "How can you tell them apart? They look the same."

"A mother's eyes," she murmured, and bent to kiss him. "Where've you been, sailor?"

"We went way, way out in the ocean and back, twice. We saw nine whales. One was like a baby. When they're all together, they're called a pod. Like what peas grow in."

"Is that so?"

"And Nate let me steer and blow the horn, and I helped chart the course. And this man on the second deck was sick the whole time, but I wasn't 'cause I've got good sea legs. And Nate says I can go with him again, so can I?"

Nearly nine years as a mother had Megan following the stream of information perfectly. "Well, I imagine you can."

"Did you know whales mate for life, and they're not really fish at all, even though they live in the water? They're mammals, just like us and elephants and dogs, and they've got to breathe. That's how come they come up and blow water out of their spouts."

Nathaniel walked in on the lecture. And stopped, and looked. Megan stood, smiling down at her son, his hand in hers and a baby on her hip.

I want. The desire streamed through Nathaniel like sunlight, warm, bright. The woman—there had never been a question of that. But he wanted, as Sloan had said, the whole package. The woman, the boy, the family.

Megan looked over and smiled at him. His heart all but stopped.

She started to speak, but the look in Nathaniel's eyes had her throat closing. Though she took an unconscious step back, he was already there, his hand on her cheek, his lips on hers with a tenderness that turned her to putty.

The baby laughed in delight and reached for a fistful of Nathaniel's hair.

"Here we go." Nathaniel took Delia, hefted her high so that she could squeal and kick her feet. When he settled her on his hip, both Megan and Kevin were still staring at him. He jiggled the baby and cocked his head at the boy. "Do you have a problem with me kissing your mom?"

Megan made a little strangled sound. Kevin's gaze dropped heavily to the floor. "I don't know," he mumbled.

"She sure is pretty, isn't she?"

Kevin shrugged, flushed. "I guess." He wasn't sure how he was supposed to feel. Lots of men kissed his mother. His granddad and Sloan—and Holt and Trent and Max. But this was different. He knew that. After all, he wasn't a baby. He shot a look up, lowered his eyes again. "Are you going to be her boyfriend now?"

"Ah . . ." Nathaniel glanced at Megan, was met with a look that clearly stated that he was on his own. "That's close enough. Does that bother you?"

Because his stomach was suddenly jittery, Kevin moved his thin shoulders again. "I don't know."

If the boy wasn't going to look up, Nathaniel figured it was time to move down. He crouched, still holding the baby. "You can take plenty of time to think about it, and let me know. I'm not going anywhere."

"Okay." Kevin's eyes slid up toward his mother's, then back to Nathaniel's. He sidled closer and leaned toward Nathaniel's ear. "Does she like it?"

Nathaniel clamped down on a chuckle and answered solemnity with solemnity. "Yeah, she does."

After a long breath, Kevin nodded. "Okay, I guess you can kiss her if you want."

"I appreciate it." He offered Kevin a hand, and the man-to-man shake had the boy's chest swelling like a balloon.

"Thanks for taking me today." Kevin took off the captain's hat. "And for letting me wear this."

Nathaniel dropped the hat back on Kevin's head, pushed up the brim. "Keep it."

The boy's eyes went blank with shocked pleasure. "For real?"

"Yeah."

"Wow. Thanks. Thanks a lot. Look, Mom, I can keep it. I'm going to show Aunt Coco."

He raced upstairs with a clatter of sneakers. When Nathaniel straightened again, Megan was eyeing him narrowly.

"What did he ask you?"

"Man talk. Women don't understand these things."

"Oh, really?" Before she could disabuse him of that notion, Nathaniel hooked his fingers in her waistband and jerked her forward.

"I've got permission to do this now." He kissed her thoroughly, while Delia did her best to snuggle between them.

"Permission," Megan said when she could breathe again. "From whom?"

"From your men." He strolled casually into the parlor, laid Delia on her play rug, where she squealed happily at her favorite stuffed bear. "Except your father, but he's not around."

"My men? You mean Kevin and Sloan." Realization dawned, and had her sinking onto the arm of a chair. "You spoke to Sloan about . . . this?"

"We were going to beat each other up about it, but it didn't come to that." Very much at home, Nathaniel walked to the side table and poured himself a short whiskey from a decanter. "We straightened it out."

"You did. You and my brother. I suppose it didn't occur to either of you that I might have some say in the matter."

"It didn't come up. He was feeling surly about the fact that you'd spent the night with me."

"It's none of his business," Megan said tightly.

"Maybe it is, maybe it isn't. It's water under the bridge now. Nothing to get riled about."

"I'm not riled. I'm irritated that you took it upon yourself to explain our relationship to my family without discussing it with me." And she was unnerved, more than a little, by the worshipful look she'd seen in Kevin's eyes.

Women, Nathaniel thought, and tossed back his whiskey. "I was either going to explain it to Sloan or take a fist in the face."

"That's ridiculous."

"You weren't there, sugar."

"Exactly." She tossed back her head. "I don't like to be discussed. I've had my fill of that over the years."

Very carefully, Nathaniel set his glass down. "Megan, if you're going to circle back around to Dumont, you're just going to get me mad."

"I'm not doing that. I'm simply stating a fact."

"And I stated a fact of my own. I told your brother I was in love with you, and that settled it."

"You should have . . ." She trailed off, gasped for air that had suddenly gone too thin. "You told Sloan you were in *love* with me?"

"That's right. Now you're going to say I should have told you first."

"I . . . I don't know what I'm going to say." But she was glad, very glad, that she was already sitting down.

"The preferred response is 'I love you, too.'" He waited, ignored the slow stroke of pain. "Can't get your tongue around that."

"Nathaniel." Be calm, she warned herself. Reasonable. Logical. "This is all moving so fast. A few weeks ago, I didn't even know you. I never expected what's happened between us. And I'm still baffled by it. I have very strong, very real feelings for you, otherwise I couldn't have stayed with you that first night."

She was killing him, bloodlessly. "But?"

"Love isn't something I'll ever be frivolous about again. I don't want to hurt you, or be hurt, or risk a misstep that could hurt Kevin."

"You really think time's the answer, don't you? That no matter what's going on inside you, if you just wait a reasonable period, study all the data, balance all the figures, the right answer comes up."

Her shoulders stiffened. "If you're saying do I need time, then yes, I do."

"Fine, take your time, but add this into your equation."

In two strides he was in front of her, dragging her up, crushing her mouth with his. "You feel just what I feel."

She did—she was very much afraid she did. "That's not the answer."

"It's the only answer." His eyes burned into hers. "I wasn't looking for you, either, Megan. My own course was plotted out just fine. You changed everything for me. So you're going to have to adjust your nice neat columns and make room for me. Because I love you, and I'm going to have you. You and Kevin are going to belong to me." He released her. "Think about it," he said, and walked out.

Idiot. Nathaniel continued to curse himself as he spun his wheels pulling up in front of Shipshape. Obviously he'd found a new way to court a woman: Yell and offer ultimatums. Clearly the perfect way to win a heart.

He snatched Dog out of the back seat and received a sympathetic face bath. "Want to get drunk?" he asked the wriggling ball of fur. "Nope, you're right, bad choice." He stepped inside the building, set the dog down and wondered where he might find an alternative.

Work, he decided, was a wiser option than a bottle.

He busied himself with an engine until he heard the familiar blat of a horn. That would be Holt, bringing in the last tour of the day.

His mood still sour, Nathaniel went out and down to the pier to help secure lines.

"The holiday's bringing in a lot of tourists," Holt commented when the lines were secured. "Good runs today."

"Yeah." Nathaniel scowled at the throng of people still lingering on the docks. "I hate crowds."

Holt's brow lifted. "You were the one who came up with the Fourth of July special to lure them in."

"We need the money." Nathaniel stomped back into the shop. "Doesn't mean I have to like it."

"Who's ticked you off?"

"Nobody." Nathaniel took out a cigar, lit it defiantly. "I'm not used to being landlocked, that's all."

Holt very much doubted that was all, but, in the way of men, shrugged his acceptance and picked up a wrench. "This engine's coming along."

"I can pick up and go anytime." Nathaniel clamped the cigar between his teeth. "Nothing holding me. All I got to do is pack a bag, hop a freighter."

Holt sighed, accepted his lot as a sounding board. "Megan, is it?"

"I didn't ask for her to drop in my lap, did I?"

"Well . . ."

"I was here first." Even when he heard how ridiculous that sounded, Nathaniel couldn't stop. "Woman's got a computer chip in her head. She's not even my type, with those neat little suits and that glossy briefcase. Who ever said I was going to settle down here, lock myself in for life? I've never stayed put anywhere longer than a month since I was eighteen."

Holt pretended to work on the engine. "You started a business, took out a mortgage. And it seems to me you've been here better than six months now."

"Doesn't mean anything."

"Is Megan dropping hints about wedding bells?"

"No." Nathaniel scowled around his cigar and snarled. "I am."

Holt dropped his wrench. "Hold on a minute. Let me get this straight. You're thinking of getting married, and you're kicking around here muttering about hopping a freighter and not being tied down?"

"I didn't ask to be tied down, it just happened." Nathaniel took a deliberate puff, then swore. "Damn it, Holt, I made a fool of myself."

"Funny how we do that around women, isn't it? Did you have a fight with her?"

"I told her I loved her. She started the fight." He paced the shop, nearly gave in to the urge to kick the tool bench. "What happened to the days when women wanted to get married, when that was their Holy Grail, when they set hooks for men to lure them in?"

"What century are we in?"

The fact that Nathaniel could laugh was a hopeful sign. "She thinks I'm moving too fast."

"I'd tell you to slow down, but I've known you too long."

Calmer, he took up a ratchet, considered it, then set it down again. "Suzanna took her lumps from Dumont. How'd you get past it?"

"I yelled at her a lot," Holt said, reminiscing.

"I've tried that."

"Brought her flowers. She's got a real weakness for flowers." Which made him think that perhaps he'd stop on the way home and pick some up.

"I've done that, too."

"Have you tried begging?"

Nathaniel winced. "I'd rather not." His eyes narrowed curiously. "Did you?"

Holt took a sudden, intense interest in the engine. "We're talking about you. Hell, Nate, quote her some of that damn poetry you're so fond of. I don't know. I'm not good at this romance stuff."

"You got Suzanna."

"Yeah." Holt's smile spread. "So get your own woman."

Nathaniel nodded, crushed out his cigar. "I intend to."

Chapter 10

The sun had set by the time Nathaniel returned home. He'd overhauled an engine and repaired a hull, and he still hadn't worked off his foul mood.

He remembered a quote—Horace, he thought—about anger being momentary insanity. If you didn't figure out a way to deal with momentary insanity, you ended up in a padded room. Not a cheerful image.

The only way to deal with it, as far as he could see, was to face it. And Megan. He was going to do both as soon as he'd cleaned up.

"And she'll have to deal with me, won't she?" he said to Dog as the pup scrambled out of the car behind him. "Do yourself a favor, Dog, and stay away from smart women who have more brains than sense."

Dog wagged his tail in agreement or sympathy, then toddled away to water the hedges.

Nathaniel slammed the car door and started across the yard.

"Fury?"

He stopped, squinted into the shadows of dusk, toward the side of the cottage. "Yeah?"

"Nathaniel Fury?"

He watched the man approach, a squat, muscled tank in faded denim. Creased face, strutting walk, a grease-smeared cap pulled low over the brow.

Nathaniel recognized the type. He'd seen the man, and the trouble he carried with him like a badge, in dives and on docks the world over. Instinctively he shifted his weight.

"That's right. Something I can do for you?"

"Nope." The man smiled. "Something *I* can do for *you*."

Even as the first flash of warning lit in Nathaniel's brain, he was grabbed from behind, his arms viciously twisted and pinned. He saw the first blow coming, braced, and took a heavy fist low in the gut. The pain was incredible, making his vision double and waver before the second blow smashed into his jaw.

He grunted, went limp.

"Folded like a girl. Thought he was supposed to be tough." The voice behind him sneered, giving him the height and the distance. In a fast, fluid movement, Nathaniel snapped his head back, rapping his skull hard against the soft tissue of a nose. Using the rear assailant for balance, he kicked up both feet and slammed them into a barrel chest.

The man behind him cursed, loosened his grip enough for Nathaniel to wrest himself away. There were only seconds to judge his opponents and the odds.

He saw that both men were husky, one bleeding profusely now from his broken nose, the other snarling as he wheezed, trying to get back his breath after the double kick to his chest. Nate snapped his elbow back, had the momentary pleasure of hearing the sound of bone against bone.

They came at him like dogs.

He'd been fighting all his life, knew how to mentally go around the pain and plow in. He tasted his own blood, felt the power sing up his arm as his fist connected. His head rang like church bells when he caught a blow to the temple. His breath burned from another in the ribs.

But he kept moving in as they circled him, lashing out, dripping sweat and blood. Avoiding a leap at his throat with a quick pivot, he followed through with a snapping, backhanded blow. The flesh on his knuckles ripped, but the pain was sweet.

He caught the quick move out of the corner of his eye and turned into it. The blow skimmed off his shoulder, and he answered it with two stinging jabs to the throat that had one of the men sinking bonelessly to his knees.

"Just you and me now." Nathaniel wiped the blood from his mouth and measured his foe. "Come on."

The loss of his advantage had his opponent taking a step in retreat. Facing Nathaniel now was like facing a wolf with fangs sharp and exposed. His partner was useless, and the man shifted his eyes for the best route of escape.

Then his eyes lit up.

Lunging, he grabbed one of the boards waiting to be nailed to the deck. He was grinning now, advancing and swinging the board like a bat. Nathaniel felt the wind whistle by his ear as he feinted left, then the wood slapping on his shoulder on the return swing.

He went in low. The rushing power took them both over the deck and smashing through the front door.

"Fire in the hole!" Bird shouted out. "All hands on deck!" His wings flapped frantically as the two men hurtled across the room.

A small table splintered like toothpicks under their combined weight. The wrestling wasn't pretty, nor was there any grace in the short body punches or the gouging fingers. The cottage rang with smashing furniture and harsh breathing.

Something new crept into the jungle scent of sweat and blood. When he recognized fear, Nathaniel's adrenaline pumped faster, and he used the new weapon as ruthlessly as his fists.

He closed his hand around the thick throat, thumb crushing down on the windpipe. The fight had gone out of his opponent. The man was flailing now, gagging.

"Who sent you?" Nathaniel's teeth were bared in a snarl as he grabbed the man by the hair and rapped his head hard on the floor.

"Nobody."

Breathing through his teeth, Nathaniel hauled him over, twisted his arm and jerked it viciously up his back. "I'll snap it like a twig. Then I'll break the other one, before I start on your legs. Who sent you?"

"Nobody," the man repeated, then screamed thinly when Nathaniel increased the pressure. "I don't know his name. I don't!" He screamed again, almost weeping now. "Some dude outa Boston. Paid us five hundred apiece to teach you a lesson."

Nathaniel kept the arm twisted awkwardly, his knee on the man's spine. "Draw me a picture."

"Tall guy, dark hair, fancy suit." The squat man babbled out curses, unable to move without increasing his own agony. "Name of God, you're breaking my arm."

"Keep talking and it's all I'll break."

"Pretty face—like a movie star. Said we was to come here and look you up. We'd get double if we put you in the hospital."

"Looks like you're not going to collect that bonus." After releasing his arm, Nathaniel dragged the man up by the scruff of his neck. "Here's what you're going to do. You're going to go back to Boston and tell your pretty-faced pal that I know who he is and I know where to find him." For the hell of it, Nathaniel rammed the man against the wall on the way out the door. "Tell him not to bother looking over his shoulder, because if I decide he's worth going after, he won't see me coming. You got that?"

"Yeah, yeah, I got it."

"Now pick up your partner." The other man was struggling onto his hands and knees. "And start running."

They didn't need any more urging. Pressing a hand to his ribs, Nathaniel watched until they'd completed their limping race out of sight.

He gave in to a groan then, hobbling painfully through the broken door and into the house.

"I have not yet begun to fight," Bird claimed.

"A lot of help you were," Nathaniel muttered. He needed ice, he thought, a bottle of aspirin and a shot of whiskey.

He took another step, stopping, then swearing, when his vision blurred and his legs wobbled like jelly. Dog came out of the corner where he'd huddled, whimpering, and whined at Nate's feet.

"Just need a minute," he said to no one in particular, and then the room tilted nastily on its side. "Oh, hell," he murmured, and passed out cold.

Dog licked at him, tried to nuzzle his nose, then sat, thumped his tail and waited. But the smell of blood made him skittish. After a few moments, he waddled out the door.

Nathaniel was just coming to when he heard the footsteps approaching. He struggled to sit up, wincing at every blow that had gone unfelt during the heat of battle. He knew that if they'd come back for him, they could tap-dance on his face without any resistance from him.

"Man overboard," Bird announced, and earned a hissing snarl from Nathaniel.

Holt stopped in the doorway and swore ripely. "What the hell happened?" Then he was at Nathaniel's side, helping him to stand.

"Couple of guys." Too weak to be ashamed of it, Nathaniel leaned heavily on Holt. It began to occur to him that he might need more than aspirin.

"Did you walk into a robbery?"

"No. They just stopped by to beat me to a pulp."

"Looks like they did a good job of it." Holt waited for Nathaniel to catch his breath and his balance. "Did they mention why?"

"Yeah." He wiggled his aching jaw and saw stars. "They were paid to. Courtesy of Dumont."

Holt swore again. His friend was a mess, bruised, bloodied and torn. And it looked as though he were too late to do anything other than mop up the spills.

"Did you get a good look at them?"

"Yeah, good enough. I kicked their butts back to Boston to deliver a little message to Dumont."

Half carrying Nathaniel to the door, Holt stopped, took another survey. "You look like this, and you won?"

Nathaniel merely grunted.

"Should have known." The news made Holt marginally more cheerful. "Well, we'll get you to the hospital."

"No." Damned if he'd give Dumont the satisfaction. "Son of a bitch told them they'd get a bonus if they put me in the hospital."

"Then that's out," Holt said with perfect understanding. "Just a doctor then."

"It's not that bad. Nothing's broke." He checked his tender ribs. "I don't think. Just need some ice."

"Yeah, right." But, being a man, Holt was in perfect sympathy with the reluctance to be bundled off to a doctor. "Okay, we're going to the next-best place." He eased Nathaniel into the car. "Take it slow, ace."

"I can't take it otherwise."

With a snap of his fingers, Holt ordered Dog into the car. "Hold on a minute while I phone Suzanna, let her know what's going on."

"Feed the bird, will you?"

Nathaniel drifted between pain and numbness until Holt returned.

"How'd you know to come by?"

"Your dog." Holt started the car and eased it as gently as possible out of the drive. "He played Lassie."

"No fooling?" Impressed, Nathaniel made the effort to reach back and pat Dog on the head. "Some dog, huh?"

"It's all in the bloodlines."

Nathaniel roused himself enough to probe his face with cautious fingers. "Where are we going?"

"Where else?" Holt headed for The Towers.

Coco squealed at the sight of him, pressing both hands to her cheeks, as Nathaniel hobbled into the family kitchen with one arm slung over Holt's supporting shoulders.

"Oh, you poor *darling*! What happened? Was there an accident?"

"Ran into something." Nathaniel dropped heavily into a chair. "Coco, I'll trade you everything I own, plus my immortal soul, for a bag of ice."

"Goodness."

Brushing Holt away, she took Nathaniel's battered face in her hands. In addition to bruises and scrapes, there was a jagged cut under one eye. The other was bloodshot and swelling badly. It didn't take her longer than a moment to see that the something he'd run into was fists.

"Don't you worry, sweetheart, we'll take care of you. Holt, run up to my room. There's a bottle of painkillers in the medicine chest, from when I had that nasty root canal."

"Bless you," Nathaniel managed. He closed his eyes, listening to her bustling around the kitchen. Moments later he hissed and jerked when a cool cloth dabbed the cut under his eye.

"There, there, dear," she cooed. "I know it hurts, but we have to get it clean so there's no infection. I'm going to put a little peroxide on it now, so you just be brave."

He smiled, but found that did nothing to help his torn lip. "I love you, Coco."

"I love you, too, sweetie."

"Let's elope. Tonight."

Her answer was to lay her lips gently on his brow. "You shouldn't fight, Nathaniel. It doesn't solve anything."

"I know."

Breathless from the run, Megan burst into the kitchen. "Holt said—Oh, God." She streaked to Nathaniel's side, grabbed his sore hand so tightly he had to bite down to suppress a yelp. There was blood drying on his face, and there were bruises blooming. "How bad are you hurt? You should be in the hospital."

"I've had worse."

"Holt said two men came after you."

"Two?" Coco's hand paused. "*Two* men attacked you?" All the softness fled from her eyes, hardening them to tough blue steel. "Why, that's reprehensible. Someone should teach them how to fight fair."

Despite his lip, Nathaniel grinned. "Thanks, beautiful, but I already did."

"I hope you knocked their heads together." After a huffing breath, Coco went back to work on his face. "Megan, dear, fix Nate an ice bag for his eye. It's going to swell."

Megan obeyed, torn into dozens of pieces, by the damage to his face, by the fact that he hadn't even looked at her.

"Here." She laid the cool bag against his eye while Coco cleaned his torn knuckles.

"I can hold it. Thanks." He took it from her, let the ice numb the pain.

"There's antiseptic in the left-hand cupboard, second shelf," Coco said.

Megan, feeling weepy, turned to get it.

The door opened again, this time letting in a crowd. Nathaniel's initial discomfort with the audience turned to reluctant amusement as the Calhouns fired questions and indignation. Plans for revenge were plotted and discarded while Nathaniel suffered the sting of iodine.

"Give the boy air!" Colleen commanded, parting her angry grandnieces and nephews like a queen moving through her court. She eyed Nathaniel. "Banged you up pretty good, did they?"

"Yes, ma'am."

Her eyes were shrewd. "Dumont," she murmured, so that only he could hear.

Nathaniel winced. "Right the first time."

She glanced at Coco. "You seem to be in able hands, here. I have a call to make." She smiled thinly. It helped to have connections, she thought as she tapped out of the room with her cane. And through them she would see that Baxter Dumont knew he had put a noose around his own neck, and that one false move would mean his career would come to an abrupt and unpleasant stop.

Nobody trifled with Colleen Calhoun's family.

Nathaniel watched Colleen go, then took the pill Coco held out to him and gulped it down. The movement sent fresh pain radiating up his side.

"Let's get that shirt off." Trying to sound cheerful, Coco attacked the torn T-shirt with kitchen shears. The angry mutters died away as Nathaniel's bruised torso was exposed.

"Oh." Tears stung Coco's eyes. "Oh, baby."

"Don't pamper the boy." Dutch came in holding two bottles. Witch hazel and whiskey. One look at Nathaniel had him gritting his teeth together so hard they ached, but he kept his voice careless. "He ain't no baby. Take a shot of this, Captain."

"He's just taken a pill," Coco began.

"Take a shot," Dutch repeated.

Nathaniel winced once as the whiskey stung his lip. But it took the edge off a great many other aches. "Thanks."

"Look at ya." Dutch snorted and dumped the witch hazel onto a cloth. "Let 'em pound all over you, like some city boy with sponges where his fists should be."

"There were two of them," Nathaniel muttered.

"So?" Dutch gently swabbed the bruises. "You getting so outa shape you can't take two?"

"I kicked their butts." Experimentally Nathaniel probed a tooth with his tongue. It hurt, but at least it wasn't loose.

"Better had," Dutch returned, with a flash of pride. "Tried to rob you, did they?"

Nathaniel's gaze flashed to Megan. "No."

"Ribs're bruised." Ignoring Nathaniel's curse, Dutch prodded and poked until he was satisfied. "Not cracked though." He crouched, peered into Nathaniel's eyes. "D'ya pass out?"

"Maybe." It was almost as bad as another thumping to admit it. "For a minute."

"Vision blurred?"

"No, Doc. Not now."

"Don't get smart. How many?" He held up two thick fingers.

"Eighty-seven." Nathaniel would have reached for the whiskey again, but Coco shoved it aside.

"He's not drinking any more on top of the pill I gave him."

"Women think they know every damn thing." But Dutch sent her a look, reassuring her that their charge would be all right. "Bed's what you need now. A hot soak and cool sheets. Want I should carry you?"

"Hell, no." That was one humiliation he could do without. He took Coco's hand, kissed it. "Thanks, darling. I'd do it all again if I knew you'd be my nurse." He looked back at Holt. "I could use a ride home."

"Nonsense." Coco disposed of that idea instantly. "You'll stay here, where we can look after you. You may very well have a concussion, so we'll take shifts waking you up through the night to be sure you don't slip into a coma."

"Wives' tales," Dutch grunted, but nodded at her behind Nathaniel's back.

"I'll turn down the bed in the rose guest room," Amanda stated. "C.C., why don't you run our hero a nice hot bath? Lilah, bring that ice along."

He didn't have the energy to fight the lot of them, so he sat back as Lilah walked over and touched her lips gently to his. "Come on, tough guy."

Sloan moved over to help him to his feet. "Two of them, huh? Puny guys?"

"Bigger than you, pal." He was floating just a little as he hobbled up the stairs between Sloan and Max.

"Let's get those pants off," Lilah said, when they'd eased him down to sit on the side of the bed.

He still had the wit to arch a brow at her. "You never said that when it counted. No offense," he added to Max.

"None taken." With a chuckle, Max bent down to

pull off Nathaniel's shoes. He knew what it was to be nursed back to health by the Calhoun women, and he figured that once Nathaniel got past the worst of the pain, he'd realize he'd landed in heaven. "Need some help getting in the tub?"

"I can handle it, thanks."

"Give a call if you run into trouble." Sloan held the door open, waiting until the room cleared. "And, when you're more up to it, I'd like the whole story."

Alone, Nathaniel managed to ease himself into the hot water. The first flash of agony passed, transforming gradually into something closer to comfort. By the time he'd climbed out again, the worst seemed to be over.

Until he looked in the mirror.

There was a bandage under his left eye, another on his temple. His right eye looked like a rotting tomato. That left the bruises, the swollen lip, the nasty scrape on his jaw. All in all, he thought, he looked like hell.

With a towel slung around his waist, he stepped back into the bedroom, just as Megan came in the hallway door.

"I'm sorry." She pressed her lips together to keep herself from saying all manner of foolish things. "Amanda thought you might want another pillow, some more towels."

"Thanks." He made it to the bed and lay back with a sigh of relief.

Grateful for something practical to do, she hurried to the bed, plumped and arranged pillows for him, smoothed the sheets. "Is there anything I can get you? More ice? Some soup?"

"No, this is fine."

"Please, I want to help. I need to help." She couldn't bear it any longer, and she laid a hand to his cheek. "They hurt you. I'm so sorry they hurt you."

"Just bruises."

"Damn it, don't be so stupid—not when I'm looking right at you, not when I can see what they did." She pulled back on the need to rage and looked helplessly into his eyes. "I know you're angry with me, but can't you let me do something?"

"Maybe you'd better sit down." When she did, he took her hand in his. He needed the contact every bit as much as she did. "You've been crying."

"A little." She looked down at his damaged knuckles. "I felt so helpless downstairs, seeing you like this. You let Coco tend you, and you wouldn't even look at me." Drenched with emotion, her eyes came back to his. "I don't want to lose you, Nathaniel. It's only that I've just found you, and I don't want to make another mistake."

"It always comes back to him, doesn't it?"

"No, no. It comes back to me."

"What he did to you," Nathaniel corrected grimly.

"All right, yes." She brought his hand to her cheek. "Please, don't walk away from me. I don't have all the answers yet, but I know when Holt said you'd been hurt—my heart just stopped. I've never been so frightened. You mean so much to me, Nathaniel. Let me just take care of you until you're better."

"Well." He was softening, and he reached out to stroke her hair. "Maybe Dumont did me a favor this time."

"What do you mean?"

He shook his head. Maybe his brain was a little addled by the drug and the pain. He hadn't meant to tell her, at least not yet. But he thought she had the right to know.

"The two guys that jumped me tonight. Dumont hired them."

Every ounce of color faded from her cheeks. "What are you saying? You're saying that Baxter paid them to attack you? To—"

"Rough me up, that's all. I'd say he was sore about me tossing him in the water and was looking for some payback." He shifted, winced. "He'd have been smarter to put his money on a couple of pros. These two were real amateurs."

"*Baxter* did this." Megan's vision hazed. She shut her eyes until she was sure it had cleared again. "My fault."

"Like hell. None of it's been yours, not from the start. He did what he did to you, Suzanna, the kids. Chickenhearted bastard couldn't even fight for himself. Hey." He tugged on her hair. "I won, remember. He didn't get what he'd paid for."

"Do you think that matters?"

"It does to me. If you want to do something for me, Megan, really want to do something for me, you'll push him right out of your head."

"He's Kevin's father," she whispered. "It makes me sick to think it."

"He's nothing. Lie down here with me, will you?"

Because she could see that he was fighting off the drug, she did as he asked. Gently she shifted his head so that it rested on her breast.

"Sleep for a while," she murmured. "We won't think of it now. We won't think of anything."

He sighed, let himself drift. "I love you, Megan."

"I know." She stroked his hair and lay wakeful while he slept.

Neither of them saw the little boy with shattered eyes and pale cheeks in the open doorway.

Nathaniel woke to the rhythm of his own pain. There was a bass drum in his head, pounding low in the skull, with a few more enthusiastic riffs at the left temple. It was more of a snare along his ribs, a solid rat-a-tat that promised to remain steady and persistent. His shoulder sang along in a droning hum.

Experimentally, he sat up. Stiff as a week-old corpse, he thought in disgust. With slow, awkward movements, he eased out of the bed. Except for the pounding in his head, it was clear. Maybe too clear, he thought with a wince as he limped into the shower. His one pleasure was that he knew his two unexpected visitors would be suffering more than he was at the moment.

Even the soft needles of spray brought a bright bloom of pain to the worst of his bruises. Teeth clenched, he waited out the pain until it mellowed to discomfort.

He'd live.

Naked and dripping, he stepped out of the shower, then filled the basin with icy water. Taking one bracing breath, he lowered his face into it until the shocking cold brought on a blessed numbness.

Steadier, he went back into the bedroom, where fresh clothes had been left folded on a chair. With a great deal of swearing, he managed to dress. He was thinking of coffee, aspirin and a full plate when the door creaked open.

"You shouldn't be up." Coco, a tray balanced in both hands, clucked her tongue. "Now get that shirt off and get back into bed."

"Darling, I've been waiting all my life to hear you say that."

"You must be feeling a little better," Coco said, and laughed, then set the tray on the bedside table and fluffed at her hair. It occurred to Nathaniel as he followed the familiar gesture that her hair hadn't changed color in a couple weeks, maybe more. Must be some mood she was in, he decided.

"I'll do."

"Poor dear." She lifted a hand to gently touch the bruises on his face. He looked even worse this morning, but she didn't have the heart to say so. "At least sit down and eat."

"You read my mind." More than willing, he eased himself into a chair. "I appreciate the service."

"It's the least we can do." Coco fit the legs of the bedside table over the chair and unfolded his napkin. Nathaniel thought she would have tucked it into his collar if he hadn't taken it himself. "Megan told me what happened. That Baxter hired those—those thugs. I've a mind to go to Boston myself and deal with that man."

The fierce look in her eyes warmed Nathaniel's heart. She was like some fiery Celtic goddess. "Sugar, he wouldn't have a chance against you." He sampled his eggs, closed his eyes on the simple pleasure of hot, delicious food. "We'll let it go, darling."

"Let it go! You can't. You have to contact the police. Of course, I'd prefer if all you boys got together and took a trip down to blacken that man's eyes . . ." She pressed a hand to her heart as the image caused it to beat fast. "But," she continued with some regret, "the proper thing to do is contact the authorities and have them handle it."

"No cops." He scooped up delicately fried hash-brown potatoes. "Dumont's going to suffer a lot more, not knowing what I'll do or when I'll do it."

"Well . . ." Considering that, Coco began to smile. "I suppose he would. Like waiting for the other shoe to drop."

"Yeah. And bringing the police in would make it tough for Megan and the boy."

"You're right, of course." Gently she brushed a hand over his hair. "I'm so glad they have you."

"I wish she felt the same way."

"She does. She's just afraid. Megan's had so much to handle in her life. And you—well, Nathaniel, you're a man who'd leave any woman a bit addled."

"You think so, huh?"

"I know so. Are you having much pain this morning, dear? You can take another pill."

"I'll settle for aspirin."

"I thought you might." Coco took a bottle out of her apron pocket. "Take these with your juice."

"Yes, ma'am." He obeyed, then went back to his eggs. "So, you've seen Megan this morning?"

"It was nearly dawn before I could convince her to leave you and get some sleep."

That information went down even better than the food. "Yeah?"

"And the way she looked at you . . ." Coco patted his hand. "Well, a woman knows these things. Especially when she's in love herself." A becoming blush bloomed on her cheeks. "I suppose you know that Niels and I—that we're . . . involved."

He made some sound. He didn't want the image in his brain of them together in the dark. Coco and Dutch were as close to parents as he'd ever had, and no child, even at thirty-three, wanted to think about that side of a parental relationship.

"These past few weeks have been wonderful. I had a lovely marriage, and there are memories I've cherished and will cherish all of my life. And over the years, I've had some nice, compatible relationships. But with Niels . . ." The dreamy look came into her eyes. "He makes me feel young and vital, and almost delicate. It's not just the sex," she added, and had Nathaniel wincing.

"Aw, jeez, Coco." He took a sip of coffee, as he was rapidly losing his appetite. "I don't want to know about that."

She chuckled, adoring him. "I know how close you are to Niels."

"Well, sure." He was beginning to feel trapped in the chair, barred by the tray. "We sailed together a long time, and he's . . ."

"Like a father to you," she said gently. "I know. I just wanted you to know I love him, too. We're going to be married."

"What?" His fork clattered against china. "*Married?* You and the Dutchman?"

"Yes." Nervous now, because she couldn't tell whether his expression was horrified or simply shocked, Coco fiddled with the jet beads at her throat. "I hope you don't mind."

"Mind?" His brain had gone blank. Now it began to fill again—the restless movements of her hands, the tone of her voice, the anxious look in her eyes. Nathaniel shifted the table away from his chair and rose. "Imagine a classy woman like you falling for that old tar. Are you sure he hadn't been slipping something into your soup?"

Relieved, she smiled. "If he has, I like it. Do we have your blessing?"

He took her hands, looked down at them. "You know, for nearly as far back as I can remember, I wanted you to be my mother."

"Oh." Her eyes filled, overflowed. "Nathaniel."

"Now I guess you will be." His gaze lifted to hers again before he kissed her, one cheek, the other, then her lips. "He'd better be good to you, or he'll answer to me."

"I'm so happy." Coco sank, weeping, into his arms. "I'm so very happy, Nate. I didn't even see it coming in the cards." Her breath hitched as she pressed her wet face to his throat. "Or the tea leaves, even the crystal. It just happened."

"The best things usually do."

"I want you to be happy." Drawing back, she fumbled in her pocket for one of her lace-trimmed hankies. "I want you to believe in what you have with Megan, and not let it slip away. She needs you, Nate. So does Kevin."

"That's what I told her." He smiled a little as he took the hankie and dried Coco's tears himself. "I don't guess she was ready to hear it."

"You just keep saying it." Her voice became firm. "Keep right on saying it until she is." And if Megan needed an extra push, Coco thought, she'd be happy to supply it herself. "Now, then." She smoothed down her hair, her slacks. "I have a million things to do. I want you to rest, so you'll be up to the picnic and the fireworks."

"I feel okay."

"You feel as if you've been run over by a truck." She marched to the bed, busying herself with smoothing sheets and fluffing pillows. "You can lie down for another hour or two, or you can sit out on the terrace in the sun. It's a lovely day, and we can fix you up a nice chaise. When Megan wakes up, I'll have her come give you a rubdown."

"Now that sounds promising. I'll take the sun." He started toward the terrace doors, but then he heard footsteps hurrying down the hall.

Megan rushed in. "I can't find Kevin," she blurted out. "No one's seen him all morning."

Chapter 11

She was pale as ice, and struggling to be calm. The idea of her little boy running away was so absurd that she continued to tell herself it was a mistake, a prank. Maybe a dream.

"No one's seen him," she repeated, bracing a hand on the doorknob to stay upright. "Some—some of his clothes are gone, and his knapsack."

"Call Suzanna," Nathaniel said quickly. "He's probably with Alex and Jenny."

"No." She shook her head slowly, side to side. Her body felt like glass, as though it would shatter if she moved too quickly. "They're here. They're all here. They haven't seen him. I was sleeping." She said each word deliberately, as if she were having trouble understanding her own voice. "I slept late, then I checked his room, like I always do. He wasn't there, but I thought he'd be downstairs, or outside. But when I went down, Alex was looking for him." The fear began to claw at her, little cat feet up and down her spine. "We hunted around, then I came back up. That's when I saw that some of his things . . . some of his things . . ."

"All right, dear, now don't you worry." Coco hurried over to slip a supporting arm around Megan's waist. "I'm sure he's just playing a game. There are so many places to hide in the house, on the grounds."

"He was so excited about today. It's all he could talk about. He's supposed to be playing Revolutionary War with Alex and Jenny. He—he was going to be Daniel Boone."

"We'll find him," Nathaniel told her.

"Of course we will." Gently Coco began to ease Megan along. "We'll organize a search party. Won't he be excited when he finds out?"

An hour later, they were spread throughout the house, searching corners and hidey-holes, retracing and backtracking. Megan kept a steel grip on her composure and covered every inch, starting in the tower and working her way down.

He had to be here, she reassured herself. Of course, she would find him any minute. It didn't make sense otherwise.

Bubbles of hysteria rose in her throat and had to be choked down.

He was just playing a game. He'd gone exploring. He loved the house so much. He'd drawn dozens of pictures of it to send back to Oklahoma so that everyone could see that he lived in a castle.

She would find him behind the next door she opened.

Megan told herself that, repeating it like a litany, as she worked her way from room to room.

She ran into Suzanna in one of the snaking hallways. She felt cold, so cold, though the sun beat hot against the windows. "He doesn't answer me," she said faintly. "I keep calling him, but he doesn't answer."

"It's such a big house." Suzanna took Megan's hands, gripped hard. "Once when we were kids we played hide-and-seek and didn't find Lilah for three hours. She'd crawled into a cabinet on the third floor and had a nap."

"Suzanna." Megan pressed her lips together. She had to face it, and quickly. "His two favorite shirts are missing, and both pairs of his sneakers. His baseball caps. The money he'd been saving in his jar is gone. He's not in the house. He's run away."

"You need to sit down."

"No, I—I need to do something. Call the police. Oh, God—" Breaking, Megan pressed her hands to her face. "Anything could have happened to him. He's just a little boy. I don't even know how long he's been gone. I don't even know." Her eyes, swimming with fear, locked on Suzanna's. "Did you ask Alex, Jenny? Maybe he said something to them. Maybe—"

"Of course I asked them, Megan," Suzanna said gently. "Kevin didn't say anything to them about leaving."

"Where would he go? Why? Back to Oklahoma," she said on a wild, hopeful thought. "Maybe he's trying to get back to Oklahoma. Maybe he's been unhappy, just pretending to like it here."

"He's been happy. But we'll check it out. Come on, let's go down."

"Been over every bit of this section," Dutch told Nathaniel. "The pantries, the storerooms, even the meat locker. Trent and Sloan are going over the renovation areas, and Max and Holt are beating the bushes all over the grounds."

There was worry in his eyes, but he was brewing a pot of fresh coffee with steady hands.

"Seems to me if the kid was just playing and heard all this shouting and calling, he'd come out to see what the excitement was all about."

"We've been over the house twice." Nathaniel stared grimly out the window. "Amanda and Lilah have combed every inch of The Retreat. He's not in here."

"Don't make a lick of sense to me. Kevin's been happy as a clam. He's in here every blessed day, getting under my feet and begging for sea stories."

"Something's got him running." There was a prickle at the back of his neck. Rubbing it absently, Nathaniel looked out toward the cliffs. "Why does a kid run? Because he's scared, or he's hurt, or he's unhappy."

"That boy ain't none of those things," Dutch said staunchly.

"I wouldn't have thought so." Nathaniel had been all three at that age, and he believed he would have recognized the signs. There had been times he ran, too. But he'd had nowhere to go.

The tickle at the back of his neck persisted. Again, he found his gaze wandering toward the cliffs. "I've got a feeling," he said almost to himself.

"What?"

"No, just a feeling." The prickle was in his gut now. "I'm going to check it out."

It was as though he were being pulled to the cliffs. Nathaniel didn't fight it, though the rocky ground jarred the pain back into his bones and the steep climb stole his breath. With one hand pressed to his aching ribs, he continued, his gaze sweeping the rocks and the high wild grass.

It was, he knew, a place that would draw a child. It had drawn him as a boy. And as a man.

The sun was high and white, the sea sapphire blue, then frothy where it lashed and foamed on the rocks. Beautiful and deadly. He thought of a young boy stumbling along the path, missing a step, slipping. The nausea churned so violently he had to stop and choke it back.

Nothing had happened to Kevin, he assured himself. He wouldn't let anything happen to Kevin.

He turned, started to climb higher, calling the boy's name as he searched.

It was the bird that caught his eye. A pure white gull, graceful as a dancer, swooped over the grass and rock, circled back with a musical call that was almost human, eerily feminine. He stood, staring at it. For one sunstruck second, Nathaniel would have sworn the gull's eyes were green, green as emeralds.

It glided down, perched on the ledge below and looked up, as if waiting for him.

Nathaniel found himself clambering down, ignoring the jolts to his abused body. The thunder of the surf seemed to fill his head. He thought he smelled a woman, sweet, soft, soothing, but then it was only the sea.

The bird wheeled away, skyward, joined its mate—another gull, blindingly white. For a moment they circled, calling together in something like joy. Then they winged out to sea.

Wheezing a bit, Nathaniel gained the ledge, and saw the shallow crevice in the rock where the boy was huddled.

His first instinct was to scoop the child up, hold him. But he checked it. He wasn't altogether certain he wasn't the reason Kevin had run.

Instead, he sat down on the ledge and spoke quietly. "Nice view from here."

Kevin kept his face pressed to his knees. "I'm going back to Oklahoma." It was an attempt at defiance that merely sounded weary. "I can take a bus."

"I guess so. You'd see a lot of the country that way. But I thought you liked it here."

His answer was a shrug. "It's okay."

"Somebody give you a hard time, mate?"

"No."

"Did you have a fight with Alex?"

"No, it's nothing like that. I'm just going back to Oklahoma. It was too late to take the bus last night, so I came up here to wait. I guess maybe I fell asleep." He hunched his shoulder, kept his face averted. "You can't make me go back."

"Well, I'm bigger than you, so I could." He said it gently, touched a hand to Kevin's hair. But the boy jerked away. "I'd rather not make you do anything until I understand what's on your mind."

He let some time pass, watching the sea, listening to the wind, until he sensed Kevin relaxing a little beside him.

"Your mother's kind of worried about you. Everybody else is, too. Maybe you ought to go back and tell them goodbye before you leave."

"She won't let me go."

"She loves you a lot."

"She should never have had me." There was bitterness in the words, words that were much too sharp for a little boy.

"That's a stupid thing to say. I figure you've got a right to get mad if you want but there's not much point in just being stupid."

Kevin's head shot up. His face was streaked with tears and dirt, and it sliced through Nathaniel's heart.

"If she hadn't had me, things would be different. She always pretends it doesn't matter. But I know."

"What do you know?"

"I'm not a baby anymore. I know what he did. He made her pregnant, then he went away. He went away, and he never cared. He went away and married Suzanna, and then he left her, too. And Alex and Jenny. That's how come I'm their brother."

Those were stormy seas, Nathaniel thought, that needed to be navigated with care. The boy's eyes, hurt and angry, latched onto his.

"Your mother's the one who has to explain that to you, Kevin."

"She told me that sometimes people can't get married and be together, even when they have kids. But he didn't want me. He never wanted me, and I hate him."

"I'm not going to argue with you about that," Nathaniel said carefully. "But your mother loves you, and that counts for a lot more. If you take off, it's going to hurt her, bad."

Kevin's lips trembled. "She could have you if I was gone. You'd stay with her if it wasn't for me."

"I'm afraid I'm not following you, Kevin."

"He—he had you beaten up." Kevin's voice hitched as he fought to get the words out. "I heard last night. I heard you and Mom, and she said it was her fault, but it's mine. 'Cause he's my father and he did it and now you hate me, too, and you'll go away."

"Little jerk." On a flood of emotion, Nathaniel yanked the boy to his knees and shook him. "You pulled this stunt because I got a few bruises? Do I look like I can't take care of myself? Those other two wimps had to crawl away."

"Really?" Kevin sniffed and rubbed at his eyes. "But still—"

"Still, hell. You didn't have anything to do with it, and I ought to shake you until your teeth fall out for worrying us all this way."

"He's my father," Kevin said, tilting his chin up. "So that means—"

"That means nothing. My father was a drunk who used to kick my butt for the pleasure of it, six days out of seven. Does that make me like him?"

"No." Tears began to roll more freely now. "But I thought you wouldn't like me anymore, and you'd never stay and be my father now, like Holt is with Alex and Jenny."

Nathaniel's hands gentled as he drew the sobbing boy into his arms. "You thought wrong." He rubbed his lips over Kevin's hair, absorbed the jolt of love. "I ought to hang you from the yardarm, sailor."

"What's that?"

"I'll show you later." He tightened his grip. "Did you stop and think that I might be hoping you'd be my son? That I want you and your mom to be mine?"

"Honest?" Kevin's voice was muffled against Nathaniel's chest.

"Do you figure I've been training you to take the helm just to have you walk off?"

"I don't know. I guess not."

"I've been looking for you, Kevin, longer than just today."

With a sigh, Kevin let his head rest in the curve of Nathaniel's shoulder. "I was awful scared. But then the bird came."

"Bird?" Remembering, Nathaniel glanced around. But the rocks were empty.

"Then I wasn't so scared. She stayed all night. She was there whenever I woke up. She flew away with the other one, but then you came. Is Mom mad at me?"

"Probably."

Kevin sighed again—a long-suffering sound that made Nathaniel smile. "I guess I'm in trouble."

"Well, let's get your things and go back and face the music."

Kevin picked up his knapsack and put his hand trustingly in Nathaniel's. "Does it hurt?" he asked, studying Nathaniel's face.

"You bet."

"Later, can I see all your bruises?"

"Sure. I've got some beauts."

Nathaniel felt every one of them as they climbed back up to the cliff path and started down the rocky slope toward home. It was worth it, worth every jar and wince, to see the look on Megan's face.

"Kevin!" She flew across the lawn, hair blowing, cheeks tracked with tears.

"Go on," Nathaniel murmured to the boy. "She'll want to hug you first."

With a nod, Kevin dropped his knapsack and raced into his mother's arms.

"Oh, Kevin..." She couldn't hold him tight enough, even kneeling on the grass, pressing him close, rocking and weeping in terrible relief.

"Where'd you find him?" Trent asked Nathaniel quietly.

"Up on the cliffs, holed up in a crevice in the rocks."

"Good God." C.C. shuddered. "Did he spend the night up there?"

"Looked that way. I had this feeling, I can't explain it. And there he was."

"A feeling?" Trent exchanged a look with his wife. "Remind me to tell you sometime how I found Fred when he was a puppy."

Max gave Nathaniel a pat on the back. "I'll go call the police, let them know we've found him."

"He'll be hungry." Coco swallowed fresh tears and burrowed closer to Dutch. "We'll go fix him something to eat."

"You bring 'em in when she's finished slobbering over him—" Dutch camouflaged the break in his voice with a cough. "Women. Always making a fuss."

"Come on, let's go in." Suzanna tugged on Alex and Jenny's hands.

"But I want to ask if he saw the ghosts," Alex complained.

"Later." Holt solved the problem by hoisting Alex onto his shoulders.

With a shuddering sigh, Megan drew back, ran her hands over Kevin's face. "You're all right? You're not hurt?"

"Nuh-uh." It embarrassed him that he'd cried in front of his brother and sister. After all, he was nearly nine. "I'm okay."

"Don't you *ever* do that again." The swift change from weeping mother to fierce parent had Nathaniel's brows rising. "You had us all worried sick, young man. We've been looking for you for hours, even Aunt Colleen. We've called the police."

"I'm sorry." But the thrill of knowing the police had been alerted overpowered the guilt.

"Sorry isn't enough, Kevin Michael O'Riley."

Kevin's gaze hit the ground. It was big-time trouble when she used all his names. "I won't ever do it again. I promise."

"You had no business doing it this time. I'm supposed to be able to trust you, and now—Oh." On another hitching sob, she pressed his head to her breast. "I was so scared, baby. I love you so much. Where were you going?"

"I don't know. Maybe Grandma's."

"Grandma's." She sat back on her heels and sighed. "Don't you like it here?"

"I like it best of anything."

"Then why did you run away, Kevin? Are you mad at me?"

He shook his head, then dropped his chin on his chest. "I thought you and Nate were mad at me because he got beaten up. But Nate says it's not my fault and you're not mad. He says it doesn't matter about *him*. You're not mad at me, are you?"

Her horrified eyes flew to Nate's, held there as she drew Kevin close again. "Oh, no, baby, I'm not. No one is." She looked at her son again, cupping his face in her hands. "Remember when I told you that sometimes people can't be together? I should explain that sometimes they shouldn't be together. That's the way it was with me and—" She couldn't refer to him as Kevin's father. "With me and Baxter."

"But I was an accident."

"Oh, no." She smiled then, kissed his cheeks. "An accident's something you wish hadn't happened. You were a gift. The best one I ever had in my life. If you ever think I don't want you again, I guess I'll have to stuff you into a box and tie it up with a bow so you'll get the point."

He giggled. "I'm sorry."

"Me too. Now let's go get you cleaned up." She rose, gripped her son's hand in hers and looked at Nathaniel. "Thank you."

In the way of children, Kevin bounced back from his night on the cliffs and threw himself into the holiday. He was, for the moment, a hero, desperately impressing his siblings with his tales of the dark and the sea and a white bird with green eyes.

In keeping with the family gathering, all the dogs attended, so Sadie and Fred raced with their puppies and the children over the rolling lawn. Babies napped in playpens or rocked in swings or charmed their way into willing arms. A few hotel guests wandered over from their own feast provided by The Retreat, drawn by the laughter and raised voices.

Nathaniel passed, reluctantly, on the impromptu softball game, figuring one slide into third would have him down for the count. Instead, he designated himself umpire and had the pleasure of arguing with every batter he called out.

"Are you blind or just stupid?" C.C. tossed down

her bat in disgust. "A sock in the eye's no excuse for missing that call. That ball was outside a half a mile."

Nathaniel clamped his cigar in his teeth. "Not from where I'm standing, sugar."

She slapped her hands on her hips. "Then you're standing in the wrong spot." Jenny took the opportunity to attempt a cartwheel over home plate, and earned some applause from the infield.

"C.C., you've got one of the best-looking strike zones I've ever had the pleasure of seeing. And that was strike three. You're out."

"If you weren't already black-and-blue . . ." She swallowed a laugh, and sneered instead. "You're up, Lilah."

"Already?" In a lazy gesture, Lilah brushed her hair away from her face and stepped into the box.

From her position at short, Megan glanced at her second baseman. "She won't run even if she connects."

Suzanna sighed, shook her head. "She won't have to. Just watch."

Lilah skimmed a hand down her hip, cast a sultry look back at Nathaniel, then faced the pitcher. Sloan went through an elaborate windup that had the children cheering. Lilah took the first strike with the bat still on her shoulder. Yawned.

"We keeping you up?" Nathaniel asked her.

"I like to wait for my pitch."

Apparently the second one wasn't the one she was waiting for. She let it breeze by, and earned catcalls from the opposing team.

She stepped out of the box, stretched, smiled at Sloan. "Okay, big guy," she said as she took her stance again.

She cracked the low curveball and sent it soaring for a home run. Amid the cheers, she turned and handed her bat to Nathaniel. "I always recognize the right pitch," she told him, and sauntered around the bases.

When the game broke for the feast, Nathaniel eased down beside Megan. "You've got a pretty good arm there, sugar."

"I coached Kevin's Little League team back in Oklahoma." Her gaze wandered to her son, as it had dozens of times during the afternoon. "He doesn't seem any the worse for wear, does he?"

"Nope. How about you?"

"The bats in my stomach have mellowed out to butterflies." She pressed a hand to them now, lowered her voice. "I never knew he thought about Baxter. About . . . any of it. I should have."

"A boy's got to have some secrets, even from his mother."

"I suppose." It was too beautiful a day, she decided, too precious a day, to waste on worry. "Whatever you said to him up there, however you said it, was exactly right. It means a lot to me." She looked over at him. "You mean a lot to me."

Nathaniel sipped his beer, studied her. "You're working up to something, Meg. Why don't you just say it?"

"All right. After you left yesterday, I spent a lot of time thinking. About how I'd feel if you didn't come back. I knew there'd be a hole in my life. Maybe I'd be able to fill it again, part of the way, but something would always be missing. When I asked myself what that would be, I kept coming up with the same answer. No matter how many ways I looked at it or juggled it around, the answer never changed."

"So what's the answer, Meg?"

"You, Nathaniel." She leaned over and kissed him. "Just you."

Later, when the sky was dark and the moon floated over the water, she watched the fireworks explode. Color bloomed into color. Waterfalls of glowing sparks rained from sky to water in a celebration of freedom, new beginnings and, Megan thought, hope.

It was a dazzling display that had the children staring upward, wide-eyed and openmouthed. The echoing booms shivered the air until, with a machine-gun crescendo, color and light spewed high in the finale. For a heart-pounding interlude, the sky was bright with golds and reds, blues and blinding whites, circles and spirals, cascades and towers, that shattered into individual stars over the sea.

Long after it was over, the dregs of the party cleared away, the children tucked into bed, she felt the power of the celebration running through her blood. In her own room, she brushed her hair until it flowed over her shoulders. Anticipation vibrating inside her, she belted her borrowed robe loosely at her waist. Quietly she slipped out the terrace doors and walked to Nathaniel's room.

It hadn't taken much pressure to persuade him to stay another night. He'd been tired and aching, and he hadn't relished even the short drive home. But the long soak in the tub hadn't relaxed him, as he hoped. He was still filled with restless urges, and with flashing images of Megan's face, lit with the glow of rockets.

Then he stepped into the bedroom and saw her.

She wore a silky robe of deep blue that flowed down

her body and clung to her curves. Her hair glinted, golden fire, and her eyes were as dark and mysterious as sapphires.

"I thought you could use a rubdown." She smiled hesitantly. "I've had a lot of experience loosening stiff muscles. With horses, anyway."

He was almost afraid to breathe. "Where did you get that?"

"Oh." Self-consciously she ran a hand down the robe. "I borrowed it from Lilah. I thought you'd like it better than terry cloth." When he said nothing, her nerve began to slip. "If you'd rather I go, I understand. I don't expect that you'd feel well enough to—We don't have to make love, Nathaniel. I just want to help."

"I don't want you to go."

Her smile bloomed again. "Why don't you lie down, then? I'll start on your back. Really, I'm good at this." She laughed a little. "The horses loved me."

He crossed to the bed, touched her hair, her cheek. "Did you wear silk robes to work the stock?"

"Always." She eased him down. "Roll onto your stomach," she said briskly. Pleased with the task, she poured liniment into her hands, then rubbed her palms together to warm it. Carefully, so that the movement of the mattress didn't jar him, she knelt over him. "Tell me if I hurt you."

She started on his shoulders, gently over the bruises, more firmly over knotted muscles. He had a warrior's body, she thought, tough and tight, and carrying all the marks of battle.

"You overdid it today."

He only grunted, closing his eyes and letting his body reap the pleasure of her stroking hands. He felt the brush of silk against his skin when she shifted. Drifting through the sharp scent of liniment was her subtle perfume, another balm to the senses.

The aches began to fade, then shifted into a deeper, more primal pain that coursed smoothly through his blood when she lowered her lips to his shoulder.

"Better?" she murmured.

"No. You're killing me. Don't stop."

Her laugh was low and soft as she eased the towel from his hips, and pressed competent fingers low on his spine. "I'm here to make you feel better, Nathaniel. You have to relax for me to do this right."

"You're doing just fine." He moaned as her hands moved lower, circling, kneading. Then her lips, skimming, whisper-soft.

"You have such a beautiful body." Her own breathing grew heavy as she stroked and explored. "I love looking at it, touching it." Slowly she took her lips up his spine, over his shoulder again, to nuzzle at his ear. "Turn over," she whispered. "I'll do the rest."

Her lips were there to meet his when he shifted, to linger, to heat. But when he reached up, groaning, to cup her breasts, she drew back.

"Wait." Though her hands trembled, she freshened the liniment. With her eyes on his, she spread her fingers over his chest. "They put marks on you," she murmured.

"I put more on them."

"Nathaniel the dragon-slayer. Lie still," she whispered, and bent close to kiss the scrapes and bruises on his face. "I'll make it all go away."

His heart was pounding. She could feel it rocket against her palm. In the lamplight, his eyes were dark as smoke. The robe pooled around her knees when she straddled him. She massaged his shoulders, his arms, his hands, kissing the scraped knuckles, laving them with her tongue.

The air was like syrup, thick and sweet. It caught in his lungs with each labored breath. No other woman had ever made him feel helpless, drained and sated, all at once.

"Megan, I need to touch you."

Watching him, she reached for the belt of the robe, loosened it. In one fluid movement, the silk slid from her shoulders. Beneath she wore a short slip of the same color and texture. As he reached up, one thin strap spilled off her shoulder.

She closed her eyes, let her head fall back, as his hands stroked over the silk, then beneath. The colors were back, all those flashing, dazzling lights that had erupted in the sky. Stars wheeled inside her head, beautifully hot. Craving more, she rose over him, took him into her with a delicious slowness that had them both gasping.

She shuddered when he arched up, gripping her hips in his hands. Now the colors seemed to shoot into her blood, white-hot, and her skin grew damp and slick. Suddenly greedy, she swooped down, devouring his lips, fingers clutching the bruised flesh she'd sought to soothe.

"Let me." She moaned and pressed his hands against her breasts. "Let me."

With a wildness that staggered him, she drove him hard, riding him like lightning. He called out her name as his vision dimmed, as the frantic need convulsed like pain inside him. Release was like a whiplash that stung with velvet.

She tightened around him like a fist and shattered him.

Weak as water, she flowed down, rested her head on his chest. "Did I hurt you?"

He couldn't find the strength to wrap his arms around her and let them lie limp on the bed. "I can't feel anything but you."

"Nathaniel." She lifted her head to press a kiss to his thundering heart. "There's something I forgot to tell you yesterday."

"Hmm . . . What's that?"

"I love you, too." She watched his eyes open, saw the swirl of emotion darken them.

"That's good." His arms, no longer weak, circled her, cradled her.

"I don't know if it's enough, but—"

He turned his lips to hers to quiet her. "Don't mess it up. 'For love's sake only,' Megan. That's enough for tonight." He kissed her again. "Stay with me."

"Yes."

Chapter 12

Fireworks were one thing, but when the Calhouns put their heads together planning Coco's engagement party, there promised to be plenty of skyrockets.

Everything from a masked ball to a moonlight cruise had been considered, with the final vote going to dinner and dancing under the stars. With only a week to complete arrangements, assignments were handed out.

Megan squeezed time out of each day to polish silver, wash crystal and inventory linens.

"All this fuss." Colleen thumped her way to the closet where Megan was counting napkins. "When a woman her age straps herself down to a man, she should have the sense to do it quietly."

Megan lost count and patiently began again. "Don't you like parties, Aunt Colleen?"

"When there's a reason for them. Never considered putting yourself under a man's thumb reason to celebrate."

"Coco's not doing that. Dutch adores her."

"Humph. Time will tell. Once a man's got a ring on your finger, he doesn't have to be so sweet and obliging." Her crafty eyes studied Megan's face. "Isn't that why you're putting off that big-shouldered sailor? Afraid of what happens after the 'I-dos'?"

"Of course not." Megan laid a stack of linens aside before she lost count again. "And we're talking about Coco and Dutch, not me. She deserves to be happy."

"Not everybody gets what they deserve," Colleen shot back. "You'd know that well, wouldn't you?"

Exasperated, Megan whirled around. "I don't know why you're trying to spoil this. Coco's happy, I'm happy. I'm doing my best to make Nathaniel happy."

"I don't see you out buying any orange blossoms for yourself, girl."

"Marriage isn't the answer for everyone. It wasn't for you."

"No, I'm too smart to fall into that trap. Maybe you're like me. Men come and go. Maybe the right one goes with the rest, but we get by, don't we? Because we know what they're like, deep down." Colleen eased closer, her dark eyes fixed on Megan's face. "We've known the worst of them. The selfishness, the cruelty, the lack of honor and ethics. Maybe one steps into our lives for a moment, one who seems different. But we're too wise, too careful, to take that shaky step. If we live our lives alone, at least we know no man will ever have the power to hurt us."

"I'm not alone," Megan said in an unsteady voice.

"No, you have a son. One day he'll be grown, and if you've done a good job, he'll leave your nest and fly off to make his own."

Colleen shook her head, and for one moment she looked so unbearably sad that Megan reached out. But the old woman held herself stiff, her head high.

"You'll have the satisfaction of knowing you escaped the trap of marriage, just as I did. Do you think no one ever asked me? There was one," Colleen went on, before Megan could speak. "One who nearly lulled me in before I remembered, before I turned him away, before I risked the hell my mother had known."

Colleen's mouth thinned at the memory. "He tried to break her in every way, with his rules, his money, his need to own. In the end, he killed her, then he slowly, slowly, went mad. But not with guilt. What ate at him, I think, was the loss of something he'd never been able to fully own. That was why he rid the house of every piece of her, and locked himself in his own private purgatory."

"I'm sorry," Megan murmured. "I'm so sorry."

"For me? I'm old, and long past the time to grieve. I learned from my experience, as you learned from yours. Not to trust, never to risk. Let Coco have her orange blossoms, we have our freedom."

She walked away stiffly, leaving Megan to flounder in a sea of emotion.

Colleen was wrong, she told herself, and began to fuss with napkins again. She wasn't cold and aloof and blocked off from love. Just days ago she'd declared her love. She wasn't letting Baxter's shadow darken what she had with Nathaniel.

Oh, but she was. Wearily she leaned against the doorjamb. She was, and she wasn't sure she could change it. Love and lovemaking didn't equal commitment. No one knew that better than she. She had loved Baxter fully, vitally. And that was the shadow. Even knowing that what she felt for Nathaniel was fuller, richer, and much, much truer, she couldn't dispel that doubt.

She would have to think it through, calmly, as soon

as she had time. The answer was always there, she assured herself, if you looked for it long enough, carefully enough. All she had to do was process the data.

She tossed down her neatly counted napkins in disgust. What kind of woman was she? she wondered. She was trying to turn emotions into equations, as if they were some sort of code she had to decipher before she could know her own heart.

That was going to stop. She was going to stop. If she couldn't look into her own heart, it was time to . . .

Her thoughts trailed off, circled back, swooping down on one errant idea like a hawk on a rabbit.

Oh, God, a code. Leaving the linens in disarray, she flew down the hall to her own bedroom.

Fergus's book was where she'd left it, lying neatly on the corner of her desk. She snatched it up and began flipping frantically through pages.

It didn't have to be stock quotations or account numbers, she realized. It didn't have to be anything as logical as that. The numbers were listed in the back of the book, after dozens of blank sheets—after the final entry Fergus had written. On the day before Bianca died.

Why hadn't she seen it before? There were no journal entries, no careful checks and balances after that date. Only sheet after blank sheet. Then the numbers, formed in a careful hand.

A message, Megan wondered, something he'd been compelled to write down but hadn't wanted prying eyes to read. A confession of guilt, perhaps? Or a plea for understanding?

She sat and took several clearing breaths. They were numbers, after all, she reminded herself. There was nothing she couldn't do with numbers.

An hour passed, then two. As she worked, the desk became littered with discarded slips of paper. Each time she stopped to rest her eyes or her tired brain, she wondered whether she had tumbled into lunacy even thinking she'd found some mysterious code in the back of an old book.

But the idea hooked her, kept her chained to the desk. She heard the blast of a horn as a tour boat passed. The shadows lengthened from afternoon toward evening.

She grew only more determined as each of her efforts failed. She would find the key. However long it took, she would find it.

Something clicked, causing her to stop, sit back and study anew. As if tumblers had fallen into place, she had it. Slowly, painstakingly, she transcribed numbers into letters and let the cryptogram take shape.

The first word to form was *Bianca*.

"Oh, God." Megan pressed her hand to her lips. "It's real."

Step by step she continued, crossing out, changing, advancing letter by letter, word by word. When the excitement began to build in her, she pushed it back. This was an answer she would find only with her mind. Emotions would hurry her, cause mistakes. So she thought of nothing but the logic of the code.

The figures started to blur in front of her eyes. She forced herself to close them, to sit back and relax until her mind was clear again. Then she opened them again, and read.

Bianca haunts me. I have no peace. All that was hers must be put away, sold, destroyed. Do spirits walk? It is nonsense, a lie. But I see her eyes, staring at me as she fell. Green as her emeralds. I will leave her a token to satisfy her. And that will be the end of it. Tonight I will sleep.

Breathless, Megan read on. The directions were very simple, very precise. For a man going mad with the enormity of his own actions, Fergus Calhoun had retained his conciseness.

Tucking the paper in her pocket, Megan hurried out. She didn't consider alerting the Calhouns. Something was driving her to finish this herself. She found what she needed in the renovation area in the family wing. Hefting a crowbar, a chisel, a tape measure, she climbed the winding iron steps to Bianca's tower.

She had been here before, knew that Bianca had stood by the windows and watched the cliffs for Christian. That she had wept here, dreamed here, died here.

The Calhouns had made it charming again, with plump, colorful pillows on the window seat, delicate tables and china vases. A velvet chaise, a crystal lamp.

Bianca would have been pleased.

Megan closed the heavy door at her back. Using the tape measure, she followed Fergus's directions. Six feet in from the door, eight from the north wall.

Without a thought to the destruction she was about to cause, Megan rolled up the softly faded floral carpet, then shoved the chisel between the slats of wood.

It was hard, backbreaking work. The wood was old, but thick and strong. Someone had polished it to a fine gleam. She pried and pulled, stopping only to flex her straining muscles and, when the light began to fail, to switch on the lamps.

The first board gave with a protesting screech. If she'd

been fanciful, she might have thought it sounded like a woman. Sweat dripped down her sides, and she cursed herself for forgetting a flashlight. Refusing to think of spiders, or worse, she thrust her hand into the gap.

She thought she felt the edge of something, but no matter how she stretched and strained, she couldn't get a grip. Grimly resigned, she set to work on the next board.

Swearing at splinters and her own untried muscles, she fought it loose. With a grunt, she tossed the board aside, and panting, stretched out on her stomach to grope into the hole.

Her fingertip rang against metal. She nearly wept. The handle almost slipped out of her sweaty hand, but she pulled the box up and free and set it on her lap.

It was no more than a foot long, a foot wide and a few pounds in weight, and it was grimy from the years it had spent in the darkness. Almost tenderly, she brushed away the worst of the dust. Her fingers hovered at the latch, itching to release it, then dropped away.

It wasn't hers to open.

"I don't know where she could be." Amanda strode back into the parlor, tossing up her hands. "She's not in her office, or her room."

"She was fussing in a closet when I saw her last." Colleen tipped back her glass. "She's a grown woman. Might be taking a walk."

"Yes, but . . ." Suzanna trailed off with a glance at Kevin. There was no point in worrying the child, she reminded herself. Just because Megan was never late, that was no reason to assume something was wrong.

"Maybe she's in the garden." She smiled and handed the baby to Holt. "I can go look."

"I'll do it." Nathaniel stood up. He didn't really believe Megan had forgotten their date for dinner and gone walking in the garden, but looking was better than worrying. "If she comes in while I'm gone—" But then he heard her footsteps and glanced toward the doorway.

Her hair was wild, her eyes were wide. Her face and clothes were smeared with dirt. And she was smiling, brilliantly. "I'm sorry I'm late."

"Megan, what on earth?" Dumbfounded, Sloan stared at her. "You look as if you've been crawling in a ditch."

"Not quite." She laughed and pushed a hand through her disordered hair. "I got a little involved, lost track of the time. Sloan, I borrowed some of your tools. They're in the tower."

"In the—"

But she was crossing the room, her eyes on Colleen. She knelt at the old woman's feet, set the box in her lap. "I found something that belongs to you."

Colleen scowled down at the box, but her heart was thrumming in her ears. "Why would you think it belongs to me?"

Gently Megan took Colleen's hand, laid it on the dusty metal. "He hid it under the floor of the tower, her tower, after she died." Her quiet voice silenced the room like a bomb. "He said she haunted him." Megan pulled the transcribed code out of her pocket, set it on top of the box.

"I can't read it," Colleen said impatiently.

"I'll read it for you." But when Megan took the sheet again, Colleen grabbed her wrist.

"Wait. Have Coco come in. I want her here."

While they waited, Megan got up and went to Nathaniel. "It was a code," she told him, before turning to face the room. "The numbers in the back of the book. I don't know why I didn't see it . . ." Then she smiled. "I was looking too hard, too closely. And today I knew. I just knew." She stopped, lifted her hands, let them fall. "I'm sorry. I should have told you as soon as I'd solved it. I wasn't thinking."

"You did what you were meant to do," Lilah corrected. "If one of us was supposed to find it, we would have."

"Is it like a treasure hunt?" Kevin wanted to know.

"Yes." Megan drew him close to ruffle his hair.

"I really don't have time right now, dear." Coco was arguing as Amanda dragged her into the room. "It's the middle of the dinner rush."

"Sit and be quiet," Colleen ordered. "The girl has something to read. Get your aunt a drink," she said to C.C. "She may need it. And freshen mine, while you're at it." She lifted her eyes, bird-bright, to Megan's. "Well, go on. Read it."

As she did, Megan slipped her hand into Nathaniel's. She heard Coco's quick gasp and sigh. Her own throat was raw with unshed tears when she lowered the page again.

"So . . . I went up and I pried up some floorboards. And I found it."

Even the children were silent when Colleen placed her thin hands on the box. They trembled once, then steadied as she worked the latch free, and opened the lid. Now it was her lips that trembled, and her eyes filled. She drew out a small oval frame, tarnished black with age.

"A photograph," she said in a thick voice. "Of my mother with me and Sean and Ethan. It was taken the year before she died. We sat for it in the garden in New York." She stroked it once, then offered it to Coco.

"Oh, Aunt Colleen. It's the only picture we have of all of you."

"She kept it on her dressing table, so that she could look at it every day. A book of poetry." Colleen drew out the slim volume, caressed it. "She loved to read poetry. It's Yeats. She would read it to me sometimes, and tell me it reminded her of Ireland. This brooch." She took out a small, simple enamel pin decorated with violets. "Sean and I gave it to her for Christmas. Nanny helped us buy it, of course. We were too young. She often wore it."

She caressed a marcasite watch, its pin shaped like a bow, and a carved jade dog hardly bigger than her thumb.

There were other small treasures—a smooth white stone, a pair of tin soldiers, the dust of an ancient flower. Then the pearls, an elegant choker of four delicate strands that had slept the decades away in a black velvet pouch.

"My grandparents gave her these as a bridal gift." Colleen ran a fingertip over the smooth orbs. "She told me it would be mine on my wedding day. He didn't like her to wear it. Too plain, he said. Too ordinary. She kept them in the pouch, in her jewel case. She would often take them out and show them to me. She said that pearls given with love were more precious than diamonds given for show. She told me to treasure them as she did, and to wear them often, because—" Her voice broke, and she reached for her glass, sipped to clear her throat. "Because pearls needed warmth."

She closed her eyes and sat back. "I thought he'd sold them, disposed of them with the rest."

"You're tired, Aunt Colleen." Suzanna went quietly to her side. "Why don't I take you upstairs? I can bring you a dinner tray."

"I'm not an invalid." Colleen snapped the words out, but her hand covered Suzanna's and squeezed. "I'm old, but I'm not feeble. I've wit enough to make some bequests. You." She pressed the brooch into Suzanna's hand. "This is yours. I want to see you wear it."

"Aunt Colleen—"

"Put it on now. Put it on." She brushed Suzanna away and picked up the book of poetry. "You spend half your time dreaming," she said to Lilah. "Dream with this."

"Thank you." Lilah bent down, kissed her.

"You'll have the watch," she said to Amanda. "You're the one who's always worrying about what time it is. And you," she continued, looking at C.C. and waving Amanda's thanks away, "take the jade. You like to set things around that gather dust."

Her eyebrow cocked at Jenny.

"Waiting for your turn, are you?"

Jenny smiled guilelessly. "No, ma'am."

"You'll have this." She offered Jenny the stone. "I was younger than you when I gave this to my mother. I thought it was magic. Maybe it is."

"It's pretty." Delighted with her new treasure, Jenny rubbed it against her cheek. "I can put it on my windowsill."

"She'd have been pleased," Colleen said softly. "She kept it on hers." With a harsh cough, she cleared her voice to briskness again. "You boys, take these, and don't lose them. They were my brother's."

"Neat," Alex whispered, reverently holding a perfectly detailed soldier. "Thanks."

"Thanks," Kevin echoed. "It's just like a treasure box," he said, grinning at her. "Aren't you going to give anything to Aunt Coco?"

"She'll have the photograph."

"Aunt Colleen." Overcome, Coco reached for her hankie. "Really, you mustn't."

"You'll take it as a wedding gift, and be grateful."

"I am grateful. I don't know what to say."

"See that you clean that tarnish off the frame." Bracing her weight on the cane, Colleen rose and turned to Megan. "You look pleased with yourself."

Megan's heart was too full for pretense. "I am."

For a moment, Colleen's damp eyes twinkled back. "You should be. You're a bright girl, Megan. And a resourceful one. You remind me of myself, a very long time ago." Gently she picked up the pearls, letting the glowing strands run through her bent fingers.

"Here." Megan stepped toward her. "Let me help you put them on."

Colleen shook her head. "Pearls need youth. They're for you."

Stunned, Megan dropped her hands again. "No, you can't give them away like that. Bianca meant them for you."

"She meant them to be passed on."

"Within the family. They . . . they should go to Coco, or—"

"They go where I say they go," Colleen said imperiously.

"It isn't right." Megan searched the room for help, but found only satisfied smiles.

"It seems perfectly right to me," Suzanna murmured. "Amanda?"

Amanda touched a hand to the watch she'd pinned to her lapel. "Completely."

"Lovely." Coco wept into her hankie. "Just lovely."

"Fits like a glove," C.C. agreed, and glanced at Lilah.

"Destined." She tilted her face up to Max. "Only a fool fights destiny."

"Then we're agreed?" Suzanna took a quick survey and received nods from the men. "The vote's in."

"Ha!" Though she was enormously proud, Colleen scowled. "As if I needed approval to dispose of what's mine. Take them." She thrust them into Megan's hands. "Go upstairs and clean yourself up. You look like a chimney sweep. I want to see you wearing them when you come down."

"Aunt Colleen . . ."

"No blubbering. Do as you're told."

"Come on." Suzanna took Megan's arm to lead her from the room. "I'll give you a hand."

Satisfied, Colleen sat again, thumped her cane. "Well, where's my drink?"

Later, when the waning moon had tipped over the edge of the sea, Megan walked with Nathaniel to the cliffs. The breeze whispered secrets in the grass and teased the wildflowers.

She wore blue, a simple summer dress with a full skirt that swirled in the wind. The pearls, glowing like small, perfect moons, circled her throat.

"You've had quite a day, Megan."

"My head's still spinning. She gave it all away, Nathaniel. I can't understand how she could give away all the things that mattered so much."

"She's a hell of a woman. It takes a special one to recognize magic."

"Magic?"

"My practical, down-to-earth Megan." He tugged on her hand until they sat on a rock together, looking out over the churning water. "Didn't you wonder, even for a moment, why each gift was so perfectly suitable? Why eighty years ago Fergus Calhoun would have been compelled to select just those things to hide away? The flower brooch for Suzanna, the watch for Amanda, Yeats for Lilah and the jade for C.C.? The portrait for Coco?"

"Coincidence," Megan murmured, but there was doubt in her voice.

He only laughed and kissed her. "Fate thrives on coincidence."

"And the pearls?"

"These." He lifted a finger to trace them. "A symbol of family, endurance, innocence. They suit you very well."

"They—I know I should have found a way not to accept them, but when Suzanna put them on me upstairs, they felt as though they were mine."

"They are. Ask yourself why you found them, why, with all the months the Calhouns searched for the emeralds, they never came across a hint of the strongbox. Fergus's book turns up after you move into The Towers. There's a numbered code. Who better to solve it than our logical CPA?"

Megan shook her head and blew out a laughing breath. "I can't explain it."

"Then just accept it."

"A magic rock for Jenny, soldiers for the boys." She rested her head against Nathaniel's shoulder. "I suppose I can't argue with that kind of coincidence. Or fate." Content, she closed her eyes and let the air caress her cheeks. "It's hard to believe that just a few days ago I was frantic with worry. You found him near here, didn't you?"

"Yes." He thought it best for her peace of mind not to mention the dicey climb down to the ledge. "I followed the bird."

"The bird?" Puzzled, she drew back. "That's odd. Kevin told me about a bird. A white one with green eyes that stayed with him that night. He's got a good imagination."

"There was a bird," Nathaniel told her. "A white gull with emerald eyes. Bianca's eyes."

"But—"

"Take magic where you find it." He slipped an arm around her shoulders so that they both could enjoy the sounds of the surf. "I have something for you, Megan."

"Mmm?" She was comfortable, almost sleepy, and she moaned in protest when he shifted away.

Nathaniel reached inside his jacket and drew out a sheaf of papers. "You might have a hard time reading them in this light."

"What's this?" Amused, she took them. "More receipts?"

"Nope. It's a life insurance policy."

"A—For heaven's sake. You shouldn't be carrying

this around. You need to put it in a safe-deposit box, or a safe. Fireproof."

"Shut up." His nerves were beginning to stretch, so he stood, then paced to the edge of the cliff and back. "There's a hospitalization policy, too, my mortgage, a couple of bonds. And a damn Keogh."

"A Keogh." Megan held the papers as if they were diamonds. "You filled out the form."

"I can be practical, if that's what it takes. You want security, I'll give you security. There are plenty of figures there for you to tally."

She pressed her lips together. "You did this for me."

"I'd do anything for you. You'd rather I invest in municipal bonds than slay dragons? Fine."

She stared at him as he stood with the sea and sky at his back, his feet braced as if he were riding the deck of a ship, his eyes lit with a power that defeated the dark. And with bruises fading on his face.

"You faced your dragon years ago, Nathaniel." To keep her hands occupied, she smoothed the papers. "I've had trouble facing my own." Rising, she walked to him, slipped the papers back into his pocket. "Aunt Colleen cornered me today. She said a lot of things, how I was too smart to take risks. How I'd never make the mistake of letting a man be too important. That I'd be better off alone than giving someone my trust, my heart. It upset me, and it frightened me. It took me a while to realize that's just what she'd meant to do. She was daring me to face myself."

"Have you?"

"It's not easy for me. I didn't like everything I saw, Nathaniel. All these years I've convinced myself that

I was strong and self-reliant. But I'd let someone so unimportant shadow my life, and Kevin's. I thought I was protecting my son, and myself."

"You did a hell of a good job, from where I'm standing."

"Too good, in some ways. I closed myself off because it was safer. Then there was you." She reached up to lay a hand on his cheek. "I've been so afraid of what I feel for you. But that's over. I love you, Nathaniel. It doesn't matter if it was magic or fate, coincidence or sheer luck. I'm just glad I found you."

She lifted her face to his, reveled in the freedom of the kiss, the scent of the sea, the promise of his arms.

"I don't need retirement plans and insurance policies, Nathaniel," she murmured. "Not that you don't. It's very important that you . . . Stop laughing."

"I'm crazy about you." Still laughing, Nathaniel scooped her off her feet and swung her in dizzying circles.

"Crazy period." She struggled to catch her breath and clung to him. "We're going to fall off the cliff."

"Not tonight we're not. Nothing can happen to us tonight. Can't you feel it? We're the magic now." He set her on her feet again and held her close, so that even the air couldn't come between them. "I love you, Meg, but damned if I'm going to get down on one knee."

She went very still. "Nathaniel, I don't think—"

"Good. Don't think. Just listen. I've sailed around the world more than once, and seen in a decade more than most people see in their lifetimes. But I had to come home to find you. Don't say anything," he murmured. "Sit."

He led her back to the rock and sat with her. "I have something more for you than paperwork. That was just to smooth the path. Take a look at it," he said as he drew a box from his pocket. "Then tell me it wasn't meant."

With trembling fingers, she opened the box. With a sound of wonder, she lifted her eyes to his. "It's a pearl," she whispered.

"I was going to go for the traditional diamond. Seemed like the right thing. But when I saw this, I knew." He took it out of the box. "Coincidence?"

"I don't know. When did you buy this?"

"Last week. I thought about walking here with you, that first time. The moon and the stars." He studied the ring, the single glowing pearl surrounded by small, bright diamonds. "The moon and the stars," he said again, taking her hands. "That's what I want to give you, Megan."

"Nathaniel." She tried to tell herself it was too fast, too foolish, but the thought wouldn't lodge. "It's lovely."

"It's meant." He touched his lips to hers. "Just as we're meant. Marry me, Megan. Start a life with me. Let me be Kevin's father and make more children with you. Let me grow old loving you."

She couldn't find the logic, or think of all the reasons they should wait. So she answered with her heart. "Yes. Yes to everything." Laughing, she threw her arms around him. "Oh, Nathaniel. Yes, yes, yes . . ."

He squeezed his eyes tight on relief and joy. "You sure you don't want to qualify that?"

"I'm sure. I'm so sure." Drawing back, she held out

her left hand. "Please. I want the moon and the stars. I want you."

He slipped the ring on her finger. "You've got me, sugar."

When he drew her close again, he thought he heard the air sigh, like a woman.

Epilogue

"Mom! We're here!"

Megan glanced up from her desk just as Kevin flew in the office door. She lifted her brow at the suit jacket and tie he wore.

"My, my, don't you look handsome!"

"You said I had to dress up 'cause it's Aunt Colleen's birthday dinner. I guess it's okay." He stretched his neck. "Dad showed me how to tie the tie by myself."

"And you did a fine job." She restrained herself from smoothing and straightening the knot. "How was the tour business today?"

"It was great. Calm seas and a freshening breeze. We sighted the first whale off the port bow."

"Oh, I love that nautical talk." She kissed his nose.

"If I didn't have to go to school, I could work with Dad and Holt every day, and not just on Saturday."

"And if you didn't go to school, you'd never know much more than you do today. Saturdays will have to do." She gave his hair a tug. "Mate."

He'd expected as much. And, really, he didn't mind school. After all, he was a whole year in front of Alex.

He grinned at his mother. "Everybody's here. When are the new babies coming?"

"Mmm . . ." With the Calhoun sisters in varying stages of pregnancy, it was an interesting question. "I'd say on and off starting next month and through the New Year."

He ran a fingertip over the corner of her desk. "Who do you think's going to be first? C.C. or Suzanna?"

"Why?" She glanced up from the ledger, and her eyes narrowed. "Kevin, you are not betting on who has the next baby."

"But, Mom—"

"No betting," she repeated, and smothered a laugh. "Give me just a minute to finish up here, and I'll be along."

"Hurry up." Kevin was bouncing. "The party's already started."

"All right, I'll just—" Just nothing, she thought, and closed the ledger with a snap. "Office hours are over. Let's go party."

"All right!" Grabbing her hand, Kevin hauled her out of the room. "Alex said Dutch made this really big cake and it's going to have about a hundred candles on it."

"Not quite a hundred," Megan said with a laugh. When they neared the family wing, she glanced toward the ceiling. "Honey, I'd better check upstairs first."

"Looking for someone?" Nathaniel came down the steps. There was a twinkle in his eye and a tiny pink bundle in his arms.

"I should have known you'd wake her up."

"She was awake. Weren't you, sugar?" He bent his

head to kiss his daughter's cheek. "She was asking for me."

"Really."

"She can't talk yet," Kevin informed his father. "She's only six weeks old."

"She's very advanced for her age. Smart, like her mama."

"Smart enough to know a sucker when she sees one." They made such a picture, she thought, the big man with a boy at his side and a baby in his arms. Her picture, she thought, and smiled. "Come here, Luna."

"She wants to go to the party, too," Kevin declared, reaching up to stroke a finger over his sister's cheek.

"Sure she does. That's what she told me."

"Oh, Dad."

Grinning, Nathaniel ruffled Kevin's hair. "I could eat a pod of whales, mate. How about you?"

"Aye, aye." Kevin made a dash for the parlor. "Come on, come on, everybody's waiting."

"I've got to do this first." Nathaniel leaned over his daughter to kiss Megan.

"Jeez." With a roll of his eyes, Kevin headed for the noise, and the real fun.

"You're looking awfully pleased with yourself," Megan murmured.

"Why shouldn't I? I've got a beautiful wife, a terrific son, an incredible daughter." He ran his knuckles over Megan's pearl choker. "What else could I ask for? How about you?"

Megan lifted her hand to pull his mouth back to hers. "I've got the moon and the stars."

* * * * *

IRISH REBEL

To Nancy Jackson and Karen Solem, who took a chance on a very green writer and made her part of the Silhouette family.

And to readers who took the story of a young Irish woman into their hearts.

Chapter 1

As far as Brian Donnelly was concerned, a vindictive woman had invented the tie to choke the life out of man so that he would then be so weak she could just grab the tail of it and lead him wherever she wanted him to go. Wearing one made him feel stifled and edgy, and just a little awkward.

But strangling ties, polished shoes and a dignified attitude were required in fancy country clubs with their slick floors and crystal chandeliers and vases crowded with flowers that looked as if they'd been planted on Venus.

He'd have preferred to be in the stables, or on the track or in a good smoky pub where you could light up a cigar and speak your mind. That's where a man met a man for business, to Brian's thinking.

But Travis Grant was paying his freight, and a hefty price it was to bring him all the way from Kildare to America.

Training racehorses meant understanding them, working with them, all but living with them. People were necessary, of course, in a kind of sideways fashion.

But country clubs were for owners, and those who played at being racetrackers as a hobby—or for the prestige and profit.

A glance around the room told Brian that most here in their glittery gowns and black ties had never spent any quality time shoveling manure.

Still, if Grant wanted to see if he could handle himself in posh surroundings, blend in with the gentry, he'd damn well do it. The job wasn't his yet. And Brian wanted it.

Travis Grant's Royal Meadows was one of the top thoroughbred farms in the country. Over the last decade, it had moved steadily toward becoming one of the best in the world. Brian had seen the American's horses run in Kildare at Curragh. Each one had been a beauty. The latest he'd seen only weeks before, when the colt Brian had trained had edged out the Maryland bred by half a neck.

But half a neck was more than enough to win the purse, and his own share of it as trainer. More, it seemed, it had been enough to bring Brian Donnelly to the eye and the consideration of the great Mr. Grant.

So here he was, at himself's invitation, Brian thought, in America at some posh gala in a fancy club where the women all smelled rich and the men looked it.

The music he found dull. It didn't stir him. But at least he had a beer and a fine view of the goings-on. The food was plentiful and as polished and elegant as the people who nibbled on it. Those who danced did so with more dignity than enthusiasm, which he thought was a shame, but who could blame them when the band had as much life as a soggy sack of chips?

Still it was an experience watching the jewels glint

and crystal wink. The head man in Kildare hadn't been the sort to invite his employees to parties.

Old Mahan had been fair enough, Brian mused. And God knew the man loved his horses—as long as they ended by prancing in the winner's circle. But Brian hadn't thought twice about flipping the job away at the chance for this one.

And, well, if he didn't get it, he'd get another. He had a mind to stay in America for a while. If Royal Meadows wasn't his ticket, he'd find another one.

Moving around pleased him, and by doing so, by knowing just when to pack his bag and take a new road, he'd hooked himself up with some of the best horse farms in Ireland.

There was no reason he could see why he couldn't do the same in America. More of the same, he thought. It was a big and wide country.

He sipped his beer, then lifted an eyebrow when Travis Grant came in. Brian recognized him easily, and his wife as well—the Irish woman, he imagined, was part of his edge in landing this position.

The man, Grant, was tall, powerfully built with hair a thick mixture of silver and black. He had a strong face, tanned and weathered by the outdoors. Beside him, his wife looked like a pixie with her small, slim build. Her hair was a sweep of chestnut, as glossy as the coat of a prize thoroughbred.

They were holding hands.

It was a surprising link. His parents had made four children between them, and worked together as a fine and comfortable team. But they'd never been much for public displays of affection, even as mild a one as handholding.

A young man came in behind them. He had the look of his father—and Brian recognized him from the track in Kildare. Brendon Grant, heir apparent. And he looked comfortable with it—as well as the sleek blonde on his arm.

There were five children, he knew—had made it his business to know. A daughter, another son and twins, one of each sort. He didn't expect those who had grown up with privilege to bother themselves overly about the day-to-day running of the farm. He didn't expect that they'd get in his way.

Then she rushed in, laughing.

Something jumped in his belly, in his chest. And for an instant he saw nothing and no one else. Her build was delicate, her face vibrant. Even from a distance he could see her eyes were as blue as the lakes of his homeland. Her hair was flame, a sizzling red that looked hot to the touch and fell, wave after wave, over her bare shoulders.

His heart hammered, three hard and violent strokes, then seemed simply to stop.

She wore something floaty and blue, paler, shades paler than her eyes. What must have been diamonds fired at her ears.

He'd never in his life seen anything so beautiful, so perfect. So unattainable.

Because his throat had gone burning dry, he lifted his beer and was disgusted to realize his hand wasn't quite steady.

Not for you, Donnelly, he reminded himself. Not for you to even dream of. That would be the master's oldest daughter. And the princess of the house.

Even as he thought it, a man with a well-cut suit

and pampered tan went to her. The way she offered her hand to him was just cool enough, just aloof enough to have Brian sneering—which was a great deal more comfortable than goggling.

Ah yes, indeed, she was royalty. And knew it.

The other family came in—that would be the twins, Brian thought, Sarah and Patrick. And a pretty pair they were, both tall and slim with roasted chestnut hair. The girl, Sarah—Brian knew she was just eighteen—was laughing, gesturing widely.

The whole family turned toward her, effectively—perhaps purposely—cutting out the man who'd come to pay homage to the princess. But he was a persistent sort, and reaching her, laid his hand on her shoulder. She glanced over, smiled, nodded.

Off to do her bidding, Brian mused as the man slipped away. A woman like that would be accustomed to flicking a man off, Brian imagined, or reining him in. And making him as grateful as the family hound for the most casual of pats.

Because the conclusion steadied him, Brian took another sip of his beer, set his glass aside. Now, he decided, was as good a time as any to approach the grand and glorious Grants.

"Then she whacked him across the back of his knees with her cane," Sarah continued. "And he fell face first into the verbena."

"If she was my grandmother," Patrick put in, "I'd move to Australia."

"Sure Will Cunningham usually deserves a whack. More than once I've been tempted to give him one myself." Adelia Grant glanced over, her laughing eyes meeting Brian's. "Well then, you've made it, haven't you?"

To Brian's surprise, she held out both hands to him, clasped his warmly and drew him into the family center. "It appears I have. It's a pleasure to see you again, Mrs. Grant."

"I hope your trip over was pleasant."

"Uneventful, which is just as good." As small talk wasn't one of his strengths, he turned to Travis, nodded. "Mr. Grant."

"Brian. I hoped you'd make it tonight. You've met Brendon."

"I did, yes. Did you lay any down on the colt I told you of?"

"On the nose. And since it was at five-to-one, I owe you a drink, at least. What can I get you?"

"I'll have a beer, thanks."

"What part of Ireland are you from?" This was from Sarah. She had her mother's eyes, Brian thought. Warm green, and curious.

"I'm from Kerry. You'd be Sarah, wouldn't you?"

"That's right." She beamed at him. "This is my brother Patrick, and my sister Keeley. Our Brady's already on campus, so we're one short tonight."

"Nice meeting you, Patrick." Deliberately he inclined his head in what was nearly a bow as he turned to Keeley. "Miss Grant."

She lifted one slim eyebrow, the gesture as deliberate as his own. "Mr. Donnelly. Oh, thank you, Chad." She accepted the glass of champagne, touched a hand briefly to the arm of the man who'd brought it to her. "Chad Stuart, Brian Donnelly, from Kerry. That's in Ireland," she added with an irony dry as dust.

"Oh. Are you one of Mrs. Grant's relatives?"

"I don't have that privilege, no. There are a few of

us scattered through the country who are not, in fact, related."

Patrick snorted out a laugh and earned a warning look from his mother. "Well now, we're cluttering up the place as usual. We'll move this herd along to our table. I hope you'll join us, Brian."

"How about a dance, Keeley?" Chad asked, standing at her elbow in a proprietary manner.

"I'd love to," she said absently and stepped forward. "A little later."

"Have a care." Brian put a hand lightly on Keeley's elbow as they walked away. "Or you'll slip on the pieces of the heart you just broke."

She slid a glance over and up. "I'm very surefooted," she told him, then made a point of taking a seat between her two brothers.

Because he'd caught the scent of her—subtle sex, with an overlay of class—*he* made a point of sitting directly across from her. He sent her one quick grin, then settled in to be entertained by Sarah, who was already chattering to him about horses.

She didn't like the look of him, Keeley thought as she sipped her champagne. He was just a little too much of everything. His eyes were green, a sharper tone than her mother's. She imagined he could use them to slice his opponent in two with one glance. And she had a feeling he'd enjoy it. His hair was brown, but anything but a quiet shade, with all those gilded streaks rioting through it, and he wore it too long, so that it waved past his collar and around a face of planes and angles.

A sharp face, like his eyes, one with a faint shadow of a cleft in the chin and a well-defined mouth that struck her as being just a little too sensuous.

She thought he was built like a cowboy—long-legged and rangy, and looking entirely too rough-and-ready for his suit and tie.

She didn't care for the way he stared at her, either. Even when he wasn't looking at her it *felt* as if he were staring. And as if he'd read her thoughts, he shifted his eyes to hers again. His smile was slow, unmistakably insolent, and made her want to bare her teeth in a snarl.

Rather than give him the satisfaction, Keeley rose and walked unhurriedly to the ladies' lounge.

She hadn't gotten all the way through the door when Sarah bulleted in behind her. "God! Isn't he gorgeous?"

"Who?"

"Come on, Keel." Rolling her eyes, Sarah plopped down on one of the padded stools at the vanity counter and prepared to enjoy a chat. "Brian. I mean he is so *hot*. Did you see his eyes? Amazing. And that mouth—makes you just want to lap at it or something. Plus, he's got a terrific butt. I know because I made sure I walked behind him to check it out."

With a laugh, Keeley sat down beside her. "First, you're so predictable. Second, if Dad hears you talk that way, he'll shove the man on the first plane back to Ireland. And third, I didn't notice his butt, or anything else about him, particularly."

"Liar." Sarah propped her elbow on the counter as her sister took out a lipstick. "I saw you give him the Keeley Grant once-over."

Amused, Keeley passed the lipstick to Sarah. "Then let's say I didn't much like what I saw. The rough-edged and proud of it type just doesn't do it for me."

"It sure works for me. If I wasn't leaving for college next week, I'd—"

"But you are," Keeley interrupted, and part of her was torn at the upcoming separation. "Besides that, he's much too old for you."

"It never hurts to flirt."

"And you've made a career of it."

"That's just to balance your ice princess routine. 'Oh hello, Chad.'" Sarah put a distant look in her eye and gracefully lifted a hand.

Keeley's comment was short and rude and made Sarah giggle. "Dignity isn't a flaw," Keeley insisted, even as her own lips twitched. "You could use a little."

"You've got plenty for both of us." Sarah hopped up. "Now I'm going to go out and see if I can lure the Irish hunk onto the dance floor. I just bet he's got great moves."

"Oh, yeah," Keeley muttered when her sister swung out the door. "I bet he does."

Not, of course, that she was the least bit interested.

At the moment she wasn't particularly interested in men, period. She had her work, she had the farm, she had her family. The combination kept her busy, involved and happy. Socializing was fine, she mused. An interesting companion over dinner, great. An occasional date for the theater or a function, dandy.

Anything more, well, she was just too busy to bother. If that made her an ice princess, so what? She'd leave the heart melting to Sarah. But, she decided as she rose, if their father hired Donnelly, she was keeping an eye on him and her guileless sister over the next week.

She'd barely taken two steps out of the lounge when Chad appeared at her side again, asking for a dance. Because the ice princess crack was still on her mind, she offered him a smile warm enough to dazzle his eyes and let him draw her into his arms.

Brian didn't mind dancing with Sarah. It would be a pitiful man who couldn't enjoy a few moments of holding a pretty young girl in his arms and listening to her bubble over about whatever came into her head.

She was a sweetheart as far as he was concerned, miraculously unspoiled and friendly as a puppy. After ten minutes, he knew she intended to study equine medicine, loved Irish music, broke her arm falling out of a tree when she was eight, and that she was an innate and charming flirt.

It was a pure pleasure to dance with Adelia Grant, to hear his own country in her voice and feel the easy welcome of it.

He'd heard the stories, of course, of how she'd come to America, and Royal Meadows, to stay with her uncle Patrick Cunnane, who was trainer in those days for Travis Grant. It was said she'd been hired on as a groom as she had her uncle's gift with horses.

But guiding the small, elegant woman around the dance floor, Brian dismissed the stories as so much pixie dust. He couldn't imagine this woman ever mucking out a stall—any more than he could picture her pretty daughters doing so.

The socializing hadn't been so bad, he acknowledged, and he couldn't say he minded the food, though a man would do better with a good beef sandwich. Still it was plentiful, even if you did have to pick your way through half of it to get to something recognizable.

But despite the evening not being quite the ordeal he'd imagined it would be, he was glad when Travis suggested they get some air.

"You've a lovely family, Mr. Grant."

"Yes, I do. And a loud one. I hope you still have your hearing left after dancing with Sarah."

Brian grinned, but he was cautious. "She's charming—and ambitious. Veterinary medicine's a challenging field, and especially when you specialize in horses."

"She's never wanted anything else. She went through stages, of course," Travis continued as they walked down a wide white stone path. "Ballerina, astronaut, rock star. But under it all, she always wanted to be a vet. I'm going to miss her, and Patrick, when they leave for college next week. Your family will miss you, I imagine, if you stay in America."

"I've been coming and going for some time. If I settle in America, it won't be a problem."

"My wife misses Ireland," Travis murmured. "A part of her's still there, no matter how deep she's dug her roots here. I understand that. But . . ." He paused and in the backwash of light studied Brian's face. "When I take on a trainer, I expect his mind, and his heart, to be in Royal Meadows."

"That's understood, Mr. Grant."

"You've moved around quite a bit, Brian," Travis added. "Two years, occasionally three at one organization, then you switch."

"True enough." Eyes level, Brian nodded. "You could say I haven't found the place that wants to hold me longer than that. But while I'm where I am, that farm, those horses, have all my attention and loyalty."

"So I'm told. The boots I'm looking to fill are big. No one's managed to fill them to my satisfaction since Paddy Cunnane retired. He suggested I take a look at you."

"I'm flattered."

"You should be." Travis was pleased to see nothing more than mild interest on Brian's face. He appreciated a man who could hold his own thoughts. "I'd like you to come by the farm when you're settled."

"I'm settled enough. I prefer moving right along if it's all the same to you."

"It is."

"Fine. I'll come round tomorrow, for the morning workout, and have a look at how you do things, Mr. Grant. After I've seen what you have, and you've heard what I'd have in mind to do about it, we'll know if it works for both of us. Will that suit you?"

Cocky young son of a bitch, Travis thought, but didn't smile. He, too, knew how to hold his thoughts. "It suits me fine. Come on back inside. I'll buy you a beer."

"Thanks just the same, but I think I'll go on back to my hotel. Dawn comes early."

"I'll see you tomorrow." Travis held out a hand, shook Brian's briskly. "I'll look forward to it."

"So will I."

Alone, Brian took out a slim cigar, lighted it, then blew out a long stream of smoke.

Paddy Cunnane had recommended him? The idea of it had both nerves and pleasure stirring in his gut. He'd told Travis he'd been flattered, but in truth, he'd been staggered. In the racing world, that was a name spoken of with reverence.

Paddy Cunnane trained champions the way others ate breakfast—with habitual regularity.

He'd seen the man a few times over the course of years, and had spoken to him once. But even with a well-fed ego, Brian had never thought that Paddy Cunnane had taken notice of him.

Travis Grant wanted someone to fill Paddy's boots. Well, Brian Donnelly couldn't and wouldn't do that. But he'd damn well make his mark with his own, and he'd make sure that would be good enough for anyone.

Tomorrow morning they would see what they would see.

He started down the path again when the light and shadows in front of him shifted briefly. Glancing over, he saw Keeley come out of the glass doors and walk across a flagstone terrace.

Look at her, Brian thought, so cool and solitary and perfect. She was made for moonlight, he decided. Or perhaps it was made for her. What breeze there was fluttered the layers of the filmy blue dress she wore as she crossed over to sniff at the flowers that grew out of a big stone urn in colors of rust and butter.

On impulse, he snapped off one of the late-blooming roses from its bush, and strode onto the terrace. She turned at the sound of his footsteps. Irritation flickered first in her eyes, so quickly here and gone he might have missed it if he hadn't been so focused on her. Then it was smoothed away, coated over with a thin sheen of cool politeness.

"Mr. Donnelly."

"Miss Grant," he said in the same formal tone, then held out the rose. "Those there are a bit too humble for the likes of you. This suits better."

"Really?" She took the rose because it would have been rude not to, but neither looked at it nor lifted it to sniff. "I like simple flowers. But thank you for the thought. Are you enjoying your evening?"

"I enjoyed meeting your family."

Because he sounded sincere she unbent enough to smile. "You haven't met them all yet."

"Your brother in college."

"Brady, yes, but there's my aunt and uncle. Erin and Burke Logan, and their three children, from the neighboring Three Aces farm."

"I've heard of the Logans, yes. Seen them round the tracks a time or two in Ireland. Don't they come to functions here?"

"Often, but they're away just now. If you stay in the area, you'll see quite a bit of them."

"And you? Do you still live at home?"

"Yes." She shifted, glanced back toward the light. "That's why it's home."

Which was where she wanted to be right now, she realized. Home. The thought of going back inside that overwarm and overcrowded room seemed unbearable.

"The music's better from a distance."

"Hmm?" She didn't bother to look at him, wished only that he would go away and give her back her moment of solitude.

"The music," Brian repeated. "It's better when you can barely hear it."

Because she agreed, wholeheartedly, she laughed. "Better yet when you can't hear it at all."

It was the laugh that did it. There'd been warmth then. The way smoke brought warmth even as it clogged your brain. He reached for her before he let himself think. "I don't know about that."

She went rigid. Not with a jerk as many women would, he noted, but by standing so absolutely still she stiffened every muscle.

"What are you doing?"

The words dripped ice, and left him no choice but to tighten his grip on her waist. Pride rammed against pride and the result was solid steel. "Dancing. You do dance, I saw you. And this is a better spot for it than in there, where you're jammed elbow to ass, don't you think?"

Perhaps she agreed. Perhaps she was even amused. Still, she was accustomed to being asked, not just grabbed. "I came out here to get away from the dancing."

"You didn't, no. You came out to get away from the crowd."

She moved with him because to do otherwise was too much like an embrace. And Sarah had been right, he had some lovely moves. Her heels brought her gaze level with his mouth. She'd been right, she decided. Entirely too sensuous. Deliberately she tilted her head back until their eyes met.

"How long have you been working with horses?" It was a safe topic, she thought, and an expected one.

"All my life, one way or another. And you? Are you one for riding, or just for looking from a distance?"

"I can ride." The question irritated her, and nearly had her tossing her collection of blue ribbons and medals in his face. "Relocating, if you do, would mean a big change for you. Job, country, culture."

"I like a challenge." Something about the way he said it, about the way his hand was spread over her back, had her eyes narrowing.

"Those that do often wander off looking for the next when the challenge is met. It's a game, lacking substance or commitment. I think more of people who build something worthwhile where they are."

Because it was no more than the truth, it shouldn't have stung. But it did. "As your parents have."

"Yes."

"It's easy, isn't it, to have that sensibility when you've never had to build something from the ground up with nothing but your own hands and wits?"

"That may be, but I respect someone who digs in for the long haul more than the one who jumps from opportunity to opportunity—or challenge."

"And that's what you think I'm doing here?"

"I couldn't say." She moved her shoulder, a graceful little shrug. "I don't know you."

"No, you don't. But you think you do. The rover with his eye on the prize, and stable dirt under his nails no matter how he scrubs at them. And less than beneath your notice."

Surprised, not just by the words but the heat under them, she started to step back, would have stepped back, but he held her in place. As if, she thought, he had the right to.

"That's ridiculous. Unfair and untrue."

"Doesn't matter, to either of us." He wouldn't let it matter to him. Wouldn't let her matter, though holding her had made him ache with ideas that couldn't take root.

"If your father offers me the job, and I take it, I doubt we'll be running in the same circles, or dancing the same dance, once I'm an employee."

There was anger there, she noted, just behind the vivid green of his eyes. "Mr. Donnelly, you're mistaken about me, my family, and how my parents run their farm. Mistaken, and insulting."

He raised his eyebrows. "Are you cold or just angry?"

"What do you mean?"

"You're trembling."

"It's chilly." She bit off the words, annoyed that he'd upset her enough to have it show. "I'm going back in."

"As you like." He eased away, but kept her hand in his, then angled his head when she tugged at it. "Even the stable boy learns manners," he murmured and walked her to the door. "Thank you for the dance, Miss Grant. I hope you enjoy the rest of your evening."

He knew it could cost him the offer of the job, but he couldn't resist seeing if there was any fire behind that wall of ice. So he lifted her hand, and with his eyes still on hers, brushed his lips over her knuckles. Back, forth, then back again.

The fire, one violent flash of it, sparked. And there it simmered while she yanked her hand free, turned her back on him and walked back into the polished crowd and perfumed air.

Chapter 2

Dawn at the shedrow was one of the magic times, when fog was eating its way along the ground and the light was a paler, purer gray. Music was in the jingle of harness, the dull thud of boot and hoof as grooms, handlers and horses went about their business. The perfume was horses, hay and summer.

Trailers had already been loaded, Brian imagined, and the horses picked by the man Grant had left in charge already gone to track for their workout or preparation for today's race. But here on the farm there was other work to be done.

Sprains to be checked, medication to be given, stalls to be mucked. Exercise boys would take mounts to the oval for a workout, or to pony them around. He imagined Royal Meadows had someone to act as clocker and mark the time.

He saw nothing that indicated anything other than first-class here. There was a certain tidiness not all owners insisted upon—or would pay for. Stables, barns, sheds, all were neatly painted, rich, glossy white with dark green trim. Fences were white too, and in perfect repair. Paddocks and pastures were all as neat as a company parlor.

There was atmosphere as well. It was a clever man, or a rich one, who could afford it. Trees in full leaf dotted the hillside pastures. Brian spotted one, a big beauty of an oak, that rose from the center of a paddock and was fenced around in white wood. In the center grass of the brown oval was a colorful lake of flowers and shrubs. Back away, curving between stables and track, were trim green hedges.

He approved of such touches, for the horses. And for the men. Both worked with more enthusiasm in attractive surroundings in his experience. He imagined the Grants had glossy photos of their pretty farm published in fancy magazines.

Of the house as well, he mused, for that had been an impressive sight. Though it had still been more night than day when he'd driven past it, he'd seen the elegant shape of the stone house with its juts of balconies and ornamental iron. Fine big windows, he thought now, for standing and looking out at a kingdom.

There'd been a second structure, a kind of miniature replica of the main house that had nestled atop a large garage. He'd seen the shapes and silhouettes of flowers and shrubberies there as well. And the big, shady trees.

But it was the horses that interested him. How they were housed, how they were handled. The shedrow—should he be offered this job and take it—would be his business. The owner was simply the owner.

"You'll want a look in the stables," Travis said, leading Brian toward the doors. "Paddy'll be along shortly. Between us we should be able to answer any questions you might have."

He got answers just from looking, from seeing, Brian mused. Inside was as tidy as out, with the sloped concrete floors scrubbed down, the doors of the box stalls of strong and sturdy wood each boasting a discreet brass plaque engraved with its tenant's name. Already stableboys were pitching out soiled hay into barrows or pitching in fresh. The scent of grain, liniment and horse was strong and sweet.

Travis stopped by a stall where a young woman carefully wrapped the foreleg of a bay. "How's she doing, Linda?"

"Coming along. She'll be out causing trouble again in a day or two."

"Sprain?" Brian stepped into the box to run his hands over the yearling's legs and chest. Linda flicked a glance up at him, then over at Travis, who nodded.

"This is Bad Betty," Linda told Brian. "She likes to incite riots. She's got a mild sprain, but it won't hold her back for long."

"Troublemaker, are you?" Brian put his hands on either side of Betty's head, looked her in the eye. A quick, hot thrill raced through him at what he saw. What he sensed. Here, he thought, was magic, ready to spring if only you could find the right incantation.

"It happens I like troublemakers," he murmured.

"She'll nip," Linda warned. "Especially if you turn your back on her."

"You don't want a bite of me, do you, darling?"

As if in challenge, Betty laid her ears back, and Brian grinned at her. "We'll get along, as long as I remember you're the boss." When he ran his fingertips down her neck, back again, she snorted at him. "You're too pretty for your own good."

He murmured to her, shifting without thought to Gaelic as Linda finished the bandage. Betty's ears pricked back up, and she watched him now with more interest than malice.

"She wants to run." Brian stepped back, scanning the filly's form. "Born for it. And more, born to win."

"One look tells you that?" Travis asked.

"It's in the eyes. You won't want to breed this one when she comes into season, Mr. Grant. She needs to fly first."

Deliberately he turned his back, and as Betty lifted her head, he glanced back over his shoulder. "I don't think so," he said quietly. They eyed each other another moment, then Betty tossed her head in the equine equivalent of a shrug.

Amused, Travis moved aside to let Brian out of the box. "She terrorizes the stableboys."

"Because she can, and is likely smarter than half of them." He gestured to the opposite box. "And who's this handsome old man here?"

"That's Prince, out of Majesty."

"Royal Meadows' Majesty?" There was reverence in Brian's voice as he crossed over. "And his Prince. You had your day, didn't you, sir?" Gently Brian stroked a hand down the dignified nose of the aged chestnut. "Like your sire. I saw him race, Mr. Grant, at the Curragh, when I was a lad, a stableboy. I'd never seen his like before, nor since for that matter. I worked with one of the stallions this one sired. He didn't embarrass his breeding."

"Yes, I know."

Travis showed him through the tack room, the breeding shed and birthing stalls, past a paddock where a yearling was going through his paces on a longe line, and then to the oval where a handsome stallion was being ponied around in the company of a well-behaved gelding.

A wiry little man with a blue cap over a white fringe of hair turned as they approached. He had a stopwatch dangling from his pocket and a merry grin on his weathered leprechaun's face.

"So you've had your tour then, have you? And what do you think of our little place here?"

"It's a lovely farm." Brian extended a hand. "I'm pleased to meet you again, Mr. Cunnane."

"Likewise, young Brian from Kerry." Paddy gave Brian's hand a firm shake. "I told them to hold Zeus until you got here, Travis. I thought you and the lad would like a look at his morning run."

"King Zeus, out of Prince," Travis explained. "He's running well for us."

"He took your Belmont Stakes last year," Brian remembered.

"That's right. Zeus likes a long run. Burke's colt snatched the Derby from him, but Zeus came back for the Breeder's Cup. He's a strong competitor, and he'll sire champions."

At Paddy's signal, an exercise boy trotted over mounted on a magnificent chestnut. The horse gleamed dark red in the strengthening sun, with a blaze like a lightning bolt down the center of his forehead. He pranced, sidestepping, head tossing.

Brian knew, at one glance, he was looking at poetry.

"What do you think of him?" Paddy asked.

"Beautiful form" was all Brian said.

Twelve hundred pounds of muscle atop impossibly

long and graceful legs. A wide chest, sleek body, proud head. And eyes, Brian saw, that glinted with ferocious pride.

"Take him around, Bobbie," Paddy ordered. "Don't rate him. We'll let him show off a bit this morning." Whistling between his teeth, Paddy leaned on the fence, pulled out the stopwatch.

With his thumbs hooked in his pockets, Brian watched Zeus trot back onto the track, prance in place until the boy controlled him. Then the rider rose up in the stirrups, leaned over that long, powerful neck. Zeus shot forward, a bright arrow from a plucked bow. Those long legs lifted, stretched, fell, flew, shooting out clumps of dirt like bullets as he rounded the first curve.

The air roared with the thunder.

Inside Brian's chest, his heart beat the same way, at a hard and joyful gallop. The boy's hat flew off as they turned into the backstretch. When they streaked by, Paddy gave a grunt and flicked his timer.

"Not bad," Paddy said dryly and held out the watch.

Brian didn't need to see it. He had a clock in his head, and he knew he'd just watched a champion.

"I think I've seen the like of your Prince at last, Mr. Grant."

"And he knows it."

"You want your hands on that one, boy?" Paddy asked him.

There was a time, Brian thought, to hold your cards close, and a time to lay them out. "I do, yes." Struggling not to dance with eagerness, he turned to Travis again. "If the job's being offered, Mr. Grant, I'll take it."

Travis inclined his head, extended a hand. "Welcome to Royal Meadows. Let's go get some coffee."

Brian simply stared as Travis walked off. "Just like that?" he murmured.

"He'd already made up his mind," Paddy said, "or you wouldn't be here in the first place. Travis doesn't waste time—his or anyone else's. After you're done with your coffee and such, come over to my place—above the garage. You'll want a look at the condition book, and have a little conversation."

"Yes, I will. Thanks." A bit dazed, Brian headed off after Travis.

He caught up, surprised, and a little embarrassed, to find his palms were sweaty. A job was only a job, he reminded himself. "I'm grateful for the opportunity, Mr. Grant."

"Travis. You'll work for it. We have high standards at Royal Meadows. I expect you to meet them. I'd like you to start as soon as possible."

"I'll start today."

Travis glanced over. "Good."

Scanning the area, Brian gestured toward another small building, with the paddock set up with jumps. "Do you train jumpers, show horses, as well?"

"That's a separate enterprise." Travis smiled slightly. "You'll work the racehorses. You can move your things into the trainer's quarters when you're ready." Travis flicked a glance toward the garage house.

Brian opened his mouth—then shut it again. He hadn't expected housing to be part of the package, but wasn't about to argue it away. If it didn't suit him, they'd deal with it later.

"You have a beautiful home. Someone likes their flowers."

"My wife." Travis turned onto a slate path. "She's particularly fond of flowers."

And Brian imagined they had a staff of gardeners, landscapers, whatever it was, to deal with them. "The horses appreciate a pretty setting."

Travis stepped onto a patio, turned. "Do they?"

"They do."

"Did Betty tell you that when you were speaking to her?"

Brian met Travis's amused eyes levelly. "She indicated she was a queen and expected to be treated as such."

"And will you?"

"I will, until she abuses the privilege. Even royalty needs a bit of a yank now and again."

So saying, he stepped through the door Travis held open.

Brian didn't know what he'd been expecting. Something sleek and sophisticated. Something grand, certainly.

He hadn't been expecting to walk into the Grants' kitchen, nor to find it big and cluttered and despite the gleam of snazzy appliances and fancy tiles, homey.

Certainly the last thing he'd expected was to see the lady of the manor herself in an old pair of jeans, bare feet and a faded T-shirt standing at the stove with a skillet while she rang a peal over the head of her youngest son.

"And I'll tell you another thing, Patrick Michael Thomas Cunnane, if you think you can come and go at all hours as you damn please just because you're going off to college, you'd best get that thick head of yours examined in a hurry. I'll be happy to do it myself, with the skillet I have in my hand, just as soon as I'm done with it."

"Yes, ma'am." At the table Patrick sat with his shoulders hunched, wincing at his mother's back. "But since you're using it, maybe I could have some more French toast. Nobody makes it like you do."

"You won't get around me that way."

"Maybe I will."

She shot a look over her shoulder that Brian recognized as one only a mother could conjure to wither a child.

"And maybe I won't," Patrick muttered, then brightened when he saw Brian at the door. "Ma, we've got company. Have a seat, Brian. Had breakfast? My mother makes world-famous French toast."

"Witnesses won't save you," Adelia said mildly, but turned to smile at Brian. "Come in and sit. Patrick, get Brian and your father plates."

"No, thank you. There's no need to trouble."

"Ma, I can't find my brown shoes." Sarah came bursting in. "Hello, Brian, morning, Dad."

"Sure I had my eyes right on them for weeks," Adelia said as she flipped sizzling bread in the pan. "I can't think how those shoes slipped out of my sight."

Sarah rolled her eyes and yanked open the refrigerator. "I'm going to be late."

"You could wear one of the other six thousand pairs of shoes jammed in your closet," her brother suggested.

Sarah rapped him on the back with the carton of juice she held and otherwise ignored him. "I don't have time for breakfast." She poured juice, glugged it down. "I'll be home by five."

"Take a muffin," Adelia ordered.

"We don't have any blueberry."

"Take what we do have."

"Okay, okay." She grabbed a muffin off a plate, gave her mother a smacking kiss on the cheek, rounded the table to give her father one in turn, crossed her eyes at her brother, then dashed out again.

"Sarah works at the vet's office during the summer," Adelia explained. "The pair of you wash up here now, and we'll get you something hot to eat."

Since the scent of that fried bread was impossible to resist, Brian started toward the sink. And saw the huge old dog stretched out by the stove. He resembled a long, black and outrageously shaggy floor mat.

"And who's this?" Automatically Brian crouched down.

"That's our Sheamus. He's an old man now, and likes to tuck himself at my feet while I'm cooking."

"My wife's fond of mutts," Travis said as he ran water in the sink.

"And they of me. He spends most of his time sleeping," she told Brian. "And isn't much for anyone but family now." Even as she said it her brows rose up. Brian had no more than stroked the old dog's head before Sheamus opened his eyes, thumped his ragged tail, and with a moan rolled over onto his back for a belly rub.

"Would you look at that? He's taken to you."

"Well mutts and I, we understand each other. You're a good old boy, aren't you? Fat and happy."

"Someone feeds him table scraps." Adelia slanted a look at her husband.

"I don't know what you're talking about." All innocence, Travis held out the soap when Brian stood up again.

"Hah" was all she said to that. "Would you have coffee, Brian, or tea?"

"Tea, thank you."

"Sit." She pointed to a chair, then shifted the finger to her son. "You, go. I'll finish with you later."

"I'll be at the stables, doing penance." With a heavy sigh, Patrick rose, then he wrapped his arms around his mother's waist, laid his chin on top of her head. "Sorry."

"Get."

But Brian saw her lay a hand over Patrick's, and squeeze. With a quick grin tossed to the room in general, he bolted.

"That boy's responsible for every other line on my face," Adelia muttered.

"What lines?" Travis asked, and made her laugh.

"That's the right answer. So, Brian, does Royal Meadows suit you?"

After drying his hands, he crossed to the table to sit. "Yes, ma'am."

"Oh, we're not so very formal around here. You don't have to ma'am me. Unless you're in trouble." She poured tea for him, and coffee for Travis, then stayed where she was, her free hand resting on her husband's shoulder.

"How did Zeus do this morning?"

"Took the oval in a minute-fifty flat."

"I'm sorry I missed it." She turned back to the stove to heap golden bread onto a platter.

"I'll offer you a one-year contract," Travis began.

"Can't you let the boy eat before you talk business?"

"The boy wants to know."

Brian took the platter, transferred three slices to his plate. "Yes, he does."

"You'll have a guaranteed annual salary." Travis named an amount that had Brian struggling not to bobble the syrup. "And, after two months, a two-percent share of each purse. In six months, we'll renegotiate that percentage."

"We'll negotiate it up." Steady again, Brian cut into his breakfast. "Because I promise you, I'll have earned it."

They discussed—haggled a bit for form sake—responsibilities, benefits, bonuses, duties.

Brian was on his second serving of toast, and Travis the last of his coffee, when Keeley came in.

She wore buff colored jodhpurs. Elegant and form-fitting. Her high black boots were shined like dark mirrors. Her white blouse draped soft with its wide collar buttoned high. She had tamed her hair into a sleek twist that left her face unframed. Small, complicated twists of gold glinted at her ears.

Her brow lifted at the sight of Brian eating breakfast in her kitchen, and her mouth thinned before it moved into a cool, practiced smile. "Good morning, Mr. Donnelly."

"Miss Grant."

"I'm pressed for time this morning." She walked to her father, bent down, rubbed her cheek against his.

"You should eat," her mother told her.

"I'll get something later." She went to the refrigerator, took out a soft drink. "I'll be done in a couple of hours." She went to her mother, bending first to scratch Sheamus on the top of the head, then in the same manner she'd used with her father, rubbed cheeks with Adelia before she headed out the back door.

"I'll come down in a bit," Adelia called after her. "I'd like to watch."

Twenty minutes later, Brian walked from the house toward the trainer's quarters. He saw Keeley in the paddock in front of the small building. She sat astride a black gelding. As she walked the horse, a man photographed her from various angles.

Brian paused to watch, hands on hips. She was getting her picture in some fancy magazine, he imagined. Royal Meadows Princess. No doubt she'd look fine and glossy in it.

She set the horse into a trot, then a canter, swinging in to sail over a jump. Brian's lips pursed. She had good form, he had to admit it. When she repeated that jump, then another, for the camera, he heard her laugh float out over the air.

He turned away, dismissing her. Trying to.

He climbed the stairs to the trainer's quarters, knocked.

"Come in, and welcome. In here," Paddy called out.

He sat at a desk in a room set up as an office. File cabinets lined one wall, and photographs of horses lined them all. The window was open, and on a shelf beside it sat a computer. If the dust on its cover was any indication, it was rarely, if ever, used.

Paddy's glasses balanced on the end of his nose as he gestured to a chair. "You and Travis worked out your details."

"We did. He's a fair man."

"Did you expect otherwise?"

"I don't expect anything from owners, and that way they don't often surprise me."

With a chuckle Paddy shoved up his glasses, scratched his nose. "This one might."

"I want to thank you for putting my name in so Mr. Grant would consider me."

"I've kept my eye and ear on things, though I've retired. Well, retired twice now, if the truth be known, and come out of it again as Travis and Dee haven't been satisfied with the trainers who've come along. This time I mean it to stick. I mean you to stick, boy."

When his glasses slid down again, Paddy grunted in annoyance and took them off. "We'll be bunking here together, if you have no objection, for the next week. After that, I'll be off, and the place is yours."

"Where are you going?"

"Home. Back to Ireland."

"After all these years?"

"I was born there. I've a mind to die there—though I've life left in me, no mistake. I've a yearning to spend the last years of it at home."

"What'll you do there?"

"Oh, go to the pub to tell lies," Paddy said with a twinkling grin. "Drink a pint of decent Guinness. You'll miss that here, I can tell you. It's just not the same built out of a Yank tap."

Brian had to laugh. "It's a long way to go for a pint, even for Guinness."

"Well now, there's a little farm in the south of Cork, not far from Skibbereen. Do you know Skibbereen, Brian?"

"Aye. It's a pretty town."

"Sloping streets and painted doorways," Paddy said, a bit dreamily. "Well, the farm's a bit of a ways from that pretty town. My Dee was raised there, by my sister after Dee's parents died. When my sister got sickly, the farm fell on hard times with Dee trying to run it and tend to her aunt Lettie. In the end, Lettie passed and the farm was lost, and Dee came here to me. A few years ago, the farm came up for sale, and though she told him not to, Travis bought it for her. The man knows her heart."

"So that's where you're going?" Brian asked, though he didn't have a clue why Paddy was telling him. "To be a farmer?"

"That's where I'm going, but I don't think I'll make much of a farmer. I'll have myself a few horses for company."

He shifted, turned his gaze to the window and the hills beyond where horses grazed in the late-morning sunshine.

"I'll miss my little Dee, and Travis, and the children. The friends I've made here. But I've a need to go. An itch, if you follow me."

"I do." There was little Brian understood more than an itch to be going.

"I imagine I'll be flying back and forth across the pond quite a bit—and they'll come to me as well. I've seen Dee married to a man I respect, and love like my own son. I've watched her children grow into fine young men and women. That's a rare thing. And I've had a hand in turning out champions. A man who has a thoroughbred put into his hands is a fortunate man."

"Have you no wish for your own place, your own champions?"

"I toyed with it—but in the end no, it wasn't for me." He turned his attention back to Brian. "Is that what you're after in the end?"

"No. Your own place means you're rooted, doesn't it? And there's no moving on if moving on strikes you. In any case, most owners leave the work and the decisions to the trainer, so you don't own, but you run."

"Travis Grant knows how to work." Paddy inclined his head. "He knows his horses. He loves them. If you earn his trust, he'll trust you, but he'll know every move you make. He's not one for strolling into the winner's circle after the day is done. Shedrow business will be his business, and Dee's, as much as it is yours. Whether you like it or not."

"His wife?"

Amused now, Paddy sat back. "You met her last night when she was done up fancy. I like seeing her looking fine that way. You're more like to see her down in the stables lancing an abscess or soothing a colicky mare. She's no delicate flower. My Dee's a thoroughbred. And she's bred true. Not one of her children would back away from a hard day's work when it's needed. You'll learn for yourself how things go around here, and you'll find it's not such a far distance from main house to shedrow as it is in some places."

"It's usually better all around if it is," Brian muttered, and Paddy cackled with laughter.

"Right you are, lad, in most cases. Owners can be a fly in your ointment without a doubt. You'll make up your own mind about this place, and these owners. And I hope you'll let me know what you think after a bit of time's passed. Now, let's take a look at the condition book to start off."

When Brian left Paddy, he was satisfied with the world in general. Or what, he thought as he trooped down the stairs, was soon to become his world in general. He'd make his mark at Royal Meadows, and live well doing it. His quarters were first-rate. The truth was, he'd have been willing to live in a hovel for the chance to work with Travis Grant's stable.

Everything he'd ever wanted was at his fingertips. He didn't intend to let it slip through.

He turned toward the stables where he'd parked his rental car. Paddy had told him to have a look at the little red lorry down that way, as he'd be selling it before leaving for Ireland. If the thing ran, it would do, Brian thought. He didn't require anything but the most elemental means of transportation. And time to get used to driving on the wrong damn side of the road.

As he rounded the garage he was scowling over that one sticking point, and nearly ran into Keeley.

She looked as fresh and perfect as she had that morning. Not a hair out of place, not a speck of dust on her boots. He wondered how the hell she managed it.

"Good day to you, Miss Grant. I saw you in the paddock earlier. That's a fine horse."

She was hot, irritable and very close to flash point since the photographer had hit on her. The photo shoot had been necessary. She needed the exposure, the publicity, but she damn well didn't need the hassle.

"Yes, he is." She made to move by, and Brian shifted to block her.

"Begging your pardon, princess. Did I neglect to pull my forelock?"

She held up a hand. Her temper was a vile thing when loose, and the drumming in her head warned her it was very close to springing free.

"I'm already annoyed. It won't take much to push

me to furious." But she drew a deep breath. If the scene in the kitchen earlier meant anything, Brian Donnelly was now part of Royal Meadows. She didn't make a habit of sniping at a member of the team.

"Sam's a nine-year-old. Hunter. A thoroughbred, Irish Draught horse cross. I've had him since he was four." She lifted the bottle she carried and sipped her soft drink.

"Is that all you put in you?" He tapped a finger on the bottle. "Bubbles and chemicals?"

"You sound like my mother."

"Maybe that's why you have a headache."

Keeley dropped the hand she'd pressed to her temple. Those eyes of his, she thought, were entirely too keen. "I'm fine."

"Turn around."

"I beg your pardon."

Brian merely stepped around her, laid his hands on the nape of her neck. Her already stiff shoulders jerked in protest. "Relax. I'm not after grabbing you in a fit of passion when any member of your family might come along. I'd like to put in at least one day on the job before I get the boot."

As he spoke he was kneading, pressing, running those strong fingers over the knots. He hated seeing anything in pain. "Blow out a breath," he ordered when she stood rigid as stone. "Come on, *maverneen,* don't be so hardheaded. Blow out a nice long breath for me."

Out of curiosity she obeyed and tried not to think how marvelous his hands felt on her skin.

"Now another."

His voice had gone to croon, lulling her. As he worked,

murmured, her eyes fluttered closed. Her muscles loosened, the knots untied. The threatening throbbing in her head faded away. She all but slid into a trance.

She arched against his hands, just a little. Moaned in pleasure. Just a little. He kept his hands firm, professional, even as he imagined skimming them down over her, slipping them under that soft white blouse. He wanted to touch his lips to her nape, just where his thumb was pressing. To taste her there.

And that, he knew, would end things before they'd begun. Wanting a woman was natural. Taking one, where the taking held such risks, was suicide.

So he let his hands drop away, stepped back. She nearly swayed before she caught herself. When she turned toward him, it felt almost like floating. "Thank you. You're very good at that."

Magic hands, she thought. The man had magic in his hands.

"So I've been told." He shot her a cocky grin. "I've a feeling you need regular loosening up." He snatched the bottle out of her hand. "Go drink some water, and change. You're dressed too warmly for the heat of the day."

She angled her head and was just annoyed enough now to give him a long, thorough look. His hair, all that mass of gold streaked brown, was windblown. That wonderfully sculpted mouth just quirked at the corners.

"Any other orders?"

"No, but an observation."

"I'm fascinated."

"No, you're irritated again, but I'll tell you anyway.

Your mouth's more appealing naked as it is now than when it's painted as it was this morning."

"So you don't approve of lipstick?"

"Not at all. Some women need it. You don't, so it's just a distraction."

Baffled, nearly amused, she shook her head. "Thanks so much for the advice." She started for the house—where she'd been going to change into something cooler in the first place.

"Keeley."

She stopped, but instead of turning merely glanced over her shoulder to where he stood, thumbs in the pockets of ancient jeans. "Yes?"

"It's nothing. I just wanted to try out your name. I like it."

"So do I. Isn't that handy?"

This time he blew out a breath as she strode off—long legs in tight pants and tall boots. He lifted her soft drink, took a deep sip. Playing with fire with that one, Donnelly, he warned himself. Since he was damned sure singed fingers wouldn't be all he would get if he risked a touch, it was best to back away before the heat became too tempting to resist.

Chapter 3

"Heels down, Lynn. Good. Hands, Shelly. Willy, pay attention." Keeley scanned each one of her afternoon students' form. They were coming along.

Six horses mounted with six children circled the paddock at a sedate walk. Two months before three of those children had never seen a horse firsthand, much less ridden one. Royal Meadows Riding Academy had changed that. It was making a difference.

"All right. Trot. Heads up," she ordered, hands on hips as she watched her students change gaits with varying degrees of success. "Heels down. Knees, Joey. That's the way. You're a team, remember. Looking good. Much better."

She moved closer, tapped the heels of one of her two boys. He grinned and turned them down. Oh, yes, much better, she thought. A month before Willy had jerked like a puppet every time she'd touched him.

It was all about trust.

She had them change leads, reverse, then attempt a wide figure eight.

It was a little messy, but she let them giggle their way through it.

It was also all about fun.

Brian watched her from a distance. He hadn't seen her for a couple of days. Nearly all of his time had been spent at the stables, or at one of the tracks where the Grants' horses ran. Apparently Keeley didn't spend much time at any of those locations.

He'd looked for her.

And had assumed she whiled away her time having lunch in some trendy spot, or shopping. Having her hair done or her fingernails painted. Whatever it was rich daughters did with their days.

But here she was, circling the paddock with a bunch of kids, obviously instructing them. He supposed it was a kind of hobby, teaching the privileged children of country club parents how to ride in proper English style.

Hobby or not, she looked good doing it. She'd chosen an informal look of jeans and a cotton shirt the color of blueberries. She'd pulled her hair back in some sort of band so that it fell in a wildly curling ponytail. Her boots appeared old, scuffed and serviceable.

She seemed to be enjoying herself. He didn't believe he'd seen her smile like that before. Not so quick and open and warm. Unable to resist, he walked closer as she stopped one of her students, stroked a hand over the horse's neck as she and the little girl had what appeared to be an earnest conversation.

By the time he'd reached the fence, Keeley had lined up all but the girl. Teaching them to control their mounts, he decided, to keep them quiet while something was going on around them.

The single rider posted prettily around the paddock, while Keeley turned a circle to keep her in sight. And circling, she saw Brian leaning on the fence.

The smile vanished, and he thought that was a true shame. But there was something almost as appealing about that cool, suspicious look she often aimed in his direction. He answered it with a grin, and settled in to watch the rest of the lesson.

Keeley didn't mind an audience. Often her parents or one of her siblings or one of the hands stopped by to watch. She'd certainly carried on her lessons with a parent or two of a student looking on. But since she didn't care for this particular observer, she ignored him.

One by one she selected a student to go through the day's routine solo. She corrected form, encouraged, pushed a little when it was needed for more effort or concentration. When she called for dismount, every one of them groaned.

"Five more minutes, Miss Keeley. Can't we ride for five more minutes?"

"I already let you ride five more minutes." She patted Shelly's knee. "Next week we're going to try a canter."

"I'm getting a horse for Christmas," Lynn announced. "And next spring, my mother says we'll enter shows."

"Then you'll have to work very hard. Cool off your mounts."

"That's a fine-looking group you have there. Miss Keeley."

Ingrained manners had her acknowledging Brian, walking over to the fence as she kept her eye on her students. "I like to think so."

"That boy there?" He nodded toward the dark-eyed,

thin-faced Willy. "He's in love with that horse. Dreams of him at night, of racing over fields and hills and adventuring."

It made her smile again. "Teddy loves him, too. Teddy Bear," she explained. "A big, gentle sweetheart."

"This lot's lucky to have the wherewithal for lessons with a good instructor, and smart mounts. You stable them here? I haven't seen any of these down in my area."

"They're mine. I stable them here." Her horses, her school, her responsibility. "Excuse me. The lesson's not over until the horses are groomed."

Here's your hat, what's your hurry? Brian thought. Well, he had a few things to see to. But that didn't mean he couldn't wander back this way in a bit.

He bothered her. There was no real explanation for it, Keeley thought. It just was. She didn't like the way he looked at her. And why was she the only one who seemed to notice that edge in his eyes when they landed on her?

She didn't like the way he talked to her. And again, she seemed to be the only one aware of that sly little lilt in his voice when he said her name.

Everyone else thought Brian Donnelly was just dandy, she mused as she ran her hands up a gelding's legs to check for heat. Her parents considered him the perfect man to replace Uncle Paddy—and Uncle Paddy had nothing but praise for him.

Sarah thought he was hot. Patrick thought he was cool. And Brendon thought he was smart.

"Outnumbered," she muttered, and lifted the horse's foreleg to check the hoof.

Maybe it was some chemical reaction. Something that caused her hackles to rise when he was in the vicinity. After all, he appeared to be perfectly competent in his work. More than, she admitted, from what she'd heard. And as they were both busy, they would rarely bump up against each other. So it shouldn't matter.

But she didn't like the fact that she was avoiding the stables and shedrow. That she was deliberately foregoing the pleasure of wandering down that way and watching the workouts, or lending a hand in grooming. She didn't like knowing that about herself.

She certainly didn't care for the fact that she suspected *he* knew it. Which gave him entirely too much importance.

Which, she admitted, she was doing even now just by thinking of him.

The horse wickered. Keeley's shoulders stiffened.

"You've a good eye for horses," Brian said.

It didn't surprise her that she hadn't heard him come in. And it didn't surprise her that despite not hearing she'd known he was there. The air changed, she thought, when he was in it.

"I come by it naturally."

"You do. Teddy Bear." He murmured it, causing her to look up as she lowered the gelding's leg. His eyes were on the horse's, his skilled and clever hands already moving over head and throat. Keeley heard the gelding blow out a soft breath. Pure pleasure.

"You've a kind and patient heart, don't you?" Brian moved into the box, those wide palmed hands still skimming, stroking, checking. "And a fine broad back for carrying small, dreamy boys. How long have you had him?"

She blinked, nearly flushed. There was something

hypnotic about those hands, about that voice. "Nearly two years."

Brian ran his hands down the flank. Stopped. His eyes narrowed as he stepped closer and examined a crosshatch of scarring. "What's this?" But he knew, and turned on Keeley so quickly she backed up to the wall before she could stop herself. "This horse has been whipped, and whipped bloody."

"His previous owner," she said, icily as a defense against that first spurt of alarm, "had a heavy hand with a whip. He wanted to show Teddy, but Teddy shied at the jumps. This was his way of showing he was the boss."

"Bloody bastard." And though his eyes still glinted with heat, his voice went soft again. "You're in a better place now, aren't you, boy. A fine home with a pretty woman to rub you down. Rescued him, did you?" he said to Keeley.

"I wouldn't go that far. There are different methods of breaking a horse. I don't happen to—"

"I don't break horses." Brian ducked under Teddy's belly, then his eyes met Keeley's over the wide back. "I make them. Any idiot can use a bat or a whip and break both spirit and heart. It takes skill and patience and a gentle hand to make a champion, or even just a friend."

She waited a moment, surprised her knees wanted to shake. "Why do you expect me to disagree with you?" she wondered aloud. She stepped out of the box, moved to the next.

The aging mare greeted her with a snort and a bump of head on shoulder. Keeley snatched up a body brush to finish off her student's sketchy grooming.

"I can't stand seeing anything mistreated." Brian spoke quietly from behind her. Keeley didn't turn, didn't answer. Now that the first spurt of anger had passed, he had just enough room for shame at the way he'd turned on her. "Especially something that has so little choice. It makes me sick, and angry."

"And you expect me to disagree, again?"

"I snapped at you. I'm sorry." He touched a hand to her shoulder, left it there even when she stiffened—as he would with a nervous horse. "You look into eyes like that one has over there, and you see inside them that huge, generous heart. Then the scars where someone beat him—because he could. It scrambles my brain."

With an effort she relaxed her shoulders. "It took me three months to get him to trust me enough not to shy every time I lifted my hand. One day, he stuck his head out when I came in and called to me the way they do when they're happy to see you. I fed him carrots and cried like a baby. Don't tell me about mistreatment and scrambled brains."

Shame wasn't something he felt often, but it was easy to recognize. He took a deep breath and hoped to start again. "What's this pretty mare's story?"

"Why do you think there's a story? She's a horse. You ride her."

"Keeley." He laid a hand over hers on the brush. "I'm sorry."

She moved her hand, but gave in and rested her cheek on the mare's neck. Rubbing, Brian noted, as she did when she hugged her parents.

"Her crime was age. She's nearly twenty. She'd been left stabled, and neglected. She was covered with nettle rash and lice. Her people just got bored with her, I suppose."

He didn't think when he stroked her hair. His hands were as much a part of his way of communicating as his voice. "How many do you have?"

"Eight, counting Sam, but he's too much for the students at this point."

"And did you save them all?"

"Sam was a gift for my twenty-first birthday. The others . . . well, when you're in the center of the horse world, you hear about horses. Besides, I needed them for the school."

"Some would expect you to stock thoroughbreds."

"Yes." She shifted. "Some would. Sorry, I have to feed the horses, then I have paperwork."

"I'll give you a hand with the feeding."

"I don't need it."

"I'll give you one anyway."

Keeley moved out of the box, rested a hand on the door. Best, she decided, to deal with this clean and simple. "Brian, you're working for my family, in a vital and essential role, so I think I should be straight with you."

"By all means." The serious tone didn't match the glint in his eye as she leaned back.

"You bother me," she told him. "On some level, you just bother me. It's probably because I just don't care for cocky, intense men who smirk at me, but that's neither here nor there."

"No, that's here and it's there. What kind do you care for?"

"You see—that's just the sort of thing that annoys me."

"I know. It's interesting, isn't it, that I find myself compelled to do just the thing that gets a rise out of you? You bother me as well. Perhaps it's that I don't care for regal, cool-eyed women who look down their lovely noses at me. But here we are, so we should try getting on as best we can."

"I don't look down my nose at you, or anyone."

"Depends on your point of view, doesn't it?"

She turned on her heel and marched away, focusing intensely on measuring out grain.

"Why don't we talk of something safe?" he suggested. "Like what I think about Royal Meadows. I've worked on farms and around tracks since I was ten. Stableboy, exercise boy, groom. Working my way up, hustling my way through. Twenty years means I've seen all sides of training, racing and breeding. The bright and the dark. And in twenty years, I've never seen brighter than Royal Meadows."

She paused, and her gaze shifted to his face before she began to add supplements to the grain.

"To my way of thinking, there aren't many people as worthy as one good horse. Your parents are admirable people. Not just for what they have, but much more for what they've done, and what they do with it. I'm honored to work for them. And," he said when she turned to him again, "they're lucky to have me."

She laughed. "Apparently they agree with you." Shaking her head, she moved by to start the feeding, and as she passed him he breathed in the scent of her hair, of her skin.

"But you're not sure you do. Though you don't seem to have much interest in the workings of the farm itself."

"Don't I?"

He studied the neatly typed list on the wall that

indicated which supplements in what amounts were added for each particular horse for the evening feed. "I see your sisters and your brothers on a daily basis," he commented as he began to fix Teddy's meal. "Everyone in your family, down at the shedrow, or at the track, but you."

She could have told him the time and placement of every horse they'd run that past week. Which were being medicated, which mares were breeding. Pride kept her silent. She preferred thinking of it as pride, and not sheer stubbornness.

"I suppose your little school keeps you busy."

Her teeth clamped together, wanted to grind, but she spoke through them. "Oh, yes, my little school keeps me busy."

"You're a good teacher." He moved to Teddy's box.

"Thank you so much."

"No need to be snotty about it. You are a good teacher. And one of those rich kids might stick it out, rather than getting bored once horse fever's passed."

"One of my rich kids," she murmured.

"It takes skill, endurance, and money, doesn't it, to compete in horse shows. I don't follow show jumping myself, though I've found it pretty enough to watch. You might be training yourself a champion. The Royal International or Dublin Grand Prix. Maybe the Olympics."

"So, let's see if I get this. Rich kids compete in horse shows and win blue ribbons and those who aren't so privileged do what? Become grooms?"

"That's how the world works, doesn't it?"

"That's how it can work. You're a snob, Brian."

He looked up, flabbergasted. "What?"

"You're a snob, and the worst kind of snob—the kind who thinks he's broad-minded. Now that I know that, you don't bother me at all."

The stable phone rang, delighting her. Whoever was on the other end not only had perfect timing but they had her gratitude. It gave her great pleasure to see the absolute shock on Brian's face as she walked to the phone.

"Royal Meadows Riding Academy. Would you hold one moment, please." With a friendly smile, she laid a hand over the receiver. "Really, I can finish up here. I'm keeping you from your work."

"I'm not a snob," he finally managed to say.

"Of course you wouldn't see it that way. Can we discuss this another time? I need to take this call."

Irked, he shoved the scoop back in the grain. "I'm not the one wearing bloody diamonds in my ears," he muttered as he stalked out.

It put him out of humor for the rest of the day. It stuck in his craw and festered there. A nasty little canker sore on the ego.

Snob? Where did the woman get off calling him a snob? And after he'd made the effort to be friendly, even compliment her on her snooty little riding academy.

He did the evening check himself, as was his habit, and spent considerable time going over the prime filly who was to head down to Hialeah to race there. Travis wanted Brian to go along for this one, and he was more than happy to oblige.

It would do him a world of good to put a thousand miles or so between himself and Keeley.

"Shouldn't be looking in that direction, even for a

blink," he muttered, then nuzzled the filly. "Especially when I've got a darling like you in hand. We'll have us a time in Florida, won't we, you and me?"

"Poker game tonight," one of the grooms called out as Brian left the stables. He added an eyebrow wiggle and a grin to the announcement.

"I'll be back then. And it'll be my pleasure to empty your pockets." But for now, he thought, he had paperwork of his own.

When he returned from Florida they'd separate the foals from their mothers. The weanlings would cause a commotion the first day or so. And the yearling training would begin in earnest. He had charts to make, schedules to outline, plans to ponder.

And he wanted to put a great deal of personal time into the forming of Bad Betty.

He had no business detouring toward Keeley's stable. Still it would only take a minute, Brian told himself, to set the woman straight.

But instead of Keeley, he found her sister. Sarah stopped her dash past him and waved. "Hi. Wonderful evening, isn't it? I'm going to take advantage of it and sneak in a ride before sunset. Want to join me?"

It was tempting. She was good company, and he hadn't felt a horse under him in weeks. But there was work. "I'd love to, another time. You riding one of Keeley's?"

"Yeah. She's always up for someone to exercise one of her babies. The kids don't give them much of a workout, so they can get stale. Or bored. Her Saturday class is a little more advanced, but still."

He fell into step beside her. "I don't suppose an hour of posture and posting does much for the horses."

"Oh, she lets them out to pasture, and rides herself

whenever she can fit it in. Which isn't as much as she'd like, but the kids are the priority. And that hour of posture and posting does a lot for them."

He made a noncommittal sound as they rounded the building. He hoped Keeley was still inside what he supposed was an office. He wanted a word with her. "I saw part of her class today."

"Did you? Aren't they cute? Today's what . . . oh, yeah, Willy. Did you notice the little guy, dark hair and eyes? He rides Teddy."

"Aye. He has good form, and he's cheerful about it."

"He is now. He was a scared little rabbit when Keeley took him on." Sarah swung into the stables, headed directly for the tack room.

"Afraid of horses?"

"Of everything. I don't know how people can do that to a child. I'll never understand it."

"Do what?"

She chose her tack, murmuring a thanks when Brian took the saddle from her. "Hurt them." She glanced back. "Oh, I thought since you'd seen the class, Keeley would have told you the whole deal about the school."

"No." He took the saddle blanket as well. "We didn't get to that. Why don't you tell me the whole deal?"

"Sure." She went to the old mare, cooed. "There's my girl. Want to go for a ride? Sure you do." She slipped the bridle on, fixed the bit, then led the mare out. "I don't know if it started with the horses or the kids. It all seemed to happen at the same time. She bought Eastern Star first. He was a thoroughbred, five years old, and he hadn't lived up to his potential. According to the owners. They pumped him up before a race."

"Drugged him."

"Amphetamines." Her pretty face went hard. "They got caught, but they'd damaged Star's heart and kidneys in the process. She bought him. We nursed him, did everything we could. He didn't last a year. It still gets me," Sarah murmured.

She shook her head and began to saddle her mount. "After that it was like a mission to Keeley. So I guess the horses came first. She put this place together, and got the word out that she was opening a small academy. The ones who can pay, pay a very stiff fee to have her teach their kids—and she's worth it. Those stiff fees help subsidize the other students."

"What other students?"

"Ones like Willy." Sarah cinched the saddle, checked the stirrups. "Underprivileged, abused, circling the system kids. She takes them for nothing—no, she hunts them up, sponsors them, outfits them, works with a child psychologist. It's why she doesn't have as much time to ride as she used to. Our Keeley doesn't do anything halfway. She'd take more on, but she wants to keep the classes small so each kid gets plenty of attention. So she's campaigning for other academies, other owners to start similar programs."

Sarah patted the mare's neck. "I'm surprised she didn't mention it. She rarely misses an opportunity to talk someone into getting involved."

With a cheerful smile, she vaulted into the saddle. "Listen, would you like to come up for dinner? I hear Dad's grilling chicken."

"Thanks all the same, but I've plans. Enjoy your ride."

He had plans all right, he thought as Sarah trotted off. To eat crow. He wasn't sure what it tasted like, but he already knew he wasn't going to enjoy it.

He walked around to the office, knocked. He supposed if he'd been wearing a hat, he'd have held it in his hands. When she didn't answer, he opened the door, glanced in.

Neat, organized, as expected. The air smelled of her—just the faintest echo of scent.

But everything inside was designed for business. A desk—with a computer he imagined was a great deal more in use than Paddy's—a two-line telephone and a little fax machine. File cabinets, two trim chairs and a small fridge. Curious, he walked in and opened it. Then had to grin when he saw it was stocked with bottles of the soft drink she seemed to live on.

A scan of the walls had the grin turning to a wince. Blue ribbons, medals, awards were all neatly framed and displayed. There were photographs of her in formal riding gear flying over jumps, smiling from the back of a horse or standing with her cheek pressed to her mount's neck.

And in a thick frame was an Olympic medal. A silver.

"Well, hell. We'll make that two portions of crow," he murmured.

Chapter 4

It was his fault. She could put the blame for this entirely on Brian Donnelly's shoulders. If he hadn't been so insufferable, if he hadn't been there *being* insufferable when Chad had called, she wouldn't have agreed to go out to dinner. And she wouldn't have spent nearly four hours being bored brainless when she could've been doing something more useful.

Like watching paint dry.

There was nothing wrong with Chad, really. If you only had, say, half a brain, no real interest outside of the cut of this year's designer jacket and were thrilled by a rip-roaring debate over the proper way to serve a triple latte, he was the perfect companion.

Unfortunately, she didn't qualify on any of those levels.

Right now he was droning on about the painting he'd bought at a recent art show. No, not the painting, Keeley thought wearily. A discussion of the painting, of art, might have been the medical miracle that prevented her from slipping into a coma. But Chad was discoursing—no other word for it—on The Investment.

He had the windows up and the air conditioning blasting as they drove. It was a perfectly beautiful night, she mused, but putting the windows down meant Chad's hair would be mussed. Couldn't have that.

At least she didn't have to attempt conversation. Chad preferred monologues.

What he wanted was an attractive companion of the right family and tax bracket who dressed well and would sit quietly while he pontificated on the narrow areas of his interest.

Keeley was fully aware he'd decided she fit the bill, and now she'd only encouraged him by agreeing to this endlessly tedious date.

"The broker assured me that within three years the piece will be worth five times what I paid for it. Normally I would have hesitated as the artist is young and relatively unknown, but the show was quite successful. I noticed T.D. Giles considering two of the pieces personally. And you know how astute T.D. is about such things. Did I tell you I ran into his wife, Sissy, the other day? She looks absolutely marvelous. The eye tuck did wonders for her, and she tells me she's found the most amazing new stylist."

Oh God, was all Keeley could think. Oh God, get me out of here.

When they swung through the stone pillars at Royal Meadows, she had to fight the urge to cheer.

"I'm so glad our schedules finally clicked. Life gets much too demanding and complicated, doesn't it? There's nothing more relaxing than a quiet dinner for two."

Any more relaxed, Keeley thought, and unconsciousness would claim her. "It was nice of you to ask me, Chad." She wondered how rude it would be to spring out of the car before it stopped, race to the house and do a little dance of relief on the front porch.

Pretty rude, she decided. Okay, she'd skip the dance.

"Drake and Pamela—you know the Larkens of course—are having a little soirée next Saturday evening. Why don't I pick you up at eightish?"

It took her a minute to get over the fact he'd actually used the word *soirée* in a sentence. "I really can't, Chad. I have a full day of lessons on Saturday. By the time it's done I'm not fit for socializing. But thanks." She slid her hand to the door handle, anticipating escape.

"Keeley, you can't let your little school eclipse so much of your life."

Her hand stiffened, and though she could see the lights of home, she turned her head and studied his perfect profile. One day, someone was going to refer to the academy as *her little school,* and she was going to be very rude. And rip their throat out. "Can't I?"

"I'm sure it amuses you. Hobbies are very satisfying."

"Hobbies." She bared her teeth.

"Everyone needs an outlet, I suppose." He lifted a hand from the wheel and gracefully waved away over two years of hard work. "But you must take time for yourself. Just the other day Renny mentioned she hadn't seen you in ages. After all, when the novelty wears off, you'll wonder where all this time has gone."

"My school is not a hobby, an amusement, or a novelty. And it is completely my business."

"Naturally. Of course." He gave her a patronizing little pat on the knee as he stopped the car, shifted toward her. "But you must admit, it's taking up an inordinate amount of your time. Why it's taken us six months to have dinner together."

"Is that all?"

He misinterpreted the quiet response, and the gleam in her eyes. And leaned toward her.

She slapped a hand on his chest. "Don't even think about it. Let me tell you something, pal. I do more in one day with my school than you do in a week of pushing papers in that office your grandfather gave you between your manicures and amaretto lattes and soirées. Men like you hold no interest for me whatsoever, which is why it's taken six months for this tedious little date. And the next time I have dinner with you, we'll be slurping Popsicles in hell. So take your French tie and your Italian shoes and stuff them."

Utter shock had him speechless as she shoved open her door. As insult trickled in, his lips thinned. "Obviously spending so much time in the stables has eroded your manners, and your outlook."

"That's right, Chad." She leaned back in the door. "You're too good for me. I'm about to go up and weep into my pillow over it."

"Rumor is you're cold," he said in a quiet, stabbing voice. "But I had to find out for myself."

It stung, but she wasn't about to let it show. "Rumor is you're a moron. Now we've both confirmed the local gossip."

He gunned the engine once, and she would have sworn she saw him vibrate. "And it's a British tie."

She slammed the car door, then watched narrow-eyed as he drove away. "A British tie." A laugh gurgled up, deep from the belly and up into the throat so she had to stand, hugging herself, all but howling at the moon. "That sure told me."

Indulging herself in a long sigh, she tipped her head back, looked up at the sweep of stars. "Moron," she murmured. "And that goes for both of us."

She heard a faint *click,* spun around and saw Brian lighting a slim cigar. "Lover's spat?"

"Why yes." The temper Chad had roused stirred again. "He wants to take me to Antigua and I simply have my heart set on Mozambique. Antigua's been done to death."

Brian took a contemplative puff of his cigar. She looked so damn beautiful standing there in the moonlight in that little excuse of a black dress, her hair spilling down her back like fire on silk. Hearing her long, gorgeous roll of laughter had been like discovering a treasure. Now the temper was back in her eyes, and spitting at him.

It was almost as good.

He took another lazy puff, blew out a cloud of smoke. "You're winding me up, Keeley."

"I'd like to wind you up, then twist you into small pieces and ship them all back to Ireland."

"I figured as much." He disposed of the cigar and walked to her. Unlike Chad, he didn't misinterpret the glint in her eye. "You want to have a pop at someone." He closed his hand over the one she'd balled into a fist, lifted it to tap on his own chin. "Go ahead."

"As delightful as I find that invitation, I don't solve my disputes that way." When she started to walk away, he tightened his grip. "But," she said slowly, "I could make an exception."

"I don't like apologizing, and I wouldn't have to—again—if you'd set me straight right off."

She lifted an eyebrow. Trying to free herself from that big, hard hand would only be undignified. "And are you referring to my little school?"

"It's a fine thing you're doing. An admirable thing, and not a little one at all. I'd like to help you."

"Excuse me?"

"I'd like to give you a hand with it when I can. Give you some of my time."

Off balance, she shook her head. "I don't need any help."

"I don't imagine you do. But it couldn't hurt, could it?"

She studied him with equal parts suspicion and interest. "Why?"

"Why not. You'll admit I know horses. I have a strong back. And I believe in what you're doing."

It was the last that cut through her defenses. No one outside of family had understood what she wanted to do as easily. She flexed her hand in his, and when he released her, stepped back. "Are you offering because you feel guilty?"

"I'm offering because I'm interested. Feeling guilty made me apologize."

"You haven't apologized yet." But she smiled a little as she began to walk. "Never mind. I might be able to use a strong back from time to time." She glanced over as he fell into step beside her. It looked like he had one, she mused, skimming her gaze over the rough jeans and plain white T-shirt he wore.

A strong, healthy body, good hands and an innate understanding of horses. She could do a great deal worse, she supposed. "Do you ride?"

"Well, of course I ride," he began, then caught her smirky little smile. "Having me on again, are you?"

"That one was easy." She turned to wander along a path that meandered through late-blooming shrubs and an arbor of gleaming moonflowers. "I won't pay you."

"I've a job, thanks."

"The kids handle a lot of the chores," she told him. "It's part of the package. This isn't just about teaching them to post and change leads at a canter. It's about trust—in themselves, in their horse, in me. Making a connection with their horse. Shoveling manure makes quite a connection."

He grinned. "I can't argue with that."

"Still they're kids, so fun is a big part of the program. And they're learning so they don't always do the best job mucking out or grooming. And there isn't always enough time to have them deal properly with the tack."

"I started my illustrious career with a pitchfork in my hand and saddle soap in my pocket."

Idly he tugged a white blossom from the vine, tucked it into her hair. The gesture flustered her—the easy charm of it—and made her remember they were walking in the moonlight, among the flowers.

Not, she reminded herself, a good idea.

"All right then. If and when you've time to spare, I've got an extra pitchfork."

When she veered toward the house he took her hand again. "Don't go in yet. It's a pretty night and a shame to waste it with sleeping."

His voice was lovely, with a soothing lilt. There was no reason she could think of why it made her want to shiver. "We both have to be up early."

"True enough, but we're young, aren't we? I saw your medal."

Distracted, she forgot to pull her hand away. "My medal?"

"Your Olympic medal. I went looking for you in your office."

"The medal lures parents who can afford the tuition."

"It's something to be proud of."

"I am proud of it." With her free hand she brushed her hair as the breeze teased it. Her fingertips skimmed over the soft petals of the flower. "But it doesn't define me."

"Not like, what was it? A British tie?"

The laugh got away from her, and eased the odd tension that had been building inside her. "Here's a surprise. With a great deal of time and some effort, I might begin to like you."

"I've plenty of time." He released her hand to toy with the ends of her hair. She jerked back. "You're a skittish one," he murmured.

"No, not particularly." Usually, she thought. With most people.

"The thing is, I like to touch," he told her and deliberately skimmed his fingers over her hair again. "It's that . . . connection. You learn by touching."

"I don't . . ." She trailed off when those fingers ran firmly down the back of her neck.

"I've learned you carry your worries right there, right at the base there. More worries than show on your face. It's a staggering face you have, Keeley. Throws a man off."

The tension was slipping away from under his fingers as he touched her, and building everywhere else.

A kind of gathering inside her, a concentration of heat. The pressure in her chest was so sudden and strong it made her breath short. The muscles in her stomach began to twist, tighten. Ache.

"My face doesn't have anything to do with what I am."

"Maybe not, but that doesn't take away the pure pleasure of looking at it."

If she hadn't trembled, he might have resisted. It was a mistake. But he'd made them before, would make them again. There was moonlight, and the scent of the last of summer's roses in the air. Was a man supposed to walk away from a beautiful woman who trembled under his hand?

Not this man, he thought.

"Too pretty a night to waste it," he said again, and bent toward her.

She jerked back when his mouth was a whisper from hers, but his fingers continued to play over her neck, keeping her close. His gaze dropped to her lips, lingered, then came back to hers.

And he smiled. *"Cushla machree,"* he murmured, and as if it were an incantation, she slid under the spell.

His lips brushed hers, wing-soft. Everything inside her fluttered in response. He drew her closer, gradually luring her body to fit against his, curves to angles, as his hand played rhythmically up and down her spine.

A light scrape of teeth, and her lips parted for him.

Her head went light, her blood hot, and her body seemed balanced on the brink of something high and thin. It was lovely, lovely to feel this soft, this female, this open. She brought her hands to his shoulders, clung there while she let herself teeter on that delicious edge.

He knew how to be gentle, there had always been gentleness inside him for the fragile. But her sudden and utter surrender to him, to herself, had him forcing back the need to grab and plunder. Resistance was what he'd expected. Anything from cool disdain to impulsive passion he would have understood. But this... giving destroyed him.

"More," he murmured against her mouth. "Just a little more." And deepened the kiss.

She made a sound in her throat, a low purr that slipped into his system like silk. His heart shook, then it stumbled, then God help him, it fell.

The shock of it had him yanking her back, staring at her with the edgy caution of a man suddenly finding himself holding a tiger instead of a kitten.

Had he actually thought it a mistake? Nothing more than a simple mistake? He'd just put the power to crush him into her hands.

"Damn it."

She blinked at him, struggling to catch up with the abrupt change. His face was fierce, and the hands that had shifted to her arms no longer gentle. She wanted to shiver, but wouldn't permit another show of weakness.

"Let me go."

"I didn't force you."

"I didn't say you did."

Her lips still throbbed from the pressure of his, and her stomach quaked. Rumor was she was cold, she thought dimly. And she'd believed it herself. Finding out differently wasn't cause for celebration. But for panic.

"I don't want this." This vulnerability, this need.

"Neither do I." He released her to jam his hands into his pockets. "That makes this quite the situation."

"It's not a situation if we don't let it be one." She wanted to rub a hand over her heart, to hold it there. It amazed her that he couldn't hear it hammering. "We're both grown-ups, able to take responsibility for our own actions. That was a momentary lapse on both our parts. It won't happen again."

"And if it does?"

"It won't, because each of us have priorities and a . . . situation would complicate matters. We'll forget it. Good night."

She walked to the house. She didn't run, though part of her wanted to. And another part, a part that brought her no pride, simply wanted him to stop her.

He'd hoped the time away in Florida with work at the center of his world would help him do just what she'd said to do. Forget it.

But he hadn't, and couldn't, and finally decided it had been a ridiculous thing for her to expect. Since he was suffering, he saw no reason why he should let her off so damn easy.

He knew how to handle women, he reminded himself. And princess or not, Keeley was a woman under it all. She was going to discover she couldn't swat Brian Donnelly aside like a pesky fly.

He walked up from the stables, his bag slung over his shoulder. He'd yet to go to his quarters, and had slept very little on the drive back from Hialeah. He could have flown back, but the choice to stay with the horses and make the drive had been his.

His horses had done all he'd asked of them, made

him proud at heart and plumper in the pocket. Seeing that they were delivered home and settled back again was the least he could do.

But right now he wanted nothing more than a hot shower, a shave and a decent cup of tea.

Though he'd have traded all of that for one more taste of Keeley.

Knowing it irritated him had him scowling in the direction of her paddock. The minute he was cleaned up, he promised himself, the two of them would have a little conversation. Very little, he decided, before he got his hands on her again. And when he did, he was going to—

The erotic image he conjured in his head burst like a bubble when he rounded the house and saw Keeley's mother kneeling at the flower bed.

It was not the most comfortable thing to come across the mother when you'd been picturing the daughter naked. Then Adelia looked over at him, and he saw the tears on her cheeks. And his mind went blank.

"Ah . . . Mrs. Grant."

"Brian." Sniffling, she wiped her cheeks with the back of her hand. "I was doing some weeding. Just tidying up the beds here." She tugged at the cap on her head, then she lowered her hands, dropped back on her heels. "I'm sorry."

"Ah . . ." Said that already, he thought, panicked. Say something else. He was never so helpless as he was with female tears.

"I'm missing Uncle Paddy. He left yesterday." She didn't quite muffle a sob. "I thought if I came by here and fiddled, I'd feel some better, but it's knowing he's not down at the stables, or up there. I know he had to go. I know he wanted to go. But . . ."

"Ah . . ." Oh hell. Frantic, Brian dug in his back pocket for his bandanna. "Maybe you should . . ."

"Thanks." She took the cloth as he crouched beside her. "You'll know what it's like, I think, being away from family."

"Well, mine's not close, so to speak."

"Family's family." She dried her face, blew out a breath.

She looked so young, he thought, and not like a mother at all, with her cap crooked on her head and her eyes drenched. He did what came natural for him, and took her hand.

For a moment, she leaned her head on his shoulder, sighed. "He changed everything for me, Paddy did, when he brought me here. I was so nervous coming all this way. New place, new people. A new country. And I hadn't seen Paddy outside pictures for years, or even been face-to-face since I was a baby, but as soon as I saw him, it was all right again. I don't know what I'd have done without him."

It loosened the fist around her heart to talk. Soothed her that he gave her the quiet that was an offer to listen.

"I didn't want to blubber in front of Travis and the children because they're missing him, too. And I was holding on pretty well until I came down here. This is where I lived when I first came to Royal Meadows. In a pretty room with green walls and white curtains. I was so young."

"I guess you're old and decrepit now," Brian said and was relieved when she laughed.

"Well, perhaps not quite decrepit, but I was greener then. I'd never seen a place like this in all my life, and I was going to be living right in the middle of it thanks to Paddy. If it hadn't been for him, I don't think Travis would ever have taken the likes of me on as a groom."

"A groom." Brian's brows lifted. "I thought that was a made-up story."

"Indeed it's not," she said with some heat—and an unmistakable touch of pride. "I earned my keep around here, make no mistake. I was a damn fine groom in my time. Majesty was mine."

Brian lowered himself until he was sitting on the ground beside her. "You groomed Majesty?"

"That I did, and was there to watch him take the Derby. Oh, I loved that horse. You know what it's like."

"I do, yes."

"We lost him only last year. A fine long life he had. I think that was when Paddy decided it was time for him to go home again. He's there by now, and I know what he sees when he stands out in front of the house, and that's a comfort. As you've been just now, Brian. Thank you."

"I didn't do anything. I fumble with tears."

"You listened." She handed him back his bandanna.

"Mostly because tears render me speechless. You've a bit of garden dirt here."

Keeley came down the path just in time to see Brian gently wipe her mother's face with a blue bandanna. The tearstains had her leaping forward like a mama bear to her threatened cub.

"What is it? What did you do?" Hissing at Brian, she wrapped an arm around Adelia's shoulder.

"Nothing. I just knocked your mother down and kicked her a few times."

"Keeley." With a surprised laugh, Adelia patted her

daughter's hand. "Brian's done nothing but lend me his hankie and his shoulder while I had a little cry over Uncle Paddy."

"Oh, Mama." Keeley pressed her cheek to Adelia's, rubbed. "Don't be sad."

"I have to be, a little. But I'm better now." She leaned over, surprising Brian with a kiss on the cheek. "You're a nice young man, and a patient one."

He got to his feet to help her up. "I don't have much of a reputation for either, Mrs. Grant."

"That's because not everyone looks close enough. You should be able to call me Dee easy enough now that I've cried on you. I'm going down to the stables, do some work."

"She never cries," Keeley murmured when her mother walked away. "Not unless she's very happy or very sad. I'm sorry I jumped at you that way, but when I saw she'd been crying, I stopped thinking."

"Tears affect me much the same way, so we'll let it be."

She nodded, then cast around for something to say that would help relieve the awkwardness. She'd been so sure she'd be controlled and composed when she saw him again. "So, I heard you did well at Hialeah."

"We did. Your Hero runs particularly well in a crowd."

"Yes, I've seen him. He lives to run." She noted the bag Brian had set down. "And here you are not even really back yet, and you've had one woman crying on your shoulder and another swiping at you. I really am sorry."

"Sorry enough to make me some tea while I clean up?"

"I . . . all right, but I've got less than an hour."

"Takes a good deal less to brew a pot of tea." Satisfied, he started up the steps. "You've a class this afternoon then?"

"Yes." Trapped, Keeley shrugged and followed him up and inside. He'd been kind to her mother, she reminded herself. She was obliged to repay that. "At three-thirty. I have some things to do before the students arrive."

"Well, I won't be long. You know where the kitchen is, I expect."

She frowned after him as he strolled off into the bedroom.

Making him cozy pots of tea wasn't how she'd expected to handle the situation, she thought. She'd given it a great deal of consideration and had decided the best thing all around would be to maintain a polite, marginally friendly distance. That business the other night had been nothing but a moment's foolishness. Harmless.

Incredible.

She gave herself a shake and got down the old teapot Paddy had favored. No, it was nothing to worry about. In fact, on one level she really should be grateful to Brian. He'd shown her she wasn't as indifferent to men as she'd believed. It had bothered her a little that she'd never felt that spark so many of her friends had spoken of.

Well, she'd certainly felt a whole firestorm of sparks when he'd put his hands on her. And that was good, that was healthy. Someone had finally caught her at the right time and the right place and the right mood. If it could happen once, it could happen again.

With someone else, of course. When she decided it was time.

She set the tea aside to steep, then opening a cupboard stretched high for a cup.

"I'll get that." He moved in behind her, handily trapping her between his body and the counter. Closed his hand over hers on the cup.

She could smell the shower on him, feel the heat of it. And her mouth went dry.

"I decided I don't care to forget it."

She had to concentrate on regulating her breathing. "I beg your pardon?"

"And that I'm not going to let you forget it, either."

She needed to swallow, but her throat wouldn't cooperate. "We agreed—"

"No, we didn't." He brought the cup down, set it aside. "We agreed we didn't want this." The ponytail she wore left a lovely curve of her neck bare. He nuzzled there. "And I'd say there's been an unspoken agreement that despite that, we want each other."

The firestorm was back, a burst at the base of her neck that showered heat down her spine. "We don't know each other."

"I know how you taste." He nipped lightly at flesh. "And feel, and smell. I see your face in my mind whether I want to or not." He spun her around, and his eyes were dark and restless. "Why should you have a choice when I don't?"

His mouth crushed down on hers, a hot and dangerous thrill. With his hands gripped in her hair, he pressed his body to hers.

And this time she felt as much anger as passion in the embrace. Now, wrapped around the thrill, was a thin snake of fear. The combination was unbearably exciting.

"I'm not ready for this." She struggled back. "I'm not ready for this. Can you understand?"

"No." But he understood what he saw in her eyes. He'd frightened her, and he'd no right to do so. "But then again, I don't want to." So he backed away. "Your mother said I was a patient man. I can be, under some circumstances. I'll wait, because you'll come to me. There's something alive between us, so when you're ready, you'll come to me."

"There's a thin line between confidence and arrogance, Brian. Watch your step," she suggested as she started for the door.

"I missed you."

Her hand closed over the knob, but she couldn't turn it. "You know all the angles," she murmured.

"That may be true. But still I missed you. Thanks for the tea."

She sighed. "You're welcome," she said, and left him.

Chapter 5

Bad Betty had more than earned her name. She didn't just make trouble, she looked for it. Nothing seemed to please her more than nipping at grooms. Unless it was kicking exercise boys. She chased other yearlings when out in pasture, then reared and kicked and snorted bad-temperedly when it was time to be stabled for the night.

For all those reasons, and more, Brian adored her.

There was a communal sigh of relief in the shedrow when he opted to deal with her personally. She tested him, and though she rarely got by Brian's guard he had an impressive rainbow of bruises with her name on them.

There were mutters that she was a man-eater, but Brian knew better. She was a rebel. And she was a winner. It was only a matter of teaching her how to start winning without damaging that wild spirit.

On the longe line he circled her into a walk while she pretended to ignore him. Still, when he spoke to her, her ears twitched, and now and then she sent him a sidelong glance. And days of hard work were rewarded when he lengthened the line and she broke into a canter.

"Ah, that's the way. What a beauty you are." He'd liked to have captured that moment—the gorgeous filly cantering gracefully in a circle, while green hills rolled up to a blue sky.

It would make a picture, and look to some like a frolic. But those who knew would see this moment—a racehorse learning to take commands from signals transmitted through her mouth—was another step toward the finish line.

He saw one more thing as he looked at her, as he studied lines and form and that unmistakable gleam in her eyes.

He saw his destiny.

"We'll go, you and I," he said quietly. "We were meant to go together. Rebels we are, or so people say who can't see where we're headed. We've races to win, don't we?"

He shortened the line, and she dropped into a trot. Shortened it still further and her gait changed to a walk. Sweat gleamed on her coat, trickled down his back. Summer wasn't just clinging to September. It was pummeling it.

They ignored the heat, and watched each other.

Again and again he used the line to signal her as she circled, and all the while he praised her.

Watching was irresistible. She had work to do, chores piled up. But if she couldn't take a few moments out on a brilliant September day to watch a little magic, what was the point?

She leaned on the paddock fence, enjoying the view

as Brian put Betty through her paces. Her father had been right in hiring him, she thought. There was a connection between man and horse that was stronger, and even more tangible than the line between them. She could feel it. Amusement, affection, challenge.

This wasn't something that could be taught. It simply was.

She knew Brian took time for every weanling on the farm when he wasn't out of town at a race. That wasn't an easy task in an operation as large as Royal Meadows. But it was the kind of touch that made a difference. A smart and caring horseman knew that the more a horse was handled, touched, communicated with during its youth, the better it would respond to later training.

"Looks good, doesn't she?" Brian said as he let out the line for one last canter.

"Very. You've made considerable progress with her."

"We've made progress with each other, haven't we *a ghra*. She's ready to feel a rider on her."

Knowing Betty's reputation, Keeley tucked her tongue in her cheek. "And who are you bribing—or threatening—to get up on her?"

Gradually Brian shortened the line, and Betty moved into an even trot. "Want the job?"

"I have a job, thanks." But it was tempting.

Brian knew when a seed planted needed to be left alone to sprout. "Well, she'll have her first weight on her tomorrow morning." He shortened the line again, moving Betty toward him, and both of them toward Keeley.

He liked the look of her there against the fence, with

her hair as glossy as the filly's coat, and her eyes as cautious. "This one won't be placid and eager to please. But she'll come round, won't you, *maverneen?*"

He stroked the filly's neck, and she sniffed at the pouch on his belt, then turned her head away.

"She wants to let me know she doesn't care that I've apples in here. No, doesn't matter a bit to her." He looped the line around the fence and took an apple and his knife from his pocket. Idly he cut it in half. "Maybe I'll just offer this token to this other pretty lady here."

He held out the apple to Keeley, and Betty gave him a solid rap with her head that rammed him into the fence. "Now she wants my attention. Would you like some of this then?"

He shifted, held the apple out. Betty nipped it from his palm with dignified delicacy. "She loves me."

"She loves your apples," Keeley commented.

"Oh, it's not just that. See here." Before Keeley could evade—could think to—he cupped a hand at the back of her neck, pulled her close and rubbed his lips provocatively over hers.

Betty huffed out a breath and butted him.

"You see?" Brian let his teeth graze lightly before he released Keeley. "Jealous. She doesn't care to have me give my affection to another woman."

"Next time kiss her and save yourself a bruise."

"It was worth it. On both counts."

"Horses are more easily charmed than women, Donnelly." She plucked the apple out of his hand, bit in. "I just like your apples," she told him, and strolled away.

"That one's as contrary as you are." He nuzzled Betty's cheek as he watched Keeley walk to her stables.

"What is it that makes me find contrary females so appealing?"

She hadn't meant to go down to the yearling stalls. Really. It was just that she was up early, her own morning chores were done. And she was curious. When she stepped inside the stables, out of the soft gray dawn, the first thing she heard was Brian's voice.

It made her smile. At least the exasperation in it made her smile.

"Come on now, Jim, you lost the draw. You can't be welshing on me."

"I'm not. I'm gearing up."

The young exercise boy was gritting his teeth and rolling his shoulders when Keeley stepped up to the box. "Good morning. I heard you drew the short straw, Jim."

"Yeah, just my luck." He shot a mournful look at Betty. "This one wants to eat me."

"Chew you up and spit you out more like," Brian said in disgust. "You're just giving her cause now by letting her know she intimidates you. You'll go down in history today—the first weight the next winner of the Triple Crown feels on her back."

As if reacting to the prediction, Betty snorted, tried to dance as Brian firmed his grip on the shortened reins. And Jim's eyes went big as moons in a pale face.

"I'll do it." Keeley wasn't sure if it was the challenge of it, or compassion for the terrified boy. "If it's an historic moment, it should be a Grant up on a Royal Meadows champion." She smiled at Jim as she said it. "Let me have the jacket and hat."

"You sure?" With more hope than shame, Jim looked from Keeley to Brian.

"She's the boss. In a manner of speaking," Brian told him. "Your loss here, Jim."

"I'll take the loss and save all my skin." A little too eagerly, he started out of the box. As if sensing her opening, Betty bunched, kicked out. Swearing, Brian shoved Jim aside with his shoulder and took the hoof in the ribs.

The air went blue, and every curse was in an undertone that only added impact. Without a second thought, Keeley moved into the box and laid her hand over his on the reins to help control the filly.

A thousand pounds of horse fought to plunge. Keeley felt the heat from her, and from Brian when their bodies bumped together. "How bad did she get you?"

"Not as bad as she'd like." But enough, he thought, to steal his breath and have the pain shooting up until he saw stars dancing.

He tossed the hair out of his eyes, blinked at the sweat stinging in them and muscled the filly down.

"Man, Bri, I'm sorry."

"You should have more sense than to turn your back on a skittish filly," Brian snapped out. "Next time I'll let her take a shot at your head. Go on out. She knows she's bested you. Stand back," he ordered Keeley in the same cold tone of command, then he jerked the reins just enough to bring Betty's head down.

"So this is how it's to be? You want all the temper and none of the glory? Am I wasting my time with you? Maybe you don't want to run. We'll just wait until you come into season and bring a stallion in to mount you, and set you out to pasture to breed. Then you'll never know, will you, what it is to win."

Just outside the box, Keeley slipped on the padded jacket and hat. And waited. There was a line of damp down the back of his shirt, his hair was a wild tangle of brown and gold. Muscles rippled in his arms, and his boots were scarred and filthy.

He looked, she decided, exactly how a horseman should look. Powerful. Confident. And just arrogant enough to believe he could win over an animal more than five times his weight.

He kept talking, but he'd switched to Gaelic now. Slowly, the rhythm of the words smoothed out, and warmed. Almost like a song, they played in the air, rising, falling. Mesmerizing.

The filly stood quiet now, her dark brown eyes focused on Brian's green ones.

Seduced, Keeley thought. She was watching a kind of seduction. She'll do anything for him, Keeley realized. Who wouldn't if he touched you that way, looked at you that way, used his voice on you that way?

"Come in here," he told Keeley. "Let her get your scent. Touch her so she can feel you."

"I know how it's done," she murmured. Though she'd never seen it done quite like this.

She slipped into the stall, ran her hands gently over Betty's neck, her side. She felt the muscles quiver under her hand, but the filly looked at nothing and no one but Brian.

"I've seen countless people work in countless ways with countless horses." Keeley spoke quietly as she stroked Betty. But like the horse, her eyes were on Brian. "I've never seen anyone like you. You have a gift."

His eyes shifted, met hers, held for a moment. One timeless moment. "She has the gift. Talk to her."

"Betty. Not-so-bad Betty. You scared poor Jim, didn't you, but you don't scare me. I think you're beautiful." She saw the filly's ears lay back, felt the slight shift under her hands, but kept talking. "You want to race, don't you? Well, you can't do it alone. I'd tell you this isn't going to hurt, but you don't care about that anyway. It's all pride with you."

Once again she looked at Brian. "It's all pride," she repeated, understanding both horse and man. "But you can't have the pride of winning without this step."

When Brian tightened the saddle, everyone seemed to hold their breath. Then Keeley let hers out, and put her knee in Brian's hands for a leg up.

She bellied over the saddle, lay still as Betty shied. She knew just what could happen if the filly wasn't controlled. A wrong move on anyone's part and she could find herself under several hundred pounds of agitated horse.

But Brian's voice whispered, soft and dreamy, and the light began to go pale gold. Slowly Keeley eased herself up until she sat, her feet sliding into the stirrups.

The new sensation had Betty fighting to toss her head, dancing back and kicking out. Now Keeley leaned forward, stroking, and added her voice to Brian's.

"Get used to it," she ordered in a no-nonsense tone directly opposed to his crooning. "You were born for this."

"There now, *cushla*." His lips twitched at the corners as he soothed Betty. "She's not so scary now, is she? She's hardly much of a thing at all up there on your big, beautiful back. She's only a princess, but you, you're a queen, aren't you?"

"So, I'm outranked?" Keeley wasn't sure if she was amused or insulted.

Gradually the restless movements stilled. Brian took a chunk of apple from his pocket, fed it to Betty with murmured praise and reassurance. "She's doing well."

"She'd like to bounce me off the ceiling."

"Oh aye, that she would, but she's not trying it at the moment. You're doing well, too." His gaze lifted until his eyes met Keeley's. "As natural at this as she is. Blue bloods, both of you."

"Are we making history, Brian?"

"Bet on it," he told her and kissed Betty just above the nose.

She gave him most of the morning. Dismounting, remounting, sitting quietly while he led them around the stall. Betty gave a couple of bucks, but everyone knew it was only for show.

"Will you try the walking ring with her?"

Keeley started to decline. She had work, and was already behind for the day. But the feel of the young, fresh horse under her was too much of a pleasure, too much of a challenge. She'd put in a few hours on paperwork that night.

"If you think she's ready."

"Oh, she's ready. It's the rest of us who have to catch up." He opened the box and led them out.

The walking ring was surrounded by a high wall, to give the student privacy and prevent distractions as she took her first steps under the control of a rider. As Brian led them toward it, several of the hands stopped work to watch. Money changed hands.

"Some of them bet we wouldn't manage her this morning," Brian said casually. "You just earned me fifty dollars."

"If I'd known there was a pool, I'd have bet myself."

He glanced up. "Which way?"

"I always bet to win."

He stopped inside the ring, handed Keeley the reins. "She's yours now."

Keeley angled her head. "In a manner of speaking," she said and nudged Betty into a walk.

They made a picture, Brian mused. A stunning one. The long-legged thoroughbred with her regal head and gleaming coat, and the delicate woman riding her.

If he'd ever wanted one horse for his own—and he didn't, hadn't—it would be this one.

If he'd ever wanted one woman for his own . . .

Well, that was the same. He'd never wanted the responsibilities that came from having. And neither of these could ever be his in any case. But he'd have something of each of them, and that was better all around.

For the horse, he'd have the knowledge that part of what he was went into the making of a champion. And the woman, before long he'd have the pleasure of knowing what it was to have her wrapped around him in the night. Maybe only once, but once would be enough.

Whatever the risks of that were, there was no stopping it. They came a bit closer to it every time they looked at each other. Today, he'd come to understand she knew it, too. Now it was only a matter of the time and place. And that would be up to her.

"They look good."

Brian didn't wince, but he wanted to. It was definitely inconvenient to have the father of the woman you were fantasizing about interrupt that particular image. Especially inconvenient when the man was also your employer.

"That they do. Betty needs a steady hand, and your daughter has one."

"Always has." Travis slapped a hand on Brian's shoulder and brought on instantaneous guilt. "I ran into Jim, who confessed all. You took a kick."

"It's nothing." He imagined his ribs would be sore for weeks.

"Have it looked at." The tone was casual, and carried command.

"I will shortly. Jim was spooked. I shouldn't have pushed him into it."

"He's young," Travis agreed. "But this is part of his job. At the moment, he feels bad enough that you could ask him to let Betty sit on him. I'd take advantage of it."

"And so I will. He's a good lad, Travis. Just a bit green yet. I'm thinking of taking him with me to the track more, letting him get some seasoning."

"That's a good idea. You have a number of them. Good ideas," Travis added.

"That's what you pay me for." Brian hesitated, then plunged. "Betty's not just your best shot at your Derby, she's the one who'll do it for you. And I'll wager my full year's contract pay she'll wear the Triple Crown."

"That's a leap, Brian."

"Not for her. I say she'll break records, smash them to bits. And when it comes time to breed her, it should be Zeus. I've done the charts," Brian continued. "I know you and Brendon manage the breeding end of the farm yourselves, but—"

"I'll look at your charts, Brian."

Brian nodded, shifted to watch Betty. "It's not the charts so much, though they'll bear me out. It's that I know her. Sometimes . . ." Despite himself, he found himself staring at Keeley. "You just recognize it all."

"I know it." Eyes narrowed in consideration, Travis scanned Betty's form. "Work out the race schedule you think will work for her—once she's ready. We'll talk about it."

Keeley walked Betty toward them, pulling her up with a tug of the reins and a quiet vocal command. "She's decided to tolerate me."

"What do you think?" Travis stroked the filly's neck, ignoring her first instinctive feint at nipping.

"She's not common," Keeley began, "though she has some behavioral problems that would make her so if they aren't corrected. She's smart. A fast learner. Which means you have to stay a step ahead of her. It's early days yet, of course, but I'd say this isn't a horse that's going to loaf. She'll work hard, and she'll race hard, under the right hand. If I were still competing, I'd want her."

"She's not meant for the show ring." Brian took out another chunk of apple. "She's for the oval."

Betty took the reward, then as if to show he was the only one of the three humans who mattered, bumped her head lightly against his shoulder.

"She still has to prove she can run in a crowd," Keeley pointed out. "You might want to put blinders on her."

"Not with this one, I'm thinking. The other horses won't be distractions to her. They'll be competitors."

"We'll see." Keeley dismounted, started to hand Brian the reins, but her father took them.

"I'll walk her back."

Irish Rebel

And that, Brian thought, absurdly bereft, was the difference between training and owning.

"No need to look so annoyed." Keeley cocked her head as Brian scowled after Betty. "She did very well. Better than I'd expected."

"Hmm? Oh, so she did, yes. I was thinking of something else."

"Ribs hurting?" When he only shrugged, she shook her head. "Let me take a look."

"She barely caught me."

"Oh, for heaven's sake." Impatient, Keeley did what she would have done with one of her brothers: She tugged Brian's T-shirt out of his jeans.

"Well, darling, if I'd known you were so anxious to get me undressed, I'd have cooperated fully, and in private."

"Shut up. God, Brian, you said it was nothing."

"It's not much."

His definition of not much was a softball-size bruise over the ribs in a burst of ugly red and black. "Macho is tedious, so just shut up."

He started to grin, then yelped when she pressed her fingers to the bruise. "Hell, woman, if that's your idea of tender mercies, keep them."

"You could have a cracked rib. You need an X ray."

"I don't need a damned—ouch! Bollocks and bloody hell, stop poking." He tried to pull his shirt down, but she simply yanked it up again.

"Stand still, and don't be a baby."

"A minute ago it was don't be macho, now it's don't be a baby. What do you want?"

"For you to behave sensibly."

"It's difficult for a man to behave sensibly when a

woman's taking his clothes off in broad daylight. If you're going to kiss it and make it better, I've several other bruises. I've a dandy one on my ass as it happens."

"I'm sure that's terribly amusing. One of the men can drive you to the emergency room."

"No one's driving me anywhere. I'd know if my ribs are cracked as I've had a few in my time. It's a bruise, and it's throbbing like a bitch now that you've been playing with it."

She spotted another, riding high on his hip, and gave that a poke. This time he groaned.

"Keeley, you're torturing me here."

"I'm just trying . . ." She trailed off as she lifted her head and saw his eyes. It wasn't pain or annoyance in them now. It was heat, and it was frustration. And it was surprisingly gratifying. "Really?"

It was wrong, and it was foolish, but a sip of power was a heady thing. She trailed her fingers along his hip, up his ribs and down again, and felt his muscles quiver. "Why don't you stop me?"

His throat hurt. "You make my head swim. And you know it."

"Maybe I do. Now. Maybe I like it." She'd never been deliberately provocative before. Had never wanted to be. And she'd never known the thrill of having a strong man turn to putty under her hands. "Maybe I've thought about you, Brian, the way you said I would."

"You pick a fine time to tell me when there's people everywhere, and your father one of them."

"Yeah, maybe that's true, too. I need that buffer, I guess."

"You're a killer, Keeley. You'd tease a man to death."

He didn't mean it as a compliment, but to her it was a revelation. "I've never tried it before. No one's ever attracted me enough. You do, and I don't even know why."

When she dropped her hand, he took her wrist. It surprised him to feel the gallop of her pulse there, when her eyes, her voice had been so cool, so steady. "Then you're a quick learner."

"I'd like to think so. If I come to you, you'd be the first."

"The first what?" Temper wanted to stir, especially when she laughed. Then his mind cleared and the meaning flashed through like a thunderbolt. His hand tightened on her wrist, then dropped it as though she had turned to fire.

"That scared you enough to shut you up," she observed. "I'm surprised anything could render you speechless."

"I've . . ." But he couldn't think.

"No, don't fumble around for words. You'll spoil your image." She couldn't think just why his dazed expression struck her as so funny, or why the shock in his eyes was endearing somehow.

"We'll just say that, under these circumstances, we both have a lot to consider. And now, I'm way behind in my work, and have to get ready for my afternoon class."

She walked away, as easily, as casually, Brian thought numbly, as she might have if they'd just finished discussing the proper treatment for windgalls. She left him reeling.

He'd gone and fallen in love with the gentry, and the gentry was his boss's daughter. And his boss's daughter was innocent.

He'd have to be mad to lay a hand on her after this.

He began to wish Betty had just kicked him in the head and gotten it all over with.

Served her right, Keeley decided. Spend the morning indulging herself, spend half the night doing the books. And she hated doing the books.

Sighing, she tipped back in her chair and rubbed her eyes. In another year, maybe two, the school would generate enough income to justify hiring a bookkeeper. But for now, she just couldn't toss the money away for something she could do herself. Not when she could use it to subsidize another student, or buy one of them a pair of riding boots.

It was tempting, particularly at times like these, to dip into her own bank account. But it was a matter of pride to keep the school going on its own merit, as much as she possibly could.

Ledgers and forms and bills and accounts, she thought, were her responsibility. You didn't have to like your responsibilities, you just had to deal with them.

She had two full-tuition students on her waiting list. One more, she calculated—two would be better—but one more and she could justify opening another class. Sunday afternoons.

That would give her eighteen full tuitions. Two years before, she'd had only three. It was working. And so, now, should she.

She swiveled back to the computer and focused on her spreadsheet program. Her eyes were starting to blur again when the door behind her opened.

She caught the scent of hot tea before she turned and saw her mother.

"Ma, what are you doing out here? It's midnight."

"Well, I was up, and I saw your light. I thought to myself, that girl needs some fuel if she's going to run half the night." Adelia set a thermos and a bag on the desk. "Tea and cookies."

"I love you."

"So you'd better. Darling, your eyes are half shut. Why don't you turn this off and come to bed?"

"I'm nearly done, but I can use the break—and the fuel." She ate a cookie before she poured the tea. "I'm only behind because I played this morning."

"From what your father tells me you weren't playing." Adelia took a chair, nudged it closer to the desk. "He's awfully pleased with how Brian's bringing Betty along. Well, he's pleased with Brian altogether, and so am I from what I've seen. But Betty's quite the challenge."

"Hmm." So was Brian, Keeley thought. "He has his own way of doing things, but it seems to work." Considering, she drummed her fingers on the desk. She'd always been able to discuss anything with her mother. Why should that change now?

"I'm attracted to him."

"I'd worry about you if you weren't. He's a fine-looking young man."

"Ma." Keeley laid a hand over her mother's. "I'm very attracted to him."

The amusement faded from Adelia's eyes. "Oh. Well."

"And he's very attracted to me."

"I see."

"I don't want to mention this to Dad. Men don't look at this sort of thing the way we do."

"Darling." At a loss, Adelia sighed out a breath. "Mothers aren't likely to look at this sort of thing the same way their daughters do. You're grown up, and you're a woman who answers to herself first. But you're still my little girl, aren't you?"

"I haven't been with a man before."

"I know it." Adelia's smile was soft, almost wistful. "Do you think I wouldn't know if that had changed for you? You think too much of yourself to give what you are to something unless it matters. No one's mattered before."

Here the ground was boggy, Keeley thought. "I don't know if Brian matters in the way you mean. But I feel different with him. I want him. I haven't wanted anyone before. It's exciting, and a little scary."

Adelia rose, wandered around the little office looking at the ribbons, the medals. The steps and the stages. "We've talked about such matters before, you and I. About the meaning and the precautions, the responsibilities."

"I know about being responsible and sensible."

"Keeley, while it is true that all that is important, it doesn't tell you—it can't tell you—what it is to be with a man. There's such heat." She turned back. "There's such a force you make between you. It's not just an act, though I know it can be for some. But even then it's more than just that. I won't tell you that giving your innocence is a loss, for it shouldn't be, it doesn't need to be. For me it was an opening. Your father was my first," she murmured. "And my only."

"Mama." Moved, Keeley reached for her hands. Her mother's hands were so strong, she thought. Everything about her mother was strong. "That's so lovely."

"I only ask you to be sure, so that if you give yourself

to him, you take away a memory that's warm and has heart, not just heat. Heat can chill after time passes."

"I am sure." Smiling now, Keeley brought her mother's hand to her cheek. "But he's not. And, Ma, it's so odd, but the way he backed off when I told him he'd be the first is why I'm sure. You see, I matter to him, too."

Chapter 6

It was amazing, really, how two people could live and work in basically the same place, and one could completely avoid the other. It just took setting your mind to it.

Brian set his mind to it for several days. There was plenty of work to keep him occupied and more than enough reason for him to spend time away from the farm and on the tracks. But he found avoidance scraped his pride. It was too close a kin to cowardice.

Added to that, he'd told Keeley he wanted to help her at the school and had done nothing about it. He wasn't a man to break his word, no matter what it cost him. And, he reminded himself as he walked to Keeley's stables, he was also a man of some self-control. He had no intention of seducing or taking advantage of innocence.

He'd made up his mind on it.

Then he stepped into the stables and saw her. He wouldn't have said his mouth watered, but it was a very close thing.

She was wearing one of those fancy rigs again—

jodhpurs the color of dark chocolate and a cream sort of blouse that looked somehow fluid. Her hair was down, all tumbled and wild as if she'd just pulled the pins from it. And indeed, as he watched she flipped it back and looped it through a wide elastic band.

He decided the best place in the universe for his hands to be were in his pockets.

"Lessons over?"

She glanced back, her hands still up in her hair. Ah, she thought. She'd wondered how long it would take him to wander her way again. "Why? Did you want one?"

He frowned, but caught himself before he shifted his feet. "I said I'd give you a hand over here."

"So you did. As it happens I could use one. You did say you could ride, didn't you?"

"I did, and I do."

"Good." Perfect. She gestured toward a big bay. "Mule really needs a workout. If you take him, I'll be able to give Sam some exercise, too. Neither of them has had enough the last couple of days. I'm sure I have tack that'll suit you." She opened a box door and led out the already saddled Sam. "We'll wait in the paddock."

As they clipped out, Brian eyed Mule, Mule eyed Brian. "She's a bossy one, isn't she now?" Then with a shrug, Brian headed to the tack room to find a saddle that suited him.

She was cantering around the paddock when he came out, her body so tuned to the horse they might have been one figure. With the slightest shift in rhythm and angle, she took her mount over three jumps. Cantering still, she started the next circle, then spotted Brian. She slowed, stopped.

"Ready?"

For an answer, he swung into the saddle. "Why are you all done up today?"

"It was picture day. We take photographs of the classes. The kids and the parents like it. Mule's up for a good run, if you are."

"Then let's have at it." With a tap of his heels he sent the horse out of the open gate at an easy trot.

"How are the ribs?" she asked as she came up beside him.

"They're all right." They were driving him mad, because every time he felt a twinge he remembered her hands on him.

"I'm told the yearling training's coming along well, and Betty's one of the star pupils—as predicted."

"She has the thirst. All the training in the world can't give a horse the thirst to race. We'll be giving her a taste of the starting gate shortly, see how she does with it."

Keeley headed up a gentle slope where trees were still lush and green despite the encroaching fall. "I'd use Foxfire with her," she said casually. "He's a sturdy one, with lots of experience. He loves to charge out of the gate. She sees him do it a couple of times, she won't want to be left behind."

He'd already decided on Foxfire as Betty's gate tutor, but shrugged. "I'm thinking about it. So . . . have I passed the audition here, Miss Grant?"

Keeley lifted a brow, and a smile ghosted around her mouth as she looked Brian over. She'd been checking his form, naturally. "Well, you're competent enough at a trot." With a light tap, she sent Sam into a canter.

The minute Brian matched her pace, she headed into a gallop.

Oh, she missed this. Every day she couldn't fly out across the fields, over the hills, was a sacrifice. There was nothing to match it—the thrill of speed, the power soaring under her, through her, the thunder of hooves and the whip of wind.

She laughed as Brian edged by her. She'd seen the quick grin of challenge, and answered it by letting Sam have his head.

It was like watching magic take wing, Brian thought. The muscular black horse soared over the ground with the woman on his back. They streaked over another rise, moving west, into the dying sun. The sky was a riot of color, a painting slashed with reds and golds. It seemed to him she would ride straight into it, through it.

And he'd have no choice but to follow her.

When she pulled up, turned to wait for him, her face flushed with pleasure, her eyes gleaming with it, he knew he'd never seen the like.

And wanting her was apt to kill him.

"I should've given you a handicap," she called out. "Mule runs like a demon, but he's no match for this one." She leaned over the saddle to pat Sam's neck. She straightened, shook her hair back. "Gorgeous out, isn't it?"

"Hot as blazes," Brian corrected. "How long does summer last around here?"

"As long as it likes. Mornings are getting chilly, though, and once the sun dips down behind the hills, it'll cool off quickly enough. I like the heat. Your Irish blood's not used to it yet."

She turned Sam so she could look down at Royal Meadows. "It's beautiful from up here, isn't it?"

The buildings spread out, neat, elegant, with the white fences of the paddocks, the brown oval, the horses being led to the stable. A trio of weanlings, all legs and energy, raced in the near pasture.

"From down there, too. It's the best I've ever seen."

That made her smile. "Wait till you see it in winter, with snow on the hills and the sky thick and gray with more—or so blue it hurts your eyes to look at it. And the foalings start and there are babies trying out their legs. When I was little, I couldn't wait to run down and see them in the morning."

They began to walk again, companionably now, as the light edged toward dusk. She hadn't expected to be so comfortable with him. Aware, yes, she always seemed aware of him now. But this simple connection, a quiet evening ride, was a pleasure.

"Did you have horses when you were a boy?"

"No, we never owned them. But it wasn't so far to the track, and my father's a wagering man."

"And are you?"

He tilted his face toward her. "I like playing the odds, and fortunately, have a better feel for them than my father. He loved the look of them, and the rush of a race, but never did he gain any understanding of horses."

"You didn't gain any, either," Keeley said and had him frowning at her. "What you've got you were born with. Just like them," she added, gesturing toward the weanlings.

"I think that's a compliment."

"I don't mind giving them when they're fact."

"Well, fact or fiction, horses have been the biggest

part of my life. I remember going along with my da and seeing the horses. When he could manage it, he liked to go early, check out the field, talk with the clockers and the grooms, get himself a feel for things—or so he said. He lost his money more often as not. It was the process that appealed to him."

That, and the flask in his pocket, Brian thought, but with tolerance. His father had loved the horses and the whiskey. And his mother had understood neither.

"One of the first times I went along, I saw an exercise boy, very young lad, ponying a sorrel around the track. And I thought, there, that's it. That's what I want to do, for there can't be anything better than doing that for your life and your living. And while I was still young enough, and small enough, I slid out of going to school as often as it could be managed and hitched rides to the track to hustle myself. Walk hots, muck stalls, whatever."

"It's romantic."

He caught himself. He hadn't meant to ramble on that way, but the ride, the evening, the whole of it made him sentimental. When he started to laugh at her statement, she shook her head.

"No, it is. People who aren't a part of the world of it don't understand, really. The hard work, the disappointments, the sweat and blood. Freezing predawn workouts, bruises and pulled muscles."

"And that's romantic."

"You know it is."

This time he did laugh, because she'd pegged him. "As a boy, when I hung around the shedrow, I'd see the horses come back through the mist of morning, steam rising off their backs, the sound of them growing louder, coming at you before ever you could see them. They'd slip out of the fog like something out of a dream. Then, I thought it the most romantic thing in the world."

"And now?"

"Now, I know it is."

He broke into a canter, riding with her until the lights of Royal Meadows began to flicker on and glow. He hadn't expected to spend a comfortable, contented hour in her company, and found it odd that underlying all the rest that buzzed between them they'd seemed to have formed a kind of friendship.

He'd been friends with women before, and was well on the way to being convinced he'd do just fine keeping it all on a friendly level with Keeley. He was the one who'd initiated the sexual charge, so it seemed reasonable and right that he be the one to dampen it again.

The logic of it, and the ride, relaxed him. By the time they reached the stables to cool down the horses, he was in an easy mood and thinking about his supper.

Since she was interested, he told her of the yearling training, the progress, the five-year-old mare with colic, and the weanling with ringbone.

Together they watered the horses, and while Brian took the saddles and bridles to the tack room, Keeley set up the small hay nets and set out the grooming kits.

They worked across from each other, in opposite boxes.

"I heard you and Brendon are heading off to Saratoga next week," she commented.

"Zeus is running. And I think Red Duke is a contender, and your brother agrees. Though I've only seen that track on paper and in pictures. We're off to Louisville as well. I want to be well familiar with that course before the first Saturday in May."

"You want Betty to run the Derby."

"She will run it. And win it." He picked up the curry comb to scrape out the body brush. "We've conversed about it."

"You've talked to Brendon about the Derby?"

"No, Betty. And your father as well. I expect Brendon and I will talk it through while we're away."

"What does Betty have to say?"

"Let's get on with it." He glanced over, saw she was running her fingers over Sam's coat, checking for lumps or irregularities. "Why aren't you still competing? With that one under you you'd need a vault for all your medals."

"I'm not interested in medals."

"Why not? Don't you like to win?"

"I love to win." She leaned gently against Sam, lifted his leg and sent Brian a long look that had his stomach jittering before she gave her attention to picking out the hoof. "But I've done it, enjoyed it, finished with it. Competing can take over your life. I wanted the Olympics, and I got it."

She shifted to clean out the next hoof. "Once I had, I realized that so much of what I was, what I felt and thought had been focused on that single goal. And then it was over. So I wanted to see what else there was out there, and what else I had in me. I like to compete, but I found out it doesn't always have to be done, and won, in the show ring."

"With the kind of school you've got going here, you should have someone working with you."

She shrugged and began to rub in hoof oil. "Up until now I'd been able to draft Sarah or Patrick into giving me a hand. Ma helps out when she can, and so does Dad. Brendon and Uncle Paddy put in hours with each one of my horses as I got them. And the cousins—Burke and Erin's kids from Three Aces—they're always willing to pitch in if I need extra hands."

"I haven't seen anyone working here but you."

"Well, that's very simple. Patrick and Sarah are off to college—and Brady, who's another I can browbeat into shoveling boxes when he's here. Brendon's doing a lot more traveling now than he used to. Uncle Paddy's in Ireland, and the cousins are just back from a holiday and in school. Either my mother or father, sometimes both, show up here at dawn half the time. Whether I ask them or not."

She got to her feet. "And now that I've got you interested, I've come up with a part-time groom/exercise boy/stablehand. That's a pretty good deal for a small riding academy."

She strolled out to start the evening feeding.

"You could get an eager young boy or girl to come in before and after school—pay them in lessons."

"Before school, eager young boys and girls should be eating breakfast, and after they should be playing with friends and doing homework."

"That's very strict."

She chuckled and mixed some sliced carrots into the feed as an extra treat. "That's what all my students say. I want them well-rounded. My family saw to it that I had interests and friendships outside the stable, that I got an education, that I saw something of the world besides the track and the barn. It matters."

They divvied up the horses, and the stables filled with the sounds of whickers and whinnies as the meal was served.

"If you don't mind my saying so, you don't seem to be getting out and about much now."

"I'm compulsive. Goal oriented. I see what I want and well, it's like putting on blinders and heading down the backstretch. All I see is the finish line."

She leaned in to rub a gelding's neck as if he were a pet dog. "Which is why my parents wouldn't let me spend my entire childhood around or on a horse. I took piano lessons, and as soon as I started I was determined to be the best student at the recital. If it was my job to clean the kitchen after dinner, then that damn kitchen was going to sparkle so bright you'd need sunglasses for your midnight snack."

"That's frightening."

Responding to the humor in his eyes, she nodded. "It can be. Focusing on the school means, even though it's still a single goal, that my compulsion to succeed is spread out to encompass so many elements—the kids, the horses as well as the academy itself. Once it's firmly established, I can delegate a bit more, but I need to learn from the ground up. I don't like to make mistakes. Which is why I haven't been with a man before now."

He was thrown off balance so quickly and completely, he could hear his own brain stumble. "Well, that's . . . that's wise."

He took one definite step back, like a chessman going from square to square.

"It's interesting that makes you nervous," she said, countering his move.

"I'm not nervous, I'm... finished up here, it seems." He tried another tactic, stepped to the side.

"Interesting," she continued, mirroring his move, "that it would make you nervous, or uneasy if you prefer, when you've been... I think it's safe to use the term 'hitting on me' since we met."

"I don't think that's the proper term at all." Since he seemed to be boxed into a corner, he decided he was really only standing his ground. "I acted in a natural way regarding a physical attraction. But—"

"And now that I've reacted in a natural way, you've felt the reins slip out of your hands and you're panicked."

"I'm certainly not panicked." He ignored the terror gripping claws into his belly and concentrated on annoyance. "Back off, Keeley."

"No." With her eyes locked on his, she stepped in. Checkmate.

His back was hard up against a stall door and he'd been maneuvered there by a woman half his weight. It was mortifying. "This isn't doing either of us any credit." It took a lot of effort when the blood was rapidly draining out of his head, but he made his voice cool and firm. "The fact is I've rethought the matter."

"Have you?"

"I have, yes, and—stop it," he ordered when she ran the palms of her hands up over his chest.

"Your heart's pounding," she murmured. "So's mine. Should I tell you what goes on inside my head, inside my body when you kiss me?"

"No." He barely managed a croak this time. "And it's not going to happen again."

"Bet?" She laughed, rising up just enough to nip his chin. How could she have known how much *fun* it was to twist a man into aroused knots? "Why don't you tell me about this rethinking?"

"I'm not going to take advantage of your—of the situation."

That, she thought, was wonderfully sweet. "At the moment, I seem to have the advantage. This time you're trembling, Brian."

The hell he was. How could he be trembling when he couldn't feel his own legs? "I won't be responsible. I won't use your inexperience. I *won't* do this." The last was said on a note of desperation and he pushed her aside.

"I'm responsible for myself. And I think I've just proven to both of us, that if and when I decide you'll be the one, you won't have a prayer." She drew a deep, satisfied breath. "Knowing that's incredibly flattering."

"Arousing a man doesn't take much skill, Keeley. We're cooperative creatures in that area."

If he'd expected that to scratch at her pride and cut into her power, he was mistaken. She only smiled, and the smile was full of secret female knowledge. "If that was true between us, if that were all that's between us, we'd be naked on the tack room floor right now."

She saw the change in his eyes and laughed delightedly. "Already thought of that one, have you? We'll just hold that thought for another time."

He swore, raked his hands through his hair and tried to pinpoint the moment she'd so neatly turned the tables on him, when the pursued had become the pursuer. "I don't like forward women."

The sound she made was something between a snort and a giggle, and was girlish and full of fun. It made him want to grin. "Now that's a lie, and you don't do it well.

I've noticed you're an honest sort of man, Brian. When you don't want to speak your mind, you say nothing—and that's not often. I like that about you, even if it did irritate me initially. I even like your slightly overwide streak of confidence. I admire your patience and dedication to the horses, your understanding and affection for them. I've never been involved with a man who's shared that interest with me."

"You've never been involved with a man at all."

"Exactly. That's just one reason why. And to continue, I appreciate the kindness you showed my mother when she was sad, and I appreciate the part of you that's struggling to back away right now instead of taking what I've never offered anyone before."

She laid a hand on his arm as he stared at her with baffled frustration. "If I didn't have that respect and that liking for you, Brian, we wouldn't be having this conversation no matter how attracted I might be to you."

"Sex complicates things, Keeley."

"I know."

"How would you know? You've never had any."

She gave his arm a quick squeeze. "Good point. So, you want to try the tack room?" When his mouth fell open, she laughed and threw her arms around him for a noisy kiss on his cheek. "Just kidding. Let's go up to the main house and have some dinner instead."

"I've work yet."

She drew back. She couldn't read his eyes now. "Brian, neither of us have eaten. We can have a simple meal in the kitchen—and if you're worried, we won't be alone in the house so I'll have to keep my hands off you. Temporarily."

"There's that." He couldn't stand it. How could he

be expected to? She'd thrown her arms around him with such easy affection. And his heart was balanced on a very thin wire. Trying to keep the movement casual, he set her aside. "Well, I could eat."

"Good."

She would have taken his hand, but his were already in his pockets. It amused and touched her how restrained he was determined to be. And if it made her naturally competitive spirit kick in, well, she couldn't help it, now could she?

"I'm hoping to get down to Charles Town and watch some of the workouts once you take Betty and some of the other yearlings to the track."

"She'll be ready for it soon enough." Relief was like a cool wave through his blood. Talking of horses would make it all easier. "I'd say she'll surprise you, but you've been up on her. You know what she's made of."

"Yeah, good stock, good breeding, a hard head and a hunger to win." She flashed him a smile as they approached the kitchen door. "I've been told that describes me. I'm half Irish, Brian, I was born stubborn."

"No arguing with that. A person might make the world a calmer place for others by being passive, but you don't get very far in it yourself, do you?"

"Look at that. We have a foundation of agreement. Now tell me you like spaghetti and meatballs."

"It happens to be a favorite of mine."

"That's handy. Mine, too. And I heard a rumor that's what's for dinner." She reached for the doorknob, then caught him off guard by brushing a light kiss over his lips. "And since we'll be joining my parents, it would probably be best if you didn't imagine me naked for the next couple of hours."

She sailed in ahead of him, leaving Brian helplessly and utterly aroused.

There was nothing like an extra helping of guilt to cool a man's blood. And it was guilt as much as the hot food and the glass of good wine that got Brian through the evening in the Grant kitchen. The size of it left little room for lust, considering.

There was Adelia Grant giving him a warm greeting as if he was welcome to swing in for dinner anytime he had the whim, and Travis getting out an extra plate himself—as if he waited on employees five days a week—and saying that there was plenty to go around as Brendon had other plans for dinner.

Before he knew it, he was sitting down, having food heaped in front of him and being asked how his day had been. And not in a way that expected a report.

He didn't know what to do about it. He liked these people, genuinely liked them. And there he was lusting after their daughter. An alley mutt after a registered purebred.

And the hell of it was, he liked her as well. It had been so simple at first, when there'd been only heat. Or he'd been able to tell himself that's all there was. For a time it had been possible to tolerate being in love with her—or at least talking himself out of believing it. But *caring* for her made it all a study in frustration.

He could certainly convince himself that he was in love with the *idea* of her rather than the woman. The physical beauty, the class, the sheer inaccessibility of her. That was all a kind of challenge, a risk he enjoyed taking. But she'd gone and opened herself up to him, so every time he was around her, she showed him more of herself.

The kindness, the humor, the strength of purpose and sense of self he admired.

And now this teasing, this sexual flirt in an innocent's body was driving him mad. And God help him, he liked it.

"Have some more, Brian."

"I'll be sorry if I do." But he took the big bowl Adelia offered him. "Sorrier if I don't. You're a rare cook, Mrs. Grant."

"Dee, I told you. And rare was just what I was for a number of years. Before Hannah retired—that was our housekeeper. She was with Travis longer than I've been with him. When she retired a few years back I just didn't want another woman, a stranger, you know, in the house day and night and so on. I figured I'd better learn to cook something more than fish and chips or we'd all starve to death."

"Nearly did the first six months," Travis commented and earned a narrow-eyed stare from his wife.

"Well, sure and the experience made you get a handle on that fancy grill outside, didn't it? The man was spoiled rotten. I wager you could even put a meal together for yourself, Brian."

Idly he rubbed Sheamus—who was snoring under the table—with the side of his boot. "If I've no choice in the matter."

Brian caught the lazy look Keeley sent him as she sipped her wine. Heat balled in his belly. In defense he turned to Travis. "I'm told you enjoy a hand or two of poker from time to time."

"I've been known to."

"The lads're talking about a game tomorrow night."

"I might come down—I've heard you're a hard man to beat."

"If you're going to play cards, you should ask Burke to join you," Adelia put in. "Then maybe Keeley, Erin and I can find something equally foolish to do with our evening."

"Good idea. More wine, Brian?" Keeley lifted the bottle, cocked a brow. The purr in her voice was subtle, but he heard it. And suffered.

"No, thanks. I've work yet."

"I'll walk down with you when you're ready," Travis told him. "I'd like a look at that colicky mare."

"The two of you go ahead. We'll see to the dishes."

Travis grinned like a boy. "No KP?"

"There's not that much to be done, and you can make up for it tomorrow." She got up to clear, and kissed his temple. "Go on, I know you've been worrying about her."

"Thank you for the fine meal, Dee," Brian added when she angled her head.

"And you're very welcome."

"Good night, Keeley."

"Good night, Brian. Thanks for the ride."

Adelia waited until the men were out, then turned to her daughter. "Keeley, I never would've thought it of you. You're tormenting the poor man."

"There's nothing poor about that man." Delighted with herself, Keeley broke off a piece of bread and crunched down on it. "And tormenting him is so rewarding."

"Well, there's not a woman with blood in her could argue with that. Mind you don't hurt him, darling."

"Hurt him?" Seriously shocked, Keeley rose to help with the dishes. "Of course I won't. I couldn't."

"You never know what you will or you can do." Adelia patted her daughter's cheek. "You've a lot to learn yet. And however much you learn you'll never really understand everything that goes on inside a man."

"I've good a pretty good idea about this one."

Adelia opened her mouth, then shut it again. Some things, she knew, couldn't be explained. They had to be lived.

Chapter 7

Brian came to know the roads leading from Maryland into West Virginia as well as he knew those in the county of Kerry. The highways where cars flashed by like little rockets, and the curving back roads where everything meandered were all part of his life now, and what some people would say led to a feeling of home.

There were times the green of the hills, the rise of them, reminded him of Ireland. The pang he felt at those moments surprised him as he didn't consider himself a sentimental man. At others, he'd drive along a winding road that followed a winding creek and the land was all so very different with its thick woods and walls of rock. Almost exotic. Then he'd feel a sense of contentment that surprised him nearly as much.

He didn't mind contentment. It just wasn't what he was looking for.

He liked to move. To travel from place to place. It was all to the good that his position at Royal Meadows gave him that opportunity. He figured in a couple of years, he'd have seen a great deal of America—even if the oval was in the foreground of each view.

He told himself he didn't think of Ireland as home—or Maryland as home, either. Home was the shedrow, wherever it might be.

Still, he felt a sense of welcome and ease when he drove between the stone pillars at Royal Meadows. And he felt pleasure when he saw Keeley in her paddock with one of her classes. He stopped to watch as she took her group from trot to canter.

It was a pretty sight, not despite the clumsiness and caution of some of the children, but because of it. This was no slick and choreographed competition but the first steps of a new adventure. Fun, she'd said, he remembered. They would learn, take responsibility, but she didn't forget they were children.

And some of them had been hurt.

Seeing her with them, looking at what she'd built herself when she could have spent her days exactly as he'd once imagined she did, brought him more than respect for what she was. It brought admiration that was a little too bright for comfort.

He could hear the squeals, and Keeley's calm, firm voice—a pretty sight and a pretty sound. He climbed out of the truck and walked over for a closer view.

There were grins miles wide, and eyes big as platters. There were giggles and there were gasps. As far as Brian could see, the mood ran from screaming nerves to wild delight. Through it all, Keeley gave orders, instruction, encouragement, and used each child's name.

Her long fire-fall of hair was roped back again. Her jeans were faded to a soft blue-gray like the many-pocketed vest she topped over it. Under that she wore a slim sweater the color of spring daffodils. She liked her bright tones, Keeley did, Brian mused. And her glitters as well, he mused as the light caught the dangle of little stones at her ears.

She'd be wearing perfume. She always had some cagey female scent about her. Sometimes just a drift that you had to get right up beside her to catch. And other times it was a siren call that beckoned you from a distance.

Never knowing which it would be was enough to drive a man mad.

He should stay away from her, Brian told himself. God knew he should stay away from her. And he figured he had as much chance of doing so as one of her riding hacks had of winning the Breeder's Cup.

She knew he was there. The ripple of heat over her skin told her so. She couldn't afford to be distracted with six children depending on her full attention. But oh, the awareness of him, of herself and that quick trip of the pulse, was a glorious sensation.

She began to understand why women so often made fools of themselves for men.

When she ordered the class to switch back to a trot, there were a few groans of disappointment. She had them change directions, then took them through all their paces, and back down to walk. Brian waited until she instructed them to stop, then applauded.

"Nicely done," he said. "Anyone here looking for a job, you just come see me."

"We have an audience today. This is Mr. Donnelly. He's head trainer at Royal Meadows. He's in charge of the racehorses."

"Indeed I am, and I've always got my eyes open for a new jockey."

"He talks pretty," one of the girls whispered, but Brian's ears were keen. He shot her a grin and had her blushing like a rosebud.

"Do you think so?"

"Mr. Donnelly's from Ireland," Keeley explained. Amazing, she thought, he even makes ten-year-old girls moon.

"Miss Keeley's mother's from Ireland. She talks pretty, too."

Brian glanced up and saw the boy he remembered as Willy studying him. "No one talks prettier than those from Ireland, lad. It's because we've all been kissed by the fairies."

"You're supposed to get money from the Tooth Fairy when you lose a tooth, but I never did."

"That's just your mother." The girl behind Willy rolled her eyes. "There aren't real fairies."

"Maybe they don't live here in America, but we've plenty where I come from. I'll put a word in for you, Willy, next time you lose a tooth."

His eyes rounded. "How did you know my name?"

"A fairy must've told me."

Keeley struggled to compose her features as Willy goggled. "Class. Dismount. Cool and water your mounts."

There was a great deal of chatter and movement now. Though Willy dismounted, he stood, holding the reins and studying Brian. Too cautious a look for one so young, Brian thought. And it tugged at his heart.

Willy took a breath, seemed to hold it. "I have one that's loose. A tooth."

"Do you?" Unable to resist, Brian climbed over the fence, hunched down. "Let's have a look."

Willy obliged by baring his teeth and poking his tongue against a wobbly incisor. "That's a good one. You'll be able to spit through where that was in a day or two."

"You're not supposed to spit." Willy slanted a look up at Brian as he began to walk.

"Who says?"

"Ladies." Bobby added a shrug. "They don't like you to burp, either."

"Ladies can be fussy about certain things. It's best to spit and burp among the men, I suppose."

"You're not supposed to run like a wild animal, either." Peeking around to make certain Keeley wasn't frowning in his direction, Willy shoved up the sleeve of his shirt. "This is from running like a wild animal on the playground at school. I skidded for*ever* and scraped lots of skin right off so it got really bloody."

Understanding his role, Brian pursed his lips, nodded. "That's very impressive, that is."

"I've got an even better one on my knee. Have you got any?"

"I've got a pretty good bruise." To play the game properly, Brian glanced around first, then tugged his shirt up to display the yellowing bruise on his ribs.

"Wow! That musta really hurt. Did you cry?"

"I couldn't. Miss Keeley was watching. Here she comes," he added in a conspirator's whisper and pulled his shirt down, whistled idly.

"Willy, you need to water Teddy."

"Yes, ma'am. I had a dream about Teddy last night."

"You tell me about it when we're grooming him, okay?"

"Okay. Bye, mister."

"Now that's a taking little creature," Brian murmured as Willy led his horse out to the water trough.

"Yes, he is. What were you talking about?"

"Man business." Brian hooked his thumbs in his pockets. "I've got to get down to the shedrow or I'd help you with the grooming. I could send you up a hand if you like."

"Thanks, but it's not necessary."

"Just ring down if you change your mind." He needed to go, let them both get on with work. But it was so nice to stand here and smell her. Today, the scent was subtle, just a hint of heat. "They looked good at the canter."

"They'll look better in a few weeks." It was time to get the horses inside, start the grooming session. But . . . What would another minute hurt? "I heard you took a few pots in the poker game last night."

"I came away about fifty ahead. Your cousin Burke's a slick one. I'd say he whistled home with double that."

"And my father?"

Brian's grin flashed. "I like thinking that's where I got the fifty. I told him he's better off sticking with the horses."

Keeley's brow rose. "And his response to that?"

"Isn't something I can repeat in polite company."

She laughed. "That's what I thought. I've got to get the horses inside. Parents will be trickling along soon."

"Don't they ever come to watch?"

"Sometimes. Actually I've asked them to give us a few weeks so the kids aren't distracted or tempted to show off. You were a good test audience."

"Keeley." He touched her arm as she turned away. "The little boy. Willy. He's got a tooth he'll be losing in a couple of days. It'd be nice if someone remembered to put a coin under his pillow."

Her heart, which had leaped at his touch, quieted. Melted. "He's with a very good foster family right now. Very nice and caring people. They won't forget."

"All right then."

"Brian." This time it was her hand on his arm. Despite the curious eyes of her students, she rose to her toes to brush her lips over his cheek. "I have a soft spot for a man who believes in fairies," she murmured, then walked away to gather her students.

A very soft spot, she thought, for a man with a cocky grin and a kind heart. She opened the terrace doors of her room, stepped out into the night. There was a chill in the air, and a sky so clear the stars flamed like torches. She could smell the flowers, the spice of the first mums, the poignancy of the last of the roses.

A breeze had the leaves whispering.

The three-quarter moon was pale gold, shedding light that gilded the gardens and shimmered over the fields. It seemed she could cup her hands, let that light pour into them and drink it like wine.

How could anyone sleep on so perfect a night?

Slowly she shifted and looked toward Brian's quarters. Light gleamed in his windows. And her pulse fluttered in her throat.

She told herself if his lights were off, she would close the doors again and try to sleep. But there they were, bright against dark, beckoning.

She closed her eyes on a shiver of anticipation and nerves. She'd prepared herself for this step, this change in her life, in her body. It wasn't an impulse, it wasn't reckless. But she felt impulsive. She felt reckless.

She was a grown woman, and the decision was hers. Quietly she stepped back and closed the doors.

Brian closed the condition book, pressed his fingers to his tired eyes. Like Paddy, he wasn't quite sure he trusted the computer, but he was willing to fiddle with it a bit. Three times a week he spent an hour trying to figure the damn thing out with the notion that eventually he could use it to generate his charts.

Graphics, they called it, he thought, shifting to give the machine a suspicious glare. Timesaving and efficient, if you believed all the hype. Well, tonight he was too damn tired to spend an hour trying to be timesaving and efficient.

He hadn't had a decent night's sleep in a week. Which had nothing to do with his job, he admitted. And everything to do with his boss's daughter.

It was a good thing he had that trip to Saratoga coming up, he decided as he pushed away from his desk and rose. A little distance was just what was needed. He didn't care for this unsteady sensation or this worrying ache around the heart.

He wasn't the type to fret over a woman, he thought. He enjoyed them, and was happy for them to enjoy him, then each moved on without regrets.

Moving on was always the end plan.

New York, he remembered, was a fair distance away. It should be far enough. As for tonight, he was going to have a shot of whiskey in his tea to help smooth out the edges. Then by God, he was going to sleep if he had to bash himself over the head to accomplish it.

And he wasn't going to give Keeley another thought.

The knock on the door had him cursing under his breath. Though she'd been doing well, his first worry was that the mare with bronchitis had taken a bad turn. He was already reaching for the boots he'd shed when he called out.

"Come in, it's open. Is it Lucy then?"

"No, it's Keeley." One brow lifted, she stood framed in the door. "But if you're expecting Lucy, I can go."

The boots dangled from his fingertips, and those fingertips had gone numb. "Lucy's a horse," he managed to say. "She doesn't often come knocking on my door."

"Ah, the bronchitis. I thought she was better."

"She is. Considerably." She'd gone and let her hair loose, he thought. Why did she have to do that? It made his hands hurt, actually hurt with wanting to slide into it.

"That's good." She stepped in, shut the door. And because it seemed too perfect not to, audibly flipped the lock. Seeing a muscle twitch in his jaw was incredibly satisfying.

He was a drowning man, and had just gone under the first time. "Keeley, I've had a long day here. I was just about to—"

"Have a nightcap," she finished. She'd spotted the teapot and the bottle of whiskey on the kitchen counter. "I wouldn't mind one myself." She breezed past him to flip off the burner under the now sputtering kettle.

She'd put on different perfume, he thought viciously. Put it on fresh, too, just to torment him. He was damn sure of it. It snagged his libido like a fishhook.

"I'm not really fixed for company just now."

"I don't think I qualify as company." Competently she warmed the pot, measured out the tea and poured the boiling water in. "I certainly won't be after we're lovers."

He went under the second time without even the chance to gulp in air. "We're not lovers."

"That's about to change." She set the lid on the pot, turned. "How long do you like it to steep?"

"I like it strong, so it'll take some time. You should go on home now."

"I like it strong, too." Amazing, she thought, she didn't feel nervous at all. "And if it's going to take some time, we can have it afterward."

"This isn't the way for this." He said it more to himself than her. "This is backward, or twisted. I can't get my mind around it. No, just stay back over there and let me think a minute."

But she was already moving toward him, a siren's smile on her lips. "If you'd rather seduce me, go ahead."

"That's exactly what I'm not going to do." Though the night was cool and his windows were open to it, he felt sweat slither down his back. "If I'd known the way things were, I'd never have started this."

That mouth of his, she thought. She really had to have that mouth. "Now we both know the way things are, and I intend to finish it. It's my choice."

His blood was already swimming. Hot and fast. "You don't know anything, which is the whole flaming problem."

"Are you afraid of innocence?"

"Damn right."

"It doesn't stop you from wanting me. Put your hands on me, Brian." She took his wrist, pressed his hand to her breast. "I want your hands on me."

The boots clattered to the floor as he went under for the third time. "It's a mistake."

"I don't think so. Touch me."

His hand closed over her. She was small, delicate, and through some momentary miracle, his. "Doesn't matter if it's a mistake," he said, giving up entirely.

"We won't let it be one." Her head fell back as his hands began to move.

"Doesn't matter. But I'll be careful with you."

Her eyes were blue and brilliant as she lifted her arms, slid her hands into his wildly waving hair. "Not too careful, I hope."

When he swept her up in his arms she let out a shuddering sigh. "Oh, I was hoping you'd do that." Thrilled, she pressed her lips to the side of his neck. "I was really hoping you'd do that."

He turned his face into her hair, drew in the scent, held it inside him. "You've only to tell me what you like."

She tipped her head back to look at him as he carried her into the bedroom. "Show me what I like."

With moonlight and cool breezes shimmering through the open windows, he laid her on the bed. There had been moonlight the first time he'd kissed her, soft fingers of it then, as there were now. He'd never forget the look of it, or of her.

There had been few gifts in his life that had mattered, that had stayed in him, in his heart and memory. She would, he knew. She was a gift he would cherish.

"This," he murmured, nibbling at her lips till they parted for him.

She opened, willing, wanting to be touched and tasted and taken. Even as he sensed her eagerness he led her slowly, patiently, thoroughly through the layers of sensations.

He caressed, his fingertips, palms, light as the air, then lingering at some secret place that had her breath catching on little jolts of pleasure. His mouth cruised lazily over her skin, sliding her into warmth, then it would come back to hers again, with a hungry bite that shot her into the heat.

Instinctively, avidly, she arched against him.

He was murmuring to her, lovely, stirring words in the old tongue, each like a tender kiss on the soul. Her heart fluttered, wings spreading wide for flight.

There were no nerves, no doubts as she raised herself to him, wrapped herself around him. When he slipped off her shirt, the breeze and his fingertips whispered over her. She felt beautiful.

Her skin was white silk, her hair rich flame. Every tremble was a gift, every sigh a treasure. In his life he'd never held anything as lovely as Keeley discovering herself.

She never shied when he undressed her, but embraced each new moment, welcomed each fresh sensation. Her curious hands moved over him, undressing him in turn. He'd never known how arousing it could be to be someone's first.

Her heart hammered under his mouth, and the scent she'd dabbed on that fragile flesh swirled into his senses until they were as clouded as hers. He took more, just a little more, and she began to move under him in mindless invitation.

So much. There was so much, was all she could think.

Her body was flooded with sensations, her flesh quivering from them. She could hear her own moans, her own ragged breaths but could do nothing to control them. The very loss of control was thrilling.

Everything inside her was tangled and straining. And desperate. Her nails bit into his back, her teeth found his shoulder. Then his hand closed over her.

She cried out from the shock of it, all that pulsing, pumping pleasure, the sheer heat of it that washed in one huge wave that crashed over her, inside her, and left her shuddering. She reared up, eyes blind, her fingers diving into his hair.

Then his mouth was on hers again, hotter now, hungrier, giving her no chance to catch her breath or her sanity.

"Give yourself to me," he whispered, the blood pounding in his head as her eyes, heavy, stunned, looked into his. "Take me in."

With her eyes on his, she opened and arched, and gave.

It was like rising into the air, each stroke another beat of wings. Pleasure climbed higher and higher still, lifting through her body, sweeping through her mind. All she could see were his eyes, dark and green and focused on her, even as his body was focused on hers. Mated and matched and moving with her.

Staggered by the beauty of it, she lifted a hand to his cheek, murmured his name.

And he was lost. Love and passion, dreams and desire stabbed through his heart. Helpless, he buried his face in her hair and let himself go.

With her eyes closed she absorbed the delights of being a well-loved woman. Her body felt gloriously heavy, her mind wonderfully muffled. There was no need to wonder or worry if she had given Brian the same pleasure. She had seen it in his face, and felt it as he lay over her with his heart still thundering.

There was a change inside her, she thought. Awareness, understanding. And a soaring kind of triumph.

Smiling to herself, she traced a finger down his back. "How are the ribs?"

"What?"

And didn't it feel grand to hear that sleepy slur in his voice? "Your ribs. That's still a nasty bruise you have there."

"I can't feel anything." His head was still spinning. "What's this scent you've put on? It's devious."

"Just one of my many secrets."

He lifted his head, started to grin at her, then it swamped him again. The look of her, the love of her. Lowering his head he brought his lips to hers in a long, dreamy kiss that came out of his soul and stirred hers.

Her hand slid limply to the mattress. "Brian."

"I'm crushing you." He said it briskly. He'd terrified himself.

He shifted away and shattered the moment. "There's not really very much of you." Suddenly aware that the breeze fluttering in the windows he left open was cold, he tugged at the bedspread until he could wrap it around her. "Are you all right then?"

"I'm fabulous, thank you." Laughing, she sat up, without a shrug for modesty as the spread slid to her waist. She caught his face in her hands and gave him a quick, affectionate kiss. "Are you all right then?" she said, mimicking his brogue.

"That I am, but I've had a bit of practice."

"I'll bet. But let's not bring up all your conquests just now. I'd hate to be obliged to punch you when I'm feeling so friendly."

"I wouldn't say they were conquests precisely. But we'll let that be."

"Wise choice."

"Let me close the windows. You're cold."

She angled her head as he rose. "There's nurturing in that bruised body of yours, Donnelly."

"I beg your pardon?"

"I'd say it comes from the horses." She pursed her lips, considered while he *thunked* a window down and scowled. "You look after them, worry about them, make plans for them, see to their needs and their comfort—oh and their training, of course. Then if you don't watch yourself you start to do it with people, too."

"I don't nurture people." He found the idea mildly insulting. "People can look after themselves. I don't even like people very much." He stalked over and shut the other window. "Present company excepted, as you're sitting naked in my bed and it would be rude to say otherwise."

"You didn't phrase that quite right. You don't like very many people. Do you have a robe?"

"No." He wasn't sure if it was the truth in what she said, or her understanding of him that irked him.

"Figures." She spied one of his work shirts tossed over a chair, and though it smelled of horses, slipped it on. "I'd say that tea's probably strong enough to hammer nails by now. Do you still want it?"

She looked . . . interesting in his shirt. Interesting enough that his blood began to churn again. "What are my options?"

"On my schedule, we have a cup of tea, a little conversation, then you get to seduce me back into bed and make love to me again before I go home."

"That's not bad, but I think it bears improving."

"Oh, and how's that?"

"We cut out the tea and conversation."

She ran her tongue over her top lip—his taste was still there—as he walked toward her. "That would take us straight to you seducing me? Correct?"

"That's my plan."

"I can be flexible."

His grin flashed. "I'd like to test that out."

They never got around to the tea.

And when she'd left him, he stood at the door and watched her run along the path. Love-struck idiot, he told himself. You can't keep her. You've never kept anything in your life that you couldn't fit in the bag you toss over your shoulder.

It was a bad turn of luck, that was all, that he would slip up and fall in love. It was bound to hurt like blazes before it was done. He'd get over it, of course. Over her and over this slippery feeling inside his heart. He wasn't so far gone as to believe this sort of madness lasted.

So best to enjoy it, he decided, and turned away when Keeley disappeared in the dark.

When he climbed into bed, her scent was on his pillow. For the first time in a week he slept deep and slept well.

Chapter 8

She missed him. It was the oddest thing to find herself thinking about Brian off and on during the day, and thinking of a dozen things she wanted to tell him, or show him when he got back from Saratoga.

She wasn't the only one.

During his next lesson Willy asked if Mr. Donnelly was coming so he could show off the fresh gap in his teeth. The man, Keeley mused, made an impression and made it fast.

It wasn't as if she didn't have enough to occupy her mind or her time. She'd found enough tuition students to add another class and was even now snaking her way through the maze of bureaucracy to arrange for three additional subsidized students.

She'd had meetings with the psychologist, the social worker, the parents and the children. The paperwork alone was enough to, well, choke a horse, she admitted. But it would be worth it in the end.

With some amusement, she flipped through the article in *Washingtonian Magazine*. She knew the exposure was responsible for netting her the new full tuition students. The photographs were gorgeous and the text made full use of her background, her Olympic medal and her social standing.

No problem there, she decided, particularly since the academy was mentioned several times.

She glanced at the phone with a little sigh as it rang. It hadn't stopped since the article had been published. The time was coming, Keeley thought, when she was going to have to break down and hire an assistant.

But for now, the school was all hers.

"Good morning, Royal Meadows Riding Academy." Her coolly professional tone warmed when she heard her cousin Maureen's voice.

Fifteen minutes later, she was hanging up and shaking her head. It appeared she was going to dinner and the races that evening. She'd said no—at least Keeley was fairly certain she'd said no five or six times. But nobody held out against Mo for long. She just rolled over you.

Keeley eyed the piles of paperwork on her desk, huffed out a breath when the phone rang again. Just do the first thing, she reminded herself, then do the second, and keep going until it was done.

She'd done the first, the second and the third, when her father came in.

He stopped in the doorway, held up a hand. "Wait, don't tell me. I know you. The face is very familiar." He narrowed his eyes as she rolled hers. "I'm sure I've seen you before, somewhere. Tibet? Mazetlan? At the dinner table a year or two ago."

"It hasn't been more than a week." She reached up as he bent to kiss her. "But I've missed you, too. I've been swamped here."

"So I've heard." He flipped open the magazine to her article. "Pretty girl. I bet her parents are proud of her."

"I hope so." When the phone rang, she muffled a shriek, waved her hands. "Let the machine get it. It's been ringing off the hook since Sunday. Half the parents who call in to inquire about lessons haven't even asked their kids if they want to ride."

She scooted her chair to the little fridge and took out two bottles of soda. "So thanks."

"For?" Travis prompted as he took the soft drink.

"For always asking."

"Then you're welcome. I hear I'm escorting two lovely women to dinner tonight."

"Mo caught you?"

He chuckled before he tipped back the bottle to drink. "'We haven't had an inter-family gathering in weeks,'" he mimicked. "'Don't you love me anymore?'"

"She always pushes the right button." Keeley studied the toe of her oldest boots. "So . . . have you heard from Brendon?"

"Late yesterday. They should be home tonight."

"That's good." You'd think the man could have called her once, she thought, scowling at her boots. Sent a telegram, a damn smoke signal.

"I imagine Brian's anxious to get back."

Her head jerked up. "Really?"

"Betty's making progress—as are several of the other yearlings. She's doing particularly well on the practice oval. She's ready for Brian to take her over full-time."

"I caught one of her morning workouts. She looks strong."

"We breed true at Royal Meadows." There was something wistful in his tone that had Keeley lifting her brows.

"What's the matter?"

"Nothing." Travis shrugged it off and rose. "Getting old."

"Don't be ridiculous."

"Yesterday you were riding on my shoulders," he murmured. "The house was full of noise. Clomping up and down the steps, doors slamming. Scattered toys. I don't know how many times I stepped on one of those damned little cars of Brady's."

Turning back, he ran a hand over her hair. "I miss that. I miss all of you."

"Daddy." In one fluid movement she rose and slid her arms around him.

"It's the way it's supposed to work. Three of you off at college, Brendon moving around to get a handle on the business of things. It's what he wants. And you, building your own. But . . . I miss the crowd of you."

"I promise to slam the door the very first chance I get."

"That might help."

"Sentimental softie. I love that about you."

"Lucky for me." He gave her a quick, hard squeeze, then glanced over as the phone rang again. "Actually I didn't stop in for sentiment, but to give you some business advice." He drew her back. "You need help around here."

"I'm thinking about it. Really," she added when he angled his head. "As soon as I straighten things out I'll look into it."

"I seem to recall you saying the same thing six months ago."

"It just hasn't been the right time. I've got it all under control." Even as she said it, the phone rang again.

"Keeley, getting help doesn't mean you won't be in charge, doesn't mean it won't be your school."

"I know, but . . . it won't be the same."

"I'm here to tell you nothing stays the same. The farm's more than it was when it passed to me, and less than it will be when it passes to you and your brothers and sisters. But I've put my mark on it. Nothing can change that."

"I guess I just don't want it to get away from me."

"You've already proven you can do it."

"You're right. Of course, you're right. But it isn't easy to find the right person. It would have to be someone good with kids and horses, and who'd be able to pitch in with the administrating to some extent and wouldn't quibble about shoveling manure. Plus I'd have to be able to depend on them, and get along with them. And they'd have to be diplomatic with parents, which is often the trickiest part."

Travis picked up his soft drink again. "I might be able to point you in the right direction there."

"Oh? Listen, Dad, I appreciate it, but you know, a friend of a friend or the son or daughter of an acquaintance. That kind of thing gets very sticky if it doesn't work out."

"Actually, I was thinking of someone a little closer to home. Your mother."

"Ma?" With a half laugh Keeley sat again. "Ma doesn't want this headache, even if she had time for it."

"Shows what you know." Smug now, he drank. "Just mention it to her, casually. I won't say a word about it."

By the time the day's lesson was over, and the last horse groomed and fed, Keeley dragged herself into the house. She wanted nothing more than a long bath and a quiet night. And if she ducked the evening plans, her cousin Mo would dog her like a hound. Better to face an evening out than weeks of nagging.

She moved through the kitchen, into the hall. Her father was right, she realized. How would any of them get used to the quiet? No one was shouting down the stairs or rushing in the door or playing music so loud it vibrated the eardrums.

She paused at the top of the steps, looking right. There was the room Brady and Patrick shared. She still remembered that during one spat Brady had run a line of black tape from the ceiling, down the wall, across the floor, and up again, cutting the room in half.

One had been marked Brady's Territory. The other he'd dubbed No Man's Land.

And how many times had she heard Brendon pound a fist on the wall between his room and theirs ordering them to keep it down before he came in and knocked their heads together?

When she passed Sarah's room, she saw her mother sitting on the bed, stroking a red sweater.

"Ma?"

"Oh." Adelia looked up. Her eyes were damp, but she shook her head and smiled. "You startled me. It's so bloody quiet in this house."

Keeley stepped in. The room had bright blue walls.

The curtains and spread picked up that bold hue and matched it with an equally vivid green in wide stripes. It should have been horrible, Keeley mused, as she often did. But it worked.

And it was completely Sarah.

"Do you and Dad share the same brain?" Keeping her voice light, Keeley sat on the bed. "He was feeling sad this morning over the same thing."

"I suppose after all these years together, you pick up the same vibrations or whatever. And Sarah called just a bit ago. She's desperately in need for this particular red sweater, which she can't think how she forgot to take with her. She sounds so happy and busy and grown up."

"They'll all be home next month for Thanksgiving, then again for Christmas."

"I know. Still, if I could think of a way to get away with it, I'd deliver this sweater myself instead of shipping it. Lord, look at the time. I've got to get myself cleaned up and changed for dinner. And so do you."

"Yeah." Keeley pursed her lips in thought while her mother smoothed the sweater one more time and rose. "I'm running behind today," she began. "I seem to be running behind a lot lately."

"That's what happens to successful people."

"I suppose so. And adding on this class is going to crowd my time and energy even more."

"You know I'll give you a hand when you need it, and so will your father." Adelia walked out of the room and into her own to lay Sarah's sweater aside.

"Yes, I appreciate that. I guess I'm going to have to seriously consider something more formal and permanent, though. I really hate to. I mean, taking on an outsider, it's difficult for me. But . . ."

Keeley let the word hang, surprised when her mother—who usually had something to say—remained silent.

"I don't suppose you'd be interested in working part-time at the school?"

Adelia turned her head, met Keeley's eyes in the mirror over the bureau. "Are you offering me a job?"

"It sounds awfully strange when you put it that way, but yes. But don't do it because you feel obliged. Only if you think you'd have the time or the inclination."

Adelia spun around, her face brilliant. "What the devil's taken you so long? I'll start tomorrow."

"Really? You really want to?"

"I've been *dying* to. Oh, it's taken every bit of my willpower not to come down there every day until you just got so used to me being around you didn't realize I *was* working there. This is exciting!" She rushed over to give Keeley a hug. "I can't wait to tell your father."

Keeping her arms tight around her daughter, Adelia did a quick dance. "I'm a groom again."

"If I'd known you were available, Dee, and looking for work, I'd've hired you." Burke Logan settled back in his chair and winked at his wife's cousin.

"We like to keep the best on at Royal Meadows." Adelia twinkled at him across the table in the track's dining room. He was as handsome and as dangerous to look at as he'd been nearly twenty years before when she'd first met him.

"Oh, I don't know." Burke trailed a hand over his wife's shoulder. "We have the best bookkeeper around at Three Aces."

"In that case, I want a raise." Erin picked up her wine and sent Burke a challenging look. "A big one. Trevor?"

Her voice was smooth, shimmering with Ireland as she addressed her son. "Do you have in mind to eat that pork chop or just use it for decoration?"

"I'm reading the *Racing Form,* Ma."

"His father's son," Erin muttered and snagged the paper from him. "Eat your dinner."

He heaved a sigh as only a twelve-year-old boy could. "I think Topeka in the third, with Lonesome in the fifth and Hennessy in the sixth for the trifecta. Dad says Topeka's generous and a cinch tip."

At his wife's long stare, Burke cleared his throat. "Stuff that pork chop in your mouth, Trev. Where's Jena?"

"She's fussing with her hair," Mo announced, and snatched a French fry from Travis's plate. "As usual," she added with the worldly air only an older sister could achieve, "the minute she turned fourteen she decided her hair was the bane of her existence. Huh. Like having long, thick, straight-as-a-pin black hair is a problem. This—" she tugged on one of the hundreds of wild red curls that spiraled around her face "—is a problem. If you're going to worry about something as stupid as hair, which I don't. Anyway, you guys have to come over and see this weanling I have my eye on. He's going to be amazing. And if Dad lets me train him . . ."

She trailed off, slanting a look at her father across the table.

"You'll be in college this time next year," Burke reminded her.

"Not if I can help it," Mo said under her breath.

Recognizing the mutinous look, Erin changed the subject. "Keeley, Burke tells me your new trainer is a natural with the horses, with Travis and with cards as well."

"And I hear he's gorgeous, too," Mo added.

"Where'd you hear that?" Keeley demanded before she could bite her tongue in two.

"Oh, word gets around in our snug little world," Mo said grandly. "And Shelley Mason—one of your kids? Her sister Lorna's in my World History class, a *huge* bore by the way. The class, that is, not Lorna, who's only a small bore. Anyway, she picked Shelley up last week from your place and got a load of the Irish hunk, so I heard all about it. Which is why I'm planning on coming over as soon as I can and getting a load of him myself."

"Trevor, give your sister your pork chop so she can stuff it in her mouth."

"Dad." Giggling, Mo snatched another fry. "I'm just going to look. So, Keeley, is he gorgeous? I respect your opinion more than Lorna Mason's."

"He's too old for you," Keeley said, a bit more sharply than she intended and had Mo rolling her eyes.

"Jeez. I don't want to marry him and have his children."

Travis's laugh prevented Keeley from snapping back with something foolish. "Good thing. Now that I've found someone who comes close to replacing Paddy, I don't intend to lose him to Three Aces."

"Okay." Mo licked salt from her fingertip. "I'll just ogle him."

Annoyed, and feeling ridiculous at the reaction, Keeley pushed back her chair. "I think I'll go down and take a look at the field, and check on Lonesome. He's always a little sulky before a race."

"Cool." Mo sprang up. "I'll go down with you."

Mo rushed out of the dining room, heading out past the betting windows at a fast clip, so that Keeley was forced to step lively to keep pace. "It's going to be so much fun for you, having your mom work at the school. There's nothing like a family operation, you know. Which is all I want. I mean, come on, I don't have to go to college to be a trainer. If I already know what I want to do, and I'm learning how to do it every day right at home, what's college going to do for me?"

"Expand your brain?" Keeley suggested.

Ignoring that, Mo hurried outside where the air had turned crisp. "I know horses, Keeley. You understand what it's like. It's instinct and experience and it's *doing*." She gestured widely. "Well, I've got time to nag my parents into submission."

"No one does it better."

With a laugh, Mo hooked her arm through her cousin's. "I'm so glad to see you. The summer just winged by, you know, with all of us so busy with stuff."

"I know."

They made the turn for the shedrow and the world was suddenly horses.

Some were being prepped for the next race. In the boxes, grooms wrapped long, thin legs that would carry those huge bodies in a blur of speed and power. Trainers with keen eyes and gentle hands moved among the horses to pamper a skittish ride or rev up another.

The hot walkers cooled down horses who'd already run. Legs were examined, iced down. Through the sharp air came the hoofbeats that signaled another field was coming back from the race. Steam rose off the horses' backs, turning into a fine and magical mist.

"Of all the shedrows in all the world." Brendon came out of the stables, grinning.

"You're back."

"Just." He strolled over to rub a hand over Mo's hair. "I talked to Ma a couple of hours ago from the road and she said you were all coming here tonight. So we swung by on the way home."

"We?"

"Yeah, Bri's taking a look at Lonesome, giving him a pep talk. Moodiest damn horse. Figured we might as well catch the race, then I can hook a ride back with you guys and Brian can trailer Zeus back home."

"Sounds like a plan." It pleased her to hear the calm of her own voice while her heart was galloping. "Actually I came down to take a look at Lonesome myself."

"He's all yours—and Bri's. Hey, I've got time to get some dinner. See you up there."

"Now you can introduce me to the hunk." Mo fell into step beside Keeley.

"I will if you can behave like you have a brain as well as glands."

"It has nothing to do with glands, I'm just curious. Don't worry, I'm taking a page out of your book there when it comes to men."

Keeley stopped at the door to the stables. "Excuse me?"

"You know, guys are fine to look at, or to hang around with occasionally. But there are lots more important things. I'm not going to get involved with one until I'm thirty, soonest."

Keeley wasn't certain whether to be amused or appalled. Then she heard Brian's voice, the lilt of it. And she forgot everything else.

He was in the box with Lonesome, a temperamental roan gelding. The horse moped, as was his habit before a race.

"They ask too much of you, there's no doubt about

it," Brian was saying as he checked the wrappings on Lonesome's legs. "It's a terrible cross you have to bear, and you show great courage and fortitude day after day. Perhaps if you win this one I can put a word in for you. You know, extra carrots and that sort of thing, a bit of molasses in the evening. A bigger brass plaque for your box at home."

"That's bribery," Keeley murmured.

Brian turned, his eyes going warm. "That's bargaining," he corrected. "But if I can interest you in a bribe," he began and opened the box door intending to snatch Keeley inside for a much anticipated welcome back kiss.

He nearly stepped over Mo. "Sorry. Didn't see you there."

"I'm short. That's my cross to bear. I'm Mo Logan." She stuck out a friendly hand. "Keeley's cousin from Three Aces."

"Pleased to meet you. You've a horse running tonight, Ms. Logan?"

"Mo. Hennessy. Sixth race. My money says he'll win laughing."

"I'll keep that in mind if I get up to the betting window."

"I want to take a look at Hennessy before his race. Come up to the dining room if you have time, Brian, for food or a drink. The family's all there."

"Thank you for that. Pretty thing," Brian murmured when Mo dashed off.

"She wanted to take a look at you, too. She heard you were a hunk."

"Is that so?" Amused, Brian shifted. "Did you tell her that?"

"I certainly did not. I have more respect for you than to speak of you in such a sexist way."

"Respect's a good thing." He yanked her into the box, crushing his mouth to hers before she could laugh. "But I'm banking on passion just at the moment. Have you passion for me, Keeley?" he murmured against her mouth.

"Apparently." Her ears were ringing. "Oh, Brian, I want—" She strained against him until they bumped into the horse. "You. Now. Somewhere. Can't we . . . it's been days."

"Four." He wanted to tear off the long slim dress she wore and mount her like a stallion, all blinding heat and primitive need.

He'd thought, convinced himself, that he'd be sensible about her, kept his wants and wishes under control. And all it had taken was seeing her. Just seeing her. It was exactly as it had been that first time he'd laid his eyes on her. A lightning strike in heart and blood.

"Keeley." He ran kisses over her face, buried his in her hair, then started all over again. "I've such a need for you. It's like burning from the inside out. Come with me, out to the lorry."

"Yes." At that moment, she'd have gone anywhere. It seemed he would swallow her whole. "Hurry. Let's hurry."

She took his hand, fumbled with the door herself. Breathless, she would have stumbled if he hadn't caught her. "Teach me to wear heels in the damn stable," she muttered. "My legs are shaking."

With a nervous laugh she turned back to him. Her legs stopped trembling. At least she couldn't feel them.

All she could feel now was the unsteady skipping of her heart.

He was staring at her, his eyes intense. When she'd turned his hands had reached up to frame her face. "You're so beautiful."

She'd never believed words like that mattered. They were so easily, and so often carelessly, said. But they didn't seem easy from him. And there was nothing careless about the tone of his voice. Before she could speak, before she could think of what could be said, there was a shout and the sound of running feet.

"Keeley, hurry, come with me." Oblivious to the intimacy of the scene she'd burst in on, Mo grabbed her hand. "I need backup. The bastard."

"What? What's happened?"

"If he thinks he's going to get away with it, he's got another think coming." Dragging Keeley, Mo barreled through the stables, turned and charged toward a stall.

Keeley could already hear the voices raised in argument. She saw the man first. She recognized him. Peter Tarmack with his oiled hair and cheap pinkie ring made a habit of picking up horses in claiming races, then running them into the ground.

The jockey was a familiar face as well. He was past his prime and, like Tarmack, was known to enjoy a few too many nips from the bottle at the track. Still, he picked up rides now and again when a regular jockey was sick or injured.

"I tell you, Tarmack, I won't ride him. And you won't get anyone else to. He's not fit to run."

"Don't you tell me what's fit. You'll get up and you'll ride, and you'll damn well place. You've been paid."

"Not to ride a sick and injured horse. You'll get your money back."

"What you haven't already put in a bottle."

Because Mo was quivering and had sucked in a breath to speak, Keeley squeezed her hand hard enough to grind bone. "Is there a problem, Larry?"

"Miss Keeley." The jockey yanked off his cap and turned his wrinkled, flustered face to hers. "I'm trying to tell Mr. Tarmack here that his horse isn't fit to race tonight. He's not fit."

"It's not your place to tell me anything. And I don't need one of the almighty Grant's damn whelps interfering in my business."

Before Keeley could respond, Brian had moved in. She blinked and he had hauled Tarmack up to his toes. "That's no way to be speaking to a lady." His voice was quiet, the eye of a storm. And the storm, with all its vengeance, was in his eyes. "You'll want to apologize for that, while you still have teeth to help you form the words."

"Brian, I can handle this."

"You'll handle what you like." He kept his eyes on Tarmack's now bulging ones. "But he'll by God apologize with his very next breath."

"I beg your pardon." Tarmack choked it out, wheezed in air as Brian relaxed his grip a little. "I'm simply trying to deal with a washed-up jockey—and one I've paid in advance."

"You'll get your money back," the jockey replied, then turned to Keeley. "Miss Keeley, I'm not getting up on this ride. He's half lame from a knee spavin, and anybody with eyes can see he's hidebound. He ain't fit to race."

"Excuse me." Her voice viciously cold, she pushed past Tarmack and moved into the box to examine the horse for herself. Within moments, her hands were shaking with rage.

"Mr. Tarmack, if you try to put a jockey on this horse, I'll have you up on charges. In fact, I'm damn well having you up on charges regardless. This gelding's sick, injured and neglected."

"Don't hang that on me. I've only had him a couple weeks."

"And in a couple weeks you haven't noticed his condition? You've been working him despite it?"

"Now you look." He started to take a step forward and found himself looking eye to eye with Brian again. "Listen," he said, his tone shifting to a whine. "Maybe you can be sentimental when you've got money. Me, I make my living moving horses. They don't run, I go in the red."

"How much?" Keeley laid a hand on the gelding's cheek. In her heart, he was already hers. "How much did he cost you?"

"Ah . . . ten grand."

Brian merely shoved a finger into Tarmack's breastbone. "Pull the other one. It has bells on it."

Tarmack shifted his shoulders. "Maybe it was five thousand. I'd have to check my books."

"You'll have a check for five thousand tomorrow. I'm taking the horse tonight. Brian, would you take a look at him, please?"

"Wait just a minute."

This time it was Keeley who turned and she who shoved Tarmack aside. "Be smart. Take the money.

Because whether you do or don't I'm taking this horse with me."

"The knee needs treatment," Brian said after a quick look. It burned his blood to see how the injury had been neglected. "We can deal with that. From the look of him, I'd say he has a good case of bots. He needs tending."

"He'll get tending."

Keeley merely glanced over her shoulder at Tarmack. "You can go." Her voice held the regal ring of dismissal—princess to peasant. "Someone will deliver the check to you in the morning."

The tone burned in Tarmack's gut. She wouldn't be so hoity-toity without her damn bodyguard, he thought. He'd have taught her a little respect if the Irish bastard hadn't been around.

He bunched a fist impotently in his pocket and tried to save face. "I'm not just letting you take the horse and leave me with nothing but your say-so. I don't give a damn who you are."

Brian straightened again, blood in his eye, but Keeley merely held up a hand. "Mo, would you please take Mr. Tarmack to the dining room. If you'd ask my father to write him a check for the five thousand, and I'll straighten it out later."

"Happy to." She grabbed Keeley by the shoulders, kissed her. "I knew you'd do it." Then with a sniff she turned away. "Come with me, Tarmack. You'll get your money."

"I'm sorry, Miss Keeley." Larry ran his cap through his hands. "I didn't know how bad it was till I saw the ride here. I couldn't get up on him seeing how he was."

"You did the right thing. Don't worry."

"He did pay me ahead, like he said."

She nodded, stepped out of the box again, gesturing to him. "How much do you have left?"

"'Bout twenty."

"Come and see me tomorrow. We'll take care of it."

"'Preciate it, Miss Keeley. That horse there, he ain't worth no five, you know."

She studied the gelding. His color was muddy, his face too square for elegance and made homelier still by an off-center blaze of dirty white. And his eyes were unbearably sad.

"Sure he is, Larry. He's worth it to me."

Chapter 9

"You don't have to help with this."

Brian said nothing, simply continued to clip the gelding's legs. Bots were a common enough problem, especially with horses at grass. But this one had been sadly neglected. He had no doubt the eggs the botfly had laid on the gelding's legs had been transferred to the stomach.

"Brian, really." Keeley continued to mix the blister for the knee spavin. "You've had a really long day. I can handle this."

"Sure you can. You can handle this, morons like Tarmack, washed-up jockeys and everything else that comes along before breakfast. Nobody's saying different."

Since the statement wasn't delivered in what could be mistaken for a complimentary tone, Keeley turned to frown at him. "What's wrong with you?"

"There's not a bloody thing wrong with me. But you could use some work. Do you have to do everything yourself, every flaming step and stage of it? Can't you just take help when help's offered and shut the hell up?"

She did shut the hell up, for ten shocked seconds. "I simply assumed that you'd be tired after your trip."

"I'll let you know when I'm tired."

"The gelding here doesn't seem to be the only one with something nasty in his system."

"Well, it's you in my system, princess, and it feels a bit nasty at the moment."

Hurt came first, a quick short-armed jab. Pride sprang in to defend. "I'll be happy to purge you, just like I'll purge this horse tomorrow."

"If I thought it would work," he muttered, "I'd purge myself. You'll want to wait until at least midday," Brian told her. "You can't be sure the last time he was fed."

"I know how to treat stomach-bots, thank you." Gently she began to apply the blister to the injured knee.

"Here, you'll get that all over your clothes."

Keeley jerked away bad-temperedly when Brian reached for the pot of blister. "They're my clothes."

"So you should have more respect for them. You've no business treating a horse in clothes like that. Silk dresses for God's sake."

"I've got a closetful. We princesses tend to."

"Nevertheless." He curled his fingers around the lip of the pot, and under the sick gelding they began a vicious little tug-of-war. He would have laughed, was on the point of it, when he looked at her face and saw that her eyes were wet.

He let go of the pot so abruptly, Keeley fell back on her butt. "What are you doing?" he demanded.

"I'm applying a non-irritating blister to a knee spavin. Now go away and let me get on with it."

"There's no reason to start that up. None at all."

Panic jingled straight to his head, nearly made him dizzy. "This is no place for crying."

"I'm upset. It's my stable. I can cry when and where I choose."

"All right, all right, all right." Desperately he dug into his pocket for a bandanna. "Here, just blow your nose or something."

"Just go to hell or something." Rather grandly, she turned her shoulder on him and continued to apply the blister.

"Keeley, I'm sorry." He wasn't sure for exactly what, but that wasn't here nor there. "Dry your eyes now, *a grha,* and we'll make this lad comfortable for the night."

"Don't take that placating tone with me. I'm not a child or a sick horse."

Brian dragged his hands through his hair, gave it one good yank. "Which tone would you prefer?"

"An honest one." Satisfied the blister was properly applied, she rose. "But I'm afraid the derisive one you've used since we got here fits that category. In your opinion, I'm spoiled, stubborn and too proud to accept help."

Though the tears appeared to have passed, he thought it wise to be cautious. "That's pretty close to the truth," he agreed, getting to his feet. "But it's an interesting mixture, and I've grown fond of it."

"I'm not spoiled."

Brian raised his eyebrows, cocked his head. "Perhaps the word means something different to you Yanks. Seems to me it's not everyone who could casually ask their father to write a check for five thousand dollars for a sick horse."

"I'll pay him back in the morning."

"I've no doubt of it."

Baffled now, she threw up her hands. "Should I have just left him there, walked away so that idiot Tarmack could find a jockey who would go up on him?"

"No, you did exactly right. But the fact's the same that you could toss around that kind of money without blinking an eye."

Brian walked to the gelding's head to examine his eyes and teeth. It grated on him. He wished it didn't, as it said little for him that her easy dismissal of money scored his pride.

But it had, at that heated moment at the track, slammed the distance between them right in his face.

"You're a generous woman, Keeley."

"But I can afford to be," she finished.

"True enough." He ran his hands down the horse's neck, soothing. "But that doesn't take away from the fact that you are." Slowly he continued to work his way over the horse. "You'll have to forgive me—Irish of my class are generally a bit resentful of the gentry. It's in the blood."

"The class system's in your head, Brian."

That, he thought, wasn't even worth commenting on. What was, was. His fingers found a small knot. "He's a bit of an abscess here. We'll want to bring this to a head."

They'd bring something else to a head, she decided and moved in so they faced each other over the gelding's back. "So tell me, how do men of your class deal with taking women of mine to bed?"

His eyes flashed to hers, held. "I'd keep my hands off you if I could."

"Is that supposed to flatter me?"

"No. It just is, and doesn't flatter either of us." He moved out of the box to get flannel to heat for a hot fermentation.

No, she thought. She'd be damned if she'd leave it at that. "Is that all there is to it, Brian?" she demanded as she followed him out. "Just sex?"

He ran water, hot as his hand could bear, and soaked a large section of flannel in it. "No." He spoke without turning around. "I care about you. That just makes it more difficult."

"It should make it easier."

"It doesn't."

"I don't understand you. Would you be happier if we just jumped each other, without any connection, any understanding or feelings?"

He hauled up the bucket. "Infinitely. But it's too late for that, isn't it?"

Baffled, she walked back into the box behind him. "You're angry with me because you care about me. This water's too hot," she said when she tested it.

"No, it isn't. And I'm not angry with you at t'all." Murmuring to the gelding, he lay the heated flannel over the abscess. "A bit with myself, maybe, but it's more satisfying to take it out on you."

"That, at least, I can understand. Brian, why are we fighting?" She laid a hand over the one he held pressed to the flannel. "We're doing the right thing here tonight. The method of how we got the gelding here isn't as important as what happens to him now."

"You're right, of course." He studied the contrast of their hands. His big, rough from work and hers small and elegant.

"And why we care for each other isn't as important as what we do about it."

About that he wasn't as sure, so he said nothing while she lifted another square of flannel and wrung it out.

Morning dawned misty and cool. As she'd slept poorly, Keeley's mind refused to click into gear. Her usual rush of morning adrenaline deserted her so that she began her daily chores with her body dragging and her brain fogged.

Brian's doing, she thought sulkily. This inconsistency of his, this off-and-on insistence to keep a distance between them was baffling. She'd never run into a problem she couldn't solve, an obstacle she couldn't overcome. But this one, this one man, might just be the exception.

He hurt her, and she hadn't been prepared for it. Could they have spent so much time together, been so intimate, and not understand each other? He cared about her, and that made it a problem. What kind of logic was that? she asked herself. Where was the sense in that kind of thinking?

Caring about someone made all the difference. She'd seen that constant well of compassion in him. It was, she admitted, as attractive, as appealing to her as that long, tough body, that thick, unkempt mane of sun-streaked hair.

The look of him, the face of planes and angles, the bold green eyes, might have stirred her blood—and had, though she'd been more annoyed than pleased initially. But it was the heart, the patience, the nurturing side he refused to acknowledge that had won her interest and respect.

Rather than being a problem, it had been, and was, the solution for her.

How could he look at her now, after all they'd shared, and see only the pampered daughter of a privileged home?

How could he, believing that, have feelings for her?

It was baffling, irritating and very close to infuriating. Or would be, she thought with a yawn, if she wasn't so damned tired.

The lack of energy struck unfairly keen when Mo bounced into the stables. "Just had to come by before I headed off to the eternal hell of school." She popped right into the box where Keeley was examining the injured knee. "How's he doing?"

"He's more comfortable." Testing, Keeley lifted the gelding's foot, bending the knee. He snorted, shied. "But you can see there's still pain."

"Poor guy. Poor big guy." Clucking, Mo patted his flank. "You were such a hero last night, Keel. I mean just stepping in and taking right over. I knew you would."

Keeley's brows drew together. "I didn't take over. I don't take over."

"Sure you did—you always do. The original take-charge gal. Very cool to watch. And this guy's grateful, aren't you, boy? Oh, and the hunk wasn't hard on the eyes, either." Grinning, she gave an obvious and deliberate shudder. "The real physical type. I thought he was going to punch that idiot Tarmack right in the face. Was kinda hoping he would. Anyway, the pair of you made a great team."

"I suppose."

"So, what about those smoldering looks?"

"What smoldering looks?"

"Get out." Mo cheerfully wiggled her eyebrows. "I got singed and I was only an innocent bystander. The guy looks at you like you were the last candy bar on the shelf and he'd die without a chocolate fix."

"That's a ridiculous analogy, and you're imagining things."

"He was going to pound Tarmack into dust for dissing you. Man, I just wanted to melt when he hauled the guy up by the collar. Too romantic."

"There's nothing romantic about a fight. And though I certainly could have handled Tarmack myself, I appreciated Brian's help."

Damn it, she thought. She hadn't even thanked him. Scowling, she stomped out of the box for a pitchfork.

"Yeah, you could have handled him. You handle everything. But not really needing to be rescued sort of makes *being* rescued more exciting, you know."

"No, I don't know," Keeley snapped. "Go to school, Mo. I've got mucking out to do."

"I'm going, I'm going. Sheesh. You must be low on the caffeine intake this morning. I'll come by later to see how the gelding's doing. I've got a kind of vested interest, you know? See you."

"Yeah, fine. Whatever." Keeley muttered to herself as she went to work on the stalls. There was nothing wrong with being able to handle things herself. Nothing wrong with wanting to. And she did appreciate Brian's help.

And she didn't need caffeine.

"I like caffeine," she grumbled. "I enjoy it, and that's entirely different from needing it. Entirely. I could give it up anytime I wanted, and I'd barely miss it."

Annoyed, she snagged the soft drink she'd left on a shelf and guzzled.

All right, so maybe she would miss it. But only because she liked the taste. It wasn't like a craving or an addiction or . . .

She couldn't say why Brian popped into her head just then. She was certain if he'd seen her staring in a kind of horror at a soft drink bottle, he'd have been amused. It was debatable what his reaction would be if he'd realized she wasn't actually seeing the bottle, but his face.

No, that wasn't a need, either, she thought quickly. She did not *need* Brian Donnelly. It was attraction. Affection—a cautious kind of affection. He was a man who interested her, and whom she admired in many ways. But it wasn't as if she needed . . .

"Oh God."

It had to be overreaction, she decided, and set the bottle aside as carefully as she would have a container of nitro. What she was going through was something as simple as overromanticizing an affair. That would be natural enough, she told herself, particularly since this was her first.

She didn't want to be in love with him. She began wielding the pitchfork vigorously now, as if to sweat out a fever. She didn't *choose* to be in love with him. That was even more important. When her hands trembled she ignored them and worked harder still.

By the time her mother joined her, Keeley had herself under control enough to casually ask Adelia to work in the office while she exercised Sam.

Keeley Grant had never run from a problem in her

life, and she wasn't about to start now. She saddled her mount, then rode off to clear her head before she dealt with the problem at hand.

The portable starting gate was in place on the practice oval. The air was soft and cool. Brian had seen the blush of color coming onto the leaves, the hints of change. Though he imagined it would all be a sight in another week or two, his attention was narrowed onto the horses.

He was working in fields of five, using two yearlings and three experienced racers at a go. This last phase of schooling just prior to public racing would teach him every bit as much as it taught the yearlings.

He needed to watch their style, learn their preferences, their quirks, their strengths. Much of it would be guesses—educated ones to be sure, but guesses nonetheless, at least until they had a few solid races under their belts.

But Brian was very good at guessing.

"I want Tempest on the rail." He chewed on a cigar as it helped him think. "Then The Brooder, then Betty, Caramel and Giant on the outside."

He glanced around at the sound of hoofbeats, then lost his train of thought as Keeley trotted toward the oval. Irritated, he looked deliberately away and slammed the door on that increasingly wide area of his mind she insisted on occupying.

"I don't want the yearlings rated," he ordered, telling the exercise boys not to hold them back. "Nor punished, either. No more than a tap of the bat to signal. My horses don't need to be whipped to run."

Despite his concentration, he was aware when

Keeley dismounted behind him. He took out his stopwatch, turning it over and over in his hand as the field was led to the gate.

"I don't know the yearling at the rail," Keeley said conversationally as she looped her reins around the top rung of the fence.

"Your father named him Tempest in a Teacup, as he's got a small build, but he's full of spirit. You don't often ride this way in the morning."

"No, but I wanted to see the progress. And my new assistant is handling things at the office."

He glanced over. She'd taken the band out of her hair. It flowed wild over her shoulders, but her face was cool and very serious. "Assistant is it? When did this happen?"

"Yesterday. My mother's working with me at the school now. Contrary to some beliefs, I don't insist on handling all the steps and stages by myself, when help is offered."

"Touchy still, are you?"

"Apparently."

"Well, you'll have to snarl at me later. I'm busy. Jim! Hold him steady now," Brian called out as Tempest shied a bit at the gate. "That one still objects a bit to being penned in. There, that's it," he murmured as the horses were loaded and the back gate shut. He held a finger over the timer, plunging when the gates sprang open.

The horses flew out.

He wondered if there was anything that gave his heart more of a knock than that instant, that first rush of speed, that blur of great bodies surging forward on the track.

But through the thrill of it, his eyes missed nothing. The stretch of legs, the clouds of dirt, the figures riding low over the necks.

"She wants the lead, right from the start," he murmured. "Wants the rest tasting her dust."

Caught up, Keeley leaned over the rail as the horses made the first turn. The thunder of hoofbeats drummed in her blood. "She runs well in a crowd. You were right about that. Tempest is a little nervy."

"We might try a shadow roll on him. He wants the outside. He's about endurance. The longer the race, the better he'll like it. There's Betty now. She wants the rail. Aye, she'll hug it like a lover."

Without thinking, he laid his hand over Keeley's on the rail. "Just look at her, will you? That's a champion. She doesn't need any of us. She knows it."

With his hand warm and firm over hers, Keeley watched the horses streak down the backstretch with Betty nearly a length in the lead. Pride and pleasure tangled inside her.

When Brian let out a shout, clicked his watch again, she started to turn, to indulge the giddy thrill by throwing her arms around him. But he was already drawing away.

"That's good time, damn good time. And she'll do better yet." He nodded, his eyes tracking as the riders rose high in their stirrups and slowed their mounts. "I'll find the right race for her, give her a taste of the real thing."

Giving Keeley an absent pat on the shoulder, he vaulted the fence.

She watched him go to the horses, to stroke and

compliment Tempest, give the rider a few words before moving on to Betty.

The filly pranced flirtatiously, then lowered her head to nibble delicately on Brian's shoulder.

You're wrong, Keeley thought. Whatever she knows, whatever she is, she needs you.

And so, damn it, do I.

After he'd stroked, nuzzled, praised, and the horses were led away to be cooled down, Brian jumped over the fence again to pick up his clipboard.

"I'd hoped your father would be down to see her first run with a field."

"I'm sure he would have. He must be tied up with something."

With a grunt in response, Brian continued to scribble notes. "Well, I'm running more of the yearlings this morning, so he'll see plenty. How's the gelding?"

"Comfortable. The swelling's down a little. I want to wait until after my class today to drench him. It's a messy business and I don't need a half dozen kids coming around once it starts to work on him."

"Best to wait till late in the day anyway. You want a good twenty-four hours between his last feeding and the drenching. I can do that for you if you're busy."

The automatic refusal was on the tip of her tongue. She nipped it off, took a breath. "Actually, I was hoping you'd find time to take a look at him later."

"I can do that." He glanced up, saw how set and serious her face was. "What is it? Are you that worried?"

"No." She took another breath, ordered herself to relax. "I'm sure everything will be fine." She'd make sure of it, she told herself. One way or the other. "I'll feel better when things are under control, that's all."

She worked it out. She felt better when she had a situation defined and a goal in mind. This one wasn't really so complicated, after all. She wanted Brian. She was fairly certain she was in love with him. Being certain of that would take a little more time, she imagined, a little more consideration.

After all this was new territory and needed to be approached with caution and preparation.

But her feelings for him were strong, and not as one-dimensional as simple attraction.

If it was love, then she needed to make him fall in love with her. She was perfectly willing to work toward what she wanted, as long as she got it in the end.

Pleasantly tired after a long day's work, she gave her horses their evening meal. There was no question about it, she decided. Having her mother help had taken a huge burden of time and effort off her shoulders.

Was it stubbornness, she wondered, that caused her to pull back from a helping hand so often? She didn't think so. But it was something nearly as mulish. She wanted the people she loved and who loved her to be proud of her. And she equated that, foolishly, she admitted, with the need to be perfect.

But she preferred thinking of it as taking responsibility.

Just as she was doing now with Brian, she mused. If she was in love with him, she was responsible for her own feelings. And it was up to her to try to generate those same feelings in him.

If she failed . . . No, she wouldn't consider that. Once you considered failure you were one step farther away from success.

Moving into the gelding's box, she hung his hay bag and measured out his feed. "It's better tonight, isn't it?" Gently she checked the swelling on his knee. When she heard the footsteps heading down on concrete, she smiled to herself.

"You're feeding him?" Brian stepped into the box. "I couldn't get up here any sooner."

"That's all right. He took the drenching without a quibble. And you can take my word for it, it worked." She straightened up, smiled. "You can see by the way he's eating, he's feeling better."

"Knows he's fallen into roses, he does." Brian examined the injury himself, nodded. "We have a stallion with the strangles, which is what held me up."

"Delicate creatures, aren't they?" She ran her hand over the gelding's withers. "Deceptive. The size of them, the speed and strength. It all shouts power. But under it all, there's the delicacy. You can be fooled by looking at something—at the face, at the form—and judging it without knowing what's inside."

"True enough."

"I'm not delicate, Brian. I have iron bred in me."

He looked at her. "I know you're strong, Keeley. And still, you've skin like a rosebud." Gently he ran his thumb over her cheek. "I have big hands, and they're hard, so I need to take care. It doesn't mean I think you're weak."

"All right."

He turned back to the horse. "Have you named him?"

"As a matter of fact, I have. We had a dog when I was a girl. My mother found him, a very homely stray who started sneaking up to the house. She fed him, gained his confidence. And before my father knew it, he had a big, sloppy mutt on his hands. His name was Finnegan." She laid her cheek on the gelding's, rubbed. "And so now is his."

"You've a sentimental streak along with that iron, Keeley."

"Yes, I do. And a latent romantic one."

"Is that so?" he murmured, a little surprised when she turned and ran her hands up his chest.

"Apparently. I didn't thank you for riding to my rescue last night."

"I don't recall riding anywhere." His lips twitched as she backed him out of the box.

"In a manner of speaking. You cut a bully down to size for me. I was upset and worried about the gelding, so I didn't really think about it at the time. But I did later, and I wanted to thank you."

"Well, you're welcome."

"I haven't finished thanking you." She bit lightly on his bottom lip, heard his quick indrawn breath.

"If that's what you have in mind, you could finish thanking me up in my bedroom."

"Why don't I just show you what I have in mind? Right here."

She had his shirt unbuttoned before he realized they were standing in an empty stall, freshly bedded with hay. "Here?" He laughed, taking both her hands to tug her out again. "I don't think so."

"Here." She countered his move by ramming his back against the side wall. "I know so."

"Don't be ridiculous." His lungs were clogged, and his mind insisted on following suit. "Anyone could come along."

"Live dangerously." She pulled the stall door shut behind them.

"I have been, since I first set eyes on you."

The thrum of the heart in her throat turned her voice husky. "Why stop now? Seduce me, Brian. I dare you."

"I've always found it hard to turn aside a dare." He reached out, tugged the band from her hair. "You cloud my senses, Keeley, like perfume. Before I know it, there's nothing there but you." He slid his hand around to cup the back of her neck, to draw her toward him. "And nothing that needs to be."

His mouth covered hers, soft, smooth in a kiss silky enough to have her gliding down on that alone. She'd asked for seduction knowing seduction wasn't needed.

"I want you, Brian. I wake up wanting you. Kiss me again."

And the way her body simply melted into his, the way her lips warmed and parted, inviting him in had every pulse in his body throbbing like a wound.

"I don't want to be gentle this time." He reversed their position until her back was against the wall, and his eyes, so suddenly dark, burned into hers. "I don't want to be so careful, just this once."

The thrill of it was a bolt through the heart. "Then don't. I'm not fragile like your horses, Brian. Don't be fooled."

"I'll frighten you." He couldn't have said if it was a threat or warning, but her answer was just another dare.

"Try it."

He tore her shirt open, sending buttons flying. He watched her eyes widen in shock even as he crushed his mouth to hers to swallow her gasp. Then his hands were on her, a rough scrape of callus over sensitive skin. Part of him expected her to object, to struggle away, but she only moaned against his savaging mouth, and held on.

When her knees gave like heated butter, he dragged her down to the mound of hay.

He used his mouth on her, his teeth, his tongue. A kind of wild fury. His hands raced over her, rough and possessive in their impatience to have more. To take all.

Her choked cries had the horses moving restlessly in their boxes. As he propelled her over that first breathless edge, she fisted her hands in his hair as if to anchor herself. Or to drag him with her.

He'd given her tenderness, shown her the beauty of lovemaking with patience and care. Now he showed her the dark glory of it with reckless demands and bruising hands.

Still she gave. Even with the whirlwind rushing inside him, he felt her give. Flesh dampened until it was slick, hearts pounded until the beat of them seemed to slap the air, but she rolled with him, accepting. Offering.

Even when her eyes were blind, the blue of them blurred as dark as midnight, she stayed with him. The sound of his name rushing through her lips seemed to sing in his blood.

She cried out, arching against his busy mouth when her world shattered into shards bright as glass. There was nothing to cling to, no thread to tie her to sanity, and still he drove her harder until the breath tearing from her lungs turned to harsh, primitive pants.

"It's me who has you." Wild to mate, he gripped her hips, jerked them high. "It's me who's in you." And plunged into her as if his life depended on it.

She heard a scream, high, thin, helpless. But it wasn't helplessness she felt. She felt power, outrageous power that pumped through her blood like a drug. Drunk on it, she reared up, her eyes locked on his as she fisted her hands in his hair once more.

She fixed her mouth on his, savaging it as he rode her, hard and fast. And she held on, held on, matching him beat for beat though she thought her body would burst, until she felt him fall.

"It's me," she said on a sob, "who has you." And still holding fast, let herself leap after him.

Chapter 10

As far as Keeley was concerned it was perfect. She'd fallen in love with a man who suited her. They had a strong foundation of common interests, enjoyed each other's company, respected each other's opinions.

He wasn't without flaws, of course. He tended to be moody and his confidence very often crossed the line into arrogance. But those qualities made him who he was.

The problem, as she saw it, was nudging him along from affair to commitment and commitment to marriage. She'd been raised to believe in permanency, in family, in the promise two people made to love for a lifetime.

She really had no choice but to marry Brian and make a life with him. And she was going to see to it he had no choice, either.

It was a bit like training a horse, she supposed. There was a lot of repetition, rewards, patience and affection. And a firm hand under it all.

She thought it would be most sensible for them to become engaged at Christmas, and marry the following summer. Certainly it would be most convenient for them to build their life near Royal Meadows as both of them worked there. Nothing could be simpler.

All she had to do was lead Brian to the same conclusions.

Being the kind of man he was, she imagined he'd want to make the moves. It was a little galling, but she loved him enough to wait until he made his declaration. It wouldn't be with hearts and flowers, she mused as she walked Finnegan around the paddock. Knowing Brian there would be passion, and challenge and just a hint of temper.

She was looking forward to it.

She stopped to check the gelding's leg for any heat or swelling. Gently she picked up his foot to bend the knee. When he showed no signs of discomfort, she gave him a brisk rub on the neck.

"Yeah," she said when he blew affectionately on her shoulder, "feeling pretty good these days, aren't you? I think you're ready for some exercise."

His coat looked healthy again, she noted as she saddled him. Time, care and attention had turned the tide for him. Perhaps he'd never be a beauty, and certainly he was no champion, but he had a sweet nature and a willing spirit.

That was more than enough.

When she swung into the saddle, Finnegan tossed his head, then at her signal started out of the paddock in a dignified walk.

She went cautiously for a time, tuning herself to him, checking for any hitch in his gait that would indicate he was favoring his leg. It pleased her so much to feel him slide into a smooth rhythm that after a few moments she relaxed enough to enjoy the quiet ride.

Fall had used a rich and varied palette this year to paint the trees in bold tones of golds and reds and orange. They swept over the hard blue canvas of sky and flamed under the strong slant of sunlight.

The fields held onto the deep green of high summer. Weanlings danced over the pastures, long legs reaching for speed as they charged their own shadows. Mares, their bellies swollen with the foals they carried, cropped lazily.

On the brown oval, colts and fillies raced in the majestic blur of power that brought thunder to the air.

This painting, Keeley thought, had been hers the whole of her life. The images that came back, repeating season after season. The beauty and strength of it, and the settled knowledge that it would go on year into year.

This she could, and would, pass on to her own children when the time came. The solidity of it, and the responsibilities, the joys and the sweat.

Sitting aside the healing gelding, she felt her throat ache with love. It wasn't just a place, it was a gift. One that had been treasured and tended by her parents. Her part in it, of it, would never be taken for granted.

When she saw Brian leaning on the fence, his attention riveted on the horses pounding down the backstretch, her aching throat seemed to snap shut.

For a moment she could only blink, stunned by the sudden, vicious pressure in her chest. Her skin tingled. There was no other word to describe how nerves swarmed over her in a wash of chills and heat.

As she fought to catch her breath, her heart pounded, a hammer on an anvil. The gelding shied under her, and had danced in a fretful half circle before she thought to control him.

And her hands trembled.

No, this was wrong. This wasn't acceptable at all. Where did this come from—how did she get this ball of terror in her stomach? She'd already accepted that she loved him, hadn't she? And it had been easy, a simple process of steps and study. Her mind was made up, her goals set. Damn it, she'd been pleased by the whole business.

So what was this shaky, dizzy, *painful* sensation, this clutch of panic that made her want to turn her mount sharply around and ride as far away as possible?

She'd been wrong, Keeley realized as she pressed an unsteady hand to her jumpy heart. She'd only been falling in love up to now. How foolish of her to be lulled by the smooth slide of it. This was the moment, she understood that now. This was the moment the bottom dropped away and sent her crashing.

Now the wind was knocked out of her, that same shock of sensation that came from losing your seat over a jump and finding yourself flipping through space until the ground reached up and smacked into you. Jolting bones and head and heart.

Love was an outrageous shock to the system, she thought. It was a wonder anyone survived it.

She was a Grant, Keeley reminded herself and straightened in the saddle. She knew how to take a tumble, just as she knew how to pick herself back up and focus mind and energy on the goal. She wouldn't just survive this knock to the heart. She'd thrive on it. And when she was done with Brian Donnelly, he wouldn't know what had hit him.

She steadied herself much as she had done before competitions. She took slow and deliberate breaths until her pulse rate slowed, focused her mind until it was calm as lake water, then she rode down to face her goal.

Brian turned when he heard her approach. The vague irritation at the interruption vanished when he saw Finnegan. He felt a keen interest there, and passing his clipboard and some instructions to the assistant trainer, moved toward the gelding.

"Well now, you're looking fit and fine, aren't you?" Automatically he bent down to check the injured leg. "No heat. That's good. How long have you had him out?"

"About fifteen minutes, at a walk."

"He could probably take a canter. He's looking good as new, no signs of swelling." Brian straightened, narrowing his eyes against the sun as he looked up at Keeley. "But you? Are you all right? You're a bit pale."

"Am I?" Small wonder, she thought, but smiled as she enjoyed the sensation of holding a secret inside her. "I don't feel pale. But you . . ." Swimming in the river of discovery, she leaned down. "You look wonderful. Rough and windblown and sexy."

His narrowed eyes flickered, and he stepped back, a little uneasy when she rubbed a hand over his cheek. There were a half a dozen men milling around, he thought. And every one of them had eyes.

"I was called down to the stables early this morning, didn't take time to shave."

She decided to take his evasive move as a challenge rather than an insult. "I like it. Just a little dangerous. If you've got time later, I thought you might help me out."

"With what?"

"Take a ride with me."

"I could do that."

"Good. About five?" She leaned down again and this time took a fistful of his shirt to yank him a step closer. "And, Brian? Don't shave."

The woman threw him off balance, and he didn't care for it. Giving him those hot looks and intimate little strokes in the middle of the damn morning so he went through the whole of the day itchy.

Worse yet the man who was paying him to work through the day, not to be distracted by his glands, was the woman's father.

It was a situation, Brian thought, and he'd done a great deal to bring it on himself. Still how could he have known in the beginning that he'd become so involved with her on so many levels inside himself? Falling in love had been a hard knock, but he'd taken knocks before. You got bruised and you went on. A bit of attraction was all right, a little flirtation was harmless enough. And the truth was, he'd enjoyed the risk of it. To a point.

But he was well past that point now. Now he was all wrapped up in her and at the same time had become fond of her family. Travis wasn't just a good and fair boss, but was on the way to becoming a kind of friend.

And here he was finding ways to make love to his friend's daughter as often as humanly possible.

Worse than that, he admitted as he strode toward her stables, he was—from time to time—catching himself dreaming. These little fantasies would sneak into his head when he was busy doing something else. He'd find himself wondering how it would all be between Keeley and him if things were different, if they were on the same level, so to speak. And he thought—well, that is if he were the settling down sort—that she might be just the one to settle down with.

If he were interested in rooting in one place with one person, that is. Which of course, wasn't in his plans at all. Even if it was—which it wasn't—it wouldn't work.

She was clubhouse and he was shedrow, and that was that.

Keeley was just kicking up her heels a bit. He understood about that, couldn't hold it against her. For all the privilege, she'd had a sheltered life and now was taking a few whacks at the boundaries of it. He'd rebelled himself against the borders of his own upbringing by sliding his way out of school and into the stables when he'd still been a boy. Nothing had stopped him, not the arguments, the threats, the punishments.

As soon as he'd been able, he'd left home, moving from stable to stable, track to track. He'd kept loose, he'd kept free and unfettered. And had never looked back. His brothers and sisters married, raised children, planted gardens, worked in steady jobs. They owned things, he thought now, while he owned nothing that couldn't easily fit in his traveling bag or be disposed of when he took to the next road.

When you owned things you had to tend them. Before you knew it, you owned more. Then the weight of them kept your feet planted in one spot.

He flicked a glance up at the pretty stone building that was his quarters, and admired the way it stood out against the evening sky. Flowers in colors of rust and scarlet and gold ran along the foundation, and the truck he'd bought from Paddy was parked like it belonged.

He stopped and, much as Keeley had that morning, turned to survey the land. It was a place, he realized, that could hold a man if he wasn't careful. The openness of it could fool you into believing it wasn't confining, then it would tempt you to plant things—yourself included—until it had you, heart and soul.

It was smart to remember it wasn't his land, any more than the horses were his horses. Or Keeley was his woman.

But when he stepped over toward her paddock, that fantasy snuck up on him again. In the long, soft shadows and quiet light of evening she saddled the big buff-colored gelding he knew she called Honey. Her hair was pinned on top of her head in an absentminded, messy knot that was ridiculously sexy. She wore jeans and a sweater of Kelly green.

She looked . . . reachable, Brian realized. Like the kind of woman a man wanted with him after a long day's work. There'd be a lot to talk about with this woman, over dinner, in the privacy of bed. Shared loves, shared jokes.

A man could wake up in the morning with a woman like that and not feel trapped, or worry that she did.

Catching himself, Brian shook his head. That was foolish thinking.

"Look at this." Brian walked up to the fence, leaned on it. "You've done all the work already."

"You've caught me on a good day." Keeley checked the cinch, stepped back. She knew his stirrup length now, and his favored bit and bridle. "I had no idea how much time I'd free up by having Ma help out on a regular basis."

"And what do you intend to do with it?"

"Enjoy it." When he opened the gate she led both horses through. "I've been so focused on the work the last couple of years, I haven't stepped back often enough to appreciate the results." She handed him the reins. "I like results."

"Then maybe you'll use some of that free time to come by the track." He vaulted into the saddle once she was mounted. "I'm looking for results there. I have Betty entered in a baby race tomorrow."

"Her maiden race? I wouldn't want to miss that."

"Charles Town. Two o'clock."

"I'll ask my mother to take my afternoon class. I'll be there."

They kept it to a walk, skirting the paddock and heading toward the rise of land swept with trees gone brilliant in the softening slants of sunlight. Overhead a flock of Canada geese arrowed across the evening sky sending out their deep calls.

"Twice daily," Brian said, watching the flight. "Off they go on their travels, honking away, dawn and dusk."

"I've always liked the sound of them. I guess it's something else that says home this time of year." She kept her eyes on the sky until the last call echoed away.

"Uncle Paddy phoned today."

"And how's he doing?"

"More than well. He'd bought himself a pair of young mares. He's decided to try his hand at some breeding."

"Once a horseman," Brian said. "I didn't figure he could keep out of the game."

"You'd miss it, wouldn't you? The smell and the sound of them. Have you ever thought of starting your own place, your own line?"

"No, that's not for me. I'm happy making another

man's horses. Once you own, it's a business, isn't it? An enterprise. I've no yearning to be a businessman."

"Some own for the love of it," Keeley pointed out. "And even the business doesn't shadow the feelings."

"In the rare case." Brian looked over, scanning the outbuildings. Yes, this was a place, he thought, built on feelings. "Your father's one, and I knew another once in Cork. But ownership can get in the blood as well, until you lose touch with that feeling. Before you know it, it's all facts and figures and a thirst for profit. That sounds like bars to me."

Interesting, she thought. "Making a living is a prison?"

"The need to make one, and still a better one, first and foremost. That's a trap. My father found his leg caught there."

"Really?" He so rarely mentioned his family. "What does he do?"

"He's a bank clerk. Day after day sitting in a little cage counting other people's money. What a life."

"Well, it's not the life for you."

"Thank God for that. These lads want a bit of a run," he said and kicked Honey into a gallop.

Keeley hissed in frustration but clicked to her mount to match pace. They'd come back to it, she promised herself. She hadn't learned nearly enough about where the man she intended to marry came from.

They rode for an hour before heading back to stable the horses and settle in the rest of her stock for the night. He was half hoping she'd ask him over to the house for dinner again, but she turned to him as they left the stables, lifted a brow.

"Why don't you ask me up for a drink?"

"A drink? There's not much of a variety, but you're welcome."

"It's nice to be asked occasionally." Before he could tuck his hand safely in his pocket, she took it, threaded their fingers together. "You have free time now and again yourself," she said easily. "I wonder if you've heard of the concept of dates. Dinner, movies, drives?"

"I've some experience with them." He glanced at his pickup as they turned toward his quarters. "If you've a yen for a drive, you can climb up into the lorry, but I'd need to shovel it out first."

She huffed out a breath. "That, Donnelly, wasn't the most romantic of invitations."

"Secondhand lorries aren't particularly romantic, and I've forgotten where I parked my glass coach."

"If that's another princess crack—" She broke off, set her teeth. Patience, she reminded herself. She wasn't going to spoil things with an argument. "Never mind. We'll forget the drive." She opened the door herself. "And move straight to dinner."

He caught the scent as soon as he stepped inside. Something aromatic and spicy that reminded him his stomach was about dead empty.

"What is it?"

"What is what?" Then she grinned and sniffed the air. "Oh, what is that? It's chili, one of my specialties. I put it on simmer before my last class."

"You cooked dinner?"

"Mmm." Amused, and very satisfied by his shock, she wandered off into the kitchen. "I didn't think you'd mind, and I knew we'd both be hungry by this time." She lifted the lid on a pot, gave it a quick stir while fragrant steam puffed out. "It's the kind of thing you can just leave and eat when you're ready, which is why it appeals to me. Oh, and I brought over a bottle of Merlot, though beer's never wrong with chili if you'd rather."

"I'm trying to remember the last time someone cooked for me—other than your mother and someone who was related to me."

Even more pleased, she turned to slide her arms around him. "Haven't any of your many women cooked for you?"

"Now and then perhaps, but not in recent memory." Because they were alone, he took her hips, brought her closer. "And I certainly remember none that smelled so appetizing."

"The women? Or the meal?"

"Both." He lowered his mouth to hers, allowed himself the luxury of sinking in. "And it reminds me I'm next to starving."

"What do you want first?" She grazed her teeth over his bottom lip. "Me, or the food?"

"I want you first. And last, it seems."

"That's handy, because I want you first, too." She drew back. "Why don't we clean up? I could use a shower." Laughing, her hands holding his, she pulled him out of the kitchen.

She'd brought over a change of clothes as well. It gave Brian a start to see her casually pulling on fresh jeans. Her hair was still wet from the shower they'd shared, her skin rosy from it. And, he noted, a bit raw in places because he hadn't shaved.

But the wild love they'd made under the hot spray in the steamy room wasn't anywhere near as intimate, anywhere near as *personal* somehow as her having a clean sweater lying neatly folded on the foot of his bed.

She reached for it, then glanced over, catching him staring at her. "What is it?"

He shook his head. There wasn't a way to explain this sense of panic and delight that lived inside him while he watched her dress. "I've rubbed your skin raw." Reaching out, he traced his fingertips over her collarbone. "I should have shaved. You're so soft." He murmured it, trailing those fingers up over her shoulder. "I don't know how I manage to forget that."

When she trembled, he looked up into her face. For a moment she saw the need flash back into his eyes, glinting like the edge of a sword. "Now you're cold. Put your sweater on. I've got some ointment."

The hot edge faded as quickly as it came. It was frustrating, she thought as he rooted into a drawer, that the only time he really broke the tether on his control was when they made love.

He got out a tube and since she'd yet to put the sweater on, squeezed ointment onto his fingers and began to gently rub it on her abraded skin. She recognized the scent.

"That's for horses."

"So?"

She laughed and let him fuss. "Does this make me your mare now?"

"No, you're too young and delicate of bone for that. You're still a filly."

"Are you going to train me, Donnelly?"

"Oh, you're out of my league, Miss Grant." He glanced up, cocked a brow when he saw her grinning at him. "And what amuses you?"

"You can't help it can you? You have to tend."

"I put the marks on you," he muttered as he smoothed on the ointment. "It follows I should see to them."

She lifted a hand to toy with the ends of his damp, gold-tipped hair. "I like being seen to by a man with a tough mind and a soft heart."

That soft heart sighed a little, ached a little. But he spoke lightly. "It's no hardship running my fingers over skin like yours." With his eyes on hers, he used the pad of his thumb to spread ointment over the gentle swell of her breast. "Particularly since you don't seem to have a qualm about standing here half naked and letting me."

"Should I blush and flutter?"

"You're not the fluttering sort. I like that about you." Satisfied, he capped the tube, then tugged the sweater over her head himself. "But I can't have such a fine piece of God's work catching a chill. There you are." He lifted her hair out of the neck.

"You don't have a hair dryer."

"There's air everywhere in here."

She laughed and dragged her fingers through her damp curls. "It'll have to do. Come on, let's have that wine while I finish up dinner."

He didn't know much about wine, but his first sip told him it was several steps up from what might be the usual accompaniment to so humble a meal as chili.

She seemed more at home in his kitchen than he was himself, finding things in drawers he'd yet to open. When she started to dress the salad, he set his glass aside.

"I'll be back in a minute."

"A minute's all you've got," she called out. "I'm putting the bread in to warm."

Since his answer was the slamming of the door, she shrugged and lit the candles she'd set on the little kitchen table. Cozy, she decided. And just romantic enough to suit two practical-minded people who didn't go in for a lot of fussing.

It was the sort of relaxed, simple meal two people could prepare together at the end of a workday. She intended to see they had more of them, until the man got a clue this was exactly how it was going to be.

Satisfied, she picked up her wine, toasted herself. "To good strong starts," she murmured and drank.

Hearing the door open again, she took the bread out of the oven. "We're set in here, and I'm starving."

She turned to put the basket of bread on the table and saw Brian, and the clutch of mums and zinnias he held in his hand.

"It seemed to call for them," he said.

She stared at the cheerful fall blossoms, then up into his face. "You picked me flowers."

The sheer disbelief in her voice had him moving his shoulders restlessly. "Well, you made me dinner, with wine and candles and the whole of it. Besides, they're your flowers anyway."

"No, they're not." Drowning in love she set the basket down, waited. "Until you give them to me."

"I'll never understand why women are so sentimental over posies." He held them out.

"Thank you." She closed her eyes, buried her face in them. She wanted to remember the exact fragrance, the exact texture. Then lowering them again, she lifted her mouth to his for a kiss. Rubbed her cheek against his.

His arms came around her so suddenly, so tightly, she gasped. "Brian? What is it?"

That gesture, the simple and sweet gesture of cheek against cheek nearly destroyed him. "It's nothing. I just like the way you feel against me when I hold you."

"Hold me any tighter, I'll be through you."

"Sorry." He pressed his lips to her forehead to give himself a moment to compose. "I forget my own strength when I'm starving to death."

"Then sit down and get started. I'll put these in some water."

"I . . ." He had to say something and cast around for a topic where he wouldn't stutter or say something that would embarrass them both. "I meant to tell you earlier, I looked up Finnegan's records."

There, he thought as he sat and began to dish up salad for both of them. Safe ground. "Of course he's registered as Flight of Fancy."

"Yes, I knew that." She tucked the flowers in a vase, and set them on the table before joining Brian. "Finnegan suits him better, I think."

"He's yours to call what you like now. His record in his first year of racing was uneven. His blood stock is very decent, but he never came up to potential, and his owners sold him off as a three-year-old."

"I was going to look up his data. You've saved me the trouble." She broke a hunk of bread in half, offered it. "He has good lines, and he responds well. Even after the abuse he hasn't turned common."

"The thing is he did considerably better in his third year. Some of his match-ups were uneven, and in my mind he was a bit overraced. I'd have done things differently if I'd have been working with him."

"You do things different, Brian, all around."

"Ah well. In any case, he went into that claiming race and that's how Tarmack got his hands on him."

"Bastard," Keeley said so coolly, Brian cocked his head.

"We won't argue there. I'm thinking you'd be wasting him in your school here. He was born for the track, and that's where he belongs."

Surprised, she frowned over her salad. "You think he should race?"

"I think you should consider it. Seriously. He's a thoroughbred, Keeley, bred to run. The need for it's in his blood. It's only that he's been misused and mismanaged. The athelete's inside him, and though your school's a fine thing, it's not enough for him."

"If he's prone to knee spavins—"

"You don't know that. It's not a hereditary thing. It was an injury a man was responsible for. You could have your father look him over if you don't think I've got the right of it."

She considered a moment, sipped her wine. "I certainly trust your judgment, Brian. It's not that. You and I both know that a horse can lose heart under mistreatment. Heart and spirit. I just wouldn't want to push him."

"Sure, it's up to you."

"Would you work with him?"

"I could." He ladled chili into bowls. "But so could you. You know what to do, what to look for."

She was already shaking her head. "Not for racing. I know my area, and it's not the track. If I consider running him again, I'd want him to have the best."

"That would be me," he said with such easy arrogance she grinned.

"Is that a yes?"

"If your father agrees to having me work your horse on the side, I'm happy to. We'll start him off easy, and see how he goes." He started to leave it at that, then because he thought she'd understand, hoped she would, finished. "It was in his eyes this morning, when you rode him down to the track. It was there. The yearning."

"I didn't see it." She reached over to touch his hand. "I'm glad you did."

"It's my job to see it."

"It's your gift," she corrected. "Your family must be proud of you." She spoke casually, began to eat again, then stared at him, baffled, when he laughed. "Why is that funny?"

"Pride wouldn't exactly be part of their general outlook to my way of thinking."

"Why?"

"People can't find pride in what they don't understand. Not all families, Keeley, are as cozy as yours."

"I'm sorry," she said, and meant it. Not only for whatever lack there was in his family feelings, but for deliberately prying.

"Sure it's not such a matter. We get on all right."

She meant to let it go, to change the subject, but the words burned inside her. "If they're not proud of you, then they're stupid." When he stared, his next bite of chili halfway to his mouth, she shrugged. "I'm sorry, but they are."

Watching her, he started to eat again. Her eyes were snapping, her cheeks flushed, her jaw set. Why the woman was fuming, he realized. "Darling, that's sweet of you to say, but—"

"It's not. It's rude, but I meant it." Snatching up the wine bottle, she topped off both of their glasses. "You have a real talent, and you've earned a strong reputation—or you damn well wouldn't be here at Royal Meadows. What's not to be proud of?" she demanded, with even more heat. "Your father, of all people, should understand."

"Why?"

Her mouth dropped open. "He's the one who introduced you to horses."

"To the track. It wasn't the horses for my father," Brian told her. He was so fascinated by her reaction it didn't occur to him that he was having an in-depth conversation about his family. Something he absolutely never did.

"They were a kind of vehicle. He admired them, certainly. But it was the wagering, the rush of gambling that called to him. Likely still does. That and the chance to take a few pulls from the flask in his pocket without my mother's silent and deadly disapproval. I told you, Keeley, he's a bank clerk."

"What difference does that make?"

All, was what Brian thought, but he struggled to find a more tangible explanation for her. "He stopped looking through the bars of his little cage years back. He and my mother, they married young, not quite the full nine months, you understand, before my oldest sister came along."

"That can be difficult, but still—"

"No, they were content with it. I think they love each other, in their way." He didn't think about those areas much, but since he was in it now, he did his best. "They made their home, raised their children. My father brought in the wage. Though he gambled, we never went hungry—and bills were paid sooner or later. My mother always set a decent table, and our clothes were clean. But it seemed to me that the both of them were just tired out at the end of the day, just from doing."

Keeley remembered an expression of her mother's. *A child could starve with a full plate.* She understood that without love, affection, laughter, the spirit hungered.

"Going your own way shouldn't stop them from being happy for you."

"My brother and my sisters, they're clerks and parents and settled sort of people. I'm a puzzle, and sooner or later when you can't solve a puzzle, you have to think there's something wrong with it. Else there's something wrong with you."

"You ran away," she murmured.

He wasn't sure he liked the phrase, but nodded. "In a sense, I suppose, and as fast as I could. What's the point in looking back?"

But he was looking back, Keeley thought. Looking back over his shoulder, because he was still running away.

Chapter 11

Keeley decided some men simply took longer than others to realize they wanted to go where you were leading them. It was hard to complain since she was having such a wonderful time. She was making it a habit to go to the track once a week, a pleasure she'd cut out of her life while she'd been organizing her academy.

There were still dozens of details that she needed to see to personally—the meetings, the reports and follow-ups on each individual child. She wanted to plan a kind of open house during the holidays, where all the parents, grandparents, foster families could come to the academy. Meet and mingle, and most importantly see the progress their children had made.

But now that her school was on course, and she'd expanded to seven days a week, she was more than happy to turn the classes over to her mother for one day.

She was thrilled to watch Betty's progress, to see for herself that Brian's instincts had been on target with the filly. Betty was, day after day and week after week, proving herself to be a top competitor and a potential champion.

But even more she was delighted to see Finnegan come to life under Brian's patient, unwavering hand.

Bundled against the chill of a frosty morning, Keeley stood at the fence of the practice oval and waited while Brian gave Larry his instructions on the workout run.

"He gets nervy in the gate, but he breaks clean. You'll need to rate him or he'll lose his wind. He likes a crowd so I want you to keep him in the pack till after the second turn. You let him know then, firm, that you want more. He'll give it to you. He doesn't like running in front, he misses the company."

"I'll keep his eye on the line, Mr. Donnelly. I appreciate you giving me the chance."

"It's Miss Grant's giving you the chance. I smell whiskey on your breath before post time tomorrow, and you won't get a second one."

"Not a drop. We'll run for you, if for nothing but to show that son of a bitch Tarmack how you treat a thoroughbred."

"Fair enough. Let's see how she goes."

Brian walked back to the fence where Keeley stood sipping her soft drink. "I don't know if you made the best choice in jockeys, but he's sober and he's hungry, so it's a good gamble."

"It's not the winning this time, Brian."

He took her bottle, sipped, winced. How the woman could drink such a thing in the morning was beyond him. "It's always the winning."

"You've done a wonderful job with him."

"We won't know that until tomorrow at Pimlico."

"Stop it," she ordered when he slipped through the split rail fence. "Take credit when it's deserved. That's a horse that's found his pride again," she said as the practice field was led to the gate. "You gave it to him."

"For God's sake, Keeley, he's your horse. I just reminded him he could run."

You're wrong, she thought. You gave him back his pride, just the way you made him your own.

But Brian was already focused on the horse. He took out his stopwatch. "Let's see how well he remembers running this morning."

Mists swam along the ground, a shallow river over the oval. Shards of frost still glittered on the grass while the sun pulsed weakly through the layers of morning clouds. The air was gray and still.

With a ringing clang the gate sprang open. And the horses plunged.

Ground fog tore like thin silver ribbon at the powerful cut of legs. Bodies, glistening from the morning damp, surged past in one sleek blur.

"That's it," Brian murmured. "Keep him centered. That's the way."

"They're beautiful. All of them."

"Got to pace him." Brian watched them round the first turn while the clock in his head ticked off the time. "See, he'll match his rhythm to the leader. It's a game to him now. Out gallivanting with mates, that's all he's thinking."

Keeley laughed, leaned out as her heart began to bump. "How do you know what he's thinking?"

"He told me. Get ready now. Ready now. Aye, that's it. He's strong. He'll never be a beauty, but he's strong. See, he's moving up." Forgetting himself Brian laid a hand on her shoulder, squeezed. "He's got more heart than brains, and it's his heart that runs."

Brian clicked the watch when Finnegan came in, half a length behind the leader. "Well done. Yes, well done. I'd say he'll place for you tomorrow, Miss Grant."

"It doesn't matter."

Sincerely shocked more than offended, he goggled at her. "That's a hell of a thing to say. And what kind of luck is that going to bring us tomorrow, I'd like to know?"

"It's enough to watch him run. And better, to watch you watching him run. Brian." Touched, she laid a hand on his heart. "You've gone and fallen in love with him."

"I love all the horses I train."

"Yes, I've seen that, and understand that because it's the same with me. But you're in love with this one."

Embarrassed because it was true, Brian swung over the fence. "That's a woman for you, making sloppy sentiment out of a job."

She only smiled as Brian walked over to stroke and nuzzle his job.

"That's a fine thing. My daughter and my trainer grooming a competitor."

She glanced over her shoulder, held out a hand for her father as he strode toward her. "Did you see him run?"

"The last few seconds. You've brought him a long way in a short time." Travis pressed a kiss to the top of her head. "I'm proud of you."

She closed her eyes. How easily he said it, how lovely to know he meant it. It made her only more sad, more angry, that Brian had cause to laugh over the idea of his own father having any pride in him.

"You taught me to care, you and Ma. When I saw

that horse, I cared because of what you put inside me." She tilted her head up, kissed her father's cheek. "So thanks."

When his arm came around her, she leaned in, warm and comfortable. "Brian was right. The horse needs to race. It's what he is. I wanted to save him. But Brian knew that wasn't enough. For some it's not enough just to get by."

"You brought this off together."

"You're right." She laughed a little as realization dawned, so clear and bright she wondered how she'd missed it before. "Absolutely right."

She'd canceled classes for the day. It was, Keeley told herself, a kind of holiday. A celebration, she thought, in compassion, understanding and hard work. It wasn't only Finnegan's return to the track, but Betty's first important race. Her parents would be there, and Brendon.

If there was ever a day to close up shop, this was it.

She rode out to the track at dawn, to give herself the pleasure of watching the early workouts, of listening to the track rats, building anticipation.

"You'd think it was the Derby," Brendon said as he walked with her back to the shedrow. "You're hyped."

"I've never owned a racehorse before. And I'm pretty sure he's my first and last. I'm going to enjoy every moment of this, but . . . It's not my passion. Not like it's yours and Dad's. Even Ma's."

"You channeled your passions into the school. I never thought you'd give up competing, Keel."

"Neither did I. And I never thought I'd find anything that satisfied me as much, challenged me as much."

Irish Rebel   435

They stopped as horses were brought back from the early workouts.

Steam rose off their backs, out of the tubs of hot water set outside the stables. It fogged the air, cushioned the sound, blurred the colors.

Hot walkers hustled to cool off the runners, stablehands and grooms loitered, waiting for their charges. Someone played a mournful little tune on a harmonica, with the ring of the farrier's anvil setting the beat.

"This is your deal here," she said, gesturing as Betty was led by. "Me, I'm happy just to watch."

"Yeah? Then what're you doing here so early?"

"Just carrying on a fine family tradition. I'm going to act as Finnegan's groom."

That was news to Brian, and he wasn't entirely pleased when she announced her intentions. "Owners don't groom. They sit in the grandstands, or up in the restaurant. They stay out of the way."

Keeley continued strapping Finnegan with straw. "How long have you worked at Royal Meadows now?"

His scowl only deepened. "Since midthrough of August."

"Well, that should be long enough for you to have noticed the Grants don't stay out of the way."

"Noticing doesn't mean approving." He studied the way she groomed Finnegan's neck and couldn't find fault. But that was beside the point. "Grooming a horse for showing or schooling or basic riding is a different matter than grooming before a race."

She let out a long-suffering sigh. "Does it look like I know what I'm doing?"

"His legs need to be wrapped."

Saying nothing, she gestured to the wrapping on the line, and the extra clothespins hooked to her jeans.

Not yet convinced, he studied her grooming kit and the other tools of a groomer's trade. The cotton batting, the blankets, the tack.

"The irons haven't been polished."

She glanced at the saddle. "I know how to polish irons."

Brian rocked back on his heels. He needed to see to Betty. She was racing in the second. "He needs to be talked to."

"This is funny, but I know how to talk, too."

Brian swore under his breath. "He prefers singing."

"Excuse me?"

"I said, he prefers singing."

"Oh." Keeley tucked her tongue in her cheek. "Any particular tune? Wait, let me guess. *Finnegan's Wake?*" Brian's steely-eyed stare had her laughing until she had to lean weakly against the gelding. The horse responded by twisting his head and trying to sniff her pockets for apples.

"It's a quick tune," Brian said coolly, "and he likes hearing his name."

"I know the chorus." Gamely Keeley struggled to swallow another giggle. "But I'm not sure I know all the words. There are several verses as I recall."

"Do the best you can," he muttered and strode off. His lips twitched as he heard her launch into the song about the Dubliner who had a tippling way.

When he reached Betty's box, he shook his head. "I should've known. If there's not a Grant one place, there's a Grant in another until you're tripping over them."

Travis gave Betty a last pat on the shoulder. "Is that Keeley I hear singing?"

"She's being sarcastic, but as long as the job's done. She's dug in her heels about grooming Finnegan."

"She comes by it naturally. The hard head as well as the skill."

"Never had so many owners breathing down my neck. We don't need them, do we, darling?" Brian laid his hands on Betty's cheek, and she shook her head, then nibbled his hair.

"Damn horse has a crush on you."

"She may be your lady, sir, but she's my own true love. Aren't you beautiful, my heart?" He stroked, sliding into the Gaelic that had Betty's ears pricked and her body shifting restlessly.

"She likes being excited before a race," Brian murmured. "What do you call it—pumped up like your American football players. Which is a sport that eludes me altogether as they're gathered into circles discussing things most of the time instead of getting on with it."

"I heard you won the pool on last Monday night's game," Travis commented.

"Betting's the only thing about your football I do understand." Brian gathered her reins. "I'll walk her around a bit before we take her down. She likes to parade. You and your missus will want to stay close to the winner's circle."

Travis grinned at him. "We'll be watching from the rail."

"Let's go show off." Brian led Betty out.

Keeley put the final polish on the saddle irons, rolled her now aching shoulders and decided she had enough time to hunt up a soft drink before giving Finnegan a last-minute pep talk.

She stepped outside and blinked in the sudden whitewash of light. The minute her eyes focused she saw Brian sitting near the stable door on an overturned bucket.

Alarm sprinted into her throat. He had his head in his hands and was still as stone.

"What is it? What's wrong?" She leaped forward to drop to the ground beside him. "Betty?" Her breath came short. "I thought Betty was racing."

"She was. She did. She won."

"God, Brian, I thought something was wrong."

He dropped his hands and she could see his eyes were dark, swarming with emotion. "Two and a half lengths," he said. "She won by two and a half lengths, and I swear I don't think she was half trying. Nothing could touch her, do you see? Nothing. Never in my life did I think to have a horse like that under my hands. She's a miracle."

Keeley laid her hands on his knees, sat back on her heels. Passion, she thought. She'd spoken to Brendon of it, but now she was looking at it. "You made her." Before he could speak, she shook her head. "That's what you said to me once. 'I don't break horses. I make them.'"

"I can't get my head round it just now. This field was strong. I put her in thinking now and then you need a lesson in humility. Time for her to grow up, you know what I mean. Face real competition."

Still staggered, he dragged his hands through his hair and laughed. "Well, she'll never learn a damn thing about humility."

"Why aren't you down with her?"

"That's for your parents. She's their horse."

"You've a lot to learn yourself." She got to her feet, brushed off the knees of her jeans. "Well, Finnegan will be going down shortly. Why don't you come in and look him over?"

Brian blew out a breath, sucked in another, then rose. "I think he'll place for you," he told Keeley as he followed her in. "It wouldn't hurt to wager on it."

"I intend to wager on him." While Brian went in to check Finnegan's leg wrappings, she got papers out of the pocket of the jacket she'd laid aside.

"The wrappings look all right." He flicked a finger over the stirrups. "And you polished the irons well enough."

"Glad you approve. Next time you can do it." She held out the papers.

"What's this?"

"Papers giving you half interest in Flight of Fancy, also known as Finnegan."

"What are you talking about?"

"He was half yours anyway, Brian. This just makes it legal."

His palms went cold and damp. "Don't be ridiculous. I can't take that."

She'd expected him to refuse initially, but she hadn't expected him to go pale and snarl. "Why? You helped bring him back. You trained him."

"A couple of weeks work, on my off time. Now put those away and stop being foolish."

When he started to push by her, she simply shifted to block his way. "First, he wouldn't be racing today if it wasn't for you. And second, you're as attached to him as I am. Probably more. If it's the money—"

"It's not the money." Though a part of him knew it was, to some extent. Because it was hers.

"Then what?"

"I don't own horses. I don't want to be an owner."

"That's a pity, because you are an owner. Or a half owner anyway."

"I said I'm not accepting it."

"We'll argue about it later."

"There's nothing to argue about."

She stepped out of the box, smiled sweetly. "You know, Brian, just because you can make a fifteen-hundred-pound horse do what you want, doesn't mean you can budge me one inch. I'm going to go bet on our horse. To win."

"He's not our—" He broke off, swore, as she'd already flounced out. "And you don't bet to win," he muttered. "It's nothing personal," he said to Finnegan who was watching him with soft, sad eyes. "I just can't be owning things. It's not that I don't have great affection and respect for you, for I do. But what happens if in a year or two down the road I move on? Even if I don't—as it's feeling more and more that I'd wonder why I would—I can't have the woman give me a horse. Even a half a horse. Well, not to worry. We'll straighten it all out later."

He shouldn't have been nervous. It was pitiful. It was just another horse, just another race. It wasn't, as Betty was, a shining gift. This was an apple-loving, sweet-natured gelding who'd already broken down once and had lost far more races than he'd won in his short career.

Brian was fond of him, of course, and wanted him to

have his day in the sun. But he had no illusions about this one being a champion.

He was simply guiding the horse toward doing what he'd been born for. And that was run his best.

And still nerves danced in Brian's belly.

"The track's dry and fast," he told Larry as they walked past the backstretch. "That's good for him. The field's crowded, and he likes that, too. Blue Devil's the number six horse, and odds-on favorite. There's reason for that."

"I know Blue Devil." Larry nodded and gnashed a mouthful of gum. "He can slither through a pack like a snake. He gets in the lead, he sets a fast pace."

"I expect that's what he'll do today. I need you to feel what Finnegan's got in him. I don't want you over-racing him, but don't hold him back past the first turn. Let him test his legs."

"I'll take care of him, Mr. Donnelly. Here's Miss Grant come to see us off. He looks fine, Miss Grant. You done good with him."

"Yes." A little breathless from the run back from the betting window, she gave Finnegan a brisk rub. "We did."

When the call sounded for riders up, she stepped back. "Good luck."

"Talk to him." Brian gave Larry a leg up. "Don't forget to talk to him all the way. Don't let him forget what he's there for."

"They look good," Keeley decided. "Here."

"What now?"

"I put fifty down for you."

"You—damn it."

"You can pay me back out of your winnings," she

said breezily. "We'd better get to the rail. I don't want to miss the start. Have you seen my family?"

"No. They're around. The lot of you's everywhere." Because she was moving through the crowd, he grabbed her hand. He could imagine her being trampled. "I don't know why you don't go up into the bar where you can watch in civilized surroundings."

"Snob."

"It's not a matter of—" He gave up. "I want you to tear up those papers."

"No. Look they're bringing them to the gate."

"I'm not taking a half interest in your horse."

"Our horse. Who's number three? I lost my *Racing Form*."

"Prime Target, eight to five, likes to come from behind. Keeley, it's a thoughtful gesture, but—"

"It's a sensible one. Okay, here we go." She shot him a brilliant smile. "Our first race."

The bell rang.

They shot out of the gate, ten muscular bodies with men clinging fiercely to their backs. Within seconds they were merged into one speeding form with legs reaching, flying, striking. Silks of red, white, gold, green streamed by in a shock of color. And the sound was huge.

Blindly Keeley groped for Brian's hand and clung.

She lost her breath, and her sense, in the sheer thrill.

Clouds of dust spewed from the dry track, jockeys slanted forward like dolls, and the pack began to break apart at the second turn.

"He's holding onto fourth," Keeley shouted. "He's holding on."

The lead horse edged forward. A head, a half a

length. Finnegan bulled up the line, nipping the distance, vying for third. Keeley heard the crowd around her, the solid roar of it, but her heart pounded to the rhythm of hoofbeats.

Those legs stretched, reached, lifted.

"He's gaining." She began to laugh, even as her hand clamped on Brian's, she laughed. From the joy bursting inside her, she might have been riding low on the gelding's back herself. "He's gaining. He's moving up, into second. Would you look at him?"

He was looking, and the grin on his face was wide. "I didn't give him enough credit for guts. Not nearly enough credit. He'll move on the backstretch. If he's still got it in him, he'll move."

And he moved, a big, unhandsome horse at twenty to one odds with a washed-up jockey in the irons. He moved like a bullet, streaking down the dirt, charging the leader, running neck-in-neck with the favorite while the crowd screamed.

Seconds before the finish line, he pulled ahead by a nose.

"He won." Keeley whirled to Brian. She wondered if the shock on his face mirrored her own. "My God, Brian, he won!"

"Two miracles in one day." He let out a short, baffled laugh, then another, longer. Riding on the thrill, he plucked Keeley off her feet and spun her in circles.

"I never expected it." She threw her arms in the air, then wrapped them around his neck and kissed him. "I never expected him to win."

"You bet on him."

"That was for love, not for reality. I never thought he'd win."

"He did." Brian gave her a last spin before setting her on her feet. "That's what counts."

"We're going to celebrate. Big time."

While Betty's win had left him shaken to the soul by that heady taste of destiny, this was sheer, stupefied delight. He snatched Keeley again and spun her into a quick waltz through the crowd.

"I'll buy you a bottle of champagne."

"Two," she corrected. "One for each of us. We have to get down to the winner's circle."

"You have to. I don't go to winner's circles."

He might behave like a mule, she mused, but he was a man. And she knew which button to push. "You don't have to go for me, or even for yourself. But you have to go for him." She held out a hand.

He wanted to swear but figured it a waste of breath. "I'll go, as his trainer. He's your horse. I don't own any part of him."

"Half," she corrected, trotting to keep up as Brian tugged her along. "But we can discuss which half."

Chapter 12

"Of course I'm seeing to him." Keeley bent to unwrap Finnegan's right foreleg.

"You should be up celebrating."

"This is part of it." She ran her hands carefully up the gelding's leg before pinning the wrapping to the line. "Finnegan and I are going to congratulate each other while I clean him up. But you could do me a favor." She pulled her ticket out of her pocket. "Cash in my winnings."

Brian shook his head. "At the moment I'm too pleased to be annoyed with you for betting my money." With one hand on the horse he leaned over to kiss her. "But I'm not taking half the horse."

Keeley hooked an arm around Finnegan's neck. "You hear that? He doesn't want you."

"Don't say things like that to him."

She laid her cheek against the gelding's. "You're the one hurting his feelings."

As two pairs of eyes studied him, Brian hissed out a breath. "We'll discuss this privately at some other time."

"He needs you. We both do."

The muscles in his belly twisted. "That's unfair."

"That's fact."

He looked so uncomfortable, she sighed. She wanted to throw up her hands, give the man a good thump. But it wasn't the time to rage or demand he take a good look at a woman who loved him.

"We will talk about it." They were going to talk about a great many things, she decided. Very soon. "But for now, we'll just be happy."

He hesitated while she went back to unwrapping Finnegan's legs. "I've been happier in the last few months than I've ever been."

"That doesn't have to change." She finished hanging the wrappings, picked up a dandy brush. "We're a good team, Brian. There's a lot we could do together."

Brian ran a hand down Finnegan's throat. "We've made quite a start here. Would you want to go out after a bit and have some fancy dinner and wine?"

Keeley slanted him a look. "Are you finally asking me for a date?"

"It seems appropriate under the circumstances." Grinning he fingered the betting ticket. "And it seems I've come in to some extra cash."

"Then I'd love to."

"I've got to go check on Betty, make sure she's transported back to the farm."

"If you run into any of my family, tell them where I am, will you?"

"I will. He's had his moment in the sun, hasn't he?" Brian murmured.

Keeley set the brush down, crossing over as Brian opened the stall door. "You've had quite a day, Donnelly."

"I have. I don't know when there's been another like it."

She put her arms around him, resting her head on his shoulder. "There'll be more." *For all of us.* She tipped back her head. "We'll make more," she promised as she raised her mouth to his.

He could have lost himself in her. It was so easy when he was holding her to slip away from the moment and into the dream.

"You're neglecting your horse." He rested his cheek against hers, closed his eyes. "I'll come back for you."

"I'll be waiting."

But he didn't move, only stood with her gathered close while the love inside him pulsed like light. Then he drew back, taking both of her hands and bringing them to his lips. "Don't forget to give him apples. He's fond of them."

"Yes, I know." It felt as though her heart were shaking. "Brian—"

"I'll be back," he said and strode away before the words rising into his throat could be spoken.

"Something's changed," Keeley whispered. "I felt it." She pressed her hands, still warm from his, to her heart. "Oh, it's been a hell of a day. And it's not over yet." She swung back into the stall where Finnegan stood, watching her patiently. "He loves me. He just can't get his tongue around the words yet, but he loves me. I know it."

She picked up the dandy brush again. "We're going to cross another finish line before the day's over. I've got to make myself beautiful. We'll have candlelight and wine, and . . ."

She trailed off as she heard the stall door open again. Thinking it was Brian come back, she turned. Her brilliant smile faded into ice when she saw Tarmack.

"You think you pulled a fast one, don't you?"

"You're not welcome here."

"Snatched this horse out from under me. No better than a horse thief. Figure you can get away with it 'cause you're a Grant."

"You were paid your asking price." She spoke coolly. She caught the stink of too much whiskey on his breath. And so, she thought, did Finnegan. The horse was beginning to quiver. Calmly, she hooked her hand in his bridle. "If you have a complaint, take it up with the Racing Commission."

"So your father can pay them off?"

Her head came up. Her eyes went from ice to fire. "Be careful what you say about my father."

"I'll say what I want to say." He moved in, his eyes glazed and mean from drinking. "Cheats, all of you, looking down on those of us just trying to make a living. Stole this horse from me." He jabbed a finger into her shoulder. "Said he wasn't fit to run."

"And he wasn't." She wasn't afraid. There were people around, she thought quickly. She had only to call out. But a Grant didn't cry for help at the first tussle. She could deal with a drunk and pitiful bully.

"Fit to run for you, though. To run and win. That purse is mine by rights."

It was only the money, she thought. Just as Brian said, with some, it was all facts and figures, and no feeling. "You've got all the money out of me you'll get." She turned away to brush the gelding. "Now I suggest you leave before I file a complaint."

"Don't you turn your back on me, you little bitch."

It was shock as much as pain that had Keeley gasping when he grabbed her arm and dragged her around. When she tried to jerk free, the sleeve of her shirt tore at the shoulder. Beside her, Finnegan whinnied nervously and shied.

"You look at me when I talk to you. You think you're better than me." He shoved her back against the gelding's side, then yanked her forward again. "You think you're special 'cause your daddy's rolling in money."

"I think," Keeley said with deceptive calm, "that you'd better take your hands off me." She reached in her pocket, closed her fingers, and they were rock steady, around a hoof pick.

It happened fast, a blur of motion and sound. Even as she tugged the makeshift defense free, Finnegan whipped his head and bit Tarmack's shoulder. For the second time Tarmack rapped her hard against the solid wall of the gelding's side, and as he drew back his fist she shouted, leaping to block it from connecting with Finnegan's head.

It skidded over her temple instead, sending a shocking ribbon of pain across her skull, and a haze of pale red over her vision. As she staggered, stumbling around to defend herself and her horse, Brian came through the doors like a vengeful god.

Instinctively Keeley grabbed Finnegan's bridle, to calm him, to balance herself. "It's all right. It's all right now."

But hearing the unmistakable sound of fists against flesh and bone, she ran out.

"Brian, don't!"

His face was blank, a mask without emotion. It seemed all sharp bones and cold eyes. He had Tarmack braced against the wall with a hand over the man's throat, an arm cocked back to deliver another blow. Tarmack's mouth and nose were already bleeding. Keeley grabbed Brian's arm, and hung on like a burr. It felt like gripping hot iron.

"That's enough. It's all right."

Without even a glance, so much as a flicker of acknowledgment, Brian shook her off, rammed a ready fist into Tarmack's gut. "He put his hands on you."

"Stop it." Panting, she grabbed his arm again, and wrapped both hers around it. "He didn't hurt me. Let him go, Brian." She could hear Tarmack struggling for air through the hand Brian had banded around his windpipe. "I'm not hurt."

Very slowly, Brian turned his head. When his eyes, flat and cold with violence, met hers, she trembled. "He put his hands on you," he said again, carefully enunciating each word. "Now step back."

"No." She could hear the shouts behind her, see out of the corner of her eye the crowd already forming. And she could smell the blood. "It's enough. Just let him go."

"It's not enough." He started to shake her off again, and Keeley had an image of herself flying free as he flicked her off like a gnat.

She hadn't feared Tarmack, but she was afraid now.

"What's the problem here?"

She could have wept with relief at the sound of her father's voice. The crowd parted for him. She'd never known one not to. He took one long look at her face, skimmed his gaze over the torn sleeve, and though the hand he laid on her shoulder was gentle, she'd seen the edge come into his eyes.

"Move back, Keeley," he said in a voice of quiet steel.

"Dad." She shook her head, twined around Brian's arm like a vine. "Tell Brian to let him go now. He won't listen to me."

Brian rapped the gasping Tarmack's head against the wall, a kind of absent violence as he once again spoke with rigid patience. "He put his hands on her."

The edge in Travis's eyes went keen, sharp as silver. "Did he touch you?"

"Dad, for God's sake." She lowered her voice. "He'll kill him in a minute."

"Let him go, Brian." Adelia hurried up, took in the situation in one glance. Gently she touched a hand to Brian's shoulder. "You've dealt with him. There's a lad. You're frightening Keeley now."

"Her shirt's torn. Do you see her shirt's torn?" He continued to speak slowly, as if in a foreign tongue. "Take her out of here."

"I will, I will. But let that pathetic man go now. He's not worth it."

Perhaps it was the voice, the lilt of his own country that broke quietly through the rage. Brian loosened his grip and Tarmack wheezed in air.

"He had her trapped in the stall. Trapped, you see, and his hands were on her."

Adelia nodded. Her gaze shifted briefly to her husband's. A lifetime ago he'd dealt with a drunk who'd had her trapped. She understood the barely reined violence in Brian's eyes. "She's all right now. You saw to that."

"I'm not finished." He said it so calmly, Adelia could only blink when his fist flashed out again and had Tarmack sagging to his knees.

"Stop it." Seeing no other way, Keeley stepped between the two men and shoved Brian with both hands. She didn't move him an inch, but the gesture made a point. "That's enough. It's just a torn shirt. He's drunk, and he was stupid. Now that's enough, Brian."

"You're wrong. It won't ever be enough. You've tender skin, Keeley, and he'll have marked it, so it won't ever be enough."

Tarmack was on his hands and knees, retching. In an almost absent move, Travis dragged him to his feet. "I suggest you apologize to my daughter and then be on your way, or I might let this boy loose on you again."

His stomach was jellied with pain, and he could taste his own blood in his mouth. Humiliation struck nearly as hard as he saw the blur of faces watching. "You can go to hell. You and all the rest. I'm bringing charges."

"Go ahead." Travis bared his teeth in a killing smile. "You're drunk and you're stupid, just as my daughter said. And you touched her."

"He was shouting at her, Mr. Grant." Larry elbowed his way through the crowd. "I heard him threatening her when I was coming in to see the horse."

Travis blocked Brian's move forward, felt Brian's muscle quiver under his hand. "Hold on," he said quietly, and turned his attention back to Tarmack. "You stay away from what's mine, Tarmack. If you ever lay hands on my girl again, what Brian can do to you will be nothing against what I will do."

Emboldened as he assumed Brian was now on a

leash, Tarmack swiped blood from his face with the back of his fist. "So what if I touched her? Just getting her attention was all. She's not so particular who has his hands on her. She wasn't minding when this two-bit mick was pawing her."

Brian surged forward, but Travis was closer, and nearly as quick. His fist cracked, one short-armed hammer blow, against Tarmack's jaw. The man's eyes rolled back as he collapsed.

"Dee, take Keeley home, will you?" Travis glanced at the crowd, one brow lifted as if he dared for comments. "Would someone call security?"

"We shouldn't have left." Keeley paced the kitchen, stopping at the windows on each pass. Why weren't they back?

"Darling, you're shaking. Come on now, sit and drink your tea."

"I can't. What's wrong with men? They'd have beaten that idiot to a pulp. I'm not that surprised at Brian, I suppose, but I expected more restraint from Dad."

Genuinely surprised, Adelia glanced over. "Why?"

As worry ate through her she raked her hands through her hair. "He's contained. Now you, I could see you taking a few swings . . ." She winced. "No offense," she said, then saw that her mother was grinning.

"None taken. My temper might be a bit, we'll say, more colorful than your father's. His tends to be cold and deliberate when it's called for. And it was. The man hurt and frightened his little girl."

"His little girl was about to attempt to gut the man with a hoof pick." Keeley blew out a breath. "I've never seen Dad hit anyone, or look like he wanted to keep right on with it."

"He doesn't use his fists overmuch because he doesn't have to. He'll be upset about this, Keeley." Adelia hesitated, then gestured her daughter to a chair. "Sit a minute. Years ago," she began, "shortly after I came to work here, I was down at the stables at night. One of the grooms had been drinking. He had me down in one of the stalls. I couldn't fight him off."

"Oh, Mama."

"He was starting to tear at my clothes when your father came in. I thought he would beat the man to death. He didn't even raise a sweat about it, just laid in with his fists, systematic like, in a cold kind of rage that was more terrifying than the fire. That's what I saw in Brian's face today." Gently she touched the faint bruise on Keeley's temple. "And I can't blame him for it."

"I don't blame him." She gripped her mother's hands. "This today, this wasn't like that. Tarmack was mad over the horse, and wanted to bully me."

"Threats are threats. If I'd gotten there first, likely I'd have waded in myself. Don't fret so, darling."

"I'm trying not to." She picked up her tea, set it down again. "Ma, what Tarmack said about Brian. About him pawing me. It wasn't like that. It's not like that between us."

"I know that. You're in love with him."

"Yes." It was lovely to say it. "And he loves me. He just hasn't gotten around to saying so yet. Now I'm worried that Dad . . . Tempers are up, and if he takes what that bastard said the wrong way." She pushed away from the table again. "Why aren't they back?"

She paced another ten minutes, then finally took some aspirin for the headache that snarled in both temples. She drank a cup of tea and told herself she was calm again.

And was up like a shot the minute she heard wheels on gravel. She got to the door in time to see Brian's truck drive by, and her father's pull in behind the house.

"I missed all the excitement." Though his voice was light, Brendon's eyes carried that same glint of temper she'd seen in their father's. "You okay?"

"I'm fine." Though she patted his arm, her gaze was fixed on her father. She could read nothing in his face as he climbed out of the truck. "I'm absolutely fine," she said again, stepping toward him.

"I'd like you to come inside."

Contained, she thought again. It was impressive, and not a little scary, to see all that rage and fury so tightly contained. "I will. I have to see Brian." Her eyes pleaded with his for understanding. "I have to talk to him. I'll be back."

With one quick squeeze of her hand on his arm, she dashed off.

"Let her go, Travis," Adelia said from the doorway. "She needs to deal with this."

Eyes narrowed, he watched his daughter run to another man. "She's got five minutes."

Keeley caught up with Brian before he climbed the steps to his quarters. She called out, increased her pace. "Wait. I was so worried." She would have leaped straight into his arms, but he stepped back. And his face was glacier cold. "What happened?"

"Nothing. Your father dealt with it. The man won't be bothering you again."

"I'm not worried about that," she said shortly. "Are you all right? I started to think you might be in trouble. I should have stayed and given a statement. Everything got so confused."

"There's no trouble, and nothing to be worried about."

"Good. Brian, I wanted to say that I . . . Oh, God! Your hands." She snatched them, the tears swimming up as she saw his torn knuckles. "Oh, I'm so sorry. Your poor hands. Let's go up. I'll take care of them."

"I can take care of myself."

"They need to be cleaned and—"

"I don't want you hovering."

He yanked his hands free, then cursed when he saw her cheeks go pale with shock, and the first tear slid down. "Damn it, swallow those back. I'm not in the mood to deal with tears on top of everything else."

"Why are you slapping at me this way?"

Guilt and misery rolled through him. "I've things to do." He turned away, started up the stairs. And fury caught up with guilt and misery. "You didn't want me standing up for you." He spun back, his eyes brilliant with temper.

"What are you talking about?"

"I'm good enough for a roll on the sheets or to help with the horses. But not to stand up for you."

"That's absurd." The tears came fast now as reaction from the last few hours set in. "Was I just supposed to stand by and watch while you beat him half to death?"

"Yes." He snapped, gripped her shoulders, shook. "It was for me to see to. You took that from me, and in the end, handed it to your father. It was for me, two-bit mick or not."

"What's going on here?" For the second time that day, Travis walked in on tempers and shouts, Adelia by his side. And this time, he saw his daughter's tear-streaked face. His eyes shot hotly to Brian. "What the hell is going on here?"

"I'm not sure." Keeley blinked at tears as Brian released her. "This idiot here seems to think I share Tarmack's opinion of him because I didn't stand back and let him beat the man to pieces. Apparently by objecting I've tread on his pride." She looked wearily at her mother. "I'm tired."

"Go up to the house," Travis ordered. "I want to speak with Brian."

"I refuse to be sent away like a child again. This is my business. Mine, and—"

"You don't speak in that tone to your father." Brian's sharp order brought varying reactions. Keeley gaped, Travis frowned thoughtfully and Adelia fought back a grin.

"Excuse me, but I'm very tired of being interrupted and ordered around and spoken to like a recalcitrant eight-year-old."

"Then don't behave like one," Brian suggested. "My family might not be fancy, but we were taught respect."

"I don't see what—"

"Be quiet."

The command left her stunned and speechless.

"I apologize for causing yet another scene," he said to Travis. "I'm not altogether settled yet. I didn't thank you for smoothing out whatever trouble there might have been with security."

"There were enough people who saw most of what happened. There'd have been no trouble. Not for you."

"A minute ago you were angry because my father smoothed things out."

Brian spared her a glance. "I'm just angry altogether."

"Oh, that's right." Since violence seemed to be the mood of the day, she gave in to it and stabbed a finger into his shoulder. "You're just angry period. He's got some twisted idea that I don't think he's good enough to defend me against a drunk bully. Well, I have news for you, you hardheaded Irish horse's ass."

Now that her own temper was fired, she curled her hand into a fist and used it to thump his chest. "I was defending myself just fine."

"You half Irish, stiff-necked birdbrain, he's twice your size and then some."

"I was handling it, but I appreciate your help."

"The hell you do. It's just like with everything else. You've got to do it all yourself. No one's as smart as you, or as clever, or as capable. Oh it's fine to give me a whistle if you need a diversion."

"Is that what you think?" She was so livid her voice was barely a croak. "That I make love with you for a diversion? You vile, insulting, disgusting son of a bitch."

She raised her own fists, and might have used them, but Travis stepped in and gripped Brian by the shirt. His voice was quiet, almost matter-of-fact. "I ought to take you apart."

"Oh, Travis." Adelia merely pressed her fingers to her eyes.

"Dad, don't you dare." At wit's end, Keeley threw up her hands. "I've got an idea. Why don't we all just beat each other senseless today and be done with it?"

"You've a right." Brian kept his eyes on Travis's and kept hands at his sides.

"The hell he does. I'm a grown woman. A grown woman," she repeated rapping a fist lightly on her father's arm. "And I threw myself at him."

She gained some perverse satisfaction when her father turned that frigid stare on her. "That's right. I *threw* myself at him. I wanted him, I went to him, and I seduced him. Now what? Am I grounded?"

"It doesn't matter how it happened. I was experienced, and she wasn't. I'd no right to touch her, and I knew it. In your place I'd be doing some pounding of my own."

"No one's doing any pounding." Adelia moved forward, laid a hand on Travis's arm. "Darling, are you blind? Can't you see what's between them? Now let the boy go. You know damn well he'll stand there and let you pummel him, and you'd get no satisfaction from it."

No, Travis wasn't blind. Looking in Brian's eyes he saw his life shift. His baby, his little girl, had become someone else's woman. The someone else, he noted, looked about as miserable and baffled by the whole business as he felt himself. "What do you intend to do?"

"I can be gone within the hour."

Amusement was bittersweet. "Can you?"

"Yes, sir." For the first time he knew he'd never pack all he needed, all he wanted into his bag. "Reivers is capable enough to hold you until you find another trainer."

Stubborn Irish pride, Travis thought. Well, he'd had a lifetime of experience on how to handle it. "I'll let you know when you're fired, Donnelly. Dee, we still have that shotgun up at the house, don't we?"

"Oh aye," she said without missing a beat. And wondered if she'd ever been more proud of the man she'd married, or had ever loved him more. "I believe I could lay my hands on it."

Yes, amusement was bittersweet, Travis thought as he watched every ounce of color drain from Brian's face. "Good to know. It's always pleased me that my children recognize and appreciate quality." He released Brian, turned to Keeley. "We'll talk later."

Tears were threatening again as she watched her parents walk off, saw her father reach for her mother's hand, forge that link that had always held strong.

"I've competed for a lot of things," she said quietly. "Worked for a lot of things, wanted a lot of things. But underneath it all, what they have has always been the goal." She turned as Brian walked unsteadily to the steps and sat down. "He won't shoot you, Brian, if you decide you still need to run."

It wasn't the shotgun that worried him, but the implication of it. "I think the lot of you are confused. It's been an emotional day."

"Yes, it has."

"I know who I am, Keeley. The second son of not-quite middle-class parents who are one generation out of poverty. My father liked the drink and the horses a bit too much, and my mother was dead-tired most of the time. We got by is all, then got on. I know what I am," he continued. "I'm a damn good trainer of racehorses. I've never stayed in one job, in one spot, more than three years. If you do, it might take hold of you. I never wanted to find myself fenced in."

"And I'm fencing you in."

He looked up then with eyes both weary and wary. "You could. Then where would you be?"

"Talk about birdbrains." She sighed then walked over

to him. "I know who I am, Brian. I'm the oldest daughter of beautiful parents. I've been privileged, brought up in a home full of love. I've had advantages."

She lifted a hand when he said nothing, and brushed at the hair that tumbled over his forehead. "I know what I am. I'm a damn good riding teacher, and I'm rooted here. I can make a difference here, have been making one. But I realize I don't want to do it alone. I want to fence you in, Brian," she murmured, framing his face with her hands. "I've been hammering at that damn fence for weeks. Ever since I realized I was in love with you."

His hands came to her wrists, squeezed reflexively, before he got quickly to his feet. "You're mixing things up." Panic arrowed straight into his heart. "I told you sex complicates things."

"Yes, you did. And of course since you're the only man I've been with, how would I know the difference between sex and love? Then again, that doesn't take into account that I'm a smart and self-aware woman, and I know the reason you're the only man I've been with is that you're the only man I've loved. Brian . . ."

She stepped toward him, humor flashing into her eyes when he stepped back. "I've made up my mind. You know how stubborn I am."

"I train your father's horses."

"So what? My mother groomed them."

"That's a different matter."

"Why? Oh, because she's a woman. How foolish of me not to realize we can't possibly love each other, build a life with each other. Now if you owned Royal Meadows and I worked here, then it would be all right."

"Stop making me sound ridiculous."

"I can't." She spread her hands. "You are ridiculous. I love you anyway. Really, I tried to approach it sensibly. I like doing things in a structured order that makes a beeline for the goal. But . . ." She shrugged, smiled. "It just doesn't want to work that way with you. I look at you and my heart, well, it just insists on taking over. I love you so much, Brian. Can't you tell me? Can't you look at me and tell me?"

He skimmed his fingertips over the bruise high on her temple. He wanted to tend to it, to her. "If I did there'd be no going back."

"Coward." She watched the heat flash into his eyes, and thought how lovely it was to know him so well.

"You won't push me into a corner."

Now she laughed. "Watch me," she invited and proceeded to back him up against the steps. "I've figured a lot of things out today, Brian. You're scared of me—of what you feel for me. You were the one always pulling back when we were in public, shifting aside when I'd reach for you. It hurt me."

The idea quite simply appalled him. "I never meant to hurt you."

"No, you couldn't. How could I help but fall for you? A hard head and a soft heart. It's irresistible. Still, it did hurt. But I thought it was just the snob in you. I didn't realize it was nerves."

"I'm not a snob, or a coward."

"Put your arms around me. Kiss me. Tell me."

"Damn it." He grabbed her shoulders, then simply held on, unable to push her back or draw her in. "It was the first time I saw you, the first instant. You walked in the room and my heart stopped. Like it had been struck by lightning. I was fine until you walked into the room."

Her knees wanted to buckle. Hard head, soft heart, and here, suddenly, a staggering sweep of romance. "Why didn't you tell me? Why did you make me wait?"

"I thought I'd get over it."

"Get over it?" Her brow arched up. "Like a head cold?"

"Maybe." He set her aside, paced away to stare out at the hills.

Keeley closed her eyes, let the breeze ruffle her hair, cool her cheeks. When the calm descended, she opened her eyes and smiled. "A good strong head cold's tough to shake off."

"You're telling me. I never wanted to own things," he began with his back still to her. "It was a matter of principle. But when a man decides to settle, things change."

Things change, he thought again. Maybe she had the right of it, and he'd been running for a long time. But in running, hadn't he ended up where he'd been meant to be in the end?

Destiny. He was too Irish not to embrace it when it kept slugging him between the eyes. "I've money put by. Considerable as I've never spent much. There's enough to build a house, or start one anyway. You'd want one close by—for your school, for your family."

She had to close her eyes again. Tears would only fluster him. "Those are the kind of details I usually appreciate, but they just aren't the priority right now. Will you just tell me, Brian. I need you to tell me you love me."

"I'm getting to it." He turned back. "I never thought I wanted family. I want to make children with you, Keeley. I want ours. Please don't cry."

"I'm trying not to. Hurry up."

"I can't be rushed at such a time. Sniffle those back or I'll blunder it. That's the way." He moved to her. "I don't want to own horses, but I can make an exception for the gift you gave me today. As a kind of symbol of things. I didn't have faith in him, not pure faith, that he'd run to win. I didn't have faith in you, either. Give me your hand."

She held it out, clasping his. "Tell me."

"I've never said the words to another woman. You'll be my first, and you'll be my last. I loved you from the first instant, in a kind of blinding flash. Over time the love I have for you has strengthened, and deepened until it's like something alive inside me."

"That's everything I needed to hear." She brought his hand to her cheek. "Marry me, Brian."

"Bloody hell. Will you let me do the asking?"

She had to bite her lip to hold off the watery chuckle. "Sorry."

With a laugh, he plucked her off her feet. "Well, what the hell. Sure I'll marry you."

"Right away."

"Right away." He brushed his lips over her temple. "I love you, Keeley, and since you're birdbrain enough to want to marry a hardheaded Irish horse's ass, I believe it was, I'll go up now and ask your father."

"Ask my—Brian, really."

"I'll do this proper. But maybe I'll take you with me, in case he's found that shotgun."

She laughed, rubbed her cheek against his. "I'll protect you."

He set her on her feet. They began to walk together past the sharply colored fall flowers, the white fences and fields where horses raced their shadows.

When he reached to take her hand, Keeley gripped his firmly. And had everything.

* * * * *